MW01411302

To: Maurice
From
Larry Menard
Larry Menard
June 24th 2012.
Thankyou,

The Vanguard Chronicles

Lawrence Menard

Order this book online at www.trafford.com
or email orders@trafford.com

Most Trafford titles are also available at major online book retailers.

Printed in the United States of America.

ISBN: 978-1-4669-2168-9 (sc)
ISBN: 978-1-4669-2169-6 (hc)
ISBN: 978-1-4669-2199-3 (e)

Library of Congress Control Number: 2012905392

Trafford rev. 04/23/2012

Trafford PUBLISHING www.trafford.com

North America & international
toll-free: 1 888 232 4444 (USA & Canada)
phone: 250 383 6864 • fax: 812 355 4082

Dedication

This Vanguard Chronicles could not have been possible, but for the support I received from a number of people, who only wanted me to follow my dreams.

Thank you, Sam Prewer (my son) for reading the original manuscript and offering ideas.

Thank you, Mathew Burns, because you kept me focused and supported all of my weird ideas.

Thank you, Marlene Menard (my loving wife) because you're the only reason this book ever made it off my computer screen.

Thank you, Richard Pavan for your Spider Drone rendering.

Contents

1. And So It Begins 1
2. Good-Bye, Dear Friend 9
3. Kyle Chandler 11
4. The Conspiracy 19
5. Fall from Grace 28
6. Sabrina "The Great" 36
7. Predator and Prey 42
8. The Decision 59
9. First Contact 70
10. Face to Face 77
11. Now We Are One 96
12. Draegon 102
13. What to Do 118
14. The Pact 131
15. The Discovery 139
16. The Mountain of Light 149
17. Enlightenment 162
18. Reciprocity 169
19. Aftermath 184

20. Treachery 197
21. The Vanguard Council 216
22. We Were Responsible 228
23. The Zorn Legacy 244
24. Shutting Down 252
25. The Siltron Solution 257
26. They've Come Again 267
27. The Siege of Bridgetown 271
28. The Death of Innocence 283

Prologue

Vanguard was the largest space-based engineering project ever conceived by man. From the nose of the Bridge to the farthest extension of the rear propulsion ports, the vessel measured twenty-eight miles in length. The articulated hull was over twelve miles wide and four miles high. The shear mass of the craft made it visible from the surface of the Earth. The logistical challenges of building such a vessel in space were astounding. Vanguard took sixty years from the planning board to finished product and required over 250,000 space-trained engineers and construction experts working virtually around the clock in the greatest labor of love ever undertaken.

Why would so many people give their lives to build a vessel most would never see completed before their deaths? The answer to that question speaks to necessity and the preservation of the human seed. Earth was a dying planet. Why and how this tragedy came about will be debated for a thousand years. For now, the only thing of importance in the minds of the people of Earth was to build Vanguard and five others like her, to save as many of their sons and daughters as possible before the time of man came crashing to an end.

Vanguard required a crew of ten thousand highly skilled men and women to protect and serve a passenger payload of 150,000 settlers. This ship was not a transport. It was an ark in the truest biblical sense, built for one purpose—to take as many people off the planet as possible and to search out a new beginning in the farthest reaches of the universe. To that end and that end alone, all the ingenuity of man was brought into play for one last great project. Vanguard was the true measure of our genius.

The hull structure of the vessel was designed to create a layered defensive barrier between the unknown risks of deep space and the precious cargo contained within. The hull covering was an overlay of 4 independent layers of specially treated titanium and polymer panels fused together to form an impenetrable barrier fifteen feet thick. Sandwiched between each layer was a one-foot buffer of emulsifying oxygen-rich Sidler Gelatin. The unique nature of the material was its value as a sealing agent. Should, for any reason, a layer of the hull suffer a breach, the Gelatin would be drawn into the break, hardening instantly and remaining in that state until repairs could be made.

Vanguard's fuselage was divided into three distinct barrel-shaped segments linked to one another through a series of sacrificial struts and passageways. This gave the vessel the appearance of a gigantic insect. The Bridge module (the head of the bug, if you will) was the smallest of these divisions, housing the navigational helm and control center for all systems aboard the vessel, including Vanguard's extensive array of weapons.

The Bridge was the brains of Vanguard. Our success on this pilgrimage depended entirely on a group of people never seen by the settlers and known only as Bridge Command. As strange as it might seem, there was no interaction between the people of Bridge Command and the settler payload. The Bridge was self-contained on twenty-one decks. These various levels constituted the living arrangements for all the people of Bridge Command. Everything required to sustain the lives of the crew was contained on this multilevel miniature world. The largest of these areas was the flight deck located on the underside of the ship's nose.

Two hundred and forty fighter craft known as Defenders were staged there and kept at the ready. This long-range primary attack ship was equipped with the most advanced weaponry and propulsion systems available at the time. In hindsight, it seems almost paradoxical that the very tools of war that helped seal mankind's fate on Earth were now being used to preserve those of us that were left.

Vanguard's defensive hardware did not end with the Defender. The vessel was equipped with one thousand Pulse Beam Turret Gatling guns, two hundred M12 Thor One Missile launchers, and two hundred Class-Three Phaser Disruptor Beam emitters. These weapons were managed from strategic emplacements positioned around the ship that were independently controlled by Bridge Command. Vanguard's defensive capabilities were impressive, to say the least.

The center segment of the vessel was denoted as The Hive. This module was far and away the largest of the three areas. Here, 150,000 men, women, and children lived out their lives in an environment designed to simulate Earth. Residents of The Hive were deliberately and completely kept unaware of what was required to maintain their existence. To Bridge Command, these settlers were known as The Payload. Although the term might seem dehumanizing, The Hive was the reason Vanguard was built, and the sole responsibility of the Bridge Command was to protect and serve it.

The Hive module was self-contained on twenty deck levels, with the top level being the primary Residence Space. Within this area, each family was assigned a Unit that was modular in design and identical to every other personal-living module. Each of these Units was contained within three tiered complexes referred to as Blocks, and each Block contained fifteen family Units. Everything one might expect to see in an urban setting was carefully reproduced in the Residence Space.

This living module was over a mile high and topped with a titanium reinforced, domed roof under laid with a series of laminated light-emitting panels designed to mimic a natural sky, complete with moving cloud formations and a soft sun—all created using holographic images. Each day, the animated sun would move across the backdrop, creating the illusion of a dawn-to-sunset cycle. As this sun completed its path, the panels were dimmed and the roof was reilluminated to simulate a night sky, complete with twinkling stars and a Harvest Moon that moved across the darkened backdrop.

The illusion was made complete with the use of discretely placed atmospheric recycling units, which removed used air, filtered it, and added heath-maintaining bacterium. The refreshed air was then reintroduced back into the space, disguised as gentle breezes. Although the residents understood the pretense of their environment, it was the only home they knew.

The Blocks were set on either side of long Boulevards running the length of the module for over fifteen miles. There were sixteen such boulevards linked to each other, forming a grid pattern using intercepting shorter pathways denoted as Lanes. Dotted throughout this checkerboard layout were 180 gathering areas referred to as Citizen Spaces. These grassy, mostly treed areas served three primary purposes: firstly, to provide family recreation areas; secondly, to help support and disguise air-purification systems; and finally, to serve as staging points to access the high-speed elevator systems that moved residents throughout the lower levels of The Hive.

There were nineteen levels below the Residence Space. Decks two through twelve were Citizen Service Areas and were comprised of such essential services as hospitals, schools, security, emergency services, food services, general supplies, and a full menu of other creature-comfort amenities. Citizens were free to access these decks as they wished without dealing with stringent security protocols. All levels below twelve were secured areas dedicated to development and maintenance services.

Every adult citizen worked in and for these support functions—medicine, engineering, hydroponics, atmospheric management, robotics, computer sciences, and the list went on and on. To control the movement of people on these secured lower decks, microchips were implanted in all residents. Once off an elevator on any level, the microchip was scanned before access was authorized.

The twentieth level represented the fail safe for The Hive. This deck housed the Secondary Bridge. Its sole purpose was to assume control of Vanguard should Bridge Command be compromised. Should such an event occur, the Primary Bridge would be jettisoned away from Vanguard, and the Secondary Bridge would assume control. It was imperative that The Hive be preserved at all costs, including—if necessary—the sacrifice of Bridge Command.

The Hive module was an enormous bubble suspended within the hull of Vanguard. A one-mile buffer zone separated it from the outer shell of the ship. Within the zone was an elaborate series of hydraulic shock buffers that flexed to absorb the shocks that might occur to the primary structure of the vessel. The intent was to maintain the balance and stability of The Hive regardless of the situation outside. Much like Bridge Command, should a catastrophic breach occur, the hull would be discarded, leaving The Hive to continue the voyage.

This buffer-zone space served other purposes as well, the most important of these being access to maintain critical ship systems. This was accomplished through the use of two high-speed monorail systems that moved down the length of the ship on either side, connecting Bridge Command to the Propulsion Engineering module of the craft and fifty high-speed maintenance lifts accessing over one hundred servicing catwalks. Ongoing maintenance to critical systems was imperative and occurred unbeknownst to The Hive population. Over a thousand specialists living in the Bridge module worked tirelessly to sustain The Hive.

The buffer zone housed eight hundred emergency escape pods, should the entire vessel be compromised. The assumption in their design was that the settlers could be evacuated while vessel repairs were being made, and then the settlers could be returned. These small shuttles had limited range and life support and could not sustain evacuees for any extended period. That reality was the driving design logic in ensuring that The Hive was self-sustaining.

The rear module of Vanguard was denoted as Propulsion Engineering and housed the primary propulsion systems for the vessel. Propulsion was provided by fifteen Phaeton Thrusters. Ten were primary, and five redundant. These thrusters at maximum power could move Vanguard through deep space at an astounding 1.7 million miles per hour. The Zion Plasma Cores that provided power for the thrusters and every other system of the ship had a useful life of one hundred thousand years. Servicing these systems and the cores required an additional two thousand technicians working in shifts around the clock without ever interacting with The Payload.

Within the rear section, as well, were staged thirty exploration crafts, aptly named Explorers. These vessels were vital to the examination of any planets being considered for colonization. Each ship carried a crew of one hundred, made up of staff, technicians, and scientists. Everything required to collect, study, and categorize samples was contained in sophisticated labs aboard each vessel.

Six Explorers flanked Vanguard at all times. These science vessels were not to be taken for granted. Quite apart from their exploratory value, their weapons systems were equally as impressive. In truth, it could be argued that Explorers were not merely survey ships to be used as defensive assets; they were battle cruisers that were used as exploratory alternatives.

On September 17, 3187, the maiden voyage of Vanguard was initiated. The event occurred with little or no ceremony. As Vanguard fired four of its Phaeton Thrusters and slowly broke from Earth's orbit, with her went the hopes of a doomed species. What would become of these naïve souls venturing into the unknown with nothing but faith to guide them?

As I stared at the Vanguard voyage tracker, I tried to calculate how long we had been in space since leaving Earth. As near as I could gather, it had been over 254 years. How many hundreds of billions of miles was that? How many generations had lived out their entire lives aboard this ship? What lessons had we learned from the folly of our ancestors that brought us to this? As daunting as these questions might be, they were for another time. Today was for celebration.

An almost overpowering excitement ran through our group as we stood waiting in the staging area to board the Explorer shuttle named The Phoenix. For most of us, this would be the first time we had ever been separated from the sanctuary of Vanguard. All our planning and rehearsing couldn't have prepared us for this moment, and yet it was this moment we had all dreamt about for generations. I couldn't remember ever being this scared, but as I looked around at the rest of my group, it was clear I wasn't alone.

We were all nervously jabbering about the adventure ahead and how great it was to be among the first humans to set feet upon this virgin planet, but I knew once The Phoenix moved away from the protective confines of Vanguard, all our bravado would be replaced with a somber silence. What had led us to this world so distant from our ancestral roots? The answer lay buried in the ancient text, and after countless hours of reviewing those writings, I had come to one inescapable conclusion.

From the moment mankind slithered from the primordial ooze tens of thousands of years ago, struggled to stand upright, learned to control fire and kill other living creatures, his arrogance and need to dominate everything around him led inevitably to the destruction of our ancestral world, Earth.

As harsh as that sounds, we were here because our forefathers had no other options available to them, and in a last gasp, almost futile gesture to preserve the human seed, they built this behemoth of a space vessel, which they called Vanguard. Then they went about selecting 150,000 of our young, mostly naïve forefathers and launched their asses into the blackness of space. We were the last hope for the human seed.

Earth was dying, and mankind with it. There would be no last-minute reprieves or divine interventions. Not this time! The arrogance and ignorance of our ancestors would finally be punished. The sad legacy of humanity was our race to self-destruction. This tragedy didn't just happen! Man wasn't the innocent victim of some unexpected or unfair natural disaster. This was a self-fulfilling prophecy that began as far back as the twentieth century.

Respected scientists and environmentalists had predicted that if we continued our destructive energy policies, our greed to consume all things around us, and our endless wars, we would devour all that was Earth. These warnings of impending doom fell on deaf ears. It wasn't that we didn't care or the warning signs weren't obvious without being told. We were fooled by our perceived self-importance and assumed supremacy over the planet into believing whatever harm we had unleashed from our Pandora's Box could be put back in whenever we wished. We were wrong! Terribly and fatally wrong!

The planet could no longer support organic life of any kind. All of the natural splendor and innocence of our Cradle of Life we called Earth had been scraped and polluted away. The sun that had warmed and enriched our existence since the very dawn of time now devoured our bodies. The atmosphere was a mixture of toxic gases and deadly pollutants. Oceans began to dry, creating lifeless deserts, while violent electrical storms unbalanced Earth's natural magnetic fields, resulting in unrelenting eruptions and quakes.

In a desperate attempt to extend human existence, our forefathers built and contained Earth's remaining few peoples within three environmentally controlled, domed super-cities, but the clock was ticking away our existence. We were merely cheating time. The history text details that in the decades preceding the Doomsday proclamation, the population of Earth had gone from twelve billion people to one billion. Almost all that loss of life was a direct consequence of man's murderous ways toward his fellow man. Genocide and war were the staples of the times. Nothing was immune from man's lust and greed.

Each war led to the development of even more destructive weapons. Each new weapon vaulted us closer to extinction. There were no winners in this madness, just the fruitless continuation of death and destruction in the name of dominance. It was the precursor to the end of Eden. When finally this unnatural carnage had ceased and governments fell, we began to understand the true magnitude of our folly.

On September 4, 3123, the People's World Council announced all was lost. They promised that some would be saved because there was a plan. Six vessels would be built to search for a New Earth somewhere in the vastness of the universe. The Council promised the masses that the children of man would find new lives beyond this dying planet and the lessons we had learned would help guide their way.

Given the state of affairs at the time, this Doomsday proclamation was probably not as much a shock as it was a confirmation of the obvious. The Council's naïve promises of a new life were no more than desperate dreams. We're probably never going to know whether the other five arks were built before our ancestors met their fates and Earth became just another lifeless mass orbiting around its young star, but that was then and this is now. The first day of rebirth is upon us.

One

And So It Begins

As The Phoenix touched down, the silence within our group was deafening. The anticipation so obvious on Vanguard was now replaced with absolute terror. Up until this very moment, it had all been simulated game-playing in mocked-up worlds on virtual-reality stages. The game was over! No one would be there to stop the program if things went terribly wrong. We were the first settlers to venture into this alien place. Should we lose our way, Vanguard would move on, and we would be the casualties of another bad choice.

For over two years, we evaluated the planet to assure ourselves we could be successful here. Three hundred scouting missions had been completed and the collected data analyzed over and over again. Based on those findings, this world held no surprises or limitations to our colonization. Yet as the gangway extended and we stood frozen by the hatch waiting for someone—anyone—to take the first step, doubt was chiseled on our faces.

When finally I made my way down the ramp and stepped timidly to the ground, I could feel the uneven terrain beneath my feet. This would take getting used to. During those first few nervous days, there would be many experiences that would take some getting used to. Once we had cleared the ramp, we stood mesmerized by the vastness of where we were and how insignificant we were in it. The body language of my fellow settlers told me there were those who already missed the sanctuary of Vanguard. How could you blame them? This was wilderness! Although beautiful to behold, it was nonetheless raw, untamed wilderness!

For what seemed an eternity, we just stood there looking in all directions and whispering back and forth, unsure of what to do next. It wasn't until our team leader emerged from The Explorer and herded us a safe distance away from the craft that we started to snap back to the reality of our situation. Minutes later, The Phoenix lifted off for its return to Vanguard. If we hadn't felt alone before, we did now.

Kyle Chandler could see we were all dangerously close to panic, and he swung into action immediately. As he led us around a large stand of trees, we were stunned by what awaited us: Spider Drones. I first heard of these robotic devices through my friend Kyle, our mission leader. He was the engineer and creator of the technology, but until today, until this moment, I had never actually seen one.

Spider Drones were robotic sentries, named because of their appearance. Each drone stood twelve feet tall and was supported by eight triple-hinged, spindly metal legs. The fully independent moving appendages terminated at an oblong canister-shaped body perhaps eight feet in length, three feet wide, and three feet deep. The entire device was powered by a Zion Micro-Core that gave the robot a twenty-five-year operating life.

Around the center of the body module was a constantly oscillating red beacon. Kyle explained that this harmless-looking light show was in fact sixty-four self-targeting laser weapons, which were managed by a motion-activated targeting program capable of firing one or all of them in virtually every direction at once. Each laser operated at 100,000 megawatts. That explanation was lost on me, but it sounded powerful.

In addition to the lasers, the robots were equipped with full 180-degree visual tracking, infrared and ultraviolet motion sensors, and microwave and radio-wave detection. Kyle bragged that "his babies" could detect a tree branch breaking at a thousand yards and be onsite in seconds to catch it in mid air. His babies were the ugliest, most intimidating pieces of hardware anyone had ever seen. To see them was to fear them.

As the Drones fixed on our location, they streaked toward us at a jaw-dropping speed, stopping perhaps twenty yards away and forming what can best be described as an assault line across our path. We were petrified! Kyle immediately instructed us to remain absolutely still until he dealt with them. With that, he removed a small, handheld keyboard module from his utility belt, entered some sort of code, and the robots withdrew. I'm not sure how the others felt at that moment, but I was never closer to absolute panic and hysteria.

Once they had withdrawn, we continued walking, being very careful never to take our eyes off the metal menaces until we reached the top of a low hill. In a clearing below, a kind of tent city had been established in preparation for our arrival—a sea of large, white tents precisely placed in long rows with roadways carefully carved out between them. Along with the tents were four aircraft-hanger-sized Quonset Huts, flanked by heavy equipment that was staged with typical military efficiency. Although it wasn't Vanguard, it was an organized environment, which made us feel less vulnerable.

As we entered the camp, we passed through a Security Recognition Post where each of us had an additional microchip inserted under our skin on the upper left arm. These chips were electronic tracking devices in case we got ourselves lost, but much more importantly, the chips identified us as authorized creatures to the Spider Drones. We were advised that without the implants, the Drones would treat us as intruders, and we would be dead. Every day after that, my first stop of the day was the scan station—just to be sure the implant was functioning.

Soon after receiving the implants, we were herded into one of the four large Quonset Huts, which had been set up as an indoctrination center. There we were introduced to the rules of the camp. There were no surprises about these protocols. Don't leave the confines of the encampment without escort! Don't work alone! Don't eat or drink anything not provided by the camp! Don't assume the small creatures you may encounter are friendly, and finally, if you are injured, report immediately to the medical tent.

These simple guidelines were intended to keep us safe, but some among us complained that they felt like prisoners, unable to explore the wonders of this new world. That was brave talk, nothing more. Every one of us was scared shitless.

We were each assigned a tent number, and each tent held eighteen cots and rows of lockers. It was a typical military-style barracks arrangement. Once we were settled in, we were given tours around the various support venues where meals, showers, provisions, and—most importantly—medical attention could be found. The compound layout was deliberately designed to keep the population away from the perimeter of the camp. Our questions were endless. For all our lives, we had lived in an artificial world where every moment of every day was exactly the same as every moment of every day before, and it would have been again tomorrow, but not anymore.

Our first night on New Earth was exciting; after all, we were the first settlers to stand upon this virgin ground. There were sounds we had never heard before. There were sights we had never seen before, and there were breezes, soft cool breezes, we had never felt before. Small, mostly unidentifiable creatures were everywhere inside and outside the security perimeter, fascinated by the illumination of the encampment. Every few minutes, we could hear the distinct sound of a laser snap as a Spider Drone exterminated another unsuspecting animal that mistakenly ventured inside our security perimeter. It was as exciting as it was terrifying!

We slept soundly in the pure air of this unspoiled world. The Children of Vanguard would need the rest because the months and years ahead would undoubtedly be filled with hardships yet unrevealed. Throughout our first night and every night thereafter, the Vanguard Militia—referred to as The Protectors—assisted by those hideous Drones stood watch.

The Militia was not part of The Hive population. Focused and without emotion, yet strong and committed to our protection, they were our guardians. Up until three years ago, these bigger-than-life men were unknown to the residents of The Hive, even though we shared the same home aboard Vanguard. They were soldiers of Bridge Command. We didn't know this at the time because no citizen was permitted on the Bridge. It had been that way from the beginning.

Our landing party consisted of six hundred people, selected in most cases not for our adventurous spirits or environmental brilliance, but because we had been hand-picked by The Vanguard Council to be the first citizens to visit New Earth. Why such an honor would be bestowed on any of us is a topic to be discussed later. For now, it is only important that we were here first.

For the next eighteen weeks, we worked harder than we had ever worked before. With all hands on the task, we had unloaded fifty shuttle crafts delivering supplies and equipment to establish the initial stages of Bridgetown. This site was to be our first settlement on this new planet. How the name was chosen or whether it had any historical significance was unknown. When I asked Kyle about it, his only response was, "When you look on the site plans, that name is embossed on the top of each drawing. Beyond that, who gives a shit?"

The response was typical of Kyle. He had very little patience for things that, in his mind, meant nothing. Maybe he was right! There was so much more to focus on and be curious about, but I promised myself that unless we were being attacked by man-eating space creatures, I'd avoid asking him anything else.

Since our group arrived, we seemed to have an overpowering sense of well-being. Our energy levels were always high, and we worked almost tirelessly. Perhaps it was the purity of the air or the sweet taste of the rain on our tongues when it fell—and it seemed to fall often. We slept deeply each night, awaking refreshed and ready to begin again. We had never experienced the sensation of raindrops splashing against our skin. The first time it happened, we ran around the compound like schoolchildren with our tongues hanging out, trying to catch the rain in our mouths. It was a silly act, but who cares? We had no idea what was causing those feelings of euphoria. There were new things to see and new sensations to experience and discover every moment of every day. I was in adrenaline overload and never wanted it to end.

Our primary job was the assembly of prefabricated dwellings recycled from The Hive. They were so modular in design that putting them up was more an exercise in tedium than a creative endeavor. Consequently, we were driven to get it done, if for no other reason than to move on to something that might be more interesting. Within six months, we had completed two thousand of these cookie-cutter cottages. This meant more of our brothers and sisters would be joining us.

As the new arrivals emerged from the shuttles, they looked terrified. We found that amusing but remembered it was exactly how we must have looked when the gangway lowered for our arrival. The difference, however, was dramatic. When we arrived, we were alone and unsure, but these settlers would have the benefit of our presence to get them through their initial confusion and nervousness. This served everyone because it made them functional members of the team in a couple of days rather than weeks. We were welcoming them home. I never thought I would be saying those words.

I had volunteered to play the role of tour guide as our nervous friends arrived. It was a break from the monotony of residence assembly, and it allowed me to be more of an administrative officer in our new world. Kyle was happy to let me do some of this stuff because it afforded him the opportunity to work closely with the other engineers as they executed the Bridgetown Plan.

I was even allowed to use the now infamous hand module to remotely control the Spider Drones. At times, I felt almost god-like as I put the Drones through their paces. Each group of new arrivals would of course now be subjected to my version of a practical joke, because I wanted them to experience the same terror we did upon seeing these mechanical monsters. The setup was always the same. I would wait until the new arrivals were unloaded from The Explorer and the craft lifted off. Right on cue, the Spider Drones would converge on our position. Like us, the new arrivals stood petrified while I pretended to advance toward the enemy, chasing them away.

There was always a hearty round of applause and back-slapping for my bravery until the new arrivals reached the encampment and someone explained how I managed to be so bold in the face of such a menace. Most took it as a harmless prank, but not all. When Kyle heard about my antics, he gave me one of his now famous lectures about respect and responsibility, all the while laughing his ass off. His laughter was an admission to me that he had done the exact same thing to us when we arrived.

New residences were now being finished at a rate of eighty per day. In twelve weeks, another five thousand homes had been completed. It seemed strange to me that these structures were exactly the same as they were on Vanguard, but here they were "Homes," and on Vanguard they were "Units." Kyle explained to me that the word "home" had more permanency. I guess that made sense at some level, but not to me.

New citizens were arriving daily, and our tent compound was bursting at the seams. We were becoming peoples of this New Earth. We had even grown accustomed to seeing the hideous Spider Drones. Kyle found our reaction to them humorous and called us a bunch of cowards. I often reminded him if wasn't for the fact he was their creator, he'd be shitting himself every time one crossed his path, just like the rest of us. He just laughed.

Bridgetown was beginning to take on the appearance of a small town that had mysteriously appeared along the sandy shores of a fairytale lake, nestled among the green and red of a lush forest below great snow-capped mountains. Could it get any better than this? Over the next three years, homes were built and citizens came. As the last shuttles arrived, there was a mixture of sadness and intimidation. Until this moment, there had always been an emotional link between those on the ground and those on Vanguard. Now it was as if the umbilical cord had been severed forever.

Up until now, our efforts had been directed at building homes and getting people in them. The next priority was to build a hospital. Aboard Vanguard, there were three medical complexes, but that was because of the size of the vessel, not the absolute need for so many. Bridgetown was far more condensed, and we needed to keep large building sites in proportion to the available space.

The plan was for a ten-thousand bed Medical Center to be positioned on the middle tier of our three-tiered city. The building would be the largest of the infrastructure developments, and even with all citizens involved, the project took two years to complete. All infrastructure buildings would be linked with the Medical Center. Much like the hospital, the plan was to reduce the number of structures. For example, the three universities on Vanguard were reduced to one building in Bridgetown and so on.

When all was said and done, the primary institutions were confined to four massive facilities. Every citizen either worked at or attended classes in these buildings, making the central location vital to traffic control. The entire design of Bridgetown was engineered to promote maximum flow efficiency. We knew no other way. The only agencies not resident to the central building campus were government and military services. This grouping of smaller structures housed the Chambers of The Vanguard Council, Space Administration, and of course The Protectors. It would take ten years to complete Bridgetown. And so it began!

Two

Good-Bye, Dear Friend

As much as our forefathers took away our futures on Mother Earth, toward the end, they committed every ounce of their being to ensuring that when we found a new home, we would be as prepared as it was possible to be. The entire concept of Vanguard was based on the premise that the vessel would provide a livable situation for however long that might be, and when we found New Earth, it would provide the basic raw materials to allow us to begin again.

Looking at Vanguard, I couldn't help but wonder if man had only put that much effort into preserving Earth, perhaps we might have avoided all this. Every detail of the vessel's design and construction was geared to sustaining human life. The ship was completely self-sufficient and regenerating. Apart from its outer hull, every internal structure and mechanical, power, and defensive system was designed to be reused. Bridgetown was the recycled version of Vanguard.

The Units of The Hive became the Homes of Bridgetown. The power for Bridgetown was provided by the same Zion Plasma Cores that powered Vanguard. The water-recycling systems and sewage-treatment systems came from Vanguard, and the list went on and on. Even the layout of Bridgetown was designed to incorporate the technologies of Vanguard. In the end, all we did was find a site that fit the plan and drop in the pieces. Perhaps somewhat oversimplistic, but when you scraped away the shiny new look of Bridgetown, you found the love and protection of Vanguard.

By the time Bridgetown was completed and we had transitioned to the planet, all that was left of our home of 260 plus years was the tired shell of a great friend and guardian. We had stripped her down to the point that two Explorers were required to hold her in orbit to prevent the skeleton from being drawn by the planet's gravitational pull and crashing down on top of us. The only element missing from the plan was what to do with her remains.

The Council decided Vanguard would be towed into deep space and destroyed. Many people had mixed emotions about this solution, but Bridge Command carried out the order, and the citizens only became aware of Vanguard's fate after the deed had been done. A monument to her was commissioned by the Council to be placed on the highest hill overlooking Bridgetown as a reminder of how we came to this place. This is Bridgetown. This is New Earth.

Three

Kyle Chandler

From as far back as Citizen's School, Kyle Chandler had seen things differently than the rest of his classmates had. Most put it down to the fact that he was not born to The Hive. Kyle was transferred in from Bridge Command. It was the first time in the history of Vanguard that any individual born beyond the bulkhead was moved to The Hive. What added to the strangeness of this event was that Kyle was an orphan and left in the care of the Citizen's Community Support Group.

Neither Kyle nor anyone else his age truly appreciated the magnitude of what had happened to him. He was barely five years old, orphaned, and cared for outside a traditional family setting. Some shunned him as an oddity. Others were attracted to him because he was different in a society where conformity was the only acceptable standard.

He was unique in more ways than most could have imagined. Kyle saw his predicament as a kind of badge of honor and a reason for challenging the status quo. All through Developmental School, Kyle bucked accepted traditions and rules of conduct. Teachers saw him as a troubled and disruptive spirit, brilliant, but difficult to manage. How could any of us relate to what he had endured and his feelings about not having parental affection in his life? Kyle never spoke much about his feelings. All he ever said was that his parents died and the system had banished him to a compassionless circumstance.

His grades were at the top of every class, proving he could be disruptive and still far exceed the expectations of the educational system. The Educational Cooperative concluded that the only way to get him under control was to move him to higher levels with more mature students; they believed this would smother his outspoken nature. With any other individual, the ploy might have worked, but not with Kyle. He now had a more influential audience to teach him, and in turn, whom he could inspire toward his brand of mischief. Our system had inadvertently created a political monster, but as it turned out, it was exactly the monster we needed.

As much as his antics were a constant source of excitement for the rest of us, more impressive was his uncanny ability to attract an audience, particularly girls, with his smooth, almost consoling style and speech. The more traditional students avoided any interaction with him and often referred to him as the outcast. Kyle seemed unaffected by the opinions of his critics, but he never resented them. He always referred to himself as an acquired taste. I know that was something he read somewhere, but it seemed to fit. Whether you liked him or not, everyone agreed he would be a catalyst for change in our future. If we had only known how prophetic that opinion would be, perhaps we might have treated him differently.

Bridgetown would not have been possible without Kyle Chandler. Twelve years ago, I completed the audio history disks from my review of all the historic written text. The exercise was sanctioned by The Vanguard Council in the hopes of creating one comprehensive reference library of the history of mankind in disc form. For me, the exercise was a labor of love because I was a historian and this was right up my alley.

My efforts would prove to be far more eye-opening than anyone could have imagined and in many ways contradicted what we had always been led to believe. Most of the revelations, although interesting, were not overwhelming in their impact on our naive society. But a few, just a few, cut to the very fabric of our belief systems. Upon completion of the work, the discs were to be used as educational tools at the university level to assist young adults in understanding our true heritage. At first, when the Council realized the implications of my findings, they were reluctant to have the discs circulated to the general population.

Their reservations only served to heighten the interest of the students in the discs, and before long, they replaced the written historical text as common fare in the reference libraries. Those discs and the Council's reactions concerning them intrigued Kyle and changed our lives.

Kyle truly was our version of a social rebel. He liked being labeled a nonconformist because it meant he was being noticed, even if it was in a negative context. Just as he had done at Citizen's University, every time the establishment made a decision without involving the people, he would publically berate them. He was young, brash, and very outspoken. In the discs, he found a platform to send his message to a steadily widening audience for change.

Probably the most provocative revelation contained on the discs—and what compelled Kyle to throw down the gauntlet to the Council—was the method by which they had managed the search for New Earth. The text revealed that during our voyage we had investigated over two hundred M-class planets as potential colonization options, but in the end, each and every one was deemed unsuitable because they failed to meet an unspoken set of criteria only the Council was privy to.

"Over two hundred Earth-like planets had been visited, studied, and disqualified based on a criteria interpreted and managed solely by the Council." This troubled me, and it certainly troubled the other young adults who were faced with living out their lives as had all those that came before. Kyle saw this as unacceptable and more evidence of the Council's Draconian handling of citizenry affairs.

When he petitioned the Council to explain the qualifying criteria, they strongly suggested he not concern himself with matters best dealt with by them. This show of arrogance was all Kyle needed to launch a campaign of resistance against their right to manage our affairs in isolation. Kyle boldly advised the Council that unless they sat in open consultation with the citizens, he would organize student protests and close the schools. He was no fool and a devoted follower of ancient Earth political history, but he was young and at times careless.

He knew that no governing body could withstand the scrutiny of the people should they determine their affairs were not being dealt with in a manner reflecting their best interests. The Council dismissed his threats as idle foolishness and insisted his energies would be better served improving the lives of his fellow citizens.

Kyle was true to his word. Within days, he organized the student bodies on a platform that the future of the youth of Vanguard was being manipulated by a small body of people who had lost touch with their needs. He went on to suggest that the Council had bestowed upon themselves additional status and powers beyond the scope of their charter.

Not only did the students take up his cause, but so did the professors and teachers, who years before thought of Kyle as a problem. The protests were loud and animated but never violent. Civil disobedience was unheard of in The Hive. In response, the Council made their first tactical error. To quell the disruption, they unleashed the Vanguard Militia, imposing military rule.

This was the first time citizens ofThe Hive had ever interacted with the Militia or even knew of their existence. Seeing an armed force entering The Hive through the bulkhead between us and Bridge Command and arresting The Hive children was unacceptable, but the Council didn't stop there. They directed the Militia to seize all the history discs from the libraries and outlawed their use.

For the first time in the history of Vanguard, the citizens pushed back against the Council. They petitioned Bridge Command, not the Council, to free their children. The admiral of the Bridge recognized that his primary responsibilities were to The Hive, and we were released. Within days, Kyle was summoned to appear before the Council to formerly discuss our concerns. He worked tirelessly to prepare for this face-to-face meeting. He had convinced and surrounded himself with scientists, doctors, and highly respected professors who shared his beliefs for open government and supported his "right to know" platform. Kyle also decided that if we were to represent the rights of citizens, we would need an identity people could relate to.

Thereafter, our group would be known as the Citizen's Review Board. Our mandate was to investigate the decision-making processes that disqualified over two hundred New Earth potentials. Kyle assured the people that the CRB was not formed to discredit the institution that was The Vanguard Council, only to understand the processes used to make decisions that were designed to protect the welfare and interests of the citizens.

So much needed explanation. There were too many anomalies uncovered in the texts. Most of these inconsistencies might never have come to light if not for my forensic examination. The inquiry brought out that there were ten qualifying requirements for any M-class planet to be considered for human colonization. These guidelines were adopted by the People's World Council before Vanguard was built and passed on to our advocates, The Vanguard Council.

Under closer examination, the criteria for the New Earth selection were not unreasonable, but they were vague and subject to a range of interpretations. Wherein lay the problem! Interpretation alone had disqualified every candidate planet for the past 250 plus years. In way of example, one of the requirements directed that "Any planet being considered must be Earth-like in most ways, including average temperature, land mass to ocean ratios, and distance to its sun." Taken literally, that meant any deviation, no matter how inconsequential, could disqualify a planet—and in our case had.

Trying to find a world that was virtually identical to Earth was never going to happen, and we would be wandering the heavens for all eternity. After considerable discussion and debate, the Council conceded that their interpretation of the requirements over the centuries may have been too severe given the primary objective, which was to find a new home planet. At length, they and the CRB found a way to simplify the criteria and remove subjective interpretation from the process.

A more realistic set of requirements was tabled and accepted. Did the planet have a breathable atmosphere? Did it have a tolerable climate where humans could live and flourish? Was the indigenous life compatible with humans? Was there sufficient potable water to support humankind, and lastly, was the soil suitable to support farming and the raising of livestock?

Philosophically at least, The Vanguard Council and the CRB agreed, what remained of our species was looking to begin a new life on a new world, and it should be expected there would be hardships as we planted our new roots. We agreed, as well, to reexamine an M-class planet visited six months earlier, identified as study case #203.3289, primarily because it met most of the original criteria and all of the revised qualifications. If we had waited to find another suitable planet as we travelled further on, we might spend more wasted years wandering aimlessly through the heavens.

Bridge Command hadn't turned the ship around to return anywhere since leaving Earth's orbit. They were unsettled and confused by the instruction, but nonetheless, back we would go. Turning a vessel the size of Vanguard around was not as easy as just cranking a steering wheel. To complete the slow turn took five days and required 100,000 miles of exaggerated arcing. Almost six months later, we arrived at the coordinates for #203.3289, and Kyle and I were invited by the admiral of Bridge Command to attend the forward viewing deck to see firsthand our potential new home. We were the first citizens of The Hive to ever pass through the bulkhead to Bridge Command. It was an unbelievable experience and one I know I'll never forget.

As we approached the planet, the first striking feature was the surface detail. This world appeared to have no oceans, but rather thousands of lakes dotting the entire surface, separated from each other by massive mountain ranges and dense forests. Around its equator was a white band perhaps two to three thousand miles wide. We surmised it had to be desert, completely void of any visual evidence of lakes, forests, or mountains. It was a stunning contrasting image.

Study case #203.3289 was a large planet, perhaps one and a half times the size of Earth. The cloud cover made it difficult to clearly make out finer detail, but what was apparent was that the mountain ranges were much higher than their counterparts back on Earth, towering in some cases over fifty thousand feet. It was a bigger than life version of Earth and would require a bigger than life effort to make it our home.

Kyle asked the admiral of the Bridge Command to call up to the monitors the survey records from Vanguard's previous visit to the planet. He was curious to see the scientific summary that caused this place to fail the acid test for colonization. Although it may have been an interesting read for him, the technical data was way beyond my understanding. I asked him if there was anything in the summary that should concern us about the planet and our hopes for calling it home.

"Well, Ryan, the desert area around the equator is truly inhospitable and can't support human life. Daytime temperatures are in excess of 160 degrees, falling to below forty degrees at night. Nothing can grow or live there because no water was detected. As for the rest of the planet, pack your bags, boy—we're home!" said Kyle.

"Pack your bags, boy—we're home!" I never thought I'd hear those words, and we had Kyle Chandler to thank for them. He wasn't a politician or a militant. Shit, at twenty-eight, he was barely old enough to be a citizen. All he wanted was a more fulfilling life for all of us.

For his never-say-die dogged determination, Kyle was given the honor of being the leader of the first group of settlers to land on the planet. For my work on the history discs and my relationship with Kyle, I was included. My name is Ryan Evans.

Four

The Conspiracy

Life in Bridgetown went on much the way it had on Vanguard, except we were no longer content with limiting our choices. This was a brave new world to explore, and we were young women and men ready to take up the challenge. With freedoms came enlightenment, whether you wanted it or not, and Kyle hungered for it.

I can't remember how we got around to it, but again it was Kyle who remarked that my entire historical review from the time we left Earth's orbit seemed to have no references to medical advances or pandemic diseases. Until he mentioned the anomaly, I hadn't even considered the significance. I guess in hindsight, everyone including myself had assumed that if it wasn't in the modern history section of the texts, the subject had no relevancy.

Kyle wasn't buying it! He knew there had to be records, and if they weren't where I was looking, they were somewhere else. Once again, he went before the Council, but this time they would not be intimidated by his rebellious nature. Not even the CRB would stand at his side, and generally speaking, the citizens saw no value in airing private medical records just to satisfy Kyle's need to know everything.

The medical history of our forefathers was not public domain. What greater good would be served? Without the support of the people, Kyle had no leverage and backed away. He was my friend, and I could see this bothered him in the deepest ways because he genuinely believed in the right of the people to have access to all information. In his mind, it was all about the principal. Kyle would often lament that it didn't matter what was in the records, only that the common person had the right to look if he or she wished. Perhaps not at all the records, but at least those records that referred to that person's personal family history. His philosophy fell on deaf ears, and he dropped it—or so it seemed.

I remember the moment my life—no, let me rephrase that—everyone's life changed forever. Kyle was holding court on the beach, as he always did when we weren't at our work stations. As usual, our little group was fully engaged, listening to his ramblings. Everything he said always seemed to make sense to us, no matter how out there some of it was. His true talent was an ability to paint pictures with words, and that day was no exception.

We were discussing our favorite topic for sunny days by the lake: girls, girls, and more girls! We were all men now, and in the case of Kyle and me, we had no female prospects. As we loafed around, joking and gawking at the girls prancing up and down along the shoreline, Kyle blurted out, "Have you ever noticed there are no homely girls in Bridgetown? Not one! They all have the same body type, legs, breasts, and asses. Their faces and hair are different, but still, don't you think that's strange?

"Forget the girls for a minute and look at us! We're all generally built the same. Mostly we're the same height and weight. Of course, I'm better looking than the rest of you, but other than that, we could all be brothers.

"Throughout human history, man has come in all shapes and sizes, but not us. Don't you guys find that odd?" Then he looked at us with kind of a wake-up grin. "That's not all! Throughout

Ryan's modern history discs, there are no references to plagues, flu pandemics, heart disease, cancer, or a million other maladies that have plagued man since the beginning of time. Ryan's a bit slow some days, but he wouldn't have missed something that significant."

His statements were compelling! The silliest part was I don't think he cared about any of what he was suggesting. Kyle was notorious for being melodramatic and controversial. Yet once he saw our reaction to what he said, his eyes lit up. He now had a new ploy to get access to the medical files, and it didn't require him spouting off about freedom of information that no one was buying into anyway. He would do as he had just done!

He would begin a subtle campaign of spreading doubt among the citizens about themselves. Once he had everyone wondering about their family trees, he knew it would get back to the Council. This time, they'd have to listen! He wouldn't demand to see any records. He would simply pose provocative questions and let the people demand the answers.

Why are our body shapes similar beyond what coincidence might suggest? Why is it there are never any reported diseases? Before Vanguard, these were part of man's frailty, but since we left Earth's orbit, nothing. Why? What changed? These were trap questions, and Kyle knew that the Council couldn't just brush them off with vague statements. They would have to prove their answers to quiet the masses. That would require providing access to the medical records. It was so indirect and devious, it was brilliant. I was sure glad this guy was on our side.

His plan was to get the citizens to demand audience with the Council and ask the CRB to represent them. His tact was simple and diabolically subliminal. He created colorful graphic posters and recruited us to hang them all around Bridgetown. He then organized rallies at schools, workplaces, and parks. Wherever citizens gathered was a forum for Kyle.

The controversial posters posed simple questions, such as, "How do you know your girlfriend isn't your half-sister?"

and "Why is it we are built nothing like our ancestors?" and my personal favorite, "Do you ever get sick? No. Why do you think that is?"

On the front of the girls' dorm, we hung this banner: "Isn't it wonderful you can all share bras because your breasts are all the same size?" That one almost caused an uprising! As simplistic and harmless as this all might seem, it was extremely effective in getting out his message. Before long, the posters became all the conversation in Bridgetown. Kyle knew it was just a matter of time before the citizens would want answers. He was right! In less than two weeks, the CRB was requested to attend consultations with The Vanguard Council.

The Council was a secretive body. To the citizens, they were faceless oracles who manipulated our destinies. To Kyle, they were people just like us that had been given the important responsibility of managing our affairs and guardianship of The Hive. He reminded us constantly that members of the Council were not voted into their positions; they had been appointed generations before, and their powers were passed down father to son or daughter, over and over again.

"Who holds them accountable if we don't? Shit, guys—for generations, they haven't even lived in The Hive! They govern our affairs as if they know us. They don't know us—our feelings, our hopes, and dreams! They're part of Bridge Command. The Hive was a lie, and all this is a lie! We need to wake up!" Kyle lectured.

He was determined to have the Council held accountable by the citizens and for a new order to begin. As the meeting began, Kyle wasted little time getting to his point. Immediately he began demanding answers. The Council tried their best to avoid answering any questions definitively, but Kyle would have none of it and kept repeating the same questions over and over again in different ways. Finally the Council uttered the words that set into motion a series of events that would define our destinies for the rest of time.

"Things were done in the past to protect and preserve the well-being of The Hive," declared Evelyn Meyers, Chairperson and Speaker of The Vanguard Council.

Kyle responded, "What in hell does that mean? What happened in the past? People have a right to know, and this Council has an obligation to tell them." He went on to say, "If things were done, they were done, but understanding is the first step to healing the wounds of distrust the citizens feel for this Council. Do not confuse your self-bestowed powers with your obligations to the people."

It had been over ten years since last they had to listen to a Kyle Chandler, "Good of the people" lecture. Our naïve innocence would end this day. Our blind faith in the Council would be replaced with a skepticism and distrust never before felt by the Children of Vanguard.

For reasons only our Earthly ancestors could speak to, they somehow rationalized that if there was a New Earth, it was imperative to deliver a new mankind to colonize it. In order to accomplish the objective, they decided that over time and through selective breeding, some of the historic frailties of men would be weeded out. We would be molded by science into a better, smarter, and healthier species.

What did all this mean? Once again, the arrogance of mankind had meddled into the natural order of things, even though we stood on the brink of extinction. Toward the end of Earth, our knowledge of DNA and genealogy had advanced to the point that, very literally, we could create the proverbial superman without leaving the lab. Whether or not that ever happened, we'll probably never know, but for the purposes of this explanation, it is only important that we could have.

Naturally conceived childbirth was a crap shoot! There was no predicting with certainty what good and bad genes the offspring would inherit from his or her parents. What if you could take the best of both and add what was missing? It was like playing God because we could, justifying our tampering by saying, "It is for the betterment of mankind."

I guess if the exercise had been limited to removing diseased DNA, we might have understood to a degree that it was done with the best of intentions, but to do so without asking the people was a trust issue and an entirely different matter. Putting things in perspective, this process was not limited to just the citizens of The Hive. Every resident of Vanguard, including the Council and Bridge Command, was enhanced in the same manner.

In some cases, the scientific intervention was minor, but in other cases, a total intervention was required to end up with what in their sick minds was the right result. The obvious question now was, "Is it still being done?" The response to the question by the Council was, "It never stopped being done."

"Almost three centuries of violating our most sacred of rights, and you guys haven't reached the ideal human form yet?" snipped Kyle.

He would never let this go. The Council justified their actions by boasting that virtually all hereditary disease and deformity had been eradicated decades ago, but, they explained, there were other reasons why the interventions continued. What came to light next unmasked the greatest conspiracy ever perpetrated on a segment of the human race.

The Council explained that once scientists realized their success with making a healthier human specimen, there really was no outer limit. These doctors, supported by Councils throughout our history, rationalized that as long as the primary DNA strands were maintained, what was the harm in fine-tuning around the edges? Not to make a superman, but a better man. If these madmen could manipulate the genes for bone structure and muscle development, they could make a stronger human, forever free of the pain from diseases like arthritis and osteoporosis. When the experiment was successful and the next generation grew to be stronger and disease-free, wasn't it worth the risk?

The Council showed no signs of remorse. They truly believed, as all the Councils before them, that what had been done made humans better prepared for the colonization of this new world. It was a madness justified by the notion that balance was critical to the success and well-being of The Hive. All other considerations were secondary, including the rights of the citizens.

Kyle demanded to know how this conspiracy was accomplished without a citizen's knowledge. The answer was disturbing and villainous. Each year, citizens were required to attend the Medical Center for physical evaluations. During these visits, DNA testing was undertaken, and that's how the masquerade began.

Should there be an imbalance in the population for any reason, and if couples were known to be sexually active, the female would be artificially impregnated with altered sperm. To the happy couple, it was a time of rejoicing. To the Council, order had been restored, but it went beyond even that. If there was a shortage of males or females during any generation, chromosomes were manipulated to maintain the desired mix. Although we had never noticed before, because I guess ignorance was bliss, the population of The Hive never fell below 148,000 or went above 152,000. This was not coincidence! Although the Council fell short of admitting to population quotas enforced through scientific intervention, Kyle was convinced they had manipulated deaths to maintain this balance.

As shocking and outlandish as all of this was, what was done was done. Now, it must stop—today! It was then that the Council delivered the final slap in the face. For decades, scientists had been moving and manipulating DNA throughout the population. Although they always tried to maintain the base strands, over time those lines had become blurred to the point they feared stopping could have disastrous consequences for future generations.

When I heard this, the first thing I thought of was the silly banner we hung over one of the university entrances. "How do you know your girlfriend isn't really your half-sister?" These were devastating admissions that our innocent society was ill-equipped to deal with.

"This is something out of a grotesque Poe novel, and we were just unwitting characters in your devious plots. You and all those before you are no more than ghouls!" shouted Kyle.

"Enough!" demanded Meyers. "We have answered your questions. Leave these Chambers now—or risk being arrested. How dare you!"

With that, we were escorted out of Chambers by armed guards. Kyle had to be restrained and kept screaming back over his shoulder, "We will have justice! You are monsters!"

Kyle insisted that all those involved would be held accountable for their actions. When he made the citizens aware of these unimaginable atrocities, the reaction was not one of repulsion. Nor was it a cry out for vengeance or punishment. It was more resigned and subdued. As a society, we just couldn't come to grips with the reality of our situation.

Kyle went silent! I think he felt he had gone too far and taken away the thing that made us who we were, our faith in each other. Even though that faith was a lie, it was the glue that kept us together; it was who we were. Who were we now? Were we something freakish, man-made in a test tube hidden in the back of a dimly lit laboratory?

Life in Bridgetown continued on as usual. As a society, we couldn't understand what had happened, and because we weren't equipped to deal with the truth, we withdrew into the only world we were comfortable in. In that world, others controlled our lives, and we were oblivious to the evils perpetrated against us. It had been that way since we left Earth.

We weren't ready to be on our own, and we certainly weren't ready for this level of drama. We needed Kyle Chandler to start leading us forward. I knew at some point he would realize we had come too far to slide backward. For weeks, every time we saw each other, I would complain about what had been done to us without consequence or at least reprimand. Each time, he would just shrug, and we would go our separate ways.

Then came the day! It started like any other day. Our little group was sitting around talking about essentially nothing. Suddenly Kyle stood up and proclaimed, "You guys are right! This is unacceptable! We will never be self-reliant if we allow others to think for us. Look how well that worked out! We are the future of Bridgetown and need to make a choice to lead our people forward." He was back, and we were ready to be led—or were we?

Five

Fall from Grace

Kyle wasted little time making his return to our ranks mean something. His first plan for change was to persuade most of the young adults of the city to stop reporting to the workplace. He spent every minute of every day focused on changing how people viewed their lives and the Council. He spoke of freedom of choice, controlling our destinies, and planning for our futures. Through all of this, The Vanguard Council remained strangely silent.

None of us were sure what triggered Kyle's next decision. He was different from us and thought about things from a very Utopian viewpoint. We lived in the moment, never curious about what was around the next corner. He cared only about what was around the next corner and how he could get there. One summer's day, without warning, he announced we would make a Proposal to the citizens.

We would ask them to recognize through a "yes" vote the authority of the CRB to represent their interests in all matters pertaining to Bridgetown. Further, this authority would supersede all other authorities in the service of the citizens. If successful, we would essentially push The Vanguard Council aside.

It was a gambit of monumental proportions. To fail would most certainly assure the status quo for generations to come.

Kyle didn't seem concerned about the risk; he felt the vote would represent the most important decision the citizens had ever been asked to make. He insisted the entire process be broadcast live into each home and the votes for or against be cast by families in consultation. He declared that once tabulated, the results would be live-streamed back to each household. Kyle was insistent that every person who cast a vote must know their vote counted whether they supported the Proposal or not.

On the day of the vote, there was no talking to Kyle. He had gone to another place in his mind. All he did was stare at the video monitor in his office, waiting for the polls to close and the tabulations to begin. We all had our own ways of dealing with the pressures of that day. After all was said and done, it took sixteen agonizing hours for the votes to be counted.

Midway during the live broadcast, all the monitors went black for a couple of hours, followed by a message that flashed up on the screen from the Communications Office. The message explained there had been technical issues, but they had been resolved. Kyle knew the Council had their fingers in this somewhere. Our suspicions were confirmed when a Protector delivered a handwritten note from Chairperson Myers addressed to Kyle three hours before the official results were known.

The note congratulated Kyle on the results of the vote. It went on to say The Council looked forward to working alongside the CRB for the betterment of the people. The note concluded by inviting us to the next Vanguard Council meeting for consultations and planning. When Kyle showed me the memo, a kind of wry smile crossed his lips.

He spoke calmly but with absolute conviction. "What will we do with unemployed Council Members?"

When the final count was aired, 97 percent of the adult-aged population had cast votes. Of the votes cast, 94 percent were in favor of the Proposal. Kyle's reaction was unanticipated and certainly not typical of Kyle Chandler. He ran out onto the boulevard and started thanking everyone he saw. He knocked on doors and thanked whoever answered. He was overwhelmed! The citizens were not accustomed to shows of extreme emotion, good or bad. I think for a moment they must have thought him mad. I did!

He explained to me later, after things had settled down, that it wasn't so much that the Proposal had passed; it had more to do with how proud he was that 97 percent of the citizens had voted. He went on to say that this proved we could do what was necessary to make a better life on this new world. We won the vote! So what do we do next?

To Kyle, the next step was a foregone conclusion. "We will dissolve The Vanguard Council immediately," he announced boldly.

Just like that! The abruptness of his words almost knocked me on my ass. Up until that moment, everything had been an adventure. We were young men defying the power of the establishment by drawing lines in the sand and daring the authority to cross them. Now the time had come to backup the promises we had made and provide the better life Kyle was constantly claiming was just beyond the horizon.

"We must move quickly and with clearness of purpose to show the people we meant what we said," continued Kyle. "We promised to act in their best interests. Removing the Council is the first step toward fulfilling the promise. The Council betrayed the sacred trust of the people since the very beginning. Those actions were not unfortunate, momentary lapses in good judgment. They were a series of calculated evils designed to manipulate our futures to serve their secret agendas. Such actions must have consequence."

Without another word, he dispatched a note to The Vanguard Council demanding immediate audience. His next action was to pay a visit to the admiral of Bridge Command. Admiral James Donner was in his late sixties. He was clearly a person other men paid attention to, and his support was critical to the authority of the CRB.

As the meeting began, Kyle thanked Donner for his tireless service to the people as well as the past contributions the Donner family had made over the decades. He went on to say that he would be proud to call the admiral the wisest of his friends and looked forward to tapping into his experience and seeking his good counsel.

Donner seemed flattered by the impassioned speech from a man so much his junior and held out his hand in a show of friendship. Kyle went on to explain that the time for change was now and we would dissolve The Vanguard Council within the hour because they had not acted in the best interests of the citizens.

Donner didn't bat an eye when he heard Kyle's intent. His only response was, "How can Bridge Command be of assistance?"

"We need the support of Bridge Command to back up the Citizen's Review Board's new mandate. This Council does not and will not recognize our authority, regardless of the vote. They have never acknowledged the will of the people. We need muscle! We need you! With your resources at our side, the Council cannot resist, and real change can begin," responded Kyle.

Donner was emotionless throughout the explanation. When he finally spoke, it was without passion and directly to the point. "The citizens have charged the CRB with managing their interests moving forward. Bridge Command serves the people, not The Vanguard Council. We will support you in this matter. We will walk you in and walk them out," declared Admiral Donner.

When I looked over at Kyle, I could see his chest heave as he breathed a deep sigh of relief. He advised the admiral that it wouldn't end there. Although it was true that the Council was the head of the serpent, the evil body of this coalition was the group of scientists who knowingly participated in this conspiracy and had for the last two and a half centuries. All that must end! We had their names, and they would be held accountable for their parts in this, but one step at a time.

When we arrived, the Council was waiting in Chambers. What happened next was direct, short, and decisive. As Donner promised, eight Protectors swung open the Chamber doors and proceeded up the aisle to the bench, where they stepped to either side. Kyle, Donner, and I followed in behind, and last but not least, fifty Protectors took positions just inside the entrance at the ready. There was a look on the faces of the Members that bordered on terror, but they were wise enough to remain stately and seated.

"What is the meaning of this?" the chairperson shouted down at us.

Kyle spoke without emotion and with clearness of purpose. "Members of The Vanguard Council, recent undertakings, discoveries, and admissions have shown that this House and its predecessors did not and have not fulfilled their charter. Your actions across many generations have violated sacred trusts and can no longer be tolerated. By the authority granted the CRB through the citizens of Bridgetown, I declare this Vanguard Council dissolved immediately. Admiral Donner, would you do the citizens of Bridgetown the service of having these people removed from these esteemed Chambers?"

There were no outbursts or excuses from any of the members! At first, their silence surprised me, but in hindsight, I think they knew that without Bridge Command to back their authority, it was over. With a simple nod from the admiral, the Protectors stepped forward and walked each of the former Council Members out. There was no emotion to the proceedings, only closure. Kyle thanked Donner for his support and requested right there that he consider a posting as the wisest new member of the CRB to represent the interests of Bridge Command.

The admiral hesitated for a moment, but I guess given Command's reduced role, it seemed like another way to make a meaningful contribution. He accepted, and Kyle quickly walked to the information center, where he instructed the Manager of Broadcasts to send the following message to all citizens via the video monitors.

"Citizens of Bridgetown, the CRB would like to thank you for your support as we move forward in your service. There have been many challenges and disappointments since we arrived here at our new home. We must put those behind us as we move forward with our futures. We must also put behind us those who betrayed our trust. Effective immediately, the governing body known as The Vanguard Council has been dissolved. It is now the duty of CRB to assume the responsibilities that were entrusted to them.

"On a brighter note, I am pleased to announce our first appointment to the new CRB. Please join me in welcoming Admiral James Donner of Bridge Command. His complete biography is available in the Hall of Records. Should you have any questions or concerns, please address them to my attention, and they will be dealt with."

That was that! Little could we have known what this alliance between the CRB and Bridge Command would mean to the future of the Children of Vanguard!

Kyle wasted little time in assembling the new sitting members of the CRB. We decided that the committee would have forty-one representatives. Seventeen would be elected by the citizens, three members would be seated from each of the infrastructure services, which included medicine, education, science and technology, agriculture, robotics, communications, fisheries (yet to be formed), and a newly named group to be hereafter known as the Protectorate. There would be one nonvoting member, the Secretariat (that's me), and finally the Chairperson (Kyle).

This was really the beginning of Bridgetown. Almost immediately, you could sense a change in the demeanor of the people. They began to feel they were a part of something much bigger than any one individual. The very first item on the agenda for the new CRB concerned the scientists involved in the Council's conspiracy. Bridgetown had no real police force or court system. Whatever we did had to be meaningful but politically astute!

We couldn't imprison them for crimes against the citizens, but we had to make sure nothing like this would ever happen again. It was decided that we would publically censure them, and they would be stripped of their autonomy as a separate unit of the medical establishment. From that moment forward, they would be accountable to the Regent of Medicine, Doctor Sabrina Weddell.

Sabrina was a no-nonsense general surgeon and administrator. Under her leadership, the Medical Center had moved steadily forward in their service to the citizens. She had always known something was going on between the Council and the scientists, but she was forced to remain hands off. Those days were now behind us. Henceforth, the policy would be openness and accountability. We'll speak more about Sabrina later. Her contribution to the future of Bridgetown is beyond measure, but that's another story.

Another sensitive subject for the CRB and the citizens was going to be the whole issue about DNA manipulation. If we were to believe what we were told, we could never go back to normal fertilization in the birth process because the risk of mutated births was too high to risk. Before we put the emotionally charged subject to the citizens, we would need scientific and medical guidance—in some cases from the very scientists that perpetrated the crime.

We would need an unbiased liaison that could interpret the data and provide us with the clearest assessment of the medical mumble jumble. Whatever those final recommendations were, they would be presented to the people, and we would let the chips fall where they may. For that independent go-between, we once again sought the assistance of Doctor Sabrina Weddell.

At first, she was reluctant because asking for help from the very people who caused the problem seemed to her to be justifying their actions. After some soul-searching, Sabrina came around, which was fortunate for us. There was no right answer here, and we knew it, but there could be a very wrong answer, and that would be devastating to the citizens who had already had their worlds turned upside down.

If anyone thought for a moment that this was going to be a quick exercise, they were wrong. The brainstorming and blame sessions took eight months to conclude, and the end result wasn't much clearer than where we began—but it was clearer.

Sabrina's interpretation of all their scientific deliberations was that natural child birth was possible. Beyond that, scientists disagreed on whether the modified DNA strands would hold their structure over time. There was no consensus on what the impact would be if they didn't. How would we present this to the people with enough certainty for them to make an informed decision? Kyle stepped in, as we knew he would, as he always did when the rest of us seemed to stall out.

"For almost three centuries, we allowed others to make decisions for us. We cannot allow that to happen again on our watch. Our recommendation to the citizens will not require a vote one way or another. It will require each family to decide what course they want to follow. We will honor their choices because they will have been made of free will.

"We will not terminate the practice of DNA intervention. What will be terminated is DNA enhancement. The extent of intervention will be chosen by each family, but be limited to maintenance of the existing strands."

All the members of the CRB and Sabrina agreed this was a reasonable approach to such a far-reaching moral dilemma. When the people were presented with the recommendations, they seemed relieved and satisfied that they would decide the direction of their lives. As time went on, it was interesting to learn that more than half chose to do it *au naturel*, if you will. So far, so good!

Six

Sabrina "The Great"

During all of this drama, something else was happening, which was far less controversial. Kyle was a thirty-plus bachelor! It wasn't that he didn't like women. His success with them in school was legendary among the young males of The Hive. He just stopped thinking about that side of his needs while he was very literally trying to jumpstart a new life for himself and the rest of us. That was about to change dramatically.

Much like Kyle, Sabrina Weddell had always been a strong critic of the status quo. Unlike Kyle, she conducted her campaigns against the establishment using the accepted methods for voicing opinions. Where Kyle ignored public opinion of his antics, Sabrina had to be ever conscious of her social position within The Hive elite.

Doctor Edward Weddell, Sabrina's father, was the dean of Medical Studies at the university and a man of considerable influence even beyond the bulkhead. His social and professional status forced Sabrina to always avoid negative press in order to secure her station in The Hive hierarchy. Sabrina was far more than just the daughter of a powerful father. She was brilliant in her own right.

Like Kyle, she was at the head of every class she enrolled in. Even to this day, Sabrina Weddell graduated university with more degrees in medicine than any student in the history of the university, including her father. That said, she was anything but a bookworm.

Sabrina's childhood had its share of tragedy. Her mother died giving her life. It was the only time that any woman had died in childbirth aboard Vanguard. After investigation, it was determined that Sara Weddell had a silent aneurism during labor and she was dead before Sabrina ever left her womb. This left a little girl to be raised by a father who had no concept of how to show his love in any meaningful way.

Throughout our university years, many of us considered her a real catch. She was strikingly attractive, unattached, and seemingly ready for the taking, but we quickly learned she was a mountain too high to climb. Her critical treatment of men was legendary. Kyle remembered her only as part of a group that steered clear of him because in their minds he was an outcast.

Sabrina had always found Kyle good to look at but someone that she would constantly be nose-to-nose with on any number of issues. Kyle was the model for everything she found intolerable about men. He was chauvinistic, self-centered, and impetuous. Yet, there was something about him—an attraction she felt but fought.

Sabrina began her career as the Assistant Chief of Surgery at the remarkably young age of twenty-three. Many of her peers at the time were insistent that the posting was influenced by her father's station within the medical community, not her readiness to take on the role. Whether that was true or not didn't seem to hold her back. Two years later, she was appointed Chief of Surgery, and two years after that as Regent of Medicine. Many considered her the most powerful woman this side of the bulkhead and arguably the most brilliant person on Vanguard—or anywhere else for that matter.

The Sabrina and Kyle saga started innocently enough, as romances go. Strange how you see things differently when you reach adulthood, but these two people who as students shared nothing were now close to sharing everything. They were exact opposites in almost every way except one. Their devotion to the betterment of our society was unequaled. Either of them would be happy to give all they had for the good of the people. From the moment they met again, so many years after university, something sparked. Sabrina was smarter than Kyle in many ways, but he was flamboyant, self-confident, and devoted to the cause of the people. Not even the brilliant man-hater could resist his charms forever.

Others saw the romantic attraction between them long before either of them even realized what those feelings were. They were like two peas from the same pod. Both were fanatical about what they were doing. Both were so preoccupied with leading change they couldn't recognize when they were changing. Both were outspoken and never knew when to shut up, and both loved to table controversial opinions for no other reason than to challenge the status quo.

They made every effort to keep their relationship private, but in a small city like Bridgetown, and given their individual notoriety, that wasn't going to happen. It began with private strategy meetings lasting well into the evening. When they ran out of excuses for having meetings, there were those chance encounters in the park near the lake twice a week. Although the couple was careful to never meet on the same days each week, they always met twice a week.

Soon those incidental encounters became routine events, and twice a week became three times and then four. When they shook hands and separated, supposedly to go their separate ways, people would witness them coming together again at one or the other's front door. This was all good! They both needed someone to complete them, and they seemed to be having so much fun with this clandestine love affair. We played the game with them. We pretended to know nothing, and they pretended not to be a couple.

Sabrina's affection for Kyle did not extend to her father. Edward Weddell disliked Kyle more than any man could dislike another man. When his pleading with Sabrina to end their relationship didn't work, he resorted to trying to use his influence to discredit Kyle. His best efforts failed on both fronts. Sabrina rejected his pleas, and Kyle was the people's choice and almost bulletproof. In time, it seemed her father began to accept that Sabrina and Kyle were destined to be together, but in the three years before his death, he would never speak to Kyle or even stay in a room if Kyle was there. This saddened Sabrina, but she would not allow the unwarranted emotions of her father to influence her love for Kyle.

Although never spoken of in Sabrina's or Kyle's presence, it was generally known that the reason her father had no use for Kyle was Evelyn Meyers, the ousted chairperson of the former Vanguard Council. Evelyn and Edward had been secretly involved for years, and Kyle's political actions against her and the Council had driven her into obscurity. Sabrina never talked about it, but at her father's funeral, Meyers was in the forefront weeping uncontrollably. Three months later, she took her own life.

Once you had a chance to interact with Sabrina on a personal level, it was obvious her impatience with men had more to do with their silly attempts to impress women than their sex. She was searching for a man who fulfilled her in ways most men couldn't understand, but Kyle was not most men. When they were together, they acted as foolishly as any other pair of young lovers, trying to mask it under the guise of lighthearted banter.

Kyle asked Sabrina to join the CRB to represent the medical community. This was controversial because there were no open seats. When I reminded him that by doing so he might be setting a dangerous precedent, his response was, "We need her intellect on the Board. What's another chair? I'll not appoint her. We'll sell the notion she should be invited in. Let me convince the members. Are you with me on this one, Ryan?"

Sabrina was unanimously appointed to the CRB the following week. Strange how that worked out! Sabrina was one of only four women sitting on the CRB. From the moment she took her seat, the business dealings of the Committee took on an entirely different dynamic. Kyle could no longer get away with pushing his pet projects through a vote without debate. She was like a lion among the lambs. That wasn't necessarily a bad thing, but it was always disruptive, because Sabrina's position on an issue automatically meant the other three women moved to her side of the debate. I guess someone had to keep Kyle's wide-eyed view of the world in check. Sabrina more than fulfilled the bill.

I remember the morning our two lovers walked into a scheduled CRB meeting, late as usual, and announced without any particular fanfare that they were to be married the following day in a simple ceremony by the lake. Admiral Donner agreed to perform the ceremony, and only a limited number of people were invited.

"Everyone on the Council that wishes to attend is welcome, but it will be your choice of course," Kyle declared.

I found his invitation style interesting. Every member would attend because not to might be seen as disappointing by the two most powerful people in Bridgetown. I know that was never Kyle's intention when he offered the invitation. Frankly, he would have preferred nobody came. As hard as Kyle tried to appear above the simple frailties of men in love, he wasn't fooling anyone, least of all his best friend. I could see the excitement in his body language. I was so happy for them. The entire CRB membership rose to our feet when we heard the announcement, and we all applauded, pretending to be shocked of course. Sabrina and Kyle were smirking as if they had fooled everyone.

Later, I took my friend aside and shared with him our ongoing Sabrina/Kyle watch. He seemed a bit pissed that their secret meetings and private lives were the talk of the town and neither Sabrina nor he had any idea. I think they knew exactly what we were up to, and it humored them to play games.

The wedding was a simple affair, as you might expect given the bride and groom. A small luncheon was served, and as subdued as the ceremony started is how it ended. Sabrina was radiant in her white business suit while Kyle wore his best grey jumpsuit because that's all he owned. Arm in arm, they strolled away to their small electric scooters and then home to do what newlyweds have done since the dawn of civilization. Noticeably absent from the celebration was Edward Weddell.

I knew two absolutes that would come from this union! They would absolutely never part until one of them died, and their children would absolutely not be genetically enhanced. I also knew that regardless of how they carried themselves, they were both deeply passionate people when out of the public eye. The strength of their love and devotion to each other would prove vital given the events that were to follow. First thing next morning, Kyle was at his seat in Chambers as we began the new business day—later than usual, but there nonetheless—yet Sabrina was not.

Seven

Predator and Prey

Although the Protectorate maintained the air patrols around Bridgetown, they were less focused and perhaps even a bit complacent. Our one constant was the Spider Drones. Day in and day out for all the years we'd been on the planet, the tin soldiers patrolled and guarded our perimeter. Over time, we had become comfortable with their presence, and since we didn't feel at risk, the Drones became curiosities for the young people. Unfortunately, that curiosity took a tragic turn.

A group of university students found a way to neutralize the microchip implants that identified them as authorized creatures to the Drones. Their motives were typical of inquisitive young men in our new unbridled society. They wanted to challenge the status quo by proving to their classmates that if an invader was stealth enough, he could elude the Drones and attack our city.

To prove their theory, the group of six students left Bridgetown and went into the forest beyond our perimeter. There they neutralized their chips with a small magnetic disruptor and began a slow, deliberate return to the city, covering themselves in branches and mud. Using what they believed were undetectable stealth maneuvers, they squirmed and crawled back through the underbrush toward the Drone patrols. The results were devastating!

The Spider Drones detected their presence as they drew nearer to the perimeter, but without the chips, they were intruders to be exterminated. As soon as the students realized the deception had failed, rather than retreat back into the forest, they panicked, leaped to their feet, and attempted to run across the perimeter to safety. The action left the Drone with no alternative programming other than its prime directive. In less than a heartbeat, they were dead!

Citizens viewed this tragic event as evidence the Drones could not be trusted. There was a public outcry for their destruction. The situation was worsened by Sabrina's active involvement in these protests. Kyle was hurt by her decision, but he understood. In Sabrina's case, it wasn't that she felt the Drones couldn't be trusted, it was simply a case where innocent people had died because of the robots' hard programming.

"Kyle, my love, I know you feel betrayed by the position I've taken, but our world is no longer just black and white. You changed that! You made everyone see there are other colors. These machines see only in black and white. We can no longer live our lives that way—not here, not now or ever again."

Sabrina's argument had merit, and her recommendation was that the Protectorate had plenty of soldiers and could easily replace the machines. She was convinced that had the sentries been human, this would not have happened. Kyle pleaded that as tragic as the student deaths were, they had deliberately put themselves in harm's way to prove a point. They were wrong, and sadly it cost them their lives. It was certainly unfortunate, but not a failure of the Drones.

He knew this argument wouldn't change the deeply rooted resentment everybody now shared for his creations. The will of the people would prevail. Three days later, the one thousand Spider Drones were removed from service and moth balled in a large hillside bunker near the Protectorate launch pads. Kyle refused to have them fully decommissioned because of his cautious nature and his uneasy feeling that all this was wrong.

During our initial assessment of the planet to determine if the conditions were viable for human colonization, it was noted that most of the indigenous animal samplings were herbivore and nonaggressive. The predatory samples that were found were small and clearly not at the top of the food chain.

Although our scientists found it strange that not a single large predator was identified out of thousands of specimens collected, we continued on. The scientists didn't buy it, but in the absence of evidence to the contrary, they were forced to take what they could prove at face value. Perhaps Nature had a different plan here. They were wrong; we were wrong!

Our introduction to the real threats around us began with the report that a group of surveyors had come up missing just inside our security perimeter at the north end of the city. The Protectorate launched an immediate blanket search for the four men, using low-level drone tracking for their chip implants and heat signatures. This was supplemented with military ground searches involving hundreds of soldiers blanketing the nearby forests and mountains. Nothing! For three weeks, the searches continued night and day. The citizens demanded results, but there were none to give them.

Admiral Donner was disappointed with his inability to find the missing surveyors or even to find evidence that they had met with an untimely end. The CRB declared the area off limits, and additional resources were put in place to patrol the north perimeter. For the first time since our arrival, an event had occurred that could not be explained away.

There was no talking to Kyle after the event. In his mind, this would not have happened had the Spider Drones been standing watch. Most of the CRB and Protectorate were of the same opinion. Even Sabrina had to admit that despite the deaths of the students, she may have been hasty in demanding the removal of the Drones.

Families were heartbroken and demands were made of the CRB to find ways to prevent a reoccurrence. In response, the roving patrols we tripled. Ever so slowly, people began to put the tragedy behind them as an unfortunate reality of the risks on this new world. Kyle asked the admiral to continue the airborne drone patrols because he couldn't wrap his mind around how a group of people could just disappear without a trace.

"This makes absolutely no sense! Given our surveillance technology, lost or dead they should have been found. The microchips were designed for exactly this eventuality. The evidence suggests to me they were removed from the area and taken somewhere beyond the range of our tracking equipment. If that's the case, and given the terrain of the area, the only way that could happen if they were carried off above the forests or beyond the mountains. I think we're looking for an airborne predator," Kyle suggested.

"Kyle, that's highly improbable. Even if they were attacked by a winged threat, how would this creature carry off four people?" responded the admiral.

"I don't know, and speculation is getting us nowhere. Let's get Sabrina involved. I want a full review of our original assessments of the indigenous animals, particularly flying animals. I can't get past this feeling I have that there's something going on here we've missed. If that's the case, I fear this is going to happen again," replied Kyle

Sabrina's team went back through every sample collected during the original planetary assessment. The only flying predators found were birds. Most consumed their small prey immediately upon kill, and even those large enough to carry off their kills could lift no more than two or three pounds.

Kyle asked Sabrina for an opinion on how large a bird would have to be to carry off a human body. Sabrina didn't know and suggested the question might be better answered by an aerodynamics expert. She recommended a young engineer by the name of Marcus Scott, a person she characterized as, "the smartest human on the planet."

Marcus Scott was summoned to appear before the CRB to give an opinion. "Mr. Scott, we need your expertise on a logic problem. How big would a bird have to be to kill and carry away a full-grown man? We know you're not a zoologist. We're looking more toward the lift dynamics of such a creature," I said.

"It's a bit outside my specialty, but I can offer this. The creature would have to be a minimum of five times larger than the weight it's lifting. Since I suspect this question relates to the mystery of the missing surveyors, I'm not surprised it's come up. I had been thinking about a similar scenario, so I took some time to consider some theories.

"If our people were attacked and carried off, dead or alive, then we're talking a very large specimen. It's highly unlikely this winged predator just swooped down and plucked these unfortunates off the ground. That would mean an animal of enormous size. Such a creature would be grossly out of scale for this planet and easy to find. I suspect our killer lands first and then stalks its prey, either consuming the kill on site or disabling it to transport to a nest of sorts.

"I think I'd be looking for blood pools or flesh evidence near the site. I envision a birdlike animal, but I'm not convinced it's a bird. I suspect a creature with a wingspan of perhaps twenty to thirty feet and a body length of twelve to fifteen feet. To lift a human and carry it away quickly requires tremendous lift and thrust. Look for these predators to move in small flocks. This was not the work of a single attacker," said Marcus.

"Wow—don't stop now! Where would we find these monsters?" I asked.

"Not in the forests, they would be too large! I might suggest focusing your attention on the mountains—in particular, deep mountain valleys. They might be cave dwellers, but that's just a guess. I wish I could be of more help," Marcus said.

Kyle thanked Marcus for his opinion and suggested we would be seeking his advice again. Although this was our first interface with the young genius, it wouldn't be the last. In fact, as time went on, Marcus would become far more than a reference resource. Far more!

Kyle asked the admiral to begin a systematic recon of the mountain ranges to the north. He asked Sabrina to assemble a full forensic team to travel under escort to the suspected attack site and search for blood and skin evidence. When Sabrina suggested she would accompany the team, Kyle would have none of it.

"I will not have you out there when we have no idea what we're dealing with. You're an administrator, not a field agent. Be an administrator!" he demanded.

Sabrina gave into Kyle's demands because she realized it was his love and fear for her driving him. As predicted by Marcus, human blood and skin was found soaked into the long grass, and DNA testing revealed the samples were in fact from the missing surveyors. Another distressing element of the find was that the evidence found was substantial. The forensic team agreed there was little hope the missing people could have survived. Kyle now had the sad task of bringing closure to the families of the taken; they were lost forever.

The search of the mountainous areas to the north of the city netted us nothing. Slowly, the event began to drift into the background. It was not so much that we were giving up; it was more that we had run out of options. Kyle would not accept any suggestion that this was a one-off event. He was convinced we were at risk and would be dealing with more loss of life.

Not everything that was happening was bad news though. While the insanity of the search continued, Sabrina announced to everyone that she was pregnant. I had never seen her look as radiant as when she delivered the news. Try as he would to appear matter of fact about the announcement, Kyle's constant casual reference to the upcoming event gave away his true feelings. He was as excited as his wife!

The joyous news was about to be upstaged by the confirmation of Kyle's prediction of another incident. This time it was at the northwest end of the Protectorate compound. A Protectorate sentry was attacked and carried off while patrolling the perimeter. Two others went to his rescue, and they too were attacked. These soldiers made every effort to defend themselves, but to no avail.

Their last emergency communications to Command suggested the attackers appeared to be dragons. Dragons, just like in the ancient fairytales. As farfetched as it sounded, it had to be taken seriously. There was an immediate deployment to the area by land and air, but in the few minutes the rescue took to get there, the battle was lost. Two of the three sentries were missing. The third was so badly wounded he fell into a deathly coma.

The city was put on alert, and full lockdown was ordered. This meant people were not permitted outside the city limits and nightly curfews were being enforced. Everyone was terrified, and in a reversal of sentiment, citizens demanded the Spider Drones be put back into service. Kyle didn't give into his urge to say, "I told you so." It wasn't his style. His only response to their demands was that before the Drones were put back into the field, he wanted to make a couple of programming changes.

The current Drone programming was limited to tracking targets on a horizontal plane. They were never intended to take the place of air-defense systems. This was about to change, as was the range of the Drone's laser weaponry. For the protection of our air-defense drones and ships, Kyle limited the new Spider Drone air-tracking capabilities to one thousand feet and advised the admiral to adjust his own drone patrols to remain above that level to avoid a conflict.

Kyle announced to the people that the Spider Drones would return to service, but not only around our perimeter. Roving Drone patrols were now to be present within Bridgetown. There was mild protest from some citizens, but the alternative was far worse than the physical appearance of the robots. As much as everyone hated to admit it, had the Drones been at their posts, likely none of this loss of life would have occurred.

Kyle reminded the CRB that before he took the Drones out of service, we had never been attacked. This couldn't be coincidence. He called upon Marcus Scott to review the internal memory chips of the robots to see if there had been any events where the Drones initiated their laser weapons for extended periods. If examples were found, it could mean they had confronted this predator before.

Kyle also wanted a full review of the last transmissions from the sentries during the attack. Our hope that the comatose soldier would shed some light on the events unfortunately died with him at the Medical Center. Admiral Donner invited Kyle and me to attend the replay of the transmissions. Kyle invited Marcus Scott. We needed his input because he was smarter than the rest of us, including Kyle.

As we sat down, another person entered the room and took the seat directly across from the admiral. "The officer seated across from me is Colonel James Donner, and yes, he is my son. I have invited James to this session because it was his men who died, and he wants to be part of tracking their killer," explained the admiral.

After some polite introductions and handshaking, the admiral requested the three transmissions be played back one at a time, starting with the first. With this, the loud speakers came to life.

"Command, Davidson here. Some sort of creature just landed about three hundred yards to the north and is moving toward my position. I think this might have something to do with the missing surveyors. I've signaled Peters and Smith to attend my position because there are three more of these things circling overhead. What are your orders? Out!"

"Davidson, Command here. If necessary, defend yourself and maintain contact. Peters, Smith—double time to his position," replied the Command officer.

"Well, that confirms Doctor Scott's theory that the creature lands to attack," I commented.

"Command, Peters here, I'm too late! Something's taken Davidson right in front of me. He's still alive, but I can't save him. I'm opening fire. Command, another one just landed! Where in hell is Peters? Shit—they're huge! They look like bloody dragons. Real, live dragons. It's coming, it's coming!"

Peter's must have dropped his communicator. We could hear the repetitive firing of his weapon. A few seconds later, there was what sounded like a muffled scream and a loud swooshing sound. It was over!

"At that range, he must have hit the creature numerous times, but it didn't stop it. What kind of fire power are we talking here?" asked Kyle.

James responded before his father. "They're urban policing weapons effective against a medium-sized target. At best, their effectiveness is as a deterrent more than a primary combat weapon. They won't be tomorrow."

The last transmission was from the only survivor of the event, albeit his wounds turned out to be fatal. "Control, Peters is being carried away. He's still discharging his weapon, but it's too late. Where are the reinforcements? I don't know where Davidson is. Peters must have wounded one of them because it's struggling to gain altitude. Wait—there's one coming for me!"

With that, Smith dropped his communicator and began firing his weapon nonstop for almost a minute. "I wounded the bastard, but he's still coming. Come on, you asshole! I'm here—come on!" Suddenly it went silent.

"Why didn't the creature take Smith?" I asked.

"We'll never know, but I have to think he inflicted enough damage to cause the predator to abandon his prey. Good men were lost needlessly," lamented Colonel Donner.

For a moment, we just sat there not saying a word. I could see tears welling up in the young Donner's eyes. He was a true leader who felt it deeply when his men died in no-win scenarios. Kyle stood and began to slowly clap in honor of our fallen. Before long, we were all up applauding. The tribute lasted a minute or so, and then we took our seats to discuss what we had just heard.

"Let's not let their sacrifices be for naught. We know more now than we knew before. At least two of these things were wounded, so they can be hurt; if we can hurt them, we can kill them. No one else dies," stated Kyle.

"We might have another way to find them. I reviewed the Drone memory discs as you requested, and you were right. There were five events of extended use of the laser weapons by five separate Spider Drones. Based on the power of the Drone lasers, if they hit any of these things, they took off pieces. When we find those pieces, it might help in hunting them down and putting an end to this. Who knows—one of these sites could have a whole specimen," suggested Marcus.

"Good—share those coordinates with the colonel, and he'll arrange to survey the sites. You may be right, Marcus. One thing's for sure—they will be back, and when they do, they're not leaving alive. Let's do our homework and get ourselves prepared," Kyle announced.

Under James's leadership, the surveys began that same day. We found nothing at the first two Drone coordinates, and it was beginning to look like a failed mission. Our luck changed at the third site. About a thousand yards into the forest, a full carcass of a creature was found. Based on its condition, the animal had been mortally wounded by a Drone, and while it struggled to escape into the air, it succumbed to its wounds and fell into the trees, getting caught up in branches. We might have missed it completely if not for the putrid smell of rotting flesh radiating back to the clearing.

As soon as the news of the discovery reached Kyle, he immediately wanted to attend the site. He had to see one of these creatures up close. I guess we all did. Were they really dragons as depicted in ancient Earth fairytales, or just something resembling a dragon, distorted in the excitement of the moment?

James agreed to include us on the recovery team. Kyle was almost dancing when he heard the news. Somewhere inside him was this adventurer waiting to get out. That could not be said for me. I was anxious to see it, but not to go out in the open to do it. Within the hour, James had an entire recovery team assembled, complete with heavy equipment to extract the remains from its precarious forest position.

We wouldn't be able to assess the extent of the challenge until we were on site. There were only two options: either we could free the creature and transport it out through the forest, or we would have to attempt the far riskier air extraction. In either case, getting a first look at an animal that had killed our people—apparently at will—was humbling!

When I think back to that day, I truly appreciate how lucky we were to have a Kyle Chandler. We were about two hundred yards from the forest, preparing to move to the creature's position. The team was made up of thirty or so soldiers and engineers. Everything was happening exactly as you would expect until one of the soldiers shouted, "Sir, we have incoming!"

Immediately, everyone's eyes shot upward. There they were—five of them circling about a thousand feet above us. James had his men form a human wall around us in a combat formation. Kyle and I were unceremoniously pushed into one of the trucks. I couldn't believe how scared I was. Kyle, however, had the truck door wide open, trying to get the best unobstructed view possible.

About five minutes later, the creatures landed just over five hundred yards from our position. Even at that distance, there was no denying their similarity to dragons. It was very disconcerting that our numbers didn't seem to intimidate them in any way. I guess they saw us as a buffet meal.

As the animals advanced, they made the most frightening squealing sound. Marcus was correct in almost every detail. The animal was around fifteen feet long when in flight, but once on the ground, they began to crouch down and walk on fours, which reduced their height to nearer eight feet. Fifteen or eight, it didn't matter. They were here to kill as many as they could.

I shouted at Kyle to close the hatch and get his ass inside the vehicle. He smiled and advised me not to worry because today was our day and the creatures were about to pay for killing our citizens. How could he be so cavalier in the face of death?

At first, I thought the figures moving toward us from across the field might be reinforcements called in by James, but it was too quick for that to be it. I tried to get Kyle's attention, but he was too preoccupied with the dragons. I found it curious that his facial expression was not that of fear, but humor. He'd lost his mind! The next time I looked, I realized it was Spider Drones advancing toward us across the clearing. I remember Kyle looking back at me with the broadest smile. "My babies are here! This ends now!"

By this time the predators had advanced to within three hundred yards, James had his hand raised, ready to give the "fire" command. As it turned out, it wasn't necessary! The creatures must have realized their worst enemy was closing in on them. They immediately changed their posture to the upright flight position, but too late! The Drones were upon them in full fire mode.

As the creatures began to lift off the ground, they were hit by Drone laser weapons over and over again. I lost count of the number of hits the animals took, but it was easily into the hundreds. The dying animals screamed in ungodly death cries as one by one their lifeless bodies tumbled to the ground. A moment later, the Drones were around them standing motionless. There was an exaggerated pause while the Drone scanners confirmed the kills, and then without warning, the six robots turned and ran off in the direction from which they came.

Slowly, ever so slowly, we moved toward what was left of the creatures. All weapons were at the ready position, but that wasn't necessary. As we watched the Drones streaking back across the clearing, there was a huge roar of gratitude and applause. Everyone knew these hideous machines were Kyle's creations, and each and every man stepped forward to shake his hand.

Looking more closely at our kills, they no longer resembled dragons. I'm not sure what they resembled, but there was something strangely familiar about them. Our initial thought was to transport the carcasses directly to the Medical Center labs for forensic examination. After considering the difficulty of trying to move these massive animals through the streets of Bridgetown without causing mass hysteria, the plan was discarded.

The last thing wanted or needed was any more drama over the deaths of our citizens. The new plan was for Defenders to airlift them to the Protectorate air field under the cover of darkness. They would be taken to one of three large hillside bunkers, and the forensic examination would be conducted there.

Kyle asked Sabrina to select the doctors best equipped for the post-mortem examination—and of course the most trustworthy. Any scientist would have given his right arm to be involved in this exploratory dissection. After all, how often would these eggheads have a chance to work on what could be a mythical dragon. It even left me excited!

Sabrina asked if she could attend and oversee the project. Someone needed to make sure everyone remained focused on the task at hand. She certainly filled that bill; she was a control freak. The actual transfer took place at three in the morning. We were all on hand for the event, and it went off without incident, thanks to James's efforts. Kyle and I were beginning to like this guy more and more.

Admiral Donner recommended we not sit around while the scientists did their work. In the morning, his son was going to try again to find where they came from. This time, we would survey the mountains to the south across the lake. Knowing our interest in putting this to rest, he asked if we would like to join the expedition. For a moment, I thought Kyle was going to kiss his feet. I, on the other hand, was somewhat less than thrilled with the prospect of going on another little safari. I hadn't gotten over yesterday's drama, but I did want to play with the big boys, and this was part of their game.

At 0:600 hours the following morning, Kyle and I were at the launch pad waiting to take our first trip ever onboard a Defender. Truth be told, it was the first time we had ever even seen this humbling piece of hardware. Up close, this craft was even more frightening than Spider Drones. The vessel carried a crew of ten, but if required could comfortably accommodate thirty for other purposes.

The fuselage was over a hundred feet long with two sets of swept back wing assemblies—one over, one under—midway down its length. From wing tip to wing tip, the assemblies were over 160 feet. The rear stabilizers were V shaped with four Phaeton Thrusters mounted two over two. Three smaller thrusters were embedded in the underside of the fuselage, evenly dispersed along the length.

There were twelve Plasma Emitter weapons, six per side, and five Pulse Ray Turret Gatling Guns, one in the nose and two on the bottom and top of the fuselage forward and aft. Finishing off this awesome inventory of weapons were eight missile launch ports, four per side firing M12 Thor One Rockets and Electro-Magnetic Disruptor warheads. This entire vessel existed for the sole purpose of dealing death quickly and efficiently.

Based on the shear mass of the craft, it was not designed for an air-to-air dogfight combat scenario. It didn't have to be! The weapons systems could detect and destroy an airborne object from over a thousand miles away with uncanny efficiency. Its arsenal of weapons was the best and most deadly mankind could conceive. Coupled with all this fire power were full cloaking and stealth operation capabilities and an almost impenetrable defensive shield.

As Kyle and I watched the last of the crew going up the gangway, a pair of hands touched our shoulders from behind.

Kyle calmly turned around to acknowledge the new arrival. I almost stroked out and gasped the word "shit."

"Sorry, guys, I didn't mean to startle you! Are you ready for our little adventure? It's a perfect day for dragon hunting, wouldn't you say?" said James with a chuckle.

"Sure is! I want to put in my order now. It's a drumstick, or I'm not going," replied Kyle.

"You two guys are made for each other." That was my great comeback. I was pathetic.

Without further conversation, James led us up the gangway and directly to the Bridge. Once inside, we were astonished by the sophistication. There we computers and monitors everywhere, and the crew moved as if born to do this stuff. Kyle was a brilliant engineer, but even he was impressed. We were seated directly behind two pilots and on either side of James. Immediately, from Lord only knows where, a crewman arrived with three mugs of hot coffee and buns.

"Well, isn't this service," chirped Kyle.

"You can't go to the movies without getting refreshments before the show starts," returned James.

I didn't say a word. These guys were obviously operating on a different plane of reality than I was. In fact, they seemed almost disinterested in what we were about to do. I was scared shitless—a feeling I seemed to get more and more since arriving on this planet. My fear was to heighten to near hysteria as soon as I heard the Phaeton Thrusters powering up, which could only mean one thing—we were about to leave.

It wasn't the search for the creatures that bothered me; it was flying in general, and especially flying in what amounted to a rocket. In an attempt to sound curious, I asked James how long the flight would take. I shouldn't have done that because his answer just about caused me to ask to be let off.

James explained it would take five minutes for the ship to lift vertically from the pad and level off at fifty thousand feet. He went on to say that the reason for such high altitude was because at the speed the craft travelled, we would see much more the higher up we were, and with the laser imaging cameras, very little would be missed. He continued by saying it was two thousand miles to the mountain range, and the actual flying time at normal cruising would be just short of twelve minutes.

Kyle sarcastically suggested I should stop worrying about it because at the speed we were moving, any problem would be fatal. I reminded him that somewhere a suitable punishment awaited him. They both laughed.

Once we reached the mountains, the Defender dramatically reduced its speed, and I could feel the lower thrusters power up. James explained we were going to go into a kind of forward-moving hover to take a closer look at some of the mountain valleys and plateaus. I don't know if that scared me more because the thing might fall out of the sky, or less because I related hovering to landing. Either way, this was going to take awhile. For over an hour, we wandered over the mountains, occasionally hovering down into a valley to examine the mountain face for caves, but nothing.

"James, do you think the creatures we brought down might be all there were?" asked Kyle.

"Hard to say, but no large life form readings have been scanned since we started this exercise. I think at some point we go home and hope the scientists have found some answers. Let's give it another thirty minutes, and if nothing, we'll return to base," replied James.

I was already doing the math to safety. Thirty minutes of hovering, five minutes to regain altitude, twelve minutes flying time, and five minutes to land. In just over an hour, my feet would be back on terra firma. Now at least I had something to look forward to. This relief was to be short lived, but for a different reason than any of us would have thought.

A few minutes later, the science officer looked over at James and announced that he was picking up life form readings, hundreds of them from a mountain dead ahead six hundred miles. He qualified his report by stating the life forms were humanoid, not the creatures we were hunting for.

"Science Officer, are you sure of your readings? There should be no other humans on this planet," said James.

"Sir, I have checked and rechecked the readings a number of times, and these are very definitely human signatures," replied the officer.

"Helmsman, take us up to fifty thousand feet, and let's go get a peak. I don't want to scare them or create an unnecessary incident. Let's set the viewing cameras at maximum zoom. We'll get some footage and leave, hopefully undetected. We can look them over later," directed James.

Any apprehension I had about flying was gone. I was as excited as everyone else and couldn't wait to get there. Imagine—other human beings on a planet we thought was uninhabited! This was amazing! Less than three minutes later, we were over the site. Cloud cover was thick, which made viewing with the naked eye impossible, but the laser cameras pierced through the haze to reveal a large group of people moving around the surface of an elevated mountain plateau. Apart from being able to distinguish them as humans, we were too high to make any other definitive observations.

"I think this is going to shake a few people up back home. This is a surprise! I'm not sure how we missed them during our original surveys of the planet. Let's call it a day," James suggested as the Defender veered off toward home.

Eight

The Decision

When we landed in Bridgetown, Kyle called an emergency session of the CRB to view the videos and discuss next actions. He was so enthused, I thought he was going to burst, but he understood the protocols for a discovery of this magnitude. Before anything could be made public, there was much to be done.

After the meeting, Kyle asked Sabrina to have her team review the videos and offer opinions on the human subjects. She seemed excited for the chance to be part of this discovery. Sabrina asked if she could view the material again before getting others involved to be sure there was enough substance to warrant full scientific evaluation. It made sense since the videos were long range and provided little in the way of real detail.

After reviewing, she asked if there was any way to get additional images from a much closer perspective. Kyle asked the admiral to have his son join us in the CRB Chambers to discuss that possibility.

"Admiral, as a tool for confirmation of human presence, these video images work fine. For anything deeper, they're inconclusive. What would be the chances of getting some closer, more definitive views?" she inquired.

"The best person to answer your question is my son because he was there and might have a better perspective of what we can or cannot do. James, please offer some direction," said the admiral.

"Doctor Chandler—is that how you would like to be called?" asked James Jr.

"No! And don't call me Mrs. Chandler either. You may call me Sabrina, as may your father. Despite my reputation, I don't bite, and I don't hate most men—just some, and only sometimes, my husband included," she replied.

There was some lighthearted chuckling, but everyone in the room knew Sabrina's reputation and at one time or another had seen or heard about her tirades with respect to men. Kyle refused to look up from his notes for fear she'd see his sarcastic smirk.

"Sabrina it is. I'm James. Getting closer images will have a level of risk. Not to human life, because we'll use unmanned surveillance drones, but a risk of detection. If the subjects are equipped with low-level detection systems, radar perhaps, the drone could move to within ten thousand feet because of its size.

"Given the camera technology in play, the images from that altitude would be as clear as viewing them from one hundred feet. If, however, their technology is refined enough for long-range detection and they possess defensive ground-to-air weaponry, they could bring down the drone once it drops below forty thousand feet.

"We're confident they don't have anything beyond that, or they would have taken a stab at us when we took this video from fifty thousand feet in a much larger target. My sense is they have no technology beyond the human eye. By the way, I've heard nothing but good things about you, albeit mostly from Kyle," James joked.

"Thanks for the assessment and the compliment, I think. Does this mean you'll get me some better images—and if so, when?" replied Sabrina.

James advised Sabrina that he would have something for her in three days. He asked if the doctors performing the post mortems on the dragons had come to any conclusions.

"I think they have knowledge to share. Let's convene in the bunker in one hour. I'll arrange for a quick presentation of their findings," she replied.

With that, she excused herself and left the four of us to talk about our failure to track down the nests of these beasts. At this point, it seemed we had limited other options to work with. All that could be done was being done. The surveillance drones were now fully armed and programmed to destroy any of the creatures should they be sighted, but we were a long way from putting this thing behind us.

True to her word, one hour later we were seated in the bunker, waiting for the scientists to finish what amounted to a pregame meeting. After a few minutes, Sabrina stepped forward and introduced Dr. William Knowles, head of organic life form studies. He was a geneticist and one of the DNA culprits who had been despised for his involvement in the conspiracy against the people.

I asked Sabrina later why she picked a person she had such revulsion for to be on the team. Her response was that we needed the best we had, and he was the best. Besides, she reminded me, he kept his mouth shut for years about the cover-up, which meant he didn't have loose lips. As soon as he began to speak, we immediately understood her point.

"Gentlemen, we have spent the better part of two full days examining the remains of the creatures, and here's what we know with certainty. Although some part of us may try and romanticize these animals as dragons from some ancient fairytale, and ourselves as knights defending the castle, forget it. These specimens are members of the *Eptesicus fuscus* family of winged rodents, most closely related to cave bats!"

Sabrina interrupted, "You're telling us these things are common bats?"

"They are bats, but obviously anything but common. Setting aside for a moment their size, which in itself is outstanding, they are far more aggressive than any common bat. We have put that down to the environment they must have come from, which by the way, we are convinced is somewhere other than this planet. On scale, their size is likely in proportion to other creatures on their home world," responded Knowles.

"This just gets better and better! You're telling us they're not indigenous to this planet. How did they get here? You're not suggesting they flew through space to make this planet their home," I said somewhat sarcastically.

"Please, if you will allow me to continue. My colleagues and I believe these creatures are out of scale for this world, and based on what they've done so far, have already begun to change the natural balance. To answer your question, Mr. Evans, no, they did not and could not fly here from another world. They are air breathers. The only opinion we can offer is the animal was deliberately introduced to the planet as a kind of ecological predator.

"Anytime you introduce a more aggressive species into an established ecosystem, the system is changed. Left unchecked, they will eventually devour every large animal on this planet. Until us, they had no natural enemies here. There's more. Whatever or whoever brought them here understood what the impact would be. To control the beast long term, they made them sterile, unable to reproduce. Call it a kind of a genetic kill switch. We have also determined their life span is around twenty-five years and these specimens are near twenty years old."

"I find that entire premise just too farfetched to believe. Frankly, I found the dragon theory more believable," I responded.

"Perhaps, but believe this—these creatures will kill and eat anything they can catch. That, as we know, includes us. With a wingspan of twenty-eight feet, a body length of seventeen feet, and weighing in at 1,500 pounds, these animals cannot be taken lightly," Knowles replied.

"Assuming what you're suggesting is true, is it likely these five bats obliterated God-only-knows-how-many indigenous life forms all on their own?" Sabrina challenged.

"No, Doctor, they're a fraction of what the main colony must be. Bats traditionally live in community groups numbering between fifty and five hundred. We're at a loss to explain why these few were hunting solo."

"Is it possible these were the last of them?" asked James.

Knowles continued, "Colonel, we recommend you do not abandon your search. There are more. Many more! In addition, normally bats are nocturnal hunters, but that behavior suggests they follow Earthly models. These specimens hunt by sight, sound, and smell—day or night. Consequently, they're at the top of the predatory food chain for this planet. Are there any other questions?"

"Where would we look to find their nests?" James asked.

"In any other case, I'd say to look for large caves, but I think that doesn't apply here. We can't help you with your search," Knowles responded.

Sabrina thanked the doctors and asked that they keep their findings Top Secret until we could confirm how extensive the problem might be. She also asked them to keep themselves available for further consultations. Knowles closed by recommending we destroy the remains quickly to prevent the possible spread of some sort of alien disease from the carcasses.

This was a wake-up call! I asked Sabrina, the only qualified medical professional in the room, what she thought about what we had just heard.

She was candid as always. "Well, gentlemen, I think all that they told us is accurate as it relates to the beast itself. These bats are likely not indigenous to this planet. They're correct about the sterility, and it probably did kill off most of its competition in its time on this planet. What I'm struggling with is this whole third-party involvement theory. It sounds too diabolical to be considered a reasonable explanation."

"Where does that leave us? They couldn't fly here, and we're not buying they were brought here. None of this makes any sense," Kyle confessed.

"Perhaps not, but what we do know is they'll kill us unless we kill them first, and that's the only thing that matters. Doctor Chandler, can science help us do that?" asked the admiral.

"I don't know, but let me pass it by the test-tube boys and see where that takes us," she replied.

We had vague information, unsupported speculation and opinion, but no direction or plan. At this stage, beyond putting more drones in play and expanding our search patterns, we were stumbling in the dark. As the meeting ended and we all went our separate ways, there was a general sense that the threat was real. Kyle committed that he and Marcus would program the surplus Spider Drones for deployment throughout the mountainous areas around Bridgetown. Perhaps they might have better luck.

As agreed, three days later, James asked us to join him in the Protectorate briefing room to view the videos taken of the encampment. Kyle asked him if the drone was detected during the surveillance exercise. James explained they were able to drop the drone below ten thousand feet because there was no evidence of defensive weaponry. The videos were taken from eight thousand feet, and based on the reaction of the people, they saw something, but not enough to panic.

Once the five of us were seated, James instructed the communications room to stream the videos to the large monitor on the wall. As the screen flickered to life, the first images to appear were from twenty thousand feet. These panoramic views were remarkably detailed. Sabrina was immediately caught up in what she was looking at. "This is great stuff, guys! Let's stop it right here and arrange for a general viewing for all of the scientific and medical community. We can organize a nerd convention and brainstorming session. I have a boat load of geniuses at the Medical and Science Centers that spend most of their time gossiping about each other. This will give them something useful to do with their time."

Kyle arranged to have the viewing held at the Central Meeting Hall. The facility held a thousand people, and Sabrina promised to fill every seat. Keeping such a large gathering secret from the general population was not a simple task, and the true purpose of the meeting could not be divulged without causing suspicion and rumor. Sabrina and Kyle were masters at getting people to do things without the audience ever knowing exactly why. It was their gift.

At eight o'clock the next evening, the eggheads slowly began filtering into the auditorium, whispering and complaining about how they were being forced to attend yet another boring presentation. None of them had any idea that what they were about to see would begin to define our place and role on this planet.

It took almost an hour to seat the group, including the really arrogant bastards that deliberately arrived late to promote their self-importance. Sabrina was very patient with it all, but we knew she had taken mental lists of everyone delaying the proceedings. Once the audience was seated, Kyle turned to the stage and raised his hand. Right on cue, the curtains slid open to reveal James standing at a podium off to the side of an enormous viewing screen.

"Ladies and gentlemen, we are very pleased you could all be here this evening to bear witness and offer your guidance regarding the videos we are about to present. The images you will see are of a mountain plateau three thousand miles from our current location. You will have questions, and I will stop the video at anytime to zoom in if requested to do so. What you are about to see is the first evidence of humanoid life on this planet that did not originate from Vanguard. We will be very interested in your feedback."

Amid the gasps from the stunned audience, James directed the playback to begin. As before, the screen flickered a second or two before the views were focused. On the large screen, it was almost like being there. The scene began by showing numerous humans milling about in a large clearing. At first glance, the human subjects didn't appear to be doing anything in particular, but as the drone slowly descended, it showed them building what appeared to be makeshift shelters. There were many more males than females and no sign of children. The drone continued to descend. The cameras were now picking up detail on the rock facings and what appeared to be cave entrances where other humans were milling about in small groups.

"Stop the video and zoom in please," came a voice from well up in the gallery.

James signaled, and the video was halted and zoomed in to maximum focus. The images were somewhat grainy, and James suggested we wait a few minutes to allow the drone to reach its lowest descent. As we watched, the images slowly became more defined. You could feel the excitement in the room. There were going to be a million questions for which we had zero answers, but isn't that how discovery works? Ask the questions, and then work together to answer them? At least that's how we hoped it would work.

Once the drone had reached its lowest point, the cameras were zoomed in as requested from the gallery minutes before. This time, the images were crystal clear, and even some of the finer details became identifiable. More voices were yelling to freeze the video, and the conversation began to sound like a scientific brainstorming session.

"Colonel, what do you make of the long knife-like items lashed to the sides of many of the male specimens?" questioned a voice from the gallery.

"I don't know, but they appear to be weapons of some kind," responded James.

I couldn't hold back! After all, I was the resident historian in the crowd. "Those knives, as you so aptly describe them, are in fact medieval swords. They were primarily a hand-to-hand combat weapon, which until now haven't been used in over three thousand years. How they came to be here on this planet billions of miles from where they originated is something I can't explain."

"Their dress and mannerisms are very simple. Could they be farmers?" asked another member of the audience.

Yet another voice answered, "They could be, but as the drone was descending, we had a view of the general area, and we didn't see any terrain that could even remotely be considered farmland."

James suggested we view more of the video and perhaps some questions might be answered as we went along. Thirty minutes later, the video ended and there were shouts from the gallery to run it again in its entirety. As it turns out, these requests were to be repeated three additional times as people continually wanted confirmations to questions no one seemed to have the answers to.

By this time, the audience had split themselves up into working groups without any direction to do so, and throughout the room, we could hear whispers as each group formulated their own versions of what they had seen. From time to time, a group would ask James to fast forward to a particular set of images or rewind to another set.

Sabrina joined a rather large group of doctors discussing the social order and physical characteristics of the humanoids. Other groups had their own agendas in play. It was amazing to sit with Kyle, James, and Marcus to watch this circus unfold in front of us. After four more hours, Sabrina approached James and indicated that her group wished to make a statement just to get the ball rolling. James went to the podium and introduced her.

The introduction was more a courtesy than a requirement. Everyone in the room called Sabrina boss. Like it or not, that extended to our table as well. "Colleagues, my group has discussed and debated for some time what we've been witness to this night, and we believe we have some interesting observations and theories to share.

"Let me begin by saying we agree these are likely farmers or herdsmen, perhaps both. Thanks to the efforts of Colonel Donner and the sophistication of the cameras used, we noticed the hands of the male subjects are the hands of people who work with tools on a regular basis. Assuming they are what we believe they are, it leaves us in a bit of a quandary.

"We have to ask ourselves, if they are farmers, why would they live on a mountain plateau and presumably in the caves we see in the background, so far from anything closely resembling farmland? This next part required a bit more imagination, but here goes.

"The swords, as Ryan points out, may be weapons, but these are not soldiers. Their weapons are solely for personal protection. Stating the obvious, these people do not belong in this place. So we asked ourselves again, why would they be here? At first, we thought perhaps this might be sanctuary from the flying predators.

"We dismissed that because the plateau would be a poor safe haven. From what we know, the forest would offer much better protection beneath the protective shroud of the trees. There's something else in play here! Whatever has happened to these people has forced them to abandon their homes. All that aside, they have other troubles.

"More than half the people in the video are sick or worse, diseased. Take note if you will of their lethargic movements, the lesions on their faces and hands, and the visible symptoms of advanced malnutrition and scurvy. Without medical intervention, they will eventually die off."

Sabrina's statements opened the flood gates. Group after group took the podium to share their viewpoints. A few teams, however, did not share the same opinion on why these humans ended up where they were. Some suggested they were exiled or were outlaws evading capture. What was agreed unanimously was they were dying a slow but inevitable death. The question, therefore, was what—if anything—could we or should we do?

Sabrina wasted little time in voicing what she believed was the general mood of the group. "Kyle, I don't think there's any question these humans are in distress. They need our help, and we must respond," Sabrina declared.

As obvious as her statement was, our intervention wasn't totally supported by all. There were a number in attendance who felt we should mind our own business and let the natural order of things run its course. Some suggested that focusing on these humans distracted us from dealing with the attacks on our citizens by the predators.

Sabrina, however, was not in agreement with those who wanted to just stand off. "Apart from those who brought us these videos, every person in this room has the word doctor in his or her title. Every person in this room has taken an oath to preserve the health, safety, and advancement of the human race, not just Vanguard humans, but all humans wherever they're from.

"Just so I'm not accused of imposing my will, I move we have a show of hands on the question of our intervention in this situation. This vote will not be binding on the CRB or the Protectorate, but it will help them gauge the general mood of the medical and scientific community on the subject. All those in favor of humanitarian intervention, signify by raising your hand. Ryan and Kyle, could you count please?" asked Sabina.

There were 941 in attendance that evening. Nine hundred and seven voted in favor of intervention. None of us could have known how prophetic the vote was to the future of the people of Bridgetown.

Nine

First Contact

It was all well and good the vote supported an intervention at some level, but there was much more to think about before we could be of any value to these people. One of the biggest obstacles was how to introduce ourselves into a society that very well might have never seen a spacecraft. We didn't want or need to appear as off-world invaders. Our initial introductions would be as important as the humanitarian effort itself.

Kyle asked Sabrina to assemble a team of doctors specializing in various disciplines to assist in the planning. She was eager to be a part of any solution that helped the humans. We met her team for the first time in the Medical Center Conference Room. Sabrina wasn't fooling around! Her choices for team members were all the best of the best in medicine and scientific development. Even Kyle felt out of place in the presence of such a prestigious gathering.

Intelligence aside, this adventure would be as new to them as it was to us. There were no recorded case studies to guide our actions. After considerable dialogue, the group agreed the best approach was to be direct but nonthreatening. James reminded us that a three-thousand-ton starship hovering down into your backyard might tend to be viewed as somewhat threatening. Of course he was right, and once he said it, we all felt a bit foolish.

James offered a less invasive approach. His suggestion was to send in a drone equipped with holographic imaging cameras. Drones were small and would be seen as far less a threat by the humans. His idea involved the drone descending into the encampment close enough to transmit a hologram of Kyle introducing us and explaining our good intentions.

This could be done in real time and would be as close to having them in the same room as was possible. The problem might be their ability to understand our language. One of the doctors suggested the hologram include a sketch artist who would draw simple pictures on a backdrop providing a visual interpretation of Kyle's words. The drone would be equipped with additional video and audio equipment to listen and watch events unfold from a variety of different perspectives. For this to work, we would have to descend to one hundred feet. That was the minimum projection altitude to assure the integrity of the holographic image would be maintained throughout the broadcast.

There was no guarantee of how such close proximity would be perceived by these humanoids. We would need to watch their body language very closely. James believed that when they saw the drone, their first reaction would be either flight or fight. Generally speaking, we were satisfied that as a first-contact plan this would work because it was the most subtle and least intrusive.

Kyle and Marcus committed to programming the drone to do all the wonderful stuff we required, and in two days, this was to be the move-forward plan. The following morning, Kyle went to the Communication Center to practice his speech in front of the laser cameras, while Sabrina visited the university to find the best graphic artist available.

At 07:00 hours on the morning of the second day, the entire team regrouped in the Command Center for one last sanity check on the details of our plan. Soon after, the drone lifted off the pad and headed toward a rendezvous with our future. The flight to the plateau took thirty minutes, with another fifteen minutes for the drone to hover down into position. James had breakfast delivered, and we discussed what we hoped would be a successful first contact with our new neighbors.

Just before the drone began its final descent, James had all the newly installed cameras and microphones activated. We were fairly certain the human population wouldn't become fully aware of the drone's presence until it dropped below ten thousand feet. James assumed that at some point they would become aware of the drone's presence and seek the protection of the caves.

"We're going to have to be patient with them," he said.

As it turned out, he wasn't far off the mark with his prediction. As the drone passed below 8,200 hundred feet, the human population started pointing toward the sky, and movement on the ground seemed to quicken, mostly directed toward the dozen or so cave entrances. The lower the drone descended, the more excited the movement on the ground became.

By the time it broke through the four-thousand-foot threshold, most of the camp was in full flight into the caves, but not all. A small group of men formed a circle directly below the path of the descending drone. They had their swords drawn and were standing in what we assumed was a combat posture.

At one thousand feet, the drone slowed to a crawl, and the tension was almost unbearable in the Command Center. Suddenly dozens of small creatures emerged from the caves and began to run across the clearing toward the circle of armed humans. At rough count, we put number of strange animals at around two hundred. They seemed familiar, yapping and jumping up toward the drone, which hadn't passed eight hundred feet yet. To us, the entire scene was surreal, but to those on the ground, the animals appeared to be part of a common defensive plan.

"Those are dogs! How in hell did dogs get on this planet? If someone tells me this is just another coincidence, I'm going to lose my mind," I spouted.

Most of the people in the room, including Sabrina, James, and Kyle, didn't appear to know what I was talking about.

"Dogs? What are dogs?" asked Sabrina.

"Canines—or dogs, if you will—are domesticated pack animals. I thought they were only indigenous to Earth. I'm with Ryan on this. It makes no sense they would be here," commented Marcus.

"Are they a threat?" asked James.

"If we were on the ground and they attacked, they would pose some problems, but clearly their purpose here is to protect their human masters. They represent no threat to the drone," replied Marcus.

When the drone finally leveled off at one hundred feet, a motionless standoff began. We had already decided to hold our position until the inhabitants accepted this was not an invasion and their curiosity replaced fear, drawing them out of the caves for a closer look. For over an hour, the only movement detected was the dogs and their curious antics of running in circles and jumping up toward the drone.

We were beginning to wonder if these few men and the animals were as much audience as we would be getting on our first visit until three elderly men walked out through the largest of the cave entrances. They moved directly toward the circle of posed men, never taking their eyes off the hovering drone.

Suddenly the obvious leader of the group of three turned to look back at the cave entrance and shouted, "Myloc, keep the women and children in the caves until we figure this out!"

As simple as the words were, they came as a new and wonderful discovery to us. These humans spoke our language! How was that possible? I don't know why, but an uncomfortable shiver ran up my back. Everyone at the table stood and clapped, as if we had solved a great mystery. Kyle quickly walked to the staging area to begin the telecast. Sabrina suggested he wait a couple more minutes until their leader settled things down.

Once the three men reached the circle, the apparent leader shouted a command toward the dogs. "Lie down!" Almost instantly, the creatures stopped and lay down on the spot. We all looked at each other in surprise. He then spoke softly to one of the encircled men, and again like magic, they all lowered their weapons, never taking their eyes off our drone.

Seconds later, a little man ran from the cave entrance, yelling, "Joshal, be careful! Please be careful!"

The leader turned, looked in the man's direction, and held up a hand in the stop position. The little man stopped dead in his tracks. Now the leader turned his attention back to the drone and shouted, "Why are you here? What do you want?"

Sabrina wanted to seize the moment and signaled to Kyle to begin the telecast. With this, the lighting was focused, and the thirty laser cameras required to create the hologram were activated. It was interesting to watch the reactions of the humans on the ground when the image of Kyle appeared in front of them.

The hologram was a bit hazy and for a few seconds difficult to hold, but suddenly there he was. The men forming the circle backed away. Once again, their swords were raised, and they began to scream in some sort of battle cry. The dogs immediately got caught up in the excitement, barking and growling making the whole scene rather chaotic.

The little man who had run out of the cave and was stopped frozen in his tracks looked at the image, screamed like a terrified woman, and ran back into the cave, waving his hands frantically over his head and shouting, "We're going to die! We're all going to die!"

I'm not sure why, but the entire scene seemed oddly comical. Only Sabrina wasn't laughing. "We're terrifying these poor people. We need to withdraw and rethink this plan," she demanded.

"Sabrina, the worse is over. They didn't all run back into the cave. We're okay here! Kyle, you need to begin your speech now before their fear does drive them away," commented one of the psychologists.

"Please do not be afraid! We come in peace! No harm will come to you," offered Kyle.

"How are you doing this? Are you wizards?" their leader shouted back.

"No, Joshal, we are not," replied Kyle.

This really shook them up! How could this specter know their leader's name? What dark magic could this be? Even the stone-faced Joshal stepped back in disbelief. He drew his sword, getting ready for what was to come.

"Please," Kyle urged again, "do not be afraid. We want to help you—nothing more!"

"We do not need your help! Leave us alone, evil spirit!" shouted the male standing just ahead of Joshal.

At that point, Joshal stepped forward and touched the man's shoulder, who immediately stepped back. "Then let us speak, spirit!"

For over an hour, Joshal and Kyle spoke. All during this exchange, none of the people hiding in the caves ventured out. To keep some order, Joshal ordered the dogs back into the caves, but his armed companions never let down their guard. When the conversation finished, the transmission was terminated and the drone slowly withdrew from the encampment.

As we watched the people emerging from the caves, they moved directly to Joshal. Phase one appeared to have been successful. Everyone immediately stood and clapped for Kyle as he returned to the meeting table.

Our success was as much as we could have hoped for. Their leader agreed to allow us to come to his camp and speak face-to-face with the elders. We knew Kyle must attend this first visit if we were to make any meaningful headway. He was now the face of the wizards to Joshal. We all understood how fragile these humans were, not only because of their illnesses and environment, but something else, something much deeper.

Phase two of our plan would begin the next morning. A Defender would be loaded with food and medical provisions, and should the opportunity present itself to be of assistance to these people, we'd be ready. Sabrina volunteered two of her very best general medicine doctors to go as well to tend the sick. Kyle reminded us that the medicine and doctors would be brought out only if Joshal consented.

Sabrina was giddy with anticipation and pleaded to come with us, but her condition and the unknown risks made it impractical. Kyle did promise, though, that once a Bridgetown visit could be arranged, she would be among the first citizens to be introduced—even if he had to have the shuttle land in the Medical Center parking lot. She was disappointed but seemed somewhat placated by his romantic pledge.

Ten

Face to Face

At 08:15 the next morning, we were standing on the launch pad, watching the last of the provisions being loaded. Kyle's demeanor was cool and calm, but I knew him well enough to know his inner child could barely contain itself. Sabrina was there to see us off, as were the admiral and Helen, James's wife.

It gave me an eerie feeling to see loved ones there waving good-bye. What was so special about this occasion? To someone like me, who is not a big supporter of soaring through the heavens in what amounted to a bullet, anything that seemed unusual only added to the anxiousness of the event. Ten minutes later, we were onboard, and the loading platform began to retract. We were on our way!

We had all listened yesterday as Kyle tried to prepare Joshal for what to expect when his people first saw the Defender arriving. He assured Joshal that the craft, although large and a bit intimidating, was coming in peace to visit friends. Joshal seemed oddly curious why Kyle made such a big deal about how we would arrive. He told Kyle his people had seen airships before and not to worry. Yet, we knew they could never be prepared for seeing this airship for the first time. James speculated there would be a moment when the people on the ground would start to second-guess their decision to welcome us in.

One small item did not go unnoticed during Kyle's conversation with Joshal. It revolved around his admission that "his people had seen airships before." Did he mean our patrols or something else? James seemed excited at the prospect of getting that question answered.

As always, the flight was short and uneventful. Through the cameras, we could see the people below running for cover just as they did when the drone made its appearance. We would land, but there'd be no welcoming party cheering as we walked down the gangway. I was convinced we'd have to coax them out of the caves before any dialogue could take place. They were simple farmers witnessing the arrival of something so horrific to their eyes the only smart thing to do was run and hide.

Once we landed, Marcus asked James how we should proceed. James suggested we simply walk down the ramp and hold position until Joshal was convinced we meant no harm. We were fairly confident that once he spotted Kyle, things would begin to calm down.

"Kyle, we'll keep it simple and open, but we must stay together and near the ship until we're sure of the reception," directed James.

It made sense to be prudent. As we made our way to the bottom of the gangway, there wasn't a sound to be heard in the encampment. The silence was uncomfortable. Even the air around us seemed to be caught up in the still-to-unfold drama. James was concerned about the dogs more than the sword-wielding citizens. He saw these creatures as an unknown complication and unpredictable risk.

Although James was confident that Kyle could talk us into or out of almost any situation, these trained animals might be an entirely different challenge. Before leaving the craft, he instructed weapons control to activate the scanning modules on the Gatling guns. If there was any sign of imminent peril, they were to be ready to shoot first and negotiate later.

We stood alone at the bottom of the ramp for what seemed an eternity. In actual time, it wasn't more than five minutes, but when you're exposed and facing an unknown risk, time moves too slowly. Finally, Joshal and two others appeared at the primary cave entrance. Joshal was a large, heavyset man perhaps six and a half feet tall and weighing something close to three hundred pounds.

He had long grey hair that reached to the small of his back. His facial features looked chiseled and weathered. He supported a full grey beard that hung down over his chest area. It was obvious by his appearance he had earned his position as leader of his people, and we weren't about to do anything that might compel him to flex his leadership muscle.

Sabrina was right! The small welcoming party moved lethargically, and almost every bit of exposed skin was covered in what appeared to be blisters and boils. Kyle's impatience drove him to decide to cut the walking distance between us by moving toward them. James called after him, but his words were lost in the moment. This was not the plan!

The farther away from the sanctuary of the Defender, the more difficult it would be if retreat was required. It was too late; we had no choice but to follow our impetuous friend. As we quickened our step to make up ground, James was cursing under his breath. By the time we caught up, Joshal and Kyle were already shaking hands and talking in low whispers, as if they had been friends for years.

That was another of Kyle's real talents. In just a few seconds, he could cut through the formalities of a first meeting and get right to the personal side of any stranger. He may have been a brilliant engineer, but it was his social skills and natural salesmanship that made him the statesman he was.

Once we were through the introductions, Joshal made a hand signal, and a large wooden table with six matching chairs appeared through one of the cave entrances. The furniture was placed just aside from where we stood, and Joshal gestured we take seats. Once seated, a number of women brought out food and some kind of homemade wine, but that wasn't the highlight of the moment.

One of these females was easily the most beautiful woman I had ever seen. Joshal seemed to notice that I couldn't take my eyes off of her and announced that her name was Cateria and she was his eldest daughter. I was a bit embarrassed because everyone, including the girl, could see that I was beguiled by her presence.

It took all my focus to get my thoughts back on the reason we were here. There would be plenty of time later for dreaming about this Cateria and her devastating beauty. I knew that once the conversation started, Kyle would get directly to the point of our visit. He was too impatient to wait for the perfect moment. Every moment was a perfect moment to Kyle, and this wasn't going to change now.

"Joshal, we are pleased you have permitted us to come here and speak with you and your people. Part of the reason we wished to make our presence known was our concern for your situation. You must be aware, of course, that many of your people are sick and need medicine," Kyle said.

"Yes, but there is no medicine for this malady that has beset us. It is a plague of evil, which has already claimed many of our number. I fear not long from now it will claim even more, including me. I shouldn't have asked you to come here because now you too may become infected," Joshal apologized.

"Joshal, your fears end today for your people, yourself, and us. We have brought special medicines and doctors that will cure these diseases. We have brought food because what you are sharing with us this day is food taken from your people during difficult times. Will you allow us to begin caring and feeding all those needing such remedies?" pleaded Kyle.

"You have medicines that can cure my people? Are such things possible? You most truly are wizards!" replied Joshal.

"In our world, there are no plagues, and people do not go without food. It's not magic, it's science, and we will speak more of this when everyone is well. May we help our new friends in their time of need as our friends would help us should there be things we required?" asked Kyle.

"Yes, and we are so grateful" responded Joshal.

With that, James stood and made a gesture toward the Defender. In seconds, crate after crate was being ferried down the gangway to the center of the encampment. James asked Joshal to have his people come out of the caves and be treated. Joshal called to the rather nervous man near the cave entrance and spoke to him for a few seconds. A moment later, people began emerging from the darkness. Some could barely walk. Others were being carried. It was a sad sight, but not surprising given the extent of the illness and malnutrition.

The two doctors didn't waste any time. While the crew set up a food line, the doctors were administering antibiotics and ointments for lesions. The people seemed nervous but ready to be helped. While all of this was going on, James asked for permission to call in another supply vessel and more doctors.

The population of the encampment was over a thousand people, and every other person had some form of sickness requiring attention. We needed more food as well. Much more food! Joshal was happy to grant his request. Kyle wanted to continue the conversation because we had many questions that needed answers if we were truly going to understand these people.

"Joshal, am I right in assuming you are farmers?"

"Farmers and herders of livestock," responded Joshal.

"Why would you, simple farmers and herdsman, be living in this place so far from your livelihood?"

At first, Joshal was reluctant to answer, but he shared their tale. "This dark place is not our home. As you can see, we do not live here, we merely survive here. Our fields are far to the west in the land of the Therons, and for as long as time has been a measured thing, we have planted our fields and tended our flocks.

"Twice each year, our people would make the dangerous trek to the city of Draegon, as did all the farms in the Great Valley. There we would trade our produce and livestock for clothing and metals. All was as it had always been. Then came the time when good King Tricus of Draegon passed on, and his sons battled for his throne. There were two sons, twins at birth, and both longed to be king of Draegon. A bloody feud erupted until finally the evil son, Uthess, slew his brother, Niterus, while he slept and declared himself king.

"This was the beginning of a sad time for citizens of Draegon and the peaceful farmers of the Valley. King Uthess was relentless in his quest to rule all the lands of the Great Valley, but his army was small. The dense forests between us and Draegon were our protection from his evil. Yet there came another death dealer from the south. Not a king, not a man, but a winged creature. It first set upon us in the summer during the harvest, attacking from the above, killing both beast and man.

"Not even the mighty Draegon could escape the hunter birds. King Uthess took his army within the castle walls and hid in his palace, leaving his subjects to perish in the streets. All seemed lost! The families of the Great Valley were forced to hide in the forests under the protection of the trees, safe from the hunter birds.

"For ten years, we were forced to live in the deep forest, afraid to return to our fields. Some of the families grew weary of hiding and ventured back to their homes. The beasts came and carried them away. We were trapped, living like animals in the dim light of the forest. Then when all seemed lost, Star Travelers like yourselves came from the heavens to save us in their Fire Breather ships. They drove the hunter birds from our lands. We rejoiced and praised these beings. They were our saviors, but their time among us was short.

"Before leaving, they shared their wisdom with the king and his generals. It is said that the visitors made a pact with the king and gifted him with ten Fire Breather ships and the riders to control them. With these ships, the king's dreams were fulfilled. His domain was assured. These flying war machines spewed out streams of fire, consuming their enemies. Not even the forest could stand against them. King Uthess was unstoppable.

"Those who dared to defend our lands were driven from their homes or devoured by fire. Those that survived became slaves to the king, and the great marketplace of Draegon was no more. One of my sons and my eldest daughter's husband fell to Uthess's fire. We were farmers, not soldiers! We fought with swords and bows. How could we hope to be victorious?

"Many families fled the Great Valley, searching for sanctuary far from the lands of Draegon. For three years, we searched while Uthess hunted us like animals. We had traded one flying predator for another. When we left our homes, we numbered thousands, but so very many of us have died. Finally, we came upon this place high above the forests where not even Uthess would look for us. Now disease has become the new hunter, and from it we cannot run," closed Joshal.

As I looked around at the people remaining of this once proud, simple society, I was sickened. My first impulse was to ask James to settle the score and make things right again, but that was not our mission or our business.

Kyle asked, "Joshal, since the visitors chased the hunter birds back over the mountains, have the beasts ever returned?"

"From time to time, small flocks—perhaps three or four—will circle above us, but they no longer attack us because they fear the Trells," responded Joshal.

"Trells? What are Trells?" James asked.

"I will show you," he responded.

He stood and put his fingers to his lips, creating an ear-piercing sound. From cave entrances all around the encampment, the yapping, nervous dogs we had seen during the drone's visit came running toward us, jumping around as if they had lost their wits. Immediately the Gatling guns pivoted in the direction of the animals, and James reached for his sidearm, but a now nervous Joshal pleaded that the creatures were of no threat to us. Cautiously, James hit his lapel communicator and instructed the Defender to stand down. That was too close!

"We call these creatures 'dogs' on our home world," explained Marcus.

"I think they are called by many names. The visitors called them 'canines' and gifted one male and one female to each of the families of the Great Valley. When we asked their purpose, the visitors assured us that as long as we kept them at our sides, the hunter birds would not attack us. It is true! Our people learned to love the creatures as family members. In our ancient writings, the guardian spirit of farmers and herdsmen is the 'Trell.' This is what we call your 'dogs'," explained Joshal.

We were astonished by his claims. The visitors referring to the animals as canines really set us back. What did it mean? Who were these visitors?

James had to know more. He asked Joshal how such a small animal could ever hope to frighten off the flying predators.

"They are our protectors! Trells attack their enemies in packs from many directions. They are fearless even against a much larger threat. It is true they are no match for the hunter birds, but even in death they have wounded many of them. The birds sense in the Trells a creature that will not surrender the fight, and instinctively they chose to avoid them. As difficult as that may be to accept, it is the truth. Colonel, even you, a great warrior, saw the Trells as a threat," stated Joshal.

James couldn't deny he was concerned about them, which is why the Gatling guns were activated. "This is absolutely fascinating. When we have more time, I would like to learn more about these tiny warriors," said James.

"Colonel, you will do so firsthand" replied Joshal. He waved his daughter over and whispered into her ear. Immediately, she retreated into a cave, returning a few minutes later with two small dogs, one in each arm.

"Colonel, we would be honored if you would accept this gift of a young male and female Trell. They will never leave your side, and they would trade their lives to protect yours," offered Joshal.

The expression on James's face was a mixture of elation and nervousness. It was a scene I shall never forget. James gently took the animals from Cateria and held them up close to his face, while the young pups licked his eyes and nose.

"James, you really do surprise me. I never would have thought in a million years you had a sensitive bone in your body," quipped Kyle.

"It's a damn long walk home from here. I'd remember that before any of you decide to say much more," replied James with an almost serious expression on his face.

We spoke of many other things that day, and as the sun began to wane, we were sorry to have to say goodnight. Some of the ill were in dire need of more focused medical attention, and Joshal consented to us transporting them to the Bridgetown Medical Center. By the time we were preparing to leave, there was a very noticeable change in the mood and energy levels within the camp. It wasn't so much the drugs and the food; it had more to do with the realization that we would return again and again until everyone was well and fed.

Kyle promised Joshal he would return with provisions the next day but that duties might limit the number of visits possible. He did promise that if he couldn't attend, either James or I would be here. Despite my hatred of flying, the chance to see this Cateria woman was enough incentive for me to happily risk my life on these visits.

As the first stars began to appear in the heavens, the Defenders initiated their thrusters, and the massive vessels slowly began to lift toward the sky. Our new additional cargo for the return home included twenty near-death individuals that would require immediate emergency attention once we were back in Bridgetown and a pair of Trell puppies.

James had called ahead to Sabrina, and they agreed there was little time to waste. The Defenders' first stop would be the vehicle parking area at the Center, where Sabrina would have a full team of emergency medicine doctors at the ready.

Twenty minutes later, the distinct sound of the landing pods could be heard beneath us. We were going home, and what a story we had to tell. It would be the first of many stories Joshal would share with us over the next couple of years. Kyle, Marcus, and I exited with the patients at the Center and went our separate ways. James returned to the launch pad to put the Defenders to bed, and shortly thereafter himself and his miniature warriors. We all agreed to debrief first thing in the morning.

As I made my way back to my residence, the day's events filled my mind, but none more than Cateria. I decided there and then that somehow, someway, this woman would be my wife. With that promise in my head, I fell asleep quickly and deeply. It had been a good day.

The next morning, we were being served breakfast in the briefing room, which was quickly becoming like a second home to most of us. Sabrina and Kyle arrived together, dragging with them the same two doctors that had volunteered the day before. The session began with the doctors providing a general assessment of the state of health of settlers. Although not a glowing report, it did sound upbeat and confident.

Unfortunately, two of the emergency cases from the colony died during the night, and we would have to break the news to Joshal. The rest were recovering and would be returned to their homes within a couple of days. As I suspected, the conversation inevitably turned to what we should do once the health of the people had been restored. Sabrina was insistent that as rough and tumble as these people seemed, they were not self-sufficient in their current situation.

"Perhaps we can airlift the entire colony to a place where they can start over and be their guardians until they're established again," I suggested.

"Perhaps," replied Kyle, "but could we consider another option, just for a moment? Before this whole dragon, bat, whatever fiasco, we were surveying land north and east of Bridgetown for farming. Our only challenge was who would farm them. Although we had asked for volunteers, very few had stepped forward.

"When you think about the easy lives we're used to, it isn't surprising. The problem is our natural food stores are depleting quickly. Living off supplements is something no one is looking forward to. Consider this: we make them an offer to come to Bridgetown and farm the lands, and in exchange, they will provide fresh food."

"What an absolutely fabulous idea!" blurted Sabrina. "It's so perfect! This is exactly why I married this guy. Enough said—let's just do it! I'll start preparing the appropriate welcome for our new citizens."

"Okay, before we get carried away, we need to share all this wonderfulness with our people. If they're in favor, then we'll begin planning. Not doing, Sabrina, just planning. If the people are not supportive, then we're back to the drawing board," cautioned Kyle.

"Kyle, my husband, there you go again playing the 'will of the people' card. You know—we all know—if Kyle wants this to happen, so will the people. No Child of Vanguard is ever going to go against the wishes of the man who brought them home, and you know it, but go ahead if that eases your mind. The rest of us will start planning," responded Sabrina.

The unspoken truth hidden in Sabrina's words was that if *she* wanted it, Kyle would want it, and he would convince everyone else. That's just the way it was!

The provisions for this day's visit were just about loaded, and once again we made our way to the launch pad. This time,

Sabrina didn't see us off because now she was on a quest to make this plan a reality. At 09:00 hours, the Defender lifted off the pad, and twenty minutes later, we were preparing to land.

Things were different today! As the Defender slowly hovered down, people were everywhere waving and shouting. James was concerned they were not clearing the area for landing, and the last thing we needed was to crush a dozen or so of the people we were trying to save. As the landing pods began to lower from their bays, the people began to back away to a safe distance, and Kyle just sat there smiling at James and calling him a woman. Had Sabrina heard him using the word with sarcastic intent, life for Kyle would have been crap for weeks! I, of course, threatened to tell her. He, of course, threatened to kill me.

As we walked down the gangway, Joshal was already waiting with a group of young men. "Mr. Chandler, welcome again! These young warriors would like to help with the unloading. It is the least we can do, and they actually drew lots for the opportunity to board your starship. Would that be okay?"

James smiled at Kyle and looked at Joshal. "It would be my pleasure to allow your men on my ship to assist with the unloading. Kyle is a passenger and a nonpaying one at that! He talks a lot, but beyond that, he's just a pain in the ass."

Everyone in the clearing was laughing even though most didn't hear James's remarks. I guess they thought it was the polite thing to do to honor their benefactors. The table we sat at the previous day remained in the same place, only today it was covered with wines and breads. There she was again, Cateria, carrying more wine to the table and chasing nosey children away, all the time laughing and dancing around, seemingly oblivious to our presence. Or was she?

Even in her tattered, tired dress and bare feet, there was something almost mystical about her. She had full breasts as part of a lean frame, with long blonde hair reaching to the small of her back. Her eyes were the deepest blue I had ever seen. Her high cheek bones and full lips made her face appear almost sculpted. Every time she came near the table, my heart would start pounding in my chest. A couple of times, Kyle nudged me back to reality because I was very close to gawking.

Although the small talk continued as we tried to learn more, James had a different focus, and he wasted little time in making it known. "Joshal, tell us more about these people who came from the heavens to Draegon and made the pact with the king. Where did they go? Did they ever say who they were?"

"They left as they came, back into the heavens. Although we never spoke at length with them, it is said they were the Vanguard," replied Joshal.

He must have noticed the color drain from our faces as we looked back and forth at each other in disbelief. "Kyle, do you know of these beings? Are they your enemies? You seem concerned about their name," he commented.

"We know of them; we're just a bit surprised they visited this planet. Joshal, it's a long story I'll share with you another time. In the meantime, there's another matter I would like to discuss with you, but not here. Would you and the elders consider returning to Bridgetown with us today? We can dine together, and it will give you a chance to see where we're from. Bring your family as well. I know my wife would love to play hostess for the day," offered Kyle.

"We would be honored to come with you, but we must return this day because my people will be alarmed if we're away too long. I have four children, but only Cateria can attend. The others have duties that will not allow them to leave this place. If this satisfies you, we will be ready within the hour," responded Joshal.

True to his word, less than an hour later, we were onboard and preparing to leave. Kyle asked the two doctors to stay behind and continue tending to the ill. They were happy to do so because, as usually happens in emergency situations, they had started developing their own relationships at a very personal level with some of their patients.

Minutes later, the Defender began to lift off the ground. Crowds gathered around, cheering and waving good-bye to their leaders. Although the flight was short, it was obvious these innocents had never been aboard anything that flew through the air. Joshal and the other elders were as white as sheets and gripping the armrests, as if letting them go would cause them to fall from the sky.

Strangely, Cateria seemed quite relaxed by this little adventure. She spent her time asking me questions about Bridgetown and the women there and what they were like. I was in my glory and so caught up in her that my own fear of flying wasn't even a thought.

Kyle asked James to delay the landing until we flew over the lands we were considering for farming. As we hovered over the area, James had the large monitors activated, and in an instant, the views of potential farmland came to life.

This was almost too much for our guests. Their fear of flying was instantly replaced by their fear of this black magic before them. Kyle saw this and immediately tried to calm their anxieties. "Joshal, you seem perplexed by the images on the screen. Have you never seen such things?" he asked.

"Kyle, this surely must be magic! How is this done?" pleaded Joshal.

"There is no magic here, Joshal. Think of the images as reflections in a mirror. These are reflections of what is beyond the walls of this vessel. No more than that! We show you these reflections because we need your advice. What we're looking at are lands we have started to clear for farming. What do you think of the site, and do you think it would be good for growing food and herding livestock?" asked Kyle.

The elders now seemed to have a purpose as they huddled together talking softly, looking back at the monitor, and talking again. At length, Joshal spoke. "These are wonderful lands, and the black soil is perfect for growing. We noticed as well a great river to the north. This is where you should put your herds because it is prime grazing land with water for the animals. Kyle, it is a beautiful place."

"Excellent! We value your knowledge and opinion. If these were your lands, would you think them fine?" asked Kyle.

"Any man would be proud to call these lands his own, but I fear my people will never again see a sight as beautiful as these reflections," responded Joshal.

With that, James had the Defender head for the launch pad. He had called ahead to make sure Sabrina was aware of the visit and arrangements were in place for dinner. As the vessel sat down and we exited, there was Sabrina. Her smile was almost too big. She seemed artificial, and I commented to Kyle, "You had better hope her face doesn't freeze like that."

Although she was cordial with the elders during the introductions, it was really Cateria she was focused on. Within a couple of minutes, they were walking side by side ahead of the rest of us in a full gab session. We headed for the Protectorate briefing room. Sabrina declined and indicated that she and Cateria had girl things to do and no time to listen to silly men talk about how manly they were. In the blink of an eye, they had disappeared across the courtyard.

"Kyle, your woman is very headstrong. Does that not concern you?" asked Joshal.

"Our societies are different," replied Kyle. "Here, women are not subordinate to men. In fact, Sabrina is the Regent of Science and Medicine and has many people, mostly men, seeking her counsel in their everyday tasks. She is very good at what she does, and her outspoken nature is why I love her and why she is successful."

"Truly, the ways of your people are strange, but I guess for you this is as it should be. My people have much to learn, and it will take time," said Joshal.

When we arrived at the briefing room, James ordered in refreshments, and we all took our seats. Once again, Kyle asked Joshal and the rest of the elders, based on what they'd seen during our flyover of Bridgetown, what their impressions were. Joshal explained that they were surprised that our city had no walls for defense or a castle where our king sat. When Marcus explained our system of government, they seemed confused but curious.

The elders asked about our religious beliefs and what gods we prayed to. Kyle explained that, for the most part, we recognized no gods. "We have abandoned such beliefs over the centuries, accepting we are alone to make our own way through life. That said, we appreciate the beliefs of others."

Joshal seemed set back by this. "There are gods, and we are their seed. I know you don't believe that, but these truths have been passed down through the ages, and I will share them with you if you wish," offered Joshal.

"Absolutely! We wish to know all we can about our new friends," Kyle replied.

"It is written that when this land was young, it was visited by The Fathers. These gods came here to plant their seed, as they had done on so many other young worlds. The Fathers were the guardians of the universe with magic that not even you, my friends, can comprehend. It is also written that The Fathers brought order to the discord of the heavens.

"The writings speak of the evil intent of The Blackness that swept across the heavens, devouring worlds with the power of the dark. The Fathers confronted The Blackness, and a great battle was waged to preserve all things good. This conflict raged on for a thousand millenniums with the light of The Fathers standing against the evil of The Blackness.

"A billion worlds were consumed by The Blackness. A billion more were saved by The Fathers. Even today, the evil seeks to claim the universe, lurking in the night, waiting, calculating, hungry to devour us all," Joshal explained.

"With all due respect to your people's beliefs, your legends are romantic tales of good versus evil. If you would allow us to read the ancient text, perhaps we might understand better," I requested.

"This we cannot do! The sacred writings are entombed in the Mountain of Light, lost for all eternity," Joshal answered.

"Where is this Mountain of Light?" James asked.

"It is near the ruins of the ancient city of The Fathers, far beyond the horizon in lands we dare not venture," responded Petra, one of the elders.

"Okay, enough of this! We did not bring Joshal and the elders here to question them about their beliefs. It is their affair, not ours," Kyle stated. "Joshal, we would like to discuss an arrangement with you and your people that will service our mutual needs. It doesn't require a decision today, because we know you will have to speak to your people, but we are confident you'll share our enthusiasm."

"Speak your words, Kyle," responded Joshal.

"We had a motive for your bringing you here today and for deliberately flying over the lands being cleared for farms. Our people are not farmers or herdsman. Until we arrived on this world, we had lived our entire lives on board a spacecraft, wandering among the stars. Our scientists understand the basic principles of farming, but apart from what is grown in our hydroponic gardens, we have no real farming skills.

"Consider for a moment an arrangement. We will gift this land to your people in exchange for some of the crops you harvest and animals you herd. Your people will become citizens of Bridgetown, and as citizens, we will stand between you and your enemies. You will bring your knowledge of this world to our people, and we will bring the knowledge of technology to your people. Could you consider such an arrangement?" asked Kyle.

There was a rather long pause while Joshal stared directly into Kyle's eyes. I think he was trying to gauge how real this offer was and what strings might be attached.

"We would be foolish to refuse such an arrangement given our situation and our enemies, but we are farmers without tools to farm and herdsman without herds to tend. We bring very little to this accommodation," responded Joshal.

"Nonsense!" replied Kyle. "It is your skills we require, not those material things. Together we will forge new tools and obtain animals from the forests to replace those you have lost. Let us share our technology and all it can provide with you. The measure of a man is the sum of his deeds, not the tools he owns."

"We will take your most generous offer back to our people with our blessings. By midmorning tomorrow, we will speak again."

"Excellent!" I replied. "Now when do we eat?"

I couldn't believe my eyes when Sabrina and Cateria walked into the dining room of the Great Hall. As beautiful as Joshal's daughter was in the rough, it was nothing compared to the goddess Sabrina had turned her into over a few short hours. The transformation truly was magical! I couldn't speak, and I couldn't take my eyes off of her. If I live for a thousand years, I will never forget that day and that moment.

Kyle again had to nudge me numerous times to help me avoid embarrassing myself in front of Joshal, but I'm sure it was way too late for that. Sabrina knew I was lost and didn't miss the opportunity to do what she loved to do, which was to put men in their place.

"Ryan, are you okay? Anyone would think by looking at you that you had never seen a beautiful woman before. You're embarrassing us. Look away please! I think Cateria is feeling uncomfortable watching the saliva running over your chin," she sniped.

With this, she picked up a cloth from the table and gently whipped my face. Everyone was roaring in laughter, but not Cateria and certainly not me. Now that Cateria and I had full eye contact, I was melting away. I had never been so captivated by anything or anyone in my life. It was embarrassing.

The dinner was wonderful, and Joshal and the elders told us many stories about their lives and the planet. Just after midnight, James suggested we call it a night, and he arranged to have the settlers moved back to the plateau. I was lost!

Eleven

Now We Are One

The next morning, we returned to the colony to receive Joshal's answer. As the Defender touched down, the people gathered around the ship, waiting for us to make our appearance. We could see through the cameras that Joshal and the rest of the elders were dressed in ornate costumes, and we were curious to know what they were intended to symbolize.

When we emerged from the vessel, Kyle didn't wait for James or me. He never did! He moved directly toward Joshal with his hand extended. As hard as Joshal was trying to look proud and regal, we could see he was as excited as a schoolboy to see us and deliver the news. He didn't waste any time.

While he was still shaking hands, he was speaking, "Kyle Chandler, my people discussed this arrangement far into the night, and we accept your offer as brothers and sisters of this planet."

"Excellent! Take my hand once again because that's how brothers make a pact when all that is necessary is our word," responded Kyle.

We all shook hands, and a deafening roar rose from the settlers. So it was done! How could we have known a simple handshake would change everything? For now, it was merely a symbolic gesture of acceptance between two distinctly different cultures.

"Joshal, my brother, we should move quickly to relocate your people from this place of sadness and disease. How many people would that be exactly?" asked James.

Joshal replied, "There are 853 adults, 211 children, and yes, over 200 Trells."

Kyle couldn't help but laugh. "James would never leave the Trells behind. I don't know if you noticed, but see the two soldiers near the ship holding the puppies you gave him? That's as far apart as they get."

"Kyle is right, but he doesn't mention that the Trells don't take my friendship for granted like some individuals who shall remain unnamed," responded James, smirking.

This led to another round of exaggerated laughter from all those gathered in the clearing.

"Please have your people collect their belongings. When the sun is high in the sky, we will send two vessels to bring you to your new home," continued James.

Joshal seemed puzzled. "Kyle, my good friend, it will take many of these machines to move my people unless you intend to make many trips!"

"The two vessels James will send are unlike these. They will carry many people but will require a large space to land, and I would ask your men to ensure the way is made clear. I don't want anyone hurt. The first craft will take all the women and children. As soon as it departs, a second will retrieve all the men and of course the Trells. By the time the sun sets this very day, we will be celebrating in Bridgetown. Together we will eat until we can eat no more and drink wine until the sun rises again. Then our work will begin," said Kyle.

Without further conversation, we boarded the Defender, and twenty minutes later, we touched down in Bridgetown. There was much to do and no group better to get it done than the Protectorate. Kyle immediately sought out Sabrina at the Medical Center to help with the feast by the lake. She was so happy and without any hesitation was already gathering her friends to start arranging the gala. The notice was short, but her determination was not.

Kyle returned to the CRB and sent out a video message asking the citizens to prepare for the arrival of new friends by helping with the indoctrination exercises. There was a buzz in Bridgetown unseen since Vanguard first deposited us on this world.

Kyle and I couldn't be there when the first Explorer arrived at the colony, now fully outfitted with seating for six hundred people. I wondered how the settlers reacted when they saw the ship hovering down to their small plateau. They were simple people with an innocent view of the things around them. This would be terrifying! James must have sensed that because he decided to make the first trip back to the encampment. I guess he wanted to be sure Joshal understood that his people would be safe aboard this flying city.

It took over three hours to load the woman, children, and their meager belongings onboard and another two hours to unload them at Bridgetown. The Protectors had already established a kind of tented community in the courtyard on the base, complete with portable showers and toilet facilities.

All manner of clothing had been gathered and was awaiting the colonists' arrival. As harsh as it sounded, one of the first requirements Sabrina insisted on was as soon the settlers were delivered, they must shower with special antibacterial soap and discard their clothing, not only what they were wearing, but anything packed in the sacks they carried with them. At first our new friends were confused by the instruction, but when they saw what had been collected for them, there was no hesitation.

Thousands of citizens were on hand to assist Joshal's people with their assimilation. It was hectic but strangely well controlled. The Protectorate kitchen resources had established cafeteria style food lines, and the Medical Center had sent a fifty-doctor triage team to provide more medical attention as the sick arrived. For all our frailties, the Children of Vanguard proved to be a cohesive team.

When the second Explorer arrived in Bridgetown, James decided to lead a clean-up team back to the plateau to recover anything of value and to cover our tracks. He had the foresight to take a video team and five of the Spider Drones along with twenty Protectors and, of course, two Trell puppies. The encampment seemed eerily quiet now that the settlers had left, and James felt a bit uneasy trespassing into what was once someone's home.

The Drones were the first to be sent into the darkness of the caves to scout and send back video. Once James was satisfied there were no risks to his people, he and his team followed. As soon as they entered, they were met by the overpowering stench of human decay. A few of the soldiers became ill and had to be sent to wait outside.

The moldy dampness and gloom was depressing even for the few moments they'd been there. The cave was in fact four cojoined caves with perhaps twenty separate entrances from the plateau. In the largest cave, an underground stream ran through cracks in the cave wall, traveling perhaps a hundred yards before falling into nothingness over a natural ledge.

James could see from ground disturbance where families had huddled for sleep and warmth. Throughout the chamber were fire pits perched on rock shelves. Even with the bright spotlights of the Spider Drones, the caves were gloomy and lifeless, with only faint trickles of light filtering in from the entrances dotting the exterior walls. The scene was foreboding and hopeless. James couldn't imagine how humans could have survived as long as Joshal's people had in such a place.

He now understood how deep their fear of the tyrant king must have been to endure all this. Later, when he returned home, he mentioned to Kyle and me that he was so overcome with grief and despair he cried. James admitting a moment of human emotion made us uncomfortable. Before he left the plateau, he had each cave fire bombed with liquid flame canisters to remove any evidence of human presence. Two rockets were launched onto the clearing, throwing mountains of rock and dirt into the air and sealing the cave openings forever.

Later as we reviewed the videos, it was agreed that neither Sabrina nor the CRB should see them. We as well agreed never to mention what we knew about the caves to Joshal. I was concerned, as was James, about how Kyle would react to the videos after he had more time to mull it over. As humanistic as Kyle could be, he had a darker and uglier side, which had to be kept in check. This could set him off.

During the video playbacks, James couldn't speak without stammering. Kyle saw James was struggling and simply said, "James, we understand, the videos say all that needs to be said. We will make a report to the CRB. The rest we will deal with ourselves."

Now I was concerned! Anytime Kyle made those types of vague comments, trouble was about to begin. Although I felt the same as they did about the situation, one of us had to take the reasonable position.

"Can we try to find a way to deal with this that doesn't result in starting a war with an enemy we haven't even met?" I pleaded.

"Relax, Ryan; no one's talking about war here. We're just talking out loud," responded Kyle, smiling.

It was time to show Joshal and his people that they were finally safe and to welcome them around our fires. None of us could come to grips with what these people had endured. What we could do was make sure they would never have to endure it again—and if it took us to the last man standing, then so be it!

After our review of James's heart-wrenching videos, we decided to go our separate ways to make sure everything was falling in place for the celebration. Kyle caught up with Sabrina at the nursery, where the colonist children were being treated, fed, and entertained. The plan was to keep them there for the night to allow their families to relish in their new surroundings.

Kyle stood motionless in the doorway for what seemed an unusual amount of time before Sabrina became concerned and asked if he was okay.

When he spoke, his voice was shaky, and she could see the tears welling up in his eyes. "We must do all we can for these children. Anything they need or want, we must provide. We cannot imagine the lives these innocents have had to endure. That can never be allowed to happen again."

Sabrina knew her husband well and knew when something cut into the very fabric of his soul. Once he had gone silent again, she cupped his head in her hands, staring directly into his moist eyes.

"Kyle, my love, these children will never again want for anything. We will feed them, and we will clothe them. We will nurse them and hold them safe as we would our own. All I ask of you is not to let their misery go without consequence to those who would harm them."

When I heard the story, I knew the king of Draegon was doomed, if not tomorrow, then a tomorrow not long away. To have Kyle hungering for revenge was bad enough. To have James ready to pull the trigger and Sabrina prepared to load the gun—that made his fate a foregone conclusion.

As the fading sun dipped behind the mountains on the far side of the lake, the celebration began. There had never been a bigger or louder party in Bridgetown! Thousands upon thousands of citizens rotated through the park, bringing wine and welcoming our new friends. To the settlers, the whole thing was a dreamscape.

People were dancing while others were splashing in the lake. Our new friends promised they would teach whoever wanted to learn, how to swim. That was cause for more celebration. Kyle and Sabrina left early because she was having pains. As it turns out, there was more to celebrate than we thought. At 05:23 the following morning, Sabrina gave birth to an eight-pound, six-ounce baby boy. Could it get better than this?

Twelve

Draegon

The next day came in with thunderous headaches, but for the CRB, it was business as usual. Kyle made it abundantly clear that as soon as the business of the day was done, he would be leaving to spend time with his wife and new son. I asked him what name they had decided on. He said he'd let us know.

The first order of business was to update the CRB on all that had transpired since last we convened. By the time James finished giving his report on the cave visit, the room was electric. Every member wanted immediate military action against Draegon.

Kyle shouted over the din to get everyone's attention. "That is not a solution! If we lay waste to their city, who speaks for their innocent, now victims of our vengeance? Regardless of our emotions, we must look at this dispassionately. There has been enough human suffering; what we need is a plan to make sure there is no more. Can we speak now to what that plan might be? If I'm not at my wife's side before lunch, well, you all know what she's like."

Everyone settled down. James was the first to speak. "I agree with Kyle, but I'm not a member of this Council. If I may be allowed a few words, perhaps it will help us toward a meaningful solution. It is true that we should not seek vengeance for acts that did not directly involve us. As sympathetic as we might be toward our new friends, our objective must be to make sure it doesn't happen again."

The voice of a scientist in the upper chamber echoed down. "That's easy to say, but how do we tame this wild beast that knows no other way than to take life?"

Kyle piped in, "We tame the beast! We don't have to do that by destroying them."

"Why get involved at all? We've moved the settlers within our protected perimeter. Their enemy would not dare to challenge us!" shouted another representative.

"That's an excellent question," responded James. "Our sophisticated defenses didn't stop the winged beasts that killed some of our citizens. There are no guarantees Draegon couldn't find a way to attack us. We already know they don't mind trying to take what they want. What if they decide they want Bridgetown? Maybe not today or tomorrow, but in a year, maybe two, will they come at us as they came at Joshal's people? We can't take that risk!"

Admiral Donner spoke very calmly in response. "James is correct. We must show them we are not simple farmers throwing rocks and waving silly swords. To nip at us is to nip at the lion. Once they understand that, they'll understand the folly of trying any move against us."

Psychologist Dr. Ann Snider asked the next question. "Admiral, what would you consider an appropriate demonstration of power that would make them abandon their instincts for violence, but wouldn't result in a loss of life on either side?"

"We will pay them a friendly visit. Let's call it a diplomatic mission of sorts. We'll be one neighbor introducing himself to another. What could be threatening about that? We'll send thirty Defenders and five Explorers as escort, just to be sure they don't do anything impetuous," replied the admiral.

The entire chamber broke into laughter. This was a show of raw power with a deliberate message and most assuredly meant to intimidate, perhaps with just a touch of diplomacy thrown in on the side.

"Humor aside, we must put these people on notice and then be done with this! The question therefore becomes—when?" asked Kyle.

James answered, "While Mr. Chandler tends to his new boy and wife, I shall attend to this task."

Kyle was not going to allow this to happen without him. "I will attend as well, and so will Ryan. Just give me a couple of hours with family, and I'll be ready to go. I do recall someone mentioning there might be a requirement for just a touch of diplomacy. That's right up my alley. I am as diplomatic as they come. If things go sour, we'll deal with them right there and then. How's that for diplomacy? So we have a plan! See you guys in a couple of hours." With that, Kyle was gone.

James too was making his way out the other door while the rest of the CRB members continued with the mundane business of Bridgetown. Without Kyle, I really had nothing to contribute, so I followed James. As it turns out, he wanted to stop at the tent city to see how our new arrivals were coming along. Perfect! I wanted to see Cateria again. I couldn't help myself; I was bewitched!

The camp was now functioning like a small city. As we walked around, I was struck by the fact that the women were much differently proportioned than what we were used to. There were big-breasted women and small-breasted women, thin and full figured, strikingly gorgeous and some rather plain. All this helped explain why there were an unusual number of young men from the university volunteering their time to carry things, and others down by the river learning to swim.

I guess an added bonus to this whole swimming lesson thing was that the female teachers wore no tops. It was kind of odd but humorous that breasts had never been a focal point for the guys until now. Interesting!

James and I wandered around the camp, and there she was. Immediately she came over to us and took our hands, thanking us excitedly. Cateria was breathtaking. When she touched me, I could see in her eyes what I'm sure she saw in mine. She smiled and went to fetch her father.

We had to look twice! Was this the same Joshal we met only a couple of days before? His hair was cut and washed, and his beard was trimmed. What we had thought was a man in his late sixties, perhaps early seventies, was actually a well-built man in his mid-fifties. I tried to do the math to figure out how old Cateria was. She beat me to the punch.

She was thirty-one but looked like she was in her early twenties. I had been seduced but didn't care. The four of us walked together, and as Joshal and James discussed how best to start preparing the farms, Cateria took me off to the side to introduce me to some of the other girls of the colony. I felt like a schoolboy left alone with the cookie jar.

As we strolled away from the group, she looked up directly into my eyes. "Ryan, I've seen you looking at me. Do you find me desirable?"

I was a bookworm. I wasn't used to such direct conversation with a woman, and certainly not with a woman of Cateria's beauty. I blurted out my response without considering the ramifications of what I was saying. "You're spectacular!"

She giggled at the abruptness and volume of my response, which really made me feel foolish, and I wished I could suck the words back, but it was too late for that. She wasn't quite finished with me apparently, and I had obviously set myself up for her next salvo.

"You're so sweet, Ryan! I find you handsome too. Would you like me to be your woman?"

I couldn't speak! I now understood the term "breathless." She had sucked the wind right out of me. When I didn't answer, she looked up at me with a rather sympathetic smile. "Ryan, I understand; you are a god, and I am merely a human woman. But when you're ready, I will be yours for the asking."

Calling me a god kind of shocked me back to reality because I didn't understand the reference. "Why would you think of me as a god? I am just a man—a human man, no more, no less."

"All my people know you are gods. You have come from the heavens in your great machines. You fear no mortal, and we are blessed you have chosen my people to save from a most certain death. Under your watchful eye, we no longer fear our enemies because they would not dare to challenge the gods," she replied.

As much as I wanted to sit her down and take whatever time was necessary to explain that her people were wrong about us, it wouldn't be now because I caught a glimpse of James waving at me. When I told Cateria we would speak again and said good-bye, she planted a full kiss on my lips, and I was screwed forever. I couldn't believe how quickly the time had passed. I wished I could have stayed with her all day, but there would be other days.

By the time we walked to the launch pad, Kyle was already there talking with the admiral. The sight of thirty Defenders all waiting to leave was something to behold. James mentioned that the five Explorers were already in low orbit over Draegon, waiting for our arrival. Kyle asked James what the plan was or if indeed we really had a plan in the first place. James shrugged and simply responded, "We'll fly to Draegon and then discuss our options."

I smirked and remarked, "You guys are soldiers. I thought that's what you did. Plan, execute, and then plan again. Take nothing for granted, and always have a contingency plan."

"You're right of course! Our plan right now is to fly to Draegon. Assuming that plan works, then we'll think of another plan. Are we going to get onboard or do I have to go directly to the contingency plan, which is to leave your sorry asses here and go alone?" responded James, smiling.

"You've got to admit, Ryan, it is a plan. Fairly basic, but I'm betting we can pull it off. Let's do this," chirped Kyle.

As we took our seats and the hatch closed, the familiar hum of the lift thrusters had already begun. The thirty Defenders seemed to all rise off the pad in perfect unison. It was a fascinating spectacle to watch this massive armada rise to fifty thousand feet together, as if joined by invisible cords. The three-thousand-mile flight to Draegon took just over twenty five minutes, during which time James had coffee and buns delivered to our seats while we talked over what would happen once we arrived.

James's idea was basic and based on one of the oldest military ploys of history: shock and awe. The logic was simple. Move over the city in full formation, bringing in the Explorers to hover five thousand feet above, with the Defenders flanking them on all sides—literally turning day into night. Once in position, we would begin multichannel hails to the surface and wait for a response. While we were waiting, we would assess their military capabilities and determine just how big a threat they might pose for Bridgetown security.

Kyle hoped someone would respond to the hails so we could arrange a face-to-face meeting with this infamous king and his cohorts. The biggest question on the table was: what will we do if they don't acknowledge the hails or can't? We were not there to impose our will, only to send the message, but we were quite prepared to stand nose-to-nose if it became necessary.

As we hovered into position over the city, James activated all the cameras, because at five thousand feet, we would be able to see the reaction of the people on the ground. We were surprised there didn't appear to be any concerted effort to defend the city, but that wasn't to say it wouldn't begin at any moment. Our ships had full shields raised, just in case. James instructed the communications officer to begin hailing on all available bands.

The city was somewhat sprawling, and the only structures of any consequence were contained inside an enormous, walled compound in the city center. The main structure within the walled area did not resemble a medieval castle, but it did have the same imposing presence and was clearly what they were passing off as one. Within the compound was a launch pad with ten fighter crafts. The crafts were small compared to Defenders, but that didn't make them any less a threat in quick assault theaters. Kyle commented they were too small to be worried about.

James corrected him by explaining, "If even one of these ships made it to Bridgetown, it could still inflict significant damage and death."

A couple of minutes later, one of the hails was answered, and we were summoned to the communications room to hear it. A monotone voice cautioned that we had strayed into Draegon air space and we needed to depart immediately or our actions would be considered as an act of war. James was really rather calm through the entire message, and his answer was direct.

"We mean your city no harm. We request audience with your king as visitors and ambassadors, but make no mistake, if we are fired upon, we will return fire, and innocent people will die. Please advise how you wish to proceed."

An exaggerated silence followed for two or three minutes. Suddenly the speakers crackled, and the same voice as earlier began to transmit. "Our all powerful King Uthess will grant you the audience you desire. You will send one emissary unarmed, and you will withdraw your airships as a show of homage to the king. Failure to do that will result in immediate reprisal. Do you understand?"

"That's easy!" replied James. "No! We will send three representatives with armed escort. As long as our people are on the ground, we will not withdraw. I will say it again: our intent is to speak with your king, not to harm your city or your people. If any aggression is directed toward this fleet, we will respond with a force you cannot imagine. Until your king accepts these terms and speaks with us, we will not leave this air space."

The radio went silent again. James asked the communications officer why the transmissions were crackling. The technician explained that it was not our equipment, but theirs. "The transmitting equipment they're using is archaic, sir," the young officer announced.

Kyle and I congratulated James on his handling of the exchanges, and more importantly that he was able to keep his composure through it all. He bowed at the hip and told Kyle that next year he was going after his job as head of the CRB.

Once again, it took awhile for a response from the ground, but we had to show we were in control of this event and that stall tactics wouldn't work. When the last transmission was received, it was far less aggressive in its tone. "Our great king has agreed to your terms. Please dispatch your emissaries to the coordinates being provided."

"How do you want to do this, James?" asked Kyle.

"We will land with two other Defenders right in the middle of the courtyard. Our escort will be fifty Protectors. I also brought twenty of your Spider Drones to deploy around our ships while we're inside. Those ugly pieces of scrap metal are enough to give anyone nightmares. We will allow ourselves to be escorted to their king, but we will not surrender our weapons! Once in front of this guy, Kyle takes over, and the real bullshit begins." James laughed, as did I, but not Kyle.

The three Defenders slowly hovered down into the central courtyard, and we could see through our cameras that apart from the fighter crafts, there was almost no advanced technology.

James commented, "That's probably the reason they didn't fire on the fleet. They have nothing to fire. They were bright enough to figure out that committing their fighters to a battle they couldn't win was foolhardy. Better to appear defenseless today and live to fight another day."

Another equally interesting observation was the compound appeared to be populated by military personnel only, and they looked disinterested in our arrival. I asked James what he made of that.

"I don't know" he replied. "You would think they'd be scattering like cockroaches, but apparently they don't feel at risk."

"Well, that doesn't give me any warm and cozies," responded Kyle. "Can't we just kick their asses and leave? I guarantee no one will be mad at us in Bridgetown."

We all laughed, but I'm not sure Kyle was really trying to be funny! If James had said, "Let's do it," or anything like that, this thing would have been over in a heartbeat.

As the three Defenders touched down and the gangways were extended, the Spider Drones were immediately deployed around our ships. When that happened, we could see an immediate change in the demeanor of the nearby soldiers. Now they looked uneasy, even terrified!

The Draegon guards carried no visible side arms beyond the same sword-like weapons as the settlers. Some of them were on horseback, and others were positioned around the walls of the compound with what I remembered from books as being crossbows. Whatever their normal routines, they were now fully focused on us.

It was like a scene from some ancient novel from the Iron Age of Europe. I found it absolutely fascinating. James and Kyle didn't. In their world, if something seemed unnatural and out of place, a red flag went up. I guess that was a prudent position, but I couldn't fathom any way these people could be a risk to us.

Once at the bottom of the ramp, we were almost completely surrounded by our Protectorate escort. Two great wooden doors opened at the front of the main structure, and a moment later, a procession of soldiers dressed in colorful costumes advanced toward us in a completely nonthreatening manner.

"James, we had better warn them off. If the Drones see them as a threat, things are going to turn really ugly, really quickly," Kyle urged.

"Shit, you're right! I almost forgot how temperamental these fucking things are. Stop! Please do not come any closer! We will come to you. Our robotic sentries will fire upon you if they determine your approach to be a threat to the ships!" yelled James.

The royal escort stopped in their tracks and stood motionless while we made our way toward them. When we were about ten feet away, their leader asked that we fall in behind and he would lead us to the king's throne room. I whispered into Kyle's ear that once we entered the building, we were at the greatest risk. He nodded and passed on the observation to James. James was always prepared, and when he lifted his arm, every Protector weapon was raised to the fire position.

Passing through the great doors, we found ourselves in an enormous reception area that had great stone staircases to either side of the room and a ceiling perhaps fifty feet high. Straight ahead of us was another massive set of wooden doors, and as we came to them, the leader of the royal escort stopped and turned to face us.

"You are not permitted to bring your armed escort beyond these doors. They must wait in this ante room until we exit," he instructed.

James wasted no time in his response. "If our escort cannot pass, then we will not pass. We will wait for your king out here."

"That's absurd! King Uthess does not come to you! You could be put to death for the mere suggesting of such a thing. I will communicate to the king your reluctance to enter."

"Communicate anything you want, but if our guards are out here, so are we. Any attempt to force a confrontation will cause my fleet to destroy your city. This isn't negotiation!"

The escort leader opened the door just wide enough to permit himself to pass and closed it immediately behind him. An exaggerated amount of time passed as we stood outside the door waiting for a response. We were all getting impatient, but none more than James. "Five more minutes, and we're leaving. This is bullshit!"

Just as the words left his lips, the great door opened, and the royal escort leader stepped back into the waiting area. "The king has reluctantly agreed to allow your escort into the chamber. They cannot go before the king but may stand along each side of the approach. If that's acceptable, how shall I announce you?"

Kyle thought about it a second or two and proudly announced, "We are The Vanguard."

The escort leader gave us an odd look and asked if we were sure that was what we wanted to call ourselves. James had just about lost all his patience with the posturing. "Can we get on with this? I'm tired of the crap and want to get home before the sun goes down. If you're the guy in charge, do your bloody job and make the announcement."

With this, the two great wooden doors were flung open, and with us in tow, the guide announced us in a booming voice from the doorway. Immediately, we could sense a stir among the costumed people lined up and down the approach hall. This made James uneasy, and he turned and instructed the Protectors to stay alert. Something was going on, and if it came to a hasty exit, James would make sure we escaped, regardless of how many of these people suffered.

The hall was the biggest room I had ever seen. It was well over two hundred yards long and eighty yards wide. The guards in this room were equally colorfully dressed and carried small crossbows held at the ready. James whispered to Kyle that if even one of the weapons were pointed in our direction, he would put the entire room down.

Kyle suggested to James that he not get caught up in the moment because these guards were not here for us and were mostly window dressing. He told James he would address it immediately. He wasn't lying. Kyle reached forward and tapped the escort on the shoulder. When he turned, Kyle looked him square in the face.

"Sir, we are uncomfortable with your guards having their weapons pointed at us. Please have them lower them to their sides," he requested.

"You are not permitted to speak once in the throne room! The guards will remain as they are," the escort responded aggressively.

Kyle was a wonderful politician and negotiator, but once cornered, he became a brutal dictator. Without warning, he pushed through the escort to the front of the procession. Immediately all the bowmen directed their weapons at him. James gave a simple signal, and all fifty Protectors directed their weapons toward the King and his entourage.

"King Uthess, we have come here today to speak to you about peaceful matters. Yet as we approach, your guards raise their weapons in our direction. Either they stand down immediately or this ends badly and many die, including you and me!" shouted Kyle.

Uthess didn't say anything directly but waved an aide to his side and whispered into his ear. With that, the aide stepped forward, made a gesture with his hands, and the entire audience, including the guards, began to exit. While this exodus was underway, we stood motionless about halfway between the entry door and the king.

It took almost five full minutes for the room to clear, until all that remained were the king's immediate advisors and us. The leader of the royal escort was waved forward to the side of the king, and more words were whispered.

"King Uthess reminds his honored guests that he has cleared the room to show his respect for your concerns, and he asks that you show the same respect by having your armed escort wait in the outer room."

"What do you think?" Kyle asked James.

"I think if we don't want this entire day to be wasted, we should comply with the request," replied James. He then turned and signaled to the Protectors to join the rest of the people in the main entry hall, but reminded the captain to remain vigilant.

As we approached the king, our pace quickened until we stood perhaps twenty feet away from the raised throne. Once there, the royal escort bowed to the king and left the area. There was a moment when neither the king nor we spoke, but anytime you have Kyle, you have a silence that won't last.

"King Uthess, we have come today to introduce ourselves as your new neighbors to the east. Our city is named Bridgetown, and we are The Vanguard," he announced.

"Really, you are The Vanguard? Prince Rupert, step forward and make yourself known to these pretenders," stated the king with a sarcastic tone.

A costumed man moved into the center of the area and stood to the right of the king. "I am Prince Rupert, adviser to the king and commander of the Military Forces of Draegon. I am of The Vanguard, and you are imposters! State your real business and leave this air space immediately."

Kyle didn't miss a beat, although we were floored by what had just been said. It was clear in this man's demeanor and how he carried himself that he was not of these people, but to appear shocked by his words might show weakness. That was something Kyle would not allow to happen.

"That, sir, is an interesting assertion, but frankly we don't care who you claim to be. King Uthess, we are here to speak with you, not your underlings, so unless this has any relevance to anything, please dispatch this little man so we can get on with it," demanded Kyle.

"Why are you here, and what do you really want?" shouted the king, quite red-faced.

"We are here to make our presence known to you and to advise you that the Therons are now under our protection. I'm sure you must remember the innocent farmers you tried to exterminate. You and your henchmen are hereby put on notice that any hostile action directed at them will be considered a hostile action directed at us. Such action will result in the complete and absolute destruction of your city.

"By the way, Rupert is it, since I'm sure your role in all this goes way beyond just being an arrogant bastard, you can tell the rest of your Vanguard buddies wherever they're hiding that if they wish to discuss this privately, we're happy to arrange a meeting. If, however, their intent is to continue to fuel this king's madness, we will hold you and them responsible for his actions. Do not test our resolve," said Kyle.

With that, Kyle spun toward James, winked, and suggested that it was time to go. Uthess shouted behind us that with one word he could have us all put to the sword. James was now in a theater he was quite comfortable in. He stopped, turning ever so slowly toward the throne.

"King Uthess, be very careful you do not bite off more than you can chew. Should we not make it safely back to our vessel, our air fleet has been given instruction to reduce this city to ashes. We will gladly give our lives in the knowledge that yours will end in microseconds after. You, Rupert, the next time we meet, I will make it my personal obligation and delight to rid this city of your presence," threatened James.

With that, he turned back around, tapped his lapel communicator, and told the Protectors to come for us. In an instant, the great wooden doors flew open. Our escort marched in, forming a circle around us while a dozen or so had their weapons trained on the king and his advisors.

"Think hard about your next command, Uthess; it could very well be your last!" James called over his shoulder.

We exited the chamber and proceeded through the entrance hall and back to our ships. As we walked up the gangway, James turned and looked at Kyle. "Perhaps we should quicken our pace before the shock of this wears off and they come looking for blood." The hatch doors sealed behind us, and the hum of the thrusters was the welcoming sound of safety.

"Now what? We just threatened to wipe out the only real neighbor we have. I don't see another invitation headed our way anytime soon. What I do see is the first chance they get over the next few days, they're going to try to take a shot at Bridgetown just to send us a message," warned James.

"We can't risk that happening. Once we're airborne, please have all of their fighters reduced to scrap metal. This king was harmless before he was given modern technology; let's put him back in his right timeline. Please make every effort to limit the damage to equipment only. We'll debrief later, but there is more to all of this. We need to have further conversations with Joshal on this whole Vanguard issue," replied Kyle.

As the fleet headed home, one lone Defender stayed behind long enough to hit the fighters with full-phased electromagnetic pulse beams, effectively frying all the operating systems and components of their fleet. I found myself torn between my eye-for-an-eye view of what we had done and my historian sensitivity that we had meddled in the affairs of a simple, closed culture and changed them forever. When I shared my thoughts with James and Kyle during the flight home, they had a different view on the event.

"Ryan, you're right, we have meddled where perhaps we shouldn't have, but I don't see that as necessarily a bad thing for the people of this planet. Someone before us altered the developmental direction of this culture and created a monster by providing weapons these simple people couldn't possibly comprehend. The result was they misused what they were given, which led to the deaths of thousands.

"All we've done is righted that ship! To help you come to peace with all of this, remember that our involvement with Joshal and his people is also meddling. We moved these folks a thousand years forward in social structure in less than a month.

Was that the right thing to do, and is it any different than our actions today?" asked Kyle.

It was difficult to argue the logic, especially since if we hadn't meddled, I would never have met Cateria.

Thirteen

What to Do

Although the pound of flesh we took at Draegon did somewhat satisfy our need to avenge our new friends, it left us with yet another mystery to unravel. Prince Rupert claimed he was of The Vanguard. This fell in line with Joshal's story about their intervention. In truth, it did appear obvious; the ten fighters in the Draegon arsenal must have been provided by these Vanguard people, but why? What purpose could be served by arming peasants and farmers with weapons that were thousands of years of technology ahead of where they were?

From what little we'd managed to glean from this so far, they gave them the weapons and the men to fly them, but what was their plan? If the plan was to conquer the planet, they didn't need the king. They could have accomplished that feat in a day. Was Joshal's story of the Vanguard's role in pushing away the predators valid, and did it somehow tie into arming Uthess?

There were so many questions and so few answers. What we knew for sure was we needed to answer them—and soon. James indicated he felt there was some sort of subplot in the play and if we wanted to avoid being part of the victim count, we'd better figure it out. The question was where to start. The answer was Joshal.

I had a much deeper concern about all these discoveries and events. We did over three hundred exploratory missions using the most technically advanced devices ever invented to assess whether this planet was suitable for us. How could we have missed that there were humans living here? How could we miss a settlement the size of Draegon so close to the site of Bridgetown? All these discoveries were making me very nervous. What else did we miss?

When I voiced my concerns to Kyle and James, they agreed that a whole bunch of what was happening to us should have been detected before we ever set foot on the planet. Like me, they were at a loss as to why. We rested for a few days after our little excursion to Draegon, and I spent the time trying to develop my budding relationship with Cateria. We hadn't gotten much past quick pecks, but that had everything to do with my nervousness and nothing to do with her willingness to go to the next level. She was much more woman than a guy like me could ever hope to have, yet here we were.

As silly as that sounds, I wasn't prepared for this big a prize, and I didn't want to do or say the wrong thing and lose her. Kyle was constantly prodding me to get on with it before some other suitor stole her from me. He was right, and I knew it, but the doing was a real leap of faith for someone like me.

We invited Joshal and the rest of the elders to attend a breakfast in the Protectorate briefing room. We would use the event as an excuse to learn more about what was really going on. How we presented our questions was as important as the questions themselves. Kyle didn't want this to come across as an inquisition, but we needed help.

Once seated and after a progress report from Joshal on how things were progressing with the new surroundings and preparations for planting the new fields, breakfast was served. Kyle used the relaxed mood to begin a slow but methodical question period.

"Joshal, we are pleased that your people are comfortable in their new surroundings. We'll be even more pleased when your farms start churning out real food instead of these supplements we've been eating for what seems a thousand years. I was hoping to pick your brain a bit more about the way things were before your exile. I know there is considerable pain attached to some of those memories, but we had an interesting meeting with your former countrymen in Draegon, including King Uthess, and I need your help in figuring out what's going on."

"Kyle, we are pleased to be of whatever value we can, however we were never part of the Draegon inner circle and know nothing of how this animal operated. Nonetheless, ask your questions, and we will answer if we can," replied Joshal.

"Excellent. Tell me, if you can, what you know about a man by the name of Prince Rupert and The Vanguard," said Kyle.

"So far, the questions are easy," he replied. "Prince Rupert is of The Vanguard, and these are the star travelers that gave Uthess his Fire Breathers. Prince Rupert commands the pilots of these evil vessels and is the real power behind the king's claim to his empire."

"Okay then, let's discuss for a moment The Vanguard and what you really know or think you know about them," requested Kyle.

"The Vanguard were star voyagers searching for a new home world. They were much like your people in many ways. Like you, they saved us from something we could not control. We were besieged by hunter birds. As I have told you before, many of my people died. Many more would have died if not for the Vanguard's intervention. They were our saviors and asked nothing in return," responded Joshal.

"I recall you mentioning you didn't know what the nature of the pact was that they made with the king to give him the Fire Breathers and the pilots, but you must have an opinion about it. If so, we'd like to hear it," said James.

"My people believe The Vanguard were concerned the creatures would return once they left and decided to leave behind the ships and pilots to provide additional protection. What else could it be?" he replied.

"What about The Vanguard pilots they left behind? Did they not protest the murderous use of these machines?" I asked.

"Perhaps at first, but Uthess showered them with power and gifts of lands and slaves in exchange for their knowledge and loyalty. They became as evil as he. We were doomed," Joshal answered.

"Where did The Vanguard go when they left?" Kyle asked.

"We don't know! Some say they returned to the heavens. Others believe they built a great city across the mountains where the sun sleeps. On these matters, we can't help," responded Joshal.

"Good, that's enough questions. Let's drink some coffee, eat some food, and listen to Joshal and the rest of the elders tell us more about happier times for their people," declared Kyle.

The rest of the meeting was uneventful. Although we didn't learn much more than we already knew, it was interesting to get a different perspective on things. After Joshal and the elders left, we remained. Kyle decided this was not the time to confuse them by declaring ourselves as the real Vanguard.

It had been a long day, and we wanted it to end. Too much was happening, and it was tiring to think of it all at once. When we separated, I went directly home and immediately to bed. Sleep came slowly as I listened to the soft rain hitting against the windows, but when finally it did, I slept soundly and awoke early and full of energy. After a quick shower, I decided to wander over to the compound. Perhaps Cateria would be up and we could have breakfast together. Time always went faster when we were together.

When I arrived, Joshal and his family were up and going about their morning routines before breakfast. I couldn't see Cateria, so I asked her sister where she had gone. She smiled that smile the way women do and told me she had gone for a shower in the bath tent behind the medical compound. I thanked her and decided to go over and sit outside. Hopefully she wouldn't be long, and we could still squeeze in some time together before I left for a long day at the virtual library checking my work.

Once at the tent, I shouted out. "Cateria, it's Ryan! I'll wait here, and we can eat together."

She called back over the sound of the water. "This is really early for you, Ryan. Come in. We'll finish the shower together."

"No, that's okay, I've already showered," I replied timidly.

"Well, at least come in and wash my back!" she called over the sound of the cascading water.

There was no place to run, and I was out of excuses. It was a big tent with a number of small cubicles for privacy. We were completely alone. Now what?

"Down here, Ryan!" she called out.

Her shower stall was at the far end of the tent. When I got to it, she threw open the curtain and dragged me in. Almost an hour later, we emerged. I was soaking wet but didn't care.

"Cateria, that was fabulous, but I have to get home and change my clothes," I stammered.

"Good. I'll go with you," she replied.

"As much as that would be a dream come true, you cannot."

She pretended to pout and then smiled, trotting off toward the family tent. "We'll do this again later!" she shouted back over her shoulder.

By the time I wandered home still dripping wet, changed my clothes, and made it to the library, a good portion of the morning was gone. No sooner had I arrived than a Protector tracked me down because I was wanted back in the briefing room.

"Boy, you sure look awake and pleased about something. Wait a minute—I've seen that stupid look before, but usually it's on my face. You've been with Cateria! Does Joshal know his daughter and you are doing the bedding down thing?" asked Kyle.

I chose to ignore him or at least to pretend to. I walked quickly over to the table and took a seat. "Okay, what's going on?" I asked, as if I'd been there all the time.

"That's a damn good question. What is going on?" repeated James.

The admiral was ready to go and started the discussion. "Well, we accomplished what we set out to do. Draegon is certainly not a threat anymore, thanks to you boys."

"There are other things in play here that we're somehow going to have to come to grips with. Mutated creatures are trying to kill everything they see, and no one seems to know why or where they came from. We found humanoids where we didn't think there were any. They read and speak our tongue, which is mind blowing. The cultures, although dated, appear to mimic ancient Earth history, and now we just learned there are people running around calling themselves The Vanguard," said Kyle.

This went way beyond coincidence, and frankly, we were beginning to think it was not as simple as a history lesson. A bigger concern was: what else about this planet might jump up and bite us in the ass? This was our home, and there were no other options available to us, so no matter what, we were going to have to face whatever lay ahead.

"If you would have asked me a year ago if we had a handle on everything, I'd have said we know all we need to know, but not anymore. James, how much of the planet's total surface have we surveyed?" asked Kyle.

"Apparently not enough," responded James. "We assumed our risks were right in front of us because we had no idea what was beyond our little patch of heaven. We were wrong! Uthess had limited technology but could have inflicted his brand of terror to an area at least twice as large as our surveyed geography.

That said, exploring the entire planet will take years, and we may not have the luxury of years to figure this out."

"What do we do then?" I asked.

"Well, for starters, we establish a wider patrol grid. As it stands today, we can detect inbound objects as far out as two thousand miles. We'll put another Explorer in permanent orbit over the planet. That enhances our long-range air-defense capabilities. While in orbit, we'll perform routine infrared heat scans and life form scans. We may find what we're looking for without committing to a lengthy, unproductive surveying exercise," replied James.

Shortly after, the admiral left us to continue discussing the events of the last few months. Of course, James and Kyle managed to find a way to get on to their new favorite subject, my infatuation with Cateria. It had become fairly common knowledge to everyone who knew me or her that something was going on between us.

I guess I secretly hoped that what they all thought was true *was true*, but what really concerned me was if Joshal was hearing the same rumors, how was he feeling about it. I had learned in my short association with his people that they had a strict code of conduct and decorum about family life, and right now I didn't know if I was following those rules or breaking them. The whole thing made me nervous every time the topic of Cateria and I came up.

To change the subject, I asked Kyle if Sabrina and he had decided on a name for their son. He shrugged and said that it was still a work in progress. I found the whole thing a bit odd. Here were two people who could make a decision in the blink of an eye, a decision that could affect the entire population, but they struggled to come up with something as simple as a boy's name. I guess I wouldn't know the challenges of such things until I had kids of my own.

The day was moving along, and I still hadn't spent any meaningful time at the library. This was important, and I was determined if the solution to the Vanguard saga lay buried in the history text, I was going to find it. I left James and Kyle and started making my way back toward the archives.

It was a short walk, but as luck would have it, it took me right by Joshal's camp. As soon as I saw the white tents, whatever focus I had was lost to my yearning to see Cateria again. After all, what could be the harm in just stopping a few minutes and saying hello to Joshal and his family?

It was now well into the late afternoon, and as I approached their tent, they were preparing to sit down for an early dinner. As soon as Joshal saw me coming up the laneway, he called my name and waved me over. When Cateria heard my name, she immediately ran in my direction. The entire scene could have been seen by a casual onlooker as the return of a long lost family member. Once she reached me, she jumped into my arms and kissed me hard.

"I thought you were never going to get here. Come, have dinner with us," she whispered in my ear.

"What makes you think I was even intending to come here, and more importantly, how do you know I'm not here just to see your father?" I responded, trying to sound as unaffected as possible.

"Your body tells me exactly why you're here, and my body tells me it feels the same. So stop talking silly and let's greet father," she whispered again.

That was that! Slightly embarrassed by the whole affair, we walked over to the table. There were two small girls who I hadn't seen before sitting at the far end.

"Ryan, sit here beside me. Here on my right! Jacob, make room for Ryan. We are so pleased you were nearby. Are you just wandering, or do you wish words with me?" asked Joshal.

"I think it's a bit of both, but if a free meal comes with it, why I'm here is not nearly as important as I thought it was. You certainly look like you've made this as comfortable as possible for yourselves. That's great," I commented.

"It's much better than where we were. Ryan, I was hoping I'd cross paths with either you or Kyle, so this works out well. When we were talking yesterday about Draegon and The Vanguard, I wanted to get into some more about our history and visitors from other worlds, such as yourselves, but I didn't think it had any bearing on anything. Later, when I had a chance to think about it, it occurred to me that perhaps the information might have some value to you. We'll discuss that after dinner. Cateria, bring us some wine to celebrate Ryan's visit. I'm sure his presence has much more to do with you than us," responded Joshal.

I wasn't quite sure how to respond to that since it was true. Cateria wasn't nearly as caught off guard, and she replied to her father immediately. "Father, although Ryan might enjoy his little get-togethers with you, of course he's here to see me, so leave him alone."

Wow! The zingers just kept on coming. Once we had gotten past the "let's embarrass Ryan" phase, we enjoyed a casual dinner together. During the meal, Joshal gave me the history of his family tree. There was much more tragedy in his life than having to lead his people into the mountains and fighting off man-eating bats. Add to this, as I now learned, the bats took his wife. When he got to Cateria's story, my heart sunk with sadness for her, and as he was sharing her loss with me, I could see she was clearly shaken by the reminder.

Joshal indicated that Cateria had a husband who loved her dearly. His name was Assome, and like Joshal, he was a herdsman. In their short three years together, they had two beautiful girls, his grandchildren, Safrina and Certa, the two children seated at the table. Immediately all eyes turned toward them, and they were bewildered by the sudden attention.

"When Uthess invaded our lands, Assome, like most of the young men of Theron, stepped forward to defend what was theirs. Bows and arrows were no match for fire. The young men fell quickly in a war they could not win," Joshal lamented. It was clear why the settlers hated the king and all he stood for.

My appreciation and, yes, my love for Cateria truly began that day. For it was then I realized that these simple people had endured more than could be expected of anyone, yet through it all, they had the drive to survive when others might have perished. Cateria now sobbed softly and left the table to hide her moment of grief.

I excused myself and followed her, leaving Joshal nodding his understanding and acceptance of my attention to his daughter. When I finally caught up to her near the lake, we embraced for hours while she completed the story her father had begun. By the time we returned to the tent, the day had all but passed us by.

My intent was to say my good-byes and leave, but Joshal insisted I stay the night because he wanted to divulge what he had missed saying during our meeting. Cateria was openly pleased that I would be there to hold her through the darkness. Although this sleepover stuff was new to me, as it would have been to anyone born on Vanguard, I welcomed the invitation. Joshal had his sons break out more wine and set a fire while he began to share with me yet another agonizing mystery.

"Ryan, there were other visitors from the heavens before Vanguard. These visitors did not come to save us or to become our friends. They came to destroy us and take our world for their own. This was in the time before the birth of my children, when I was still a young man.

"The visitors were a warrior species determined to end our time on this planet. They were not human but seemed human-like in many ways. Their armies swarmed across our lands, killing all that stood in their way. Those spared were made slaves to mine for a strange substance buried in the mountains to the south. Many people of our lands died in the three years the invaders were here, and even as a young man, I had accepted my fate to die in the mines like so many of my friends.

"As I said before, they were not human. Their skin and hands were dark with the texture of an animal, and they spoke in a language that was strange and ugly to hear. Standing erect, these beings were over eight feet tall and weighed twice that of the largest men in the Great Valley. They were hunters and killers, and we were their prey.

"Over the passage of time, something happened! Something strange! The invaders became infected with a sickness—a plague that only affected them. Their eyes that had been green and black became pink and distant, followed by blindness. Their hard skin became covered in oozing sores. Every breath they took became a struggle to find air. They were dying! My people believed this to be the punishment of The Fathers for the creatures' murderous ways.

"As quickly as they arrived, they were gone! We were saved, but how? I believe it wasn't The Fathers. We were the plague, humans. Something on our skin or in our breath poisoned them over time. Our bodies treated the invaders as a disease and fought them back. I know how silly that sounds, but it is what I believe."

"Joshal, it is an amazing story! So, after they left, you never saw them again?"

"Oh, they did return in their ships many times, but never again did they set foot on this planet," he responded.

We were now well into the night and exhausted. As I walked hand-in-hand with Cateria to the tent, I couldn't get Joshal's story out of my mind. Cateria drifted off to sleep in my arms, but for me, sleep came slowly. When I finally did sleep, it seemed only minutes before streaks of sunlight pierced through the fibers of the tent roof. Cateria was already up and about. As I staggered out of the tent, she called to me to wash up for breakfast. Another day began!

"Ryan, your theory that this invading race returned with the bats years later is interesting, but I'm not sure I see it. Think about it. Joshal's people defeated the invaders by breathing on them. The aliens, in turn, counter by genetically altering a creature from another world, which they transport here solely for the purpose of killing Joshal's people and eating their remains, essentially consuming the disease. To make sure this giant flying rodent is out of the way after the job is done, the alien makes sure the creature can survive only one life cycle. Are you kidding me?" James seemed almost irritated by the concept.

"James, I know it's farfetched, perhaps even silly," piped in Kyle, "but is there a better story to tell? We can't possibly understand the mind-set of an alien creature. Maybe in their minds we were the disease and the bats were the cure. I think before we dismiss the idea, we should find a way to test it. Admiral, what's your take on all this?"

"You guys think too much for my liking. Whether someone brought them to the planet or they were always here doesn't change anything, other than confuse what we need to do. We need them dead. Rather than trying to figure out where they came from, we need to know where they are. Let's become the hunters, find their nests, and neutralize the threat. Commit additional resources to the campaign and be done with this. Once the threat has passed, then we can all sit around and offer opinions about how this all started," said the admiral.

He was right, and we knew it. Within hours, James tasked four Explorers over the mountains to the south and west, focusing on valleys that might contain caves. We continued our drone patrols over Draegon, watching for any signs of them trying to rebuild their small combat fleet. There was nothing!

Kyle suggested that perhaps we had an obligation to Joshal's people to offer the option of returning them to their original farms in the Great Valley. Without aircrafts, Uthess had no resource to enforce his claim over the distant countryside.

As soon as the words left his mouth, my heart sank. Should the settlers decide to return to their homelands, my relationship with Cateria would likely be over before it started! There would be too much geography between us to nurture a budding love affair. As much as I wanted to disagree and suggest we say nothing, I knew he was right.

I asked to be the one to speak to Joshal and bring his answer back to the CRB. Who knows—perhaps I could convince Cateria to be my wife and have her stay behind to raise a family. Even as I walked toward the tent city, my step was slow and reluctant. I got a bit of a reprieve because when I arrived at Joshal's tent, there was no one around. In fact, most of the compound was empty. This baffled me for a moment until one of the remaining settlers saw me looking totally confused.

"If you're looking for Joshal and his family, they've gone to the farm sites to continue clearing the land. In fact, just about everyone's there. If you come back later, they always return at the dinner hour. You're Ryan, right? When they get back, I'll tell them you stopped by," she offered.

I thanked her and headed for the library to start my research and to kill time until later in the day. For hours, I reviewed text after text involving the building of Vanguard. There was nothing! Nowhere could I find even a reference to a Vanguard before us. The entire history spoke only of our Vanguard. I was disappointed because I wanted to be the one to step forward with the missing pieces of the puzzle.

Fourteen

The Pact

When I arrived back at the compound, Joshal was sitting in his normal chair at the head of the makeshift table, and his daughters were serving up the dinner for the night. As I approached, he stood and extended his hand. "Come sit beside me at the table."

Once again, his eldest son vacated the much sought after seat beside the family patriarch. I was a bit embarrassed and apologized for having him uprooted.

He smiled. "You are a guest at our table. When you become family, you will no longer be so well treated." With that, he smiled at Cateria, and she smiled back.

I felt a bit like a lamb being led to the slaughter. Cateria walked over to me and without any shame bent over and planted a full kiss on my lips. I'm not sure how many shades of red I must have turned, but Joshal chuckled and waved a hand for all to sit and eat. As usual, the conversation was light with no subject of any particular importance put up for discussion. I was so relieved.

My life had become a series of dramas, most of which I wasn't equipped to deal with. Part of the conversation centered on the food available and how generally tasteless it was. Joshal had no qualms about expressing his opinion even when the food was given.

"Ryan, if we are to become citizens, we need to have some serious discussion about what your people are eating. Most of it tastes like grass and lake-weed. Do you not eat meat?" he said.

I explained to him that we used to have freeze-dried and powdered beef and pork meat, but those rations were exhausted decades ago. Our scientists developed this food along with supplements to keep us healthy. We do raise chickens, and on occasion bird meat is served, but mostly we raise them for eggs. By the time they become bird meat, they're so old you need a laser cutter to eat them. I told him I'd give anything to taste real meat.

"And you shall! Tomorrow, my sons will go to the forest and kill a forest hog. We will build a fire, and my daughters will skin, clean, and roast the animal. We will dine like kings," he promised.

No living citizen had ever tasted real meat. When I told him that, he laughed and said, "Here I thought gods never did without. It would appear that too was only legend."

Then Cateria commented, "Father, not to worry, I will make sure he eats as a man should eat. He is so skinny. They all are! We'll fatten them up."

I was intrigued. "Tell me about these forest hogs. Are they dangerous, and where would you find one?" As soon as I asked, I was embarrassed.

"Forest hogs are very plentiful and can be found in the forest. They make excellent livestock as well. Before this whole ugly mess with hunter birds, we had herds numbering in the thousands. Most of them escaped back to the forest when we were attacked, but we'll build another herd over time," responded Joshal.

"Are they big?" I asked.

"I guess it depends on what you mean by big. The average hog might weigh six hundred pounds," he responded. "We have seen them over a thousand pounds, but rarely."

"How do you kill one?" I asked.

"Our Trells sniff them out, and we bring them down with bow and arrow, but I think for tomorrow we're going to convince one of those Protector soldiers to join us on the hunt. With that thing he carries, we can have a hog down and roasting in a couple of hours." Joshal chuckled.

I was actually looking forward to trying real meat. It had to be healthy because these people were certainly much stronger and more durable than the average citizen, including the Protectors.

I regretted the message I had to deliver, but delaying it any longer only made it a harder pill to swallow. "Joshal, I need to speak with you in private before all this wine we're drinking clouds my mind too much."

Without ceremony, he rose from the table and began to walk down the lane toward the lake with me trailing behind. Once we were side by side, he turned and asked me what was on my mind. The words were slow to my lips but required.

"Joshal, as you know, we destroyed Uthess's ability to spread his evil much beyond the city of Draegon. This could be very important for you and your people. If you wish to return to your farms across the mountains, we as your friends will assist in that relocation. These words do not come easily to me because I love your daughter, and the thought of losing her is almost more than I can bear." There, I said it; my speech was over.

"Ryan, our home is here with you. We are soon to be citizens of Bridgetown, and our loyalty is and shall ever be to Bridgetown. History is just that—history—and all creatures evolve and change. We have evolved and changed. Tell James and Kyle there is no way we're going anywhere. We have lands to clear and soon herds to tend.

"As for you and Cateria, my greatest wish is her happiness, and if she has chosen you to provide that, then so it shall be. However, it is far more complicated than you might think. Ask her about The Pact, and then we shall speak again. For now, let's end this conversation and get back to the family tent. You and I have much wine to drink before this day ends."

I couldn't have asked for a better response. My world had returned to where it should be. There was more to this conversation than his decision to stay. He accepted me as part of it all and, potentially, part of his family. The only caveat was this Pact thing Cateria would tell me about. I was back to being scared shitless and had no idea why.

Most of the rest of the night was spent consuming wine and listening to more settler stories. I did have one more stop before calling it a day, and I was determined to leave the camp while I was still able to focus on what I had to do. When I rose from the table and announced my need to leave, Cateria was openly disappointed.

Joshal saw her expression and reminded her of how the duties of men came before the pleasuring of women. That was really embarrassing, and I wanted to take her aside and explain that it was not how I viewed such things, but now was not the time. As I walked toward the camp entrance, Cateria ran up beside me and asked when she would see me again.

I assured her I would be back the next day, perhaps for breakfast. She seemed placated and planted a full kiss on my lips. As soon as we separated, she slapped me once on the butt and reminded me I had duties to take care of there too. Then she was gone.

By the time I walked to Kyle's residence and delivered the news that Joshal's people were staying, the stresses of the day were finally catching up to me. I was exhausted, and as much as I might have wanted to be with Cateria, it wasn't going to be tonight. As I staggered up to my front door, my last thought was, *finally, I'm going to sleep for a week.* As it turns out, that wouldn't be happening.

When I opened the door, Cateria was resting in the day lounger. She was absolutely ravishing in the pale moonlight that streamed through the door behind me. I had to jerk myself back to reality. I walked over and kissed her lightly on the forehead. Her eyes opened, and she pulled me down beside her. It could have very well been the greatest night of my life. By the time we finished making love, the first rays of the morning sun were sneaking through the front windows. We were exhausted. Together, we fell into a deep dreamless sleep, not waking again until well into the early afternoon.

When I did come back to life, I was startled to see Cateria in the kitchenette preparing food. No Protectorates at the door dragging me away for some other calamity. No task I just had to have done. Just an afternoon brunch with the woman I loved. I thought about how easy it would be to get used to this domestic bliss.

We ate our meal, and I figured what a perfect time to ask her about this Pact thing. I had the very distinct impression somehow this unknown obligation was vital to any future between us. Even as I thought about it, my stomach started to knot up the same way it did when Joshal suggested I speak to her.

"Cateria, while I was strolling with your father yesterday, your name came up in conversation. He seemed very supportive of our relationship but suggested that before we went much further you should explain something he referred to as The Pact. So I'm asking!"

"Ryan, courtship with my people is a very serious commitment and is based on the union of a man and a woman that can produce offspring to continue the family bloodlines. Trial and error is not tolerated if the union is to succeed. The Pact is merely an agreement between us and my family that we will not marry—cannot marry—until you have proven yourself by making me pregnant. Once that has been accomplished, and allowing for a period of confirmation, you then may ask Father for my hand in marriage. It's as simple as that," she explained.

"You're just fooling around, right? In order to marry you, I have to get you pregnant during premarital sex? Make you a mother out of wedlock to prove I'm worthy of being your husband? That is absolutely astonishing! I guess when in Rome you do as the Romans," I replied sarcastically.

"Where is Rome? I thought this was Bridgetown! Ryan, this is serious. Please don't make light of the traditions of my people," she scolded.

I stopped myself from saying anything else that might offend her right out of my arms. "I'm so sorry, and you're right; this is important, and we're wasting time sitting here. There is work to be done!" I lifted her into my arms, and we retreated back to the lounge.

By the time we were upright again, the sun was waning over the distant mountain peaks. We were exhausted, but the smiles on our faces would be frozen there for the rest of the night. Cateria suggested we start making our way back to the settlement. Tonight was to be the big feast Joshal had promised me, and to be late would be an insult. *Wow*, I thought to myself, *there are a lot of things I still had to learn about these people and their customs*.

When we finally arrived at the compound, there was a strange, sweet smell permeating through the air. I had never experienced anything like it. The odor made my taste buds tingle. "What is that?" I asked.

"That, my love, is forest hog roasting on the spit. Get ready for the meal of your life," she replied.

As soon as we rounded the shower tent, we could see a mass of people encircling what had to be a fire. Cateria sensed my excitement as I pulled her toward the crowd. I could hear her laughing heartily, but I didn't care. I had to see it. As we made our way through the jumble of bodies to the center of the circle, there it was. It was the biggest creature I had ever seen that wasn't trying to eat me.

Somehow they had managed to truss it to what appeared to be four lengths of tree limb supported at each end by massive wooden tripods. At each end were huge wooden cranks with two men per crank slowly rotating the beast over a blazing fire. Off to the side, Joshal was spraying bottles of wine on the creature as it roasted to perfection. I was dumbfounded by the entire scene, and Cateria just couldn't stop laughing.

"Ryan, for such a smart man, you look like a young boy seeing his first naked woman," she chuckled.

I paid no attention to her. Instead I walked over to Joshal and put my hand on his shoulder. "Sir, when you say we're going to have a feast, you mean it. This is outstanding."

"If you think this is good, wait until you taste it," he replied.

It was a long night, and we ate until we couldn't eat another bite. Every family in the camp was able to get a meal off the animal. When it was over, only the skull and ribs remained intact over the dying flames. Joshal, his sons, and I were silly drunk and singing settler folksongs, which I didn't understand and didn't care to. Cateria never left my side, and we were covered in hog grease and wine from head to foot.

Eventually, Joshal did what he always did when he drank too much. He passed out! His sons did what they always did, which was to carry their father into the tent and get him and themselves down for the night. Cateria and I were exhausted as well, but decided we would shower and I would stay in her tent for the night. We were too drained to do anything but shower together and collapse. As we lay on her blanket, we let the sound of the rain on the tent lull us to sleep. It was a great night!

Early the next morning, I awoke in much better physical condition than I had a right to be in. Too much wine, food, and sex should have left me lethargic and hurting, but for some reason, I was full of enthusiasm and energy. Cateria was still fast asleep, and I decided there was no reason to wake her. For one of the first times in days, there was to be a meeting of the CRB to review the long list of events over the last little while, and I didn't want to miss it.

As I came out of the family tent, Joshal was sitting in his usual position at the head of the large makeshift table, with his remaining children setting out the morning breakfast. We didn't speak for long, but I did mention to him that Cateria and I had spoken and agreed to The Pact. He smiled and commented that based on what he saw yesterday, we were obviously working hard at fulfilling the requirement. I was never so embarrassed! I said my good-byes and quickly left.

Fifteen

The Discovery

Things had never been quieter in Bridgetown. There had not been another bat sighting in well over a year. Cateria and I were working overtime trying to fulfill the obligations of The Pact. More than half the farms were up and running, and we had gathered over three thousand forest hogs and wild hens. The Protectorate was helping in the construction of new residences. The citizens even agreed that as ugly as they were, our safety was assured because Kyle's Spider Drones had our backs.

A bit of a population explosion was underway in our once predictable society. It wasn't only because of the addition of the settlers. Natural childbirth was making a comeback because people felt confident enough to begin new families. The Bridgetown headcount went from 160,000 when we landed to 193,000 in what seemed overnight. The maternity ward at the Medical Center had suddenly become a beehive of activity. It was great to see!

We should have known anything this good and lasting this long wouldn't continue before new drama was introduced. The strange part of what happened was how innocently it started and how complicated it became. The event began with James sending for Kyle, Marcus, and me to join him in the briefing room. It was getting so that every time I heard the term "briefing room," I wanted to run and hide. As it turns out, I probably should have.

When we arrived, James was there with his father, and they wasted little time getting to the meat of the matter. "Guys, we want to play back a communication exchange that took place earlier today between the orbiting Explorer Windsurfer and Command. Rather than trying to explain it all, let's just listen to the recording," suggested James.

"Control, Commander Diamond here! We have an anomaly with our equipment. I wanted to put the life form scanning equipment through its paces, so we settled into a fixed orbit about one hundred miles directly over you folks, and unless you're all dead, we're not picking up any readings. My technicians can't explain it because we've done a diagnostic and everything pings as good. Diamond out!"

"Commander, please have your science officer recalibrate the equipment. Perhaps it's set to fine and you're too far out," replied the Command Officer on duty.

"Done, but there's more! When we drop inside the planet's atmosphere, it works just fine and you folks light up my screens. I have requested for the Pegasus to join me at these coordinates, and we'll think this thing through. Diamond out!"

"Let us know the results as soon as you can. Command out!"

James took a break to bring some clarity to the transmissions. "To put things into perspective before we move to the follow-up transmission, it's not uncommon for systems to occasionally go haywire. With all the technicians we have aboard these Explorers, the issues are usually dealt with quickly, and life goes on—but enough, let's hear some more."

"Command, Diamond here again. We're back in fixed orbit now, joined by the Pegasus and Commander Lewis. They're having the same problem. They're not receiving any life form readings from the planet's surface. We're shifting across to Draegon to try again since we know it's a populated area. Maybe it's just an atmospheric anomaly over Bridgetown."

A few minutes passed before the speakers came to life again. "Okay, we're here! Same problem! I can't tell you how long this has been going on because I think this is the first time we've tested the system on a known population. Please advise. Diamond out!"

"Commander, this will take some time. We'll be back to you. Command out!

"What do you guys make of that?" asked James.

"I think it speaks to an earlier concern I had that when we surveyed the planet before colonization, there were no human life form readings recorded. Yet, as we now know, that was wrong by a country mile," I responded. "Kyle, any impressions?"

"If what you're saying is true, Ryan, our entire survey was flawed, and we're here because of a technical malfunction. That might explain a lot of things!" he responded.

"There must be something in the upper atmosphere absorbing the scan signals—not deflecting them, or we would have noticed. I'm not aware of any natural phenomenon that would cause the effect. James, we need to get the physicists involved, but before we do, can we get some atmospheric samples?" said Kyle.

"I would suggest a sample be taken every one thousand feet from the ground all the way through the outer atmosphere. I think it might be prudent as well to examine the samples taken when we first arrived to see if anything has changed or if there was a problem then that we just didn't detect," Marcus recommended.

"Good idea. I'll have thirty drones collect the samples and deliver them to the Science Center in three hours. Once we have those, Marcus, how long do you think it will take to conduct the tests?" asked James.

"Well, we're looking at perhaps five hundred samples. If we can get Mrs. Chandler's support on this, I'm thinking a day, perhaps two. If I may, I'd like to offer an opinion based on our experiences here so far. This latest discovery is not some naturally occurring event. It's not a coincidence that we can't detect life on the surface from outside the atmosphere.

"Someone or something deliberately wanted to hide the fact that the planet had a human population, but let's not go running around shouting 'the sky is falling' before the tests come back. I'd rather look silly than be right on this one, because being right would just create more complications," Marcus responded.

Kyle pledged he would get Sabrina's support—right after he warned Marcus never to call her Mrs. Chandler to her face. Only the admiral could get away with that. James committed to getting the samples, and I committed to reviewing the original air sample tests. Two days after the samples were taken to the lab, Marcus requested a meeting with us to discuss their findings, which he hinted were interesting but not comforting. Sabrina insisted she attend to make sure a man, even if he was a genius, didn't distort the hard work of her people. The truth was she was intrigued and wanted to know what this big secret was all about.

We all met back in the briefing room the next morning. Of course Sabrina and Kyle were late, but we were used to that, and it gave everyone else a chance to have coffee and buns before things got serious. Once they arrived, Marcus wasted little time getting to the point.

"I spent the last two days working with Mrs. Chand—I mean Sabrina's team on the tests. If James would put them up on the viewing screen, I think we can get through this quickly and get down to deciding what you gentlemen would like to do next," said Marcus.

James had the reports loaded to the monitor. Sabrina sat there smiling, and I knew she was gloating over the impact she had on men.

Marcus continued, "The tests found a small concentration of an organic particle in the lower atmosphere. However, as we moved higher in altitude, the concentrations increased at an exponential rate, with the maximum readings at 65,000 feet. These particles are interwoven with the normal elements you would expect to find in our atmosphere. Above that altitude, the presence of the element decreases and finally dissipates to zero at eighty miles.

"For the next examination, we separated a sample of the particle from the base elements and ran two separate tests. The first test was to determine what the particles were charged with. That was unsuccessful. Whatever radiation is in play here doesn't exist on the known tables. The second test was a practical exercise to determine if this unknown particle was the cause of the scan failures. It confirmed what we suspected. The particle absorbed the life sign scans at a ratio of ten thousand to one. Simply stated, nothing gets past this stuff.

"Here's where it gets interesting and disturbing. Because the particles eventually dissipate into space or fall to the ground, you would think their intensity would decrease even at 65,000 feet. They do not! The high levels found at 65,000 remained consistent throughout. Although the scientists couldn't offer a reason for this, I think I can.

"As I suspected, the presence of the particle is not naturally reoccurring. It's being introduced to the upper atmosphere—I'm assuming from a surface-based source. I suspect the idea is to seed the atmosphere in concentration at 65,000 feet using the upper jet stream to move the particles. As time passes, some are brought down by rain, and what remains is lost in the thin air, finally dissipating into near space, but the density is being constantly maintained," Marcus summed up.

"Wow! Another conspiracy theory! Whoever is doing all this must really want us to go away. Flying assassins from other worlds, people pretending to be us, and now scan blockers to fool us. I'm not sure how much more of this I can take," responded James.

"James, lighten up! He didn't invent these situations. He's trying to help us. If you have a better idea, spit it out!" sniped Kyle

"The problem is I don't, and I apologize, Marcus. My frustration was not intended for you. I just find it difficult to deal with things I can't explain or control. I feel like a pawn in a sick chess game. Assuming your right—and so far I've never known you to be wrong—what's our next move?"

"That's okay, James. I have that effect on a lot of people, which is why you guys are my only friends. Here's what I think you might consider. I've fabricated a small sampling device to help find the source of the transmissions. I only have one, but if Kyle can find a way to install it on a drone and slowly fly it around the planet at 65,000 feet, I think we'll find the source. What we do then I leave to you guys because I'll be way out of my comfort zone," Marcus replied.

"Marcus, we're your friends, and we're going to do what you suggest because it makes sense. Does everyone agree?" Kyle asked.

Everyone in Bridgetown knew Marcus was a genius. He barely looked older than fifteen. He was actually twenty-eight and had completed his university studies at sixteen. He was the only man I ever met that Sabrina actually had to admit was smarter than she was. I asked her if she saw that as a problem, given he was "one of those pesky men."

"No, I don't think so. He's really still a boy and hasn't picked up all your bad traits yet, but he will if he keeps hanging around with you, and then he'll be just another man," she replied.

Beyond his obvious intelligence was his almost sickening humility. He never set himself apart because of his genius. He often said, "Every day, people teach me more than I knew yesterday." I doubted that very much!

For as far back as Marcus could remember, his fellow engineers seemed to avoid him. He knew his junior years made him an oddity among his more senior peers, but he had tried everything to fit in. They never questioned his right to be there or his contributions in his field, but that was as far as it ever went.

There were times over the years when he felt he had been shunned and pushed away because of his intelligence. To make others feel comfortable around him, he was happy to blend into the background and let his colleagues take credit for his work at times. It was better that way for them and him.

Marcus couldn't remember ever having a friend, male or female. All through his educational years, he had been the baby of the class. The older boys would bully him, and the girls would giggle every time he walked into school. He hated school, and in the end, he learned to hate everyone associated with it. His thirst for knowledge was his salvation, and books were his only real relationships. It was a sad state of affairs. With us, his age meant nothing. His intelligence, on the other hand, would prove absolutely vital to our future.

Later, Kyle mentioned to me that he was impressed with the device Marcus threw together for this single use. He explained that when installed, the device would collect an air sample every thirty seconds, assess the concentration of the particle, and save the data for ongoing comparison to the next samples. It would then discard the last sample back into the atmosphere.

Through this collecting, comparing, and recording, a determination of the source within miles would be identified. It gets better! The exact coordinates for the source would be automatically uploaded into the navigational system of the drone, and it would return to the area and drop down to take pictures of the terrain, live streaming back to us.

"That sounds like a long, drawn out process. Not that there's any particular hurry because it is what it is, but how long do you think this will take?" I asked.

"I don't know, but you're right—what's the hurry. Whatever damage these particles have done to the credibility of our scanners has long since screwed us," he responded resolutely.

The next day, James sent the Protectors to find and deliver us to the briefing room. James didn't have the pictures yet, but he had tracked that the drone had dropped below twenty thousand feet, which could only mean video was likely and soon. Once again, Sabrina wanted to be there front and center. Fifteen minutes later, we were all having coffee and buns in front of the monitor.

As always, the screen flickered slightly before the image cleared and we were looking at a downward view of a landscape eighteen thousand feet below. Marcus asked where the drone was, which no one knew, causing James to touch his communicator and speak.

"Control, can you give us an idea in miles where the drone is transmitting from?"

"Sir, Drone #7412 is exactly 16,762.3 miles south, southwest of our position. Out," responded an unknown voice.

"That's essentially on the other side of the planet, which kind of makes sense," remarked Marcus.

"How so?" I asked.

"If the particle accelerator was closer, we would have seen evidence before now. We've covered some extensive territory over the last few years," Marcus responded.

At first, there was nothing unusual about the initial images, just more forest and more mountains. As the drone descended, the first interesting anomaly was a rather large area devoid of any trees or ground cover. From the images, it seemed almost desert-like, which was odd given the surroundings. But there was something else, and as the drone continued its downward drift, the image became clearer.

Suddenly Sabrina blurted out, "Look, it's a miniature mountain all lit up!"

We could all see it! Although it wasn't a mountain at all, it had the distinct shape of one—except the object was no more than a thousand feet tall and perhaps a thousand feet wide at its base. I don't know who saw the connection first, but Kyle was first to shout it out. "It's Joshal's Mountain of Light! He should be here to see this. I bet he'd fall out of his chair."

The mountain-shaped object had a number of large appendages protruding from the side, which gave it a rather ominous appearance, but the most prominent feature was the bright orange beam firing out of its apex into the clouds, with such intensity it was difficult to look at directly.

"Okay, now what! Marcus, if you say I told you so, you'll never make it out of this room alive. What is that thing? I vote we just blow the fucking rock up and put this all down as another surprise this planet has introduced us to," James said.

"Not yet!" responded Kyle. "I think we need to send in a study group and see what we're dealing with. Until we understand its purpose, blowing it up might begin a series of events, which may be far worse than just screwing up our scanning devices. How soon can we get a team on the ground?"

As eager as we were to get there, it was bit more complicated than merely saying so. James was insistent we take a military escort along. Although we couldn't see anything or anyone near the structure, that didn't mean there wasn't a threat. James decided that we would use three Defenders, fifty Protectors, and ten Spider Drones. It sounded like a lot of hardware, but better too much than not enough.

Sabrina suggested we take a couple of physicists along to help with the examination. It made sense, and it allowed her to keep her fingers in the pie.

"We'll leave at first light. It will take us ninety minutes from launch to landing. I want to take some provisions in case our stay stretches out a bit," advised James.

I could feel myself swallowing my tongue. "James, did you say ninety minutes to travel seventeen thousand miles?" I asked nervously.

"No, my squeamish friend, I didn't. It will only take an hour to cover the distance; the rest is for launching and landing. That's a conservative estimate, of course."

"Ryan, you should be pleased. The faster we get there, the less time we're in the air," said Kyle, smiling.

"You know, Ryan, while inside our atmosphere, we've governed the Defenders down to a top speed of twenty thousand miles an hour; otherwise the friction would rip them apart. In space, they'll do 2.4 million miles per hour in a straight line. Now that's speed!" advised Marcus.

"Marcus, go bury your face in a book or something. Seventeen thousand miles in one hour is craziness," I replied.

Sixteen

The Mountain of Light

As we stood watching the Spider Drones half-walk, half-hop up the gangway of one of the Defenders, it was almost cartoonish in its animation, and I found myself smiling. I don't know if she did it as a joke or punishment, but the physicists Sabrina sent to assist in the assessment went by the names of Doctor Simpson and Doctor Simon. They seemed bright enough but kept to themselves, speaking only when spoken to. I could tell this was going to be a long day.

Once aboard, we went immediately to the small briefing area behind the Bridge where, as usual, coffee and buns awaited us. James had some of the video images converted to stills; they were hung around the room to reacquaint us with what to expect. Kyle took a few minutes to bring our newest additions up to speed on the purpose of the exercise, and before long, they were adding their opinions right along with ours.

In just over an hour, I heard the familiar hum as the lower thrusters were activated, which meant we were about to descend. James had all the cameras initiated, and in an instant, twelve separate videos were running on the overhead monitor. It seemed odd that the object was positioned in the largest clearing we had ever seen on the planet, with no other structure anywhere near it.

"Marcus, assuming this device was placed here for the purpose we've proposed, why do you think they left it so exposed?" Kyle asked.

"I'm not sure, unless it has defensive systems we haven't come across yet. I agree, it is an odd placement," replied Marcus.

"Well, I don't like it! It's too exposed, which suggests to me it's a trap of some kind. No one goes near this thing until the Spider Drones do a recon of the area. I've picked a landing spot about five hundred yards north of the site. We'll make that our staging point, and based on the recon, we'll decide how best to approach this thing," James instructed.

Even as I was looking at it, I remembered the legend Joshal shared with us about the ancient text being kept within the Mountain of Light. If that was truly the case, this could be a monumental discovery. Doctor Simon pointed out that the object didn't appear to have any entry ports to explore the interior, and perhaps it was what it appeared to be—just a machine.

James was first off the ship and stood watching as the other two crafts hovered into position in a triangular shaped staging layout. Kyle, Marcus, and I, along with our guests, were told to stand aside while the soldiers went about the task of setting up our camp. With typical Protectorate efficiency, the site began to take shape.

"Kyle, we need to send a couple of the Drones to the object to recon and send back videos of the entire surface. If there are weapons, we need to know where they are and how to neutralize them. A close-up of those strange antenna-like protrusions wouldn't hurt either. How long will it take to program them for the task?" asked James.

"Give us twenty minutes, and we're ready," Kyle replied.

Marcus went with Kyle aboard one of the Defenders to do the programming while I found a large crate to sit on. What seemed strange to me about this entire scene was that there were no animals anywhere to be seen or heard in the area. That was a bit unsettling, but I thought perhaps our arrival might have spooked them away. Add to that, the area was void of any plant life whatsoever. I wondered if perhaps the object emitted some sort of energy field that killed the local plants and animals.

When I asked the two physicists about it, they seemed disinterested, except that Doctor Simpson suggested, somewhat off the cuff, that it looked like some time ago a significant seismic event might have occurred. Although his delivery was patronizing, what he said had a ring of fact to it, and I decided to bring it up to the guys once we were all back in one spot.

Twenty minutes later, three Spider Drones came trotting down the gangway and stood motionless at the bottom. They were followed in close order by Kyle and Marcus. Kyle took out his handheld keyboard module, and immediately the three Drones started hopping toward the object. Marcus asked Kyle how fast the units could move at full speed. He replied they were designed for speeds in excess of eighty miles per hour over uneven terrain. He added that, if required, they were quite capable of jumping on a horizontal plane. Marcus seemed impressed by this. I know I was!

As the Drones drew near the object, we began to understand why James wanted them to lead the way. Three of the hundred or so appendages mounted on the side of the object swiveled in the direction of the advancing Drones. A moment later, three intense blue beams were discharged from what we thought were antennae directly at the Drones. At first, the beams just seemed to stop the Drones in their tracks. A second later, another volley from the same weapons hit the Drones again, which resulted in three explosions. The flash and concussion of the detonations knocked us to the ground. What was left of our Drones was scattered across the clearing.

I don't think it was so much that the structure had a defensive solution that left us lying on the ground with our mouths wide open. I think it was the absolute ease with which it dispensed with our perfect robotic weapons.

"Well, Kyle, I guess we know why they didn't feel they had to hide it. Sorry about your babies, but better them than us," stated James as he got to his feet and wiped the dust off his uniform. "It would appear that the object has a rather sophisticated proximity alert system that triggers its weapons."

"I don't care what it has. It killed my babies!" responded Kyle.

Immediately, his fingers began to dance frantically across the tiny keyboard, and suddenly six more Drones emerged through the hatch of the Defender, down the ramp, and across the clearing between us and the mountain structure. Unlike the first approach, Kyle had the Spider Drones fan out, forming a rather large circle around the structure about a thousand feet out. Then with a sinister expression on his face, he shouted "Take this, you bastard!" hitting the enter button as he finished.

Instantly, the Drones unleashed the full power of their laser arsenals, destroying every exposed armature and lighting up the face of structure. When he was satisfied his eye-for-an-eye response had been delivered, he just smiled and blew softly on the end of the keyboard module as if blowing the residual smoke away from the end of a gun.

"Gentlemen, we have met the enemy, and victory is ours. Let's get started!" Kyle announced.

"That was too easy, which makes me believe the builders armed the object to protect it from a far less sophisticated enemy than us," commented Marcus.

"How long do you think this thing has been here shooting these particles into the upper atmosphere?" Kyle asked.

"Looking at its surface, I'd guess only a couple of years, but if we follow Joshal's story, it would have to be hundreds of years old at least. Remember, he said that the Mountain of Light was referenced in their ancient text," I replied.

"Maybe it's all just a coincidence. Maybe Joshal's story and this structure have nothing to do with each other" suggested James.

Just as we began to collect ourselves for the trek out to the object, it started to rain. As soon as the rain started, the beam, which had been cycling every six minutes between on and off, shut down completely.

"Was it something I said?" Kyle joked.

Before we could get ourselves moving, the two physicists were already out to the structure, examining its outer surface.

"Who gave them permission to just go off on their own? That thing could have other defensive weapons, and their asses could be lying right beside our Drones in a heartbeat," spouted James.

"Good, at least we'd know where the other weapons were placed," responded Kyle lightheartedly.

We stood for a minute or two to see if James might be right, but nothing happened. Once he was satisfied it was safe to leave, the rest of us followed. The two physicists seemed perplexed because they had no idea what the wall covering was. I asked them if they thought it might be a type of coated metal. They replied it wasn't, more likely an engineered composite.

When I told them the structure was likely over a thousand years old, they looked at me and then at each other before Doctor Simpson replied, "No, it's not!" I wanted to smack the arrogant bastard, but that would have put Sabrina in my face. What they did say earlier, which seemed to hold true now that we were up close, was that the object had no access points, which left us wondering about what to do next.

"There has to be a way in. Even if it's only a giant machine, it has moving parts that needed to be installed and serviced. There must be an access port of some kind," commented James.

I shared with the group what the physicist had suggested about a potential seismic event. My first thought was that perhaps the entrance had been covered over with dirt. Marcus agreed it was a strong possibility and asked James to send up one of the Defenders to scan the object from above. James issued the order, and five minutes later, a Defender was hovering near our position taking readings.

The scans did show an entrance to the object, but not where we expected. A tunnel was identified a hundred feet below the surface and extending away from the object horizontally five hundred feet to the west. To get to the passageway, we would have to go through a hatch further into the clearing. Immediately, we all started moving toward the coordinates with three Spider Drones leading the way.

One might have thought that an entrance not accessed for hundreds if not thousands of years and exposed to all manner of weather might require a bit of effort to find. Not the case! The hatch was fully exposed exactly where the scans indicated it would be. The cover was circular in shape and no less than twenty feet in diameter. It appeared to be made of a kind of bronzed alloy that gleamed when lights were directed on it.

"This isn't possible. If this place is as old as we thought, this hatch sure as hell wouldn't look like this. Shit, this could have been put here yesterday. Either that, or it's not old at all, and we're about to trespass where we don't belong," stated James, looking less than happy about the entire situation.

"James, old or new, the mountain is spewing crap into the air that is affecting our equipment—let alone what it might be doing to us breathing it in. I'd ring the doorbell, but there isn't one, so the way I see it, we're here—let's go for it." Kyle grinned.

In the center of the hatch, there was a small recess. At first glance, we assumed that the hatch release must be there, but under closer examination, we were surprised to find what appeared to be a palm scanner.

"Well, I guess that's the end of this adventure. Obviously, access involves security protocols and authorities we don't have. We rang the doorbell, no one's answering, so let's go home," James commented.

"Maybe, but let's try our luck first," responded Kyle.

With that, Kyle placed his hand on the palm reader and held it there. Almost instantly, the scanner began to glow a pale blue before Kyle blurted out, "Shit! The fucking thing bit me!"

A few seconds later, there was a soft humming below his feet, and Kyle immediately jumped off the hatch. Ever so slowly, the cover began to rise straight up into the air until it exposed what appeared to be nothing more than yet another cover. Even more confusing was that the hatch, now hovering above us, had nothing supporting it—no cables or pistons or compressed air stream, nothing.

"What in hell's holding that thing up? It must weigh at least ten thousand pounds. Marcus, Kyle, you guys are the engineers—what do you make of this?" asked James.

"I don't know about Marcus, but I have absolutely no idea," replied Kyle.

"I don't know either, but there are bigger questions than that in play here. We have a structure in the middle of the wilderness equipped with a weapon that destroyed our Drones with little or no effort. We have a secured hatch made of some kind of material that apparently doesn't rust or tarnish. Imbedded in this hatch is a security palm scanner, which would suggest selective access, yet it accepted Kyle's palm imprint as authority to release the hatch," stated Marcus with a perplexed expression on his face.

"Don't forget the fact that it bit me. What was all that about?" asked Kyle.

"Personally, I think it took a blood sample to confirm the palm print matched some kind of security profile for persons permitted access to the complex," replied Marcus.

"That's impossible. Why would the security system let Kyle access the complex?" I asked, now feeling really uncomfortable.

"Everything about this place is impossible. In my simple world, if you can't explain it or understand it, walk away," replied James.

"Well, if this complex has been here for centuries and has technologies that are way beyond anything we could reproduce, then all of this seems to confirm Joshal's statement that The Fathers possessed magic far beyond ours. I'm not sure who these creatures were, but they knew who we are, hence allowing us this access. That's unsettling and intimidating," responded Marcus.

"Now what? There's another cover, and I don't see any scanner," declared Kyle.

"Kyle, if you step onto the cover, I think it will answer that question for us," suggested Marcus.

Kyle tilted his head to the side, looking at Marcus like he was some kind of weird curiosity. Then he shrugged and stepped onto the platform. Almost instantly, a small pedestal began to rise up in the center of the pad, stopping about three feet above the floor. As it came to a halt, a cover opened on the top, revealing a small screen and keyboard.

None of us moved. I'm not sure any of us could. Kyle was staring directly at Marcus, who in turn was looking around at the rest of us to see if anyone had any idea what was going on. The two physicists were less impressed and immediately started examining the floor and pedestal, looking for something, which none of us paid much attention to.

"Well, Mister Scott, since it would seem you have all the answers," get your ass over here and explain what we do next," spouted Kyle.

Marcus immediately joined Kyle at the pedestal, and they began talking a million miles an hour about the device. James and I were far less eager to step on the platform because, quite frankly, we didn't understand it; consequently, we didn't trust it. A few seconds later, Kyle turned toward us and advised that the platform was actually a lift device triggered by a retinal scan, which apparently was another security protocol that he passed. He admitted that all of this had him baffled.

"Get everyone on the platform; we're going for a ride. There's a menu of levels, so we're going to start at the top," directed Kyle.

Once James led the way, the rest of us followed. Nothing happened for about two minutes, and James commented, "This is embarrassing! I hope no aliens are watching because we're all clustered together on this thing with a giant metal umbrella over our heads. For all we know, this could be a fancy mousetrap. Any second, the roof is just going to drop and crush us all. If that happens, we're screwed." Everyone chuckled.

Suddenly, the platform began to descend, but there was little in the way of jerking or noise of any kind. We were virtually sinking into a tube-like passage, but ever so slowly. Once we had lowered perhaps twenty feet, the cover that had been suspended above us began to lower back into position. I mentioned that we were about to be in total darkness, descending into a hole on a device we had no control over.

"Don't any of you guys see a problem with this?" I asked in a somewhat panicked voice.

Immediately after the cover closed, the walls of the shaft illuminated in a bright white light. Although it defied explanation, Marcus commented that there was no perceptible source for the light. He suspected the shaft itself must have light-emitting rods embedded within a translucent acrylic of some kind. I wished that he and Kyle would start speaking in a language the average person could actually make sense of, but I knew that wasn't likely.

The ride took almost five minutes before we slowly came to a stop without any kind of jolt. As soon as it stopped, a tunnel appeared to our right, fully illuminated using the same technology as the shaft.

"Men, I think we're here," said Kyle as he began moving down the tunnel.

The passageway was at least twenty feet wide and fifteen feet high. The walls were as smooth as glass, and when we spoke, there was no echo. None! Now I was really freaked, and I wasn't alone. It took us another five minutes of walking before we reached what at first glance seemed to be a dead end, until James noticed a small palm scanner mounted on the tunnel wall to one side. By this time, Kyle was feeling empowered and immediately walked over and positioned his hand. Almost instantly, the wall in front of us seemed to evaporate, exposing an enormous room. It was the most unnatural thing I had ever seen.

"Marcus, this is absolutely amazing. Whoever built this place was centuries ahead of where we are from a technology perspective," Kyle proclaimed.

As we stepped forward, we entered an enormous chamber, which apart from a massive central column, had no visible supports. The chamber itself was cylindrical in shape, tapering as the perimeter walls extended hundreds of feet above us. We could only see upward a few yards because the illuminated walls went dark above a certain level.

It was apparent we were inside the Mountain of Light. The central column appeared to come through the floor and continue up as far as the naked eye could see. We assumed the pillar covered the dispersion tube from which the particles were being directed into the atmosphere. Under closer examination, the tube itself was over forty feet across.

The chamber was nearly a thousand feet in diameter, and like the walls, the floors were fully illuminated. Around the perimeter every thirty or forty feet were work stations. This intrigued me, so I headed directly toward the closet one. The work station had a number of screens, but there were no visible keypads or CPUs. Each screen contained moving images of various components within the facility and their current operating status. I knew Kyle and Marcus would find this discovery more than just mildly exciting.

I left my friends at the station to examine the programs while I continued my search for the only prize I was interested in, which was the ancient texts Joshal suggested were stored here. I stopped at each station and examined the materials for some hint I was getting close—but nothing. Things weren't looking good until on the far side of the chamber I came across a work station unlike any of the others.

The first striking difference was the three large storage cabinets with row after row of indexed discs and a device that appeared to be a disc reader of some kind, although I was guessing, having never seen anything like it. One of these discs was conspicuously left on the work station beside the reader. When I examined its label, it read simply, "Insert First." I remember thinking to myself that it was either a strange title for a disc or an instruction.

Now I was intrigued! Taking a chance, I tried plugging it into what I hoped was a reader, and after a bit of fumbling, it slid into place. I wasn't prepared for what happened next. There was a soft whirling sound as the reader began to track. Almost instantaneously, a hatch in the floor about ten feet away slid open, and like magic, a clear acrylic dome rose up. The dome was perhaps seven or eight feet tall and four feet in diameter. I immediately called out to the guys in kind of an excited shrill, and they came running. I think they thought I had been injured.

"What do you boys make of this?" I said.

"Don't know, but I bet if we push that green button beside the reader, we'll have a better idea," smirked James.

Almost instantly, a holographic image materialized within the dome. The image was of a woman looking like she was in her late forties and wearing a white robe that reached down to her feet. She was definitely human and anything but ordinary in her stance and presentation. When she spoke, it was husky but still feminine.

I can't remember ever seeing Kyle as excited as he was at that moment. Even the normally calm, reserved Marcus was bug-eyed. When the woman began to speak, every set of eyes was frozen on her image.

"To those that may be viewing my image and hearing my words, you are the direct descendants of the Zorn Collective, and the information contained on these discs will help you understand your heritage. Your DNA profiles have allowed you to pass through the securities of this facility, which means you are ready to receive these enlightenments.

"Contained in the indexed discs to follow are drawings, formulas, and instructions to move you to the next level of your development. Use this knowledge for the good of the Zorn Collective. Our mission on this world was twofold. Firstly, it was to collect the precious Siltron Powder from this planet's core reserves, synthesize it, and return to Gaelon in time to save our people. The second objective was to establish another Zorn colony, as we've done across the vastness of this universe on many worlds, in the hopes of giving young Zorn citizens new direction and hope.

"Your ancestors were among those early settlers. They were left in this place with simple tools and knowledge in the hopes that over the millenniums to follow, they would multiply and prosper. You will have no knowledge of these things because time erases the clarity of such events. These discs will enlighten you about the goodness of the Zorn Collective.

"We have left the Siltron synthesizer and accelerator in operation as part of this facility. When this site is depleted, you have only to relocate the unit to another site and begin again. This planet has sufficient deposits to provide for your needs for ten million Zorn time phases. Please access the disc titled The Zorn Collective—Disc One."

With that, the hologram slowly faded, and the dome retracted back into the floor. The disc automatically ejected, and we were left staring at where the woman's image had been. None of us could have imagined we would ever find something as important as these discs.

"That was incredible!" announced Kyle. "We need to collect these discs and the reader thing and get them back to Bridgetown. I bet we can learn more from them in a few weeks than we would in a thousand years scratching our way around this planet. James, I don't think we're going to get much more out of this first visit. We'll investigate more of the complex after we acquaint ourselves with the material on the discs. I suggest we take what we've found and head back to our encampment."

"I agree!" James responded as he hit his communicator. "Science Officer, we'll be up top in twenty minutes. Please empty as many of those provision crates as you can. There are materials down here we need to collect and transport. Donner out!"

The transport of the disc inventory took considerable time, given the number of them and the distance underground they had to be carried. It was well into the evening by the time all our treasure had been collected and loaded. Exhausted, we decided to make use of the already established camp for the night. The rain had stopped, and the beam was once again operating.

The strangest thing happened after we had been sitting around the fire pit talking for about three hours. It rained again! Normally rain wouldn't be a big deal since it rained frequently on this planet, but once again, when the first sprinkle of rain fell to the ground, the Mountain of Light shut down. Here was yet another confusing anomaly to add to a growing list of confusing anomalies.

Call it a second wind or just too much excitement, but by the time the rain had ended, we were full of energy. Sleep was out of the question, and James suggested that we just break down the camp and spend the night at home in our beds. Everyone seemed ready to do that, and twenty minutes later, we were lifting off.

Seventeen

Enlightenment

The Zorn discs were moved to the Science Center where Marcus and I volunteered to systematically go through each and every one. This was no small task since there were over two thousand of them. In most cases, they were quite short, and each disc focused on a single topic. If we were going to have a story to tell, we would have to record highlights from each disc and assemble our notes chronologically. We immediately began searching through the crates for the first disc, as directed by the holographic woman.

I didn't know how Marcus was feeling about the project. He was really hard to read. I hadn't seen him really excited, sad, or happy. He was just Marcus. For my part, I considered myself the luckiest man in Bridgetown. We estimated it would take about eight months to review all the discs and publish a detailed overview. After all, what was the rush! Kyle did make us commit to providing weekly updates on our progress, and if we found something of significance, to call a CRB session.

When I mentioned to Joshal and Cateria that we had found his legendary Mountain of Light and the potential value of information contained within it, his reaction was one more of concern for us than the affirmation of his beliefs.

"Ryan, I fear my friends are trespassing into things they cannot possibly understand. The secret ponderings of our gods should remain secret. There may be wisdoms contained within texts that will damn you to hell," he warned.

Cateria was equally as concerned about the find because, like her father, she was raised to respect the legend of their gods. I did understand, given the Zorn technology, how they would have been considered gods to any society, including Earthlings a couple thousand years ago. Truth sometimes had a cruel way of destroying romantic myths to the detriment of innocence. I promised myself that whatever the results of our investigations, I would not volunteer them to Joshal's family.

The conversation did get me thinking about who we were and where we came from. I thought I'd share my thoughts with Marcus when we met at the Center the following morning.

"Marcus, we know from the first disc that the Zorn spread their human seed across many worlds. Do you think we may be descendants of these travelers? Do you think that may be why Kyle was able to access the complex—because of his Zorn DNA?" I asked. He just shrugged and smiled. I didn't ask again.

Our first real revelation came three weeks into the disc reviews. So significant was the find in our minds that we decided we had better share it with our group sooner than later. When I requested the meeting with Kyle, I made it a point to avoid giving away the plot as much as he tried to coax it out of me. My only tease was that "what we thought we knew, we really didn't know."

At noon the same day, we gathered in the briefing room. All the usual players were there, including Sabrina because she was party to the original assessment. James was his usual laid back self, suggesting we have lunch before getting started. Not this time!

"James, lunch will taste the same in an hour as it does now. This news is too hot to wait!" I insisted.

"Fair enough. Why don't you and your nerdy friend get on with it then," he responded jokingly.

"Marcus, you're the technical wizard. Lead us through this," I directed.

"Okay, we were wondering why our orbiting scans were not detecting life forms. We did a big study and found out that there were charged organic particles mixed in with the usual elements in the upper atmosphere that were absorbing our scans, resulting in negative readings. Based on the discovery, we assumed the particles were deliberately put there to hide the fact that there was a human presence on the planet. We than went about tracking down the source of the particles, which as we now know was Joshal's Mountain of Light."

"Interesting," butted in Kyle, "but if we're missing lunch to rehash history, I vote we eat first and reminisce later."

"Are you going to let him continue or not?" I snapped. "Marcus, go on please!"

Kyle glanced over and thumbed his nose at me playfully.

"Anyway, the entire premise of our search was to find the generator and put an end to it. Are you guys ready for the punch line? The particles are not being introduced into the atmosphere to block anything. That's a nonrelated side effect. The primary purpose of the particle is as a health-giving medicinal substance, put up there to be dispersed by raindrops onto the human population of the planet. Has that got your attention?" asked Marcus.

"You're telling us these Zorn people somehow found a drug buried deep within the planet? You've got to be kidding me! I take back my earlier statements about how smart you are," responded a skeptical Sabrina.

"We're telling you what the Zorn told us on the discs. Have you ever noticed how full of energy you feel after it rains? Just the other night, we were dragging our asses at the end of the day. In fact, we decided to stay with the object for the night. Then it rained! As soon as the rain ended, we were inexplicably full of energy and decided to come home," I said.

"Remember what the woman said on the first disc we listened to? They were here to collect the Siltron Powder and synthesize it to take back home to save their people. We didn't see the connection, but now the discs have gone into more detail. It was right in front of us all the time. We can confirm this with some simple tests of the powder on humans," replied Marcus

"So now what? If we shut it down, we all get sick and die?" said James.

"Nothing that dramatic. I don't think it cures diseases or anything so radical. I think it stimulates something in the human body and mind. Perhaps in so doing, it extends our life cycles or improves our quality of life in some way. Without it, we just carry on, but I'd bet right now if it was gone, we'd notice. I'll go even further out on a limb and suggest it may even be a contributor to the recent population explosion we're experiencing. People have more energy and zest for life than they would otherwise," I commented.

"If what you've discovered is real, this is a big one. Sabrina, how long will it take to test what the Zorn people think this powder does?" Kyle asked.

"I don't know, but we'll start setting up a test group and expose them to the powder in a more concentrated dose. I think this is just another legend, but if what you say is true, Kyle's right, this would be huge," she replied.

"Good. Can we eat now?" joked James.

When the meeting ended, I wasn't sure how I felt about their reaction. Maybe when the tests were done, they might come around and understand the importance of this discovery. For now, Marcus and I would have to be content with solving a mystery.

Six days later, a Protector arrived at the Science Center to fetch Marcus and me and deliver us across the courtyard to Sabrina's office. When we arrived, Kyle, James, and the admiral were already there. I glanced over at Sabrina, and she had a smile from ear to ear. I tried to decide if it was a satirical smile because our story was a fairytale or a happy smile because everything we said was true. Suddenly, her expression turned deadly serious.

"Gentlemen, just over five days ago, we heard an unbelievable story about some magic powder sucked out of the ground, thrown into the air to rain down on people and make them feel good. It seemed farfetched, but to humor you, we established a test group and exposed them to this Siltron stuff. I called you all here today to give you the results. Everything Marcus and Ryan shared with us from the Zorn discs is . . . absolutely correct.

"This could be the greatest medical and scientific discovery in a thousand years. It's even beyond what they thought. Administered in concentrated form, it stimulates damaged tissue and restores cognizance for short periods in the elderly suffering from dementia. The stuff stimulates brain activity and speeds post-operative recovery. The best part of all is we have absolutely no idea how it works. What we do know is that it doesn't last long. I have my labs working around the clock now on finding a way to synthesize it.

"We do have a concern with it though. We don't know if there are any long-term side effects. By the way, Marcus, I take back what I said last week. You are far and away the smartest man I know, and, Ryan, you're a nice guy too." She chuckled.

"Finally, some redemption," Marcus answered.

This was never going to end now that Sabrina had gotten into the mix. Again two days later, she requested an emergency briefing. My first fear was she had found something in the powder that made you grow extra feet or something. When we met in the briefing room, she got immediately to the point.

"Our beaker boys have been unable to replicate the attributes of the powder in the labs, which means you guys have to do something," she demanded.

James looked bewildered. "Do something about what? What are you talking about?"

"We can't have what may be a limited supply of this powder being wasted. My scientists have estimated that 96 percent of this precious material being introduced into the atmosphere is lost either because it rains all over the planet where there are no humans or it's being spun off into space. Ninety-six percent is ridiculous!

"We need to put a tap on this machine. We need control over how the powder is being dispersed. Rather than having its delivery limited to rain falls, it should be part of a controlled health regime administered properly to our citizens," she responded.

"I thought you were concerned about its long-term side effects," I said.

"Side effects we can deal with; losing the source forever is another matter," she replied.

"The woman on the disc assured us there were plenty of deposits on this planet," advised Marcus.

"What does she know? She's likely been dead for a thousand years. We're here now, and this stuff is ours to manage. When can we get control over the source?" she asked.

"It's not as simple as that. We don't even know how the machine works. It's technology millenniums beyond anything we can duplicate. I'm not even sure it has an on/off switch. Sabrina, we agree it needs to be controlled, but this will take some time. You need to be patient," James answered.

"This is me being patient," she snapped. "How long?"

"Ryan, Marcus, do you think any of those discs describe the workings of that machine and how it extracts the powder?" asked Kyle.

"I'm sure they do because essentially the control of it is being passed down to us. There must be operating instructions somewhere. We'll just have to jump around through the discs until we find them. I don't know how long that will take. Could be an hour; could be a month," I replied.

"Sabrina, we have to do this right because if we screw it up, we could lose what we have—or worse, we start a chain of events that results in something much more devastating," cautioned Kyle.

"I got it, but please hurry. Now that we've found it, I don't want to lose it, Kyle," she replied sheepishly.

That was it. Marcus and I were dispatched back to the Science Center to track down the discs, and Kyle was preparing to break the news of our discovery to the CRB and then the people. Sabrina was never more upbeat about anything. I promised myself there was no way I was missing that CRB meeting.

Eighteen

Reciprocity

Even after all these years, I still get emotional about the way the events unfolded and the subsequent impact that changed Bridgetown forever. Shortly after I arrived in Chambers, Kyle, who was as usual a few minutes late, sauntered in. We took our seats while the other thirty-nine members slowly drifted in from the adjacent cafeteria. Sabrina could not attend because of pressing Medical Center matters.

Kyle had just stepped up to the podium when suddenly an aide burst through the doors and ran up the stairs to where the admiral sat. He whispered something into the admiral's ear, which caused Donner Sr. to leap to his feet and say in a very clear voice. "Recall the patrols now and tell them our situation. Tell my son I'm on my way and to contact the orbiting Explorers. We need them to take positions over Bridgetown as quickly as possible."

He then turned to the committee and announced there were unidentified aircrafts on a direct path to Bridgetown. He cautioned that it could mean nothing, except they were not ours and were not responding to any of the hailing frequencies. He suggested we adjourn and return to our homes. With that, he moved quickly out of Chambers, leaving us all kind of dumbfounded.

The rest of the members left quickly, but Kyle and I lingered around the courtyard searching the skies for any evidence of these approaching ships. Everything seemed peaceful enough, almost too quiet. About a minute into our sky watch, I noticed something across the lake. It was too far away to clearly identify, but it was moving our way fast.

My heart started to race. This couldn't be good! As the objects drew nearer, it became clear they were fighter crafts, and we were the target. There were thirty small crafts flying in six separate arrowhead formations, approaching at varying altitudes across the surface of the lake.

"Kyle, we're going to be attacked. We need to find cover now!" I urged.

He wouldn't move! It was like he was frozen in shock or disbelief. I couldn't leave his side even though I had never been this scared. He was my friend, and whatever happened would happen. We just stood there staring, watching the drama unfold before our eyes. What happened in the next couple of minutes gets played back over and over in my mind whenever I'm alone recalling the tragic events of that day.

Perhaps a mile before land break, two of the formations veered off. One banked to the left, and one to the right directly over the launch pads and the Medical Center. The remaining four began to do the same, but suddenly the Pulse Gatling gun installations around the lakefront began to fire at a feverish rate, and almost instantly, eight attackers were incinerated, exploding into balls of fire. That didn't stop the remaining invaders that had already launched twenty or more missiles.

Five airborne torpedoes hit the main tower of the Administrative Complex, reducing it to rubble in an instant. As soon as I saw the building we had just left reduced to smoldering ash, I thought to myself that had the alert been delayed a couple more minutes, we'd all be dead now. Two other torpedoes missed the tower and hit somewhere in the residential block. Although we couldn't see where, from the deafening noise of the explosions and the plumes of dense black smoke bellowing up into the sky, we knew citizens were dying. There was nowhere to run!

For almost five minutes, the attackers repeatedly attacked while we stood there in horror as helpless spectators to mass murder. Suddenly, Defenders appeared from all directions swooping down on the attackers. In less than a minute, they had destroyed eight more enemy crafts, but the small ships were difficult to lock onto so near the city structures. Another four were destroyed over the residential area, but not before launching another twelve missiles into the very heart of the once quiet neighborhoods. Not even the Spider Drones could protect us from this kind of assault.

Our fortunes changed dramatically when the Explorers arrived. In another five minutes, the attackers were reduced to three remaining ships, which attempted to withdraw from the city but flew directly into the path of the Pegasus. As much as they surprised us, our response did the same to them. The fighters fell like flaming stones into the lake. We had won the day, but it would be at a devastating cost of life.

Four missiles had already hit the Medical Center at the surgical wing, and three others that were directed at the launch pad missed their target and flew into the tented compound. As soon as I heard the explosions, I shouted to Kyle that I had to go. With that, I left him standing in the courtyard. As much as I was concerned about his state of mind, I was more concerned that the only true love I had ever known had been torn away from me.

When I arrived at the compound—or what was left of it—most of the tents were gone, and those still standing were engulfed in flames. All the time I was running, I was praying that maybe today Joshal and the family had gone to the ranch. There were bodies strewn everywhere. Some were killed by the concussion wave of the exploding missiles. Others were dismembered, spewing blood into the dirt.

Now I was frantic! Off to the side, I saw that Sabrina had already organized a triage team. I was happy she was safe, but I wasn't thinking clearly and continued stumbling around, calling Cateria's name over and over again. The medical staff was administering first aid to survivors, and I stopped at every table to see if Cateria was among the wounded.

I remember stopping to ask Sabrina if she had seen Cateria or Joshal. She said they hadn't made their way that far into the compound yet. In turn, she asked about Kyle, and as I was running away, I yelled behind me that he was safe. When I reached what was left of Joshal's family tent, there was only fire and bodies.

I fell to my knees and remember cupping my head in my hands and wailing uncontrollably. Nothing could have survived this! One of those bodies had to be Cateria! My Cateria, it wasn't fair. I couldn't bring myself to go find her body. I wished I was dead with her. What else did I have left? Then I heard a tortured voice over by the shower tents. It was weak but familiar. My eyes danced around trying to determine where it was coming from. It was Cateria! It had to be! Thank God!

When I found her, she was half-hidden under what was left of the shower tent. She was covered in black soot, some of her skin was seared almost black on her arms, and her clothes were mostly torn or burnt away, exposing one of her breasts, but she was alive! She was weeping uncontrollably, partly because of the pain of her wounds, but mostly because she knew in her heart that her family was gone.

Cateria tried to speak, but I wouldn't allow it. I sat on the ground holding her in my arms, screaming for help until at last Sabrina heard me and rushed over to offer care. After a few minutes, Cateria stopped crying and with our help struggled to her feet. "We must say good-bye to my family."

As much as I dreaded the thought of viewing the remains of Joshal, this had to be done for closure. Slowly she led me over to the bodies of people we both loved. Suddenly her legs gave out, and before she could completely fall, I grabbed her, and together we stumbled the remaining few feet.

I felt completely useless at a time when she needed me to be strong for her. I had no answers and could offer no reflection. There, beside the makeshift dinner table lay the bodies of Joshal, his two sons, and his other daughter. When I saw the bodies, I thanked God again for sparing Cateria and for sparing the bodies from being hideously deformed.

We stooped, and she touched and kissed each of her family on the forehead, saying good-bye to each by name, but lingering longest over Joshal. I managed to recover a large piece of tent and covered their remains while she continued to sob. When at last I approached her, she jumped to her feet and began beating me with her fists so hard that I had to fend off her attacks with my arms.

"You bloody meddling bastards! Had you just left us alone in the mountains, they would still be here with me. We were safe there! You killed them as much as those monsters killed them. What will I do? What will I do?" With this, she stopped hitting me, and we embraced for what seemed an eternity.

When she recovered from the initial shock, she looked at me and spoke. "I'm sorry, Ryan, it isn't your fault. If you ever loved us, find who did this and kill them. Promise me you'll kill them all," she sputtered.

At that moment, I knew there was little choice but to make that promise. With that, she fainted, and the air became deathly still. I sat on the bloodied ground just holding her, rocking ever so slowly. I was confused! No—more than that. I was overwhelmed by what had happened. I can't remember how much time passed before I called again to Sabrina. When she finally came with a small group of nurses, they gathered Cateria onto a stretcher and took her away to the hospital tent.

Sabrina looked at me squarely and with resolute calm. "Don't worry, Ryan, she'll be okay. This isn't right! People shouldn't die this way! Tell the admiral I don't care what he does or how he does it, this can never be allowed to happen again. Do you hear me, Ryan?"

"Yes, Sabrina, we'll deal with it. Where are the girls? Cateria's girls, where are they?" I pleaded.

"They're safe. Most of the children are safe. They were all in classes, and the schools were spared," she replied.

As she was saying the words, I was leaving to find my friend. When I arrived back where I left Kyle, he wasn't there. Once the explosions had stopped, he'd gone looking for Sabrina and his son. As I wandered through the streets confused and lost in my own anguish, destruction and death were everywhere. Women were wailing, and toddlers wandered unattended, looking for their parents. I even felt a deep sadness seeing scores of our greatest protectors, the Spider Drones, destroyed with their parts scattered among the bodies of the very people they were built to protect.

What had we done? Was Cateria right? Did we bring death to our door because we involved ourselves in matters that didn't concern us? I stopped and got sick over and over again. How would our people ever come to grips with this? How would I ever face Cateria again? We had promised to protect them. We failed!

Someone or something had decided we needed a lesson in humility. Their mistake was not finishing the job. I knew as I stood there staring at the bodies and collapsed buildings a new order was about to be unleashed on an unsuspecting planet. I went back to the hospital tent and spent the night holding Cateria's hand and crying for my friend Joshal and all those who had died pointlessly that day.

In the morning, a pair of Protectors entered the tent and requested that I go with them to the briefing room. I was tired and reluctant to leave Cateria's side.

Sabrina stepped forward and announced, "I'll take care of her. I'll tell her you had to leave to avenge those who died for nothing. She'll understand, as I do. Ryan, remember what I told you. This can't just pass. You must seek reciprocity for these murders."

I nodded, forced my stiff, exhausted body to a standing position, and left with the escort. In a matter of a few minutes, we entered the briefing room where Kyle, James, Marcus, and the admiral were sitting at the table going over the casualty lists from the previous day's attack. There would be no chirpy cracks or smiles. Today would be a day of reflection and grieving.

Four thousand, two hundred and twelve people had died in the space of twelve minutes before we managed to get the situation under control. Our wounded numbered into the tens of thousands, but our enemies missed the big prize. In their zeal to inflict death and total destruction, they had overlooked most of our counter-offensive resources stored in cave bunkers near the launch pad. Worse still, they never allowed for a Kyle Chandler.

Kyle commented that some of the citizens were packing up their belongings and moving into the hills to escape what they feared would be another attack. How could we blame them for seeking sanctuary? The Children of Vanguard weren't warriors. They had no concept of war. They had never seen anything like this because they shouldn't have had to. It was the job of the Protectorate and the CRB to shield the people, and we failed. That was the first thing we had to come to grips with on the day after because it was etched on the face of each one of us.

The admiral spoke first and set the tone. He was calm, but the strain in his voice did not go unnoticed. "We had a sworn duty to protect our citizens from events just like this. That responsibility had been passed down through generations, and it was never taken for granted. We allowed ourselves to become complacent rather than focusing on our duties as protectors and managers. This failure occurred on my watch! I am resigning, effective immediately. James will assume command of the Protectorate, and I support all his decisions from here on."

We tried to explain to the admiral that this was not his fault and we had no control over the actions of our unknown enemies. Admiral Donner would have none of it. He rose from the table and left the room. For a moment, we sat there confused. I think we all wished we could just quit and let others deal with the aftermath, but there were no others.

James was the first to speak once the door closed behind the admiral. "We will deal with my father later. For now, we have to ensure there's no chance of this happening again. Consequently, I have increased our patrols from three ships to ten and have tasked an additional Explorer into stationary orbit over Bridgetown.

"If anything flies into our airspace, it will be destroyed without hails or discussion. If anything is detected moving in the forest or on the lake, it too will be destroyed. Until further notice, we are in full lockdown. We are retrieving all the settlers from their farms until we understand the magnitude of this threat."

There was no debate on the subject. James was doing what he was charged to do, and the time for discussion had long passed. "Our next challenge is to figure out who attacked us and their motives. It wasn't Draegon, although the ships used appeared to be the same as those we destroyed. And it wasn't some alien invasion because the orbiting Explorers would have detected it," summed up James.

With this, an aide entered the room to whisper something to James. He would have none of it. "The time for secret messages is over. Spit it out, Corporal!" barked James

I kind of felt sorry for the young Protector, but James was right. The aide said that a video transmission was being received, and it was not from our ships or within Bridgetown. James instructed for the transmission to be sent to the briefing room monitor. He also told the aide to get in contact with the orbiting Explorer.

"I want to know exactly where this signal is being transmitted from. Make sure the commander of the Explorer understands

I want exact coordinates, not guesses. You're dismissed, Corporal."

Kyle waited for the door to close before he spoke. "James, if this is our attackers, you need to let me do the talking because you'll declare war immediately, and that won't serve our need to figure out our next play."

"Agreed, but I don't want to hear any ass-kissing political commentary. There are thousands of citizens looking to us to deal with this enemy in the manner they deserve," responded James abruptly.

Seconds later, the giant monitor flickered to life, and the first image was a shape we recognized immediately, but that conversation could wait. The intro screen was replaced with a female speaker dressed in a type of military attire. She was humanoid, perhaps in her late thirties with an exaggerated nose and chin, yet not unattractive.

She wasted little time in getting to the point. "Do you represent and speak for your people?" Kyle responded that we did. "Then hear me well. Yesterday, you were punished for your actions against the innocent citizens of Draegon. We are The Vanguard, and Draegon is under our protection. Be grateful we decided only to teach you a minor lesson," she stated arrogantly.

She paused. That was her first error. The silence lasted just long enough for the fire in Kyle's stomach to settle. When he spoke, it was clear and without emotion. "We don't care what you call yourselves. We care that you committed a treacherous and cowardly act against our people. Let me be clear so you understand our resolve in this matter.

"You have awoken the sleeping lion. We will find you! When we do, we will unleash upon your cities and peoples the greatest armada this planet has ever known. Everything that is precious to you will be taken, and we will eradicate all evidence of your seed from this world. On this you have our word!"

With that, Kyle signaled for James to terminate the transmission. The screen went dark. James smiled ever so slightly. "If that's how diplomats conduct business, then I'm on the wrong side of the table. Now let's go kick their asses," declared James.

I thought at least one cool head should prevail, and I guess for the moment that had to be me. "Should we not try to have meaningful dialogue with these people? Shouldn't we try to get to the bottom of this before we just set ourselves to killing everyone and everything in sight?"

"Ryan, this isn't about killing people," responded Kyle. "It's about making sure we go on record with this enemy that there will be consequences to their actions. There isn't a citizen of Bridgetown who wants dialogue with these murderers. Cateria lost her entire family yesterday. Do you think she cares about dialogue while she weeps over her father and our friend? After we set the record straight and those who hurt us feel our sting, then and only then will there be dialogue. Make no mistake, more people will die over the next few hours, and they won't be ours."

Just then, the speakers came to life, and a voice from the communications room came on line. "We have a live transmission from Explorer Windsurfer, sir. Should I pass it through?"

"Yes," James responded. "Windsurfer, what have you to report? And it had better be that you've found the source of the video transmission."

"James, is that you? Commander Lucas here. What we have is the exact location, which we are now in stationary orbit over with videos for your viewing. Would you like us to stream them to you or just wipe these bastards out and be home in time for dinner?"

"Let's look at the videos first. Stand down for the time being. If, however, there's any activity that suggests they're about to send more fighters in our direction, you have my permission to neutralize the threat—but with minimal civilian casualties. Are we clear on that?" directed James.

"Understood. Here are the videos," responded Diamond.

The city was a metropolis! There were no less than four military compounds, all with launch pads and all with the same small fighters we had destroyed in Draegon. Not similar, but the same, exactly the same. The videos only lasted a few minutes before the feed ended. As soon as the video was off, James spoke.

"Commander, the feed went down," James stated.

"Yes, sir," Diamond responded. "They scrambled fighters and took out our spy drones, but they don't know we're in orbit over their city.

"Kyle, now's the time! They're in our sights! At the very least, we need to make sure they can't launch another attack on us," James announced.

"Can we get videos to show our citizens that we responded to their terrorism?" asked Kyle.

"Absolutely! Communications, link us with Diamond again please. Commander, you may be home for dinner, but before that, I need you to vaporize all four launch pads and anything that's staged on them. If you hit one nonmilitary target, you'll rot in space for all eternity. Drop a couple more drones in; we need more video," James directed.

"Drones away, no innocents hurt, got it!" responded Diamond.

There was a thirty-second delay while the drones reached position and Pulse Beams targeted each of military compounds. The Pulse Beams were calibrated to sweep back and forth across laser-marked coordinates set at four feet below ground zero.

"Based on the size of the installations, sir, this will take five minutes or so, just to be thorough. Here we go!" advised Diamond.

Four separate intense blue rays passed by the drones from space, directly at each military installation. It was fascinating to watch as the beams moved back and forth across the ground, chewing up everything in their path. I can remember thinking to myself, what a monster mankind could be as a death dealer.

Only humans would invent such a devastating weapon to be used almost exclusively to destroy other men. It was a sad statement and testament to the cruelty of the human animal. Within a couple of minutes, the military installations were engulfed in flames that shot up thousands of feet. When the barrage ended, the sites we reduced to smoldering patches of destruction.

"Commander, stay for fifteen minutes and monitor any activity. If there is none, return to your normal orbit," directed James.

"So I guess that means you lied about the home for dinner part," replied Diamond, smiling.

"Tomorrow, we'll send replacements, and I'll bring you home. Donner, out."

Everything went eerily silent. "I know you guys saw the same thing I did on the video intro screen. What do you make of that?" I asked.

There was absolutely no doubt that the emblem and the patch on the lapel of the uniformed woman were images of Vanguard. How was it possible? There had to be an explanation.

"This goes way beyond coincidence. We're missing something! I'm going back to reread the historic Vanguard equipment specifications from the archived engineering files," Marcus said.

I agreed to join Marcus in searching records, but first I had to go to Cateria. In my mind, everything else could wait. There would be no counterattack. The damage inflicted by the Windsurfer would keep our enemies ducking for days. When I finally arrived back at the compound, the makeshift hospital tent had been dismantled, and the injured had been moved to the undamaged wing of the Medical Center.

I wasn't sure I could face Cateria, but I loved her dearly, and my place was with her now more than ever. It was difficult to come to grips with the pain and suffering people had endured and were continuing to endure all through the corridors of the hospital. Occupied gurneys were everywhere with injured and wounded moaning in pain and begging for help. The entire medical team was on duty, trying to save as many of the critically injured as possible. It was organized chaos. I saw Sabrina, but only briefly. She looked drawn and defeated but determined to do her part for friends and neighbors. I asked her where Cateria was. She told me Cateria had gone to my residence to wait for me. She added that Cateria was okay and didn't want to tie up a bed needed by someone else.

When I arrived home, I found her sitting on the side of the bed weeping softly. I sat with her, and we embraced for hours before drifting off into a troubled sleep. In the morning, we travelled to the Great Hall where all the fallen were being held awaiting next of kin. Row after row of body bags were placed in alphabetical order with family names prominently displayed on labels affixed to each bag. There was something strangely unnatural about the entire scene. I understood why it had to be done this way, but it all seemed surreal.

The attack had been hard on the settlers. Over six hundred had breathed their last breath in a microsecond after the missiles hit. Included in the casualty count were all the elders and fifty-two babies and toddlers. Cateria explained to me that the only reason she wasn't among the dead was she had walked over to the shower tent to bathe and had just arrived when the explosions began. The force of the shockwave had thrown her into the back of the tent, and it collapsed around her.

"What will happen to all these people?" she asked through tear-stained eyes.

"I don't know," I responded. "I think Kyle and James are preparing a mass funeral service. Those wishing to make their own arrangements are free to collect their loved ones and leave. If you're ready, we'll find Kyle and have your family released and buried on your father's land beside the river. I know that's what he would have wanted," I replied.

We finally found Kyle with Sabrina having a coffee in the Medical Center cafeteria. They both looked exhausted. The

Center had lost the entire surgical wing along with eight highly prominent doctors, thirty nurses, and six support staff. It would be a long time before Bridgetown looked anything like it did a scant twenty-four hours earlier.

The mass funeral was held in a secluded meadow by the lake about a mile west of Bridgetown. Most of the citizens attended the funeral, and as each body was lowered into the community plot, their full family name was announced by Kyle over a public address system. The event took over twelve hours to complete, and he stood at the podium throughout it all.

As much as we all had suffered in our private lives because of this event, it had touched Kyle in a very different way. Each of us grieved lost friends and loved ones, but Kyle's grief was more profound. As strange as it sounds, he felt that all the people were his responsibility because that's the way he had wanted it, but when they had needed him most, he wasn't there. It tore at him beyond anything we could have imagined.

Cateria had held up well, but she wasn't the same person. She would never be quite the same person again. There were too many wounds that would never heal. She had lost more than any one family and although I knew she would get better over time, I also knew she would need all of my love and support.

Three weeks had passed since the attack and our response. We had remained on high alert. We would never again be caught so unaware. Kyle and Marcus immediately swung into action and developed a new first-response weapon that would detect and destroy incoming aircrafts from over three thousand miles away using another form of burst ray technology. It required a satellite link, which was placed in stationary orbit a week later. We had learned quickly from our mistakes, and so would our enemies.

Sabrina used the Siltron powder to speed the healing process for many of the wounded. She indicated that another fifteen hundred might have died on the operating table if not for Siltron's amazing stimulus attributes, which promoted rapid tissue regeneration.

Each day, Cateria, the girls, and I made the trek to the Joshal Ranch. There was a sad sidebar to these trips. Before his death, Joshal told me that in honor of our rescue of his people, he had named his ranch "New Beginnings." I asked Cateria if she wanted me to remove the sign hanging over the main gate, but she insisted it stay as a constant reminder of her father's eternal optimism.

Every chance we could, we socialized with Sabrina, Kyle, Marcus, and James. On occasion, James would bring his wife, Helen, and together, even if for only brief periods, we would forget our pain. I absolutely needed to keep Cateria distracted while she mended.

Nineteen

Aftermath

I had made it my mission to bring some sense to this whole Vanguard who's who. For weeks, I kept going over the early Vanguard text, but I found nothing about any other missions. While I was doing that, Marcus was examining the archived engineering records to see if he could find a link from a different approach.

He was obsessed with solving the aircraft mystery to bring some sense to all that had happened. We had set aside the whole Zorn disc examination because now was not the time. It had waited a thousand years. It could wait a little longer. Together and on our own, we poured over thousands of pages, searching for any technical drawings relating to the origins of the Defender.

Finally, one afternoon, Marcus leapt from his desk and shouted, "I think I've found something! Listen to this! Almost thirty years ago, the engineers aboard Vanguard developed an advanced version of the Phaeton Thruster. Get this, Ryan—the engineers that developed the modified technology were a wife and husband team going by the name Chandler. Do you think there's a connection?

"Anyway, these advances increased the speed of the Defenders from 1.6 million miles per hour to their current speed. So what—right? Well, here's the nut: the new thrusters would not fit on the original Defender, so they redesigned the ship completely. I have the schematics right here!" he exclaimed.

"I don't get it, Marcus," I replied.

"It's simple! If they remade the Defender to what we see today, what did the original look like? Clearly, it had to be smaller to require redesign. What if the old fighter looked like the ones that attacked us? Since the original version existed before Vanguard launched, we should be trying to find the specs for it in the ancient engineering text. They have to be there somewhere! If they are, and it's a match, like it or not there was another Vanguard mission," he stated.

"If this is true, we have a problem to present to our friends," I replied.

"How so?" asked Marcus.

"Firstly, the engineers that redesigned the thrusters were Kyle's deceased parents. When he hears this, it will only rekindle unpleasant memories. Secondly, right now our enemies are faceless murderers who attacked us without provocation. If, however, we put faces to them and a shared beginning, the entire dynamic changes.

"Think about it. Two groups leave Earth in the hopes of finding a new beginning, free from war and death. One doesn't know the other exists, but fate throws them back together, and they start killing each other all over again, which is the very reason they had to leave Earth in the first place. It reads like some kind of Shakespearean tragedy," I explained.

"Ryan, you're thinking too much about what it might mean in a philosophical context. That's not our job. We're fact-finders. That's our job, and we'll present the facts as we know them. How this all plays out is something others will have to debate to find a deeper meaning," Marcus replied.

Much of my time over the next couple of weeks was spent bouncing back and forth between Cateria and Marcus, trying to give each of them the attention they required. Cateria seemed a bit more resigned to the loss of her family and the understanding that the girls and I were the last ones she had left of the people she loved. She was spending a lot of time with Sabrina these days, and that worked out great since it meant she was almost never alone. There were no closer friends than Sabrina and Cateria. Sabrina had made Cateria and the girls her responsibility to help through these tough times.

It must have been two weeks after the discussion with Marcus that we met in his office. He had found what we were looking for and wanted to make sure I understood exactly how it all played out before we took our findings to the CRB. I kind of knew what he was going to say, but we had to put it into some kind of format that would make sense to the audience.

"Ryan, let me begin by stating the obvious; the people attacking us are indeed who they claim to be. I've found the original schematics for the Defenders we destroyed in Draegon, and these same crafts were used to attack Bridgetown. They're almost identical in every detail. There are two good things to come from that discovery. Firstly, they're still using that same version of fighter, which means they have nothing more powerful in reserve.

"I know you're going to say, 'What about the Explorers, which are bigger and more menacing?' The Explorers were prototypes designed exclusively for our Vanguard. They began as purely light armored exploration vehicles. We modified them into the war machines they've become. If they're still using the original Defenders, then that's all they have," explained Marcus.

"Here's the catch! I think their version of Vanguard was launched before ours. I know how the history texts read, but I think the information is misleading, and here's why. As I mentioned earlier, their Defenders are almost identical to the original designs. That design was slightly modified twenty-six years later, three years before our launch. I have those drawings as well.

"The change was subtle but visible to the naked eye. The videos of their attack on Bridgetown show they're flying a wing thrust propulsion system. The thrusters were moved to the rear to make room for the added weaponry on the wing assemblies. All Defenders were modified to the new designs," Marcus summed up.

"That's huge, Marcus! It blows the shit out of our entire history record. Where was your ass when I was suffering through two years of rewriting our history with a bunch of half-truths?" I asked, just a bit miffed by it all.

"Preschool," he answered.

This news had to be delivered to the CRB and soon. I contacted Kyle and requested an emergency session of the CRB and asked that James be in attendance. The information in our possession now might help direct us on how best to approach any future contact with our homegrown enemies. When I gave Kyle the brief overview of our findings, he almost fell on his ass.

"Isn't this just a great fucking mess we're in now!" exclaimed Kyle.

When Marcus and I arrived in Chambers, every seat in the room was filled, save the admiral's. Everyone wanted to know what we had found out, and Kyle wanted to be sure that our evidence was solid before any move-forward recommendations were offered. Marcus and I took our positions at the speaker's podium. We had brought everything necessary to make the point. The most important of this evidence were the three sets of dated schematics Marcus had put on video disc to display.

"Ladies and gentlemen, to steal a line from Marcus's playbook, let me begin with the bombshell and explain how we arrived at it. The people who attacked us claimed they are The Vanguard. They are!" I stated.

At this point, I paused while the shouts came from all directions. It became so loud that Kyle had to step forward and get them back in line. "Members of the CRB, we are here to listen to the people we charged with fact-finding and discovery. Everyone needs to shut up and let them do that. Once they get through the presentations, then we can ask questions. Thank you."

The gallery went silent, because when you piss Kyle off enough to have him get up and shout at you, it's time to rethink your actions. They did! With that, I gave the podium to Marcus, and he immediately began to lead the group through the same detailed analysis he shared with me, including his opinion about who came first. The entire presentation took over an hour. At that point, we asked for questions and got ready for the assault. To our surprise, the detail we shared was so cut and dry that only a few questions were asked, and they came primarily from James and Kyle.

"Good job, guys. I just have one clarification item. I think we're all in agreement that they're one of the expeditions from Earth. Why do they call themselves Vanguard? Wouldn't their ship have had another name?"

"There were no records found to explain that, but we have a theory. All the vessels built for these pilgrimages were called Vanguard. We believe the distinction between them was call numbers. For instance, they could have been tracked as Vanguard 1, Vanguard 2, and so on up to Vanguard 6 if they were all built," I explained.

"I can buy that," said James, "but what difference does it make when trying to come to grips with what happened? It doesn't alter the fact that they attacked us and killed our people. Sharing a common origin does not change the reality of our situation, does it?" James questioned.

"Marcus and I discussed whether this shared heritage should alter our approach to this, and we agreed it was a matter for those in these Chambers to decide—not us. James, I wish we could offer more than that," I replied.

"Do you think they know what we know?" asked a representative further back in the gallery.

"We doubt it. We think they're quite likely treating us as alien invaders. Marcus believes their attack was a reaction to how our actions in Draegon were portrayed to them, probably by their own people," I replied.

The room suddenly went silent, and Kyle took that opportunity to step forward and thank us for our work. He requested that Marcus stay in Chambers and join in the discussion about what we do next, if anything. Marcus was happy to continue to be part of any solution.

"James, I spoke to your father this morning, and he has appointed you to take his seat. Please do so, and then we'll get on with this. The debate about who these people are is over. The concern about their ability to wage an all-out war is over as well because we vastly out-gun them. The questions before this Council therefore is, do we make our citizens aware of the shared origins between us? And do we make our enemies aware of what we know?" asked Kyle.

James was not going to be silent on this matter. Everyone could tell by his body language that he wasn't ready to give up wanting to extract his pound of flesh for their actions. "I get it. I really do! They're us, and we're them—good and meaningless. They murdered our people! They weren't interested in going after only military targets. Their objective was clear: to kill as many men, women, and children as possible. Had we been a bit less fortified, we'd all be dead now.

"Regardless of their motivation for the attack, their actions went way beyond defending the small guy. They tried to murder us all. We need to respond in kind," James declared from his newly acquired seat.

"James, if the lean of your commentary is the CRB sanctions sending a force to wipe them out, that isn't going to happen on my watch. We have already delivered a measured response for their actions. To do more at this stage will make us as bad as them," answered Kyle.

"You misunderstand. I don't want to wipe out anyone, least of all a city of a million innocents because of the actions of their leadership. I want this Council to recognize that any discussions moving forward with these people, regardless of our shared heritage, must be guided by the knowledge that they're treacherous killers of the innocent," replied James.

"I think we all agree they're not to be trusted. What we do about that, short of going to the extreme, is something you and I can discuss. Let's talk about whether we make our people aware of the connection between us. I would suggest the time isn't right, and we should make sure this conflict is fully behind us first," Kyle explained.

There was whispering throughout the gallery. The mandate of the CRB was to always make the people aware, and Kyle agreed, but he reminded the group that making them aware without a solution would only unsettle them even more. In the end, we all knew he'd have his way, and more importantly, we knew he was right.

When this portion of the meeting ended, Marcus was excused, and the CRB began discussing the rebuilding of the city and damaged infrastructure. There was so much to consider if we were ever to restore our city and regain the confidence of the citizens. Kyle, James, Marcus, and I met the next morning to discuss the right approach for a video transmission to our enemies, but first we had breakfast. James did nothing without food and coffee.

While we waited, we joked about the dinner the night before and how silly we had gotten on the wine. Of special humor was Marcus's reaction to the young nurse Sabrina had invited to meet him. Her name was Susan, and she had the same baby-face look about her as Marcus. She was pretty without being beautiful, which was right up Marcus's alley. He was all stutter when speaking to her, but Sabrina was careful to select a girl that she knew would be able to relate to Marcus.

Although he wouldn't admit it to us, we were betting that last night was the best night of his young life. We also knew they had arranged to meet again, not because Marcus told us, but because Susan told Sabrina. Cateria had a great time as well. She was near being back to her former self, and that pleased everyone, but most of all me. Now a new day brought us back to the drama.

After eating, we were at it, sharing ideas on how to manage a video conference with our new enemies. Kyle wanted to employ a diplomatic approach where both parties accepted their part in the deaths of innocents and moved toward further dialogue in a more formal setting. James and Marcus were at the other end of the spectrum. They wanted a strong-arm approach where we reminded them of what we're capable of and that we would not tolerate further aggressive action.

I was undecided. On one hand, both Sabrina and Cateria made me commit to reciprocity toward our enemy—an eye-for-an-eye approach. On the other hand, I wanted things to settle down. I missed the boring days of making love to Cateria as often as possible.

Suddenly the intercom buzzed, and a voice advised James that there was another video feed arriving from the same source as before. For a moment, we all froze with our mouths wide open because once again they beat us to the punch. James said to delay the feed for a few minutes while we prepared ourselves.

"I'm getting awfully tired of these assholes upstaging us. I guess we'll be winging it as usual," piped in Kyle. "I have an idea purely for shock value. In the reception area as you enter the Protectorate is a model of our Vanguard; it's about six feet tall and made from composites. Is that something we can move here, James?"

"We put it there; we can bring it here. Why?" replied James.

"If we position it right behind my chair when the video conference begins, the first thing they'll see will be the replica of Vanguard, and that should put them off their game momentarily. Somewhat in the same way we were caught off guard when we saw the insignia of Vanguard for the first time during their transmission to us. If their intent is to saber rattle, this might just change the conversation in our favor."

With that, James picked up the phone and issued the instruction. While we waited for delivery, we discussed what might be our strategy. Come at them hard or play the negotiation card. Suddenly the briefing room's double doors burst open, and in came eight Protectors carrying the giant composite model Vanguard. As agreed, James had it placed just behind Kyle's chair so that the model filled the entire backdrop. Marcus was the first to offer an opinion of what should be done.

"When they come on line, they will announce themselves as the Vanguard. As soon as they do, my recommendation is for Kyle to interrupt the dialogue by declaring he does not speak to the underling and demands a higher authority. That will immediately put them in a defensive posture, and we will have taken control of the meeting before it begins," suggested Marcus.

We all agreed that would be our opening gambit in this chess match to gain the high ground. James called Communications and told them to put through the video conference call. Almost instantly, the video screen came to life, and as before, the Vanguard insignia appeared on the screen as a lead in to the call, followed by the live image of the same woman who had spoken to us previously.

"We are The Vanguard," she proclaimed. Kyle wasted little time in putting our plan in motion.

"Before this goes any further, what is your authority to speak with us? It doesn't matter! We will speak only with the leadership of your people. If that's not you, then get them. You have one hour. Failure to comply will result in the extermination of your people," Kyle said.

It was immediately obvious that Kyle's outburst shocked the woman. His proclamation coupled with the Vanguard model positioned behind him had set the tone. Her next words were what we had hoped they would be and clear evidence that we had won the first volley.

"Please be patient! I will summon my superiors," she replied.

The screen went dark. James called Communications to make sure the link was cut. We all stood and gave Kyle a round of applause. He smiled, stood, and bowed. "What more could a man ask than recognition from his peers? But wait a minute, you're not my peers."

It was Marcus that put us back on point. "Gentlemen, we did gain a temporary position of power, but don't let this minor victory cloud what is likely a story yet to unfold. When they come back online, they'll have a strategy designed to deflect our aggression."

"Do you have any ideas as to what they'll come back with?" I asked.

"Not really, but we need to put ourselves on their side of the table and decide what we'd do, and then develop our counter," responded Marcus.

"I think they'll come across as apologetic for their actions and blame Draegon, but I don't see them admitting they got there asses kicked," suggested Kyle.

"Then we should remind them," commented James. "We should leave no doubt in their minds that we have more in our pockets if they want it. I don't trust them," James added.

"James, the biggest mistake we could make is becoming the bullies of the schoolyard. Everyone hates the bully. Isn't that right, Marcus?" I said.

Just then, the intercom came to life again. "Okay, that was quick; they're back online. Kyle, do you want more time?" asked James.

"No, I've got an idea. Bring them on," he responded.

The Vanguard insignia was no longer part of the opening screen. It was an interesting tactic. Remove the controversial symbolism. This time, there were five people seated at a table, and the woman who had up until now done all the talking was sitting at the end in a subordinate position. The male in the middle was older, perhaps in his midsixties, and based on his authoritative posture, he was the head of this group.

"Good afternoon. I am Prime Minister Dennison, and these people on either side of me represent the various departments of our government. We are the top leadership of the Supreme Governing Council of Salmon. We understand a grievous error has been made by our actions against your city. We cannot undo what has been done, but we can offer our most sincere apologies to the families who suffered because of it. Lives have been lost on both sides. More than half of our air-defense fleet has been destroyed because of bad counsel we received from Draegon. We are a peaceful people who under normal circumstances would never inflict harm on a neighbor. Ours was poor judgment. We find ourselves in the unusual position of being in the wrong."

Kyle was ready. "You have much to answer for. Not only the preemptive attack on our people, but for the arming of the tyrant in Draegon who used what you gave him to slaughter the innocent for no other reason than to fuel his ego. These are not the acts of humane societies. They are the cold, calculated, evil conspiracies of murderous regimes. Since your people are clearly from one of the six Vanguard missions to leave planet Earth in search of new lives, we would have thought you would have learned from the folly of our ancestors. Apparently, those lessons got lost somewhere in your voyage to this new world. We will not allow this planet to follow the same path as Earth."

I could tell by their body language that Kyle's reference to shared origins had thrown them for a loop.

"You are from Earth? How could this be? Our history texts tell us we were the only successful Vanguard launch," Dennison replied, rather wide-eyed.

"Well, your text is wrong, but that's a discussion for another time and has no value to this exchange. We will not attack you again, assuming we can come to a mutual understanding. We can't make the same concessions for Draegon. They are a warrior horde led by a mass murderer made more deadly because of your involvement. As long as your regime supports his treacherous ways, we will be at odds. When we've finished dealing with your involvement in all this, we will turn our attention to the Draegon madman," Kyle declared.

Dennison was quick to respond, "We vowed a decade ago to protect the peaceful peoples of what is now Draegon. In those times, it was a series of small farming communities that had been all but exterminated by some unknown alien predator. We did not wish to intervene since we were new to this world, but we couldn't allow these creatures to kill defenseless, indigenous humanoid life forms. Once we dispatched the menace, we organized the remaining inhabitants under their young King Uthess and helped them develop an infrastructure. We gave them the tools to protect themselves and the skilled manpower to operate those tools. We could not have anticipated they would misuse our gift to kill innocents.

"Our attack on your city was initiated because their king insisted they were besieged by another alien who, without provocation, attacked and murdered thousands of women and children while they slept. He lied, and we reacted partly because of our vow to protect them and partly to protect ourselves. How could we have known?" Dennison pleaded.

James responded, "Uthess didn't fly the fighters. Your pilots did, and they're responsible for the slaughter of thousands of innocents. Suggesting you didn't know what was going on is just further proof of your deceit. How could you not know? I think you chose to ignore what was going on because it didn't affect you. Guess what? Now it does. Be advised, if your pilots get in our way, I will dispose of them as well."

"We understand," replied the Prime Minister, clearly shaken by James's verbal assault.

"Good. Go to your people, and we will do the same. There is a lasting peace to be had, and it is within your grasp. We will contact you in a few days, and arrangements will be made for a Peace Summit," said Kyle.

With that, the feed was terminated.

"Well, how do you think it went?" asked Kyle.

"You were both brilliant. Where do guys come up with this shit? You were so smooth I wanted to surrender," I responded. We all had a good laugh, but there was more to be done. Tomorrow!

Twenty

Treachery

Cateria, the girls, and I spent the rest of the afternoon visiting one of the settlement farms just outside Bridgetown. It was great fun and reminded me of happier times. Cateria was her old self, teasing and poking at me every chance she had. The girls were running around the fields with other kids and a dozen or so silly dogs. We laughed a lot, ate too much meat, and drank way too much wine. In my case, I drank myself senseless. In the end, they had to carry me into the farm house to sleep it off. I was gone for the night. The next morning when they woke me, I thought I was dying.

As much as I wanted to just lie under a shade tree for the day and sleep, Cateria would have none of it. She hinted she had something to tell me and was afraid of how I would react given all that had happened. I reminded her that she had all my love and support regardless of what she had to say.

"I'm pregnant," she blurted out as she walked down the hill.

I would still be sitting there to this day staring blankly after her if she hadn't called out over her shoulder. "Are you coming? We have a lot to do. We can discuss this later—along with when you're finally going to marry me."

As I ran down the hill after her, I was yelling, "You're pregnant! I'm the father! I'm going to be a daddy! This is great news! I've fulfilled The Pact!"

Suddenly she stopped in her tracks, whipped around, and stared straight at me. "Are you going to marry me or not?" she demanded.

"Of course I am! How do we do this?" I asked.

"Three days from now, we will speak with Dravon. He's not only a family friend; he's my godfather. You will ask him for my hand in marriage, and he will grant your request. Sabrina, Serri, Susan, and Helen will do the rest. Men are useless in such things."

"Shouldn't I formally propose to you?" I asked.

"Ryan, we have been sharing a bed for what seems forever. For a while, I was considering turning you in for a better model. Now your child is in my belly! Why are you being silly?" she replied.

When we arrived back at the residence, I was still hung-over and felt like crap, but I was as happy as any man had a right to be. I left Cateria and the kids at the school drop-off and headed to the briefing room. No one was there yet, and I fell asleep with my head on the conference table and a cup of coffee in my hand.

The next sound I heard was James and Kyle laughing loudly and calling me a drunk. When I opened my eyes, they were sitting on either side of me. I was not amused. James had ordered an aide to fetch a headache remedy from the clinic. If the medicine didn't fix my problem, the taste of it sure brought me back to life. It was the most-foul tasting concoction the chemists had ever made. Truly the cure was worse than the disease.

I couldn't wait to break the news to my two very best friends, and I wasn't about to let my splitting headache ruin my announcement. "James, Kyle, I have something to tell you, and I need both of you to shut up!"

"Let me guess—you're a homosexual! That's it isn't it? Just the other day, Kyle was saying that for years you've been staring at his ass. I thought he meant you followed him everywhere, but now the truth comes out," joked James.

"Kyle, tell him to shut up! This is really important! It's life-changing!" I exclaimed.

"James, shut up! Ryan is trying to tell us he's had a sex change or something," he chuckled.

"Cateria's pregnant!" I blurted out. "Before you say it, yes, I am the father."

The room went silent, and they just stared at me. "It's true! I'm going to be a daddy. In fact, I'm going to be a great daddy. What do you have to say to that?" I boasted.

"Well, it confirms the rumor I heard from Helen," said James.

"Sabrina told me a week ago after the test," Kyle responded.

"You mean I was the last to know? Cateria told everyone before she told me, the father?" I asked, now pissed.

"No, we didn't know until just now. We just wanted to take some of the wind out of your sails," replied James.

"So, now that you've gotten it off your chest, congratulations and let's get to work," said James.

"You know what? You two guys are real assholes, but that's okay, because nothing you do or say is going to ruin my day," I replied, pushing out my chest in a show of indifference.

I don't know if I was disappointed with the lightness with which they took my earth-shattering announcement, but it was said, and whatever their response, I knew they were very happy for Cateria and me. James indicated that Marcus would be joining us shortly, and we would start planning for our meeting with Salmon.

As soon as Marcus arrived, I told him my good news.

"That's really wonderful! Is that why I'm here?" he replied nonchalantly.

"Remind me never to share any more good news with any of you guys. You're all shitheads. Let's get on with this," I barked.

James and Kyle laughed. Marcus just sat there wondering what I was talking about. Finally, he shrugged and waited for the discussion to begin. Kyle asked James if the admiral was feeling any better about what had happened. James's mood turned somber as he told us that his father had become withdrawn, and he worried about his health. The admiral was close to eighty-five years old, and this entire ordeal had sapped most of what energy he had left. We quickly changed the subject because it was obvious that James was concerned about him.

We talked at length about the peace conference and what we were looking to gain from the exercise. The Peace Accord had to address the painful events of the last few weeks, while ensuring our security and peace of mind moving forward.

Kyle began, "We need to establish the ground rules for a lasting peace and show our enemy that it's better and safer to be our friends. We will insist on a formal apology to our people. We will not deny their right to rebuild their air-defense infrastructure. We cannot leave them unprotected from enemies as yet unknown," continued Kyle "We will ask them—"

Suddenly the intercom came to life, and an excited voice spoke nervously, "Sir, we have incoming. It looks like they've committed their entire fleet!"

James was unnaturally calm. "Are our boys ready?"

"Yes, sir, we've dropped eight Explorers out of orbit at sixty thousand feet above their city and another ten between them and us. Forty Defenders are in position over the mountains to the south, and twenty more are flanking from the east and west. Our new satellite defensive shield is fully functional and has already slowed their advance. Our boys have engaged their fleet just beyond the mountains to the south.

"Estimates put the enemy assets at three hundred fighters. Early reports indicate we've taken out over 120 since the skirmish began fifteen minutes ago. The enemy is in retreat. Should we chase them down, sir?"

"Allow them to return to their airspace above their city and box them in. None of them land, and none of them escape. Is that clear, Commander?" James asked.

"Crystal, sir. Control, out"

"Who's coming? What's going on, James?" Marcus asked.

"Who else? Those lying bastards from Salmon, that's who," James responded.

The rest of us were in shock. Why were they attacking again? What did they hope to gain from this? Did they really think after their last attempt that we wouldn't be on full alert?

"Control, send the Scorpion to pick us up," James instructed through his communicator. "Gentlemen, if we want to be there when the final blow is delivered, let's get our asses moving. Kyle, these guys are trying to kill us. It ends today."

"James, I know you're pissed, but wiping out their city isn't the answer," Kyle pleaded.

"I told you before that I have no intention of wiping out their city. I do have every intention of wiping out their ability to do us harm. These guys want us dead. They had this planet all to themselves, and then we butted in. You don't really think they give a shit about shared origins, do you? That's just more incentive to get rid of us. We know all their dirty little secrets." James smiled.

James knew the Explorers above Salmon were likely drawing ground fire from land-based defensive emplacements; he was counting on it to pinpoint their positions. He seemed fairly lighthearted about the whole affair, which made me a bit nervous about what his real intentions were.

"James, if the Explorers are taking fire, shouldn't you be concerned we'll lose assets?" I asked.

"Ryan, by the time we get there, the ground fire will be a thing of the past. Every time they fire a volley, our tracking devices pinpoint the source and hit it with laser-guided disruptor beams. My only concern is that if some of the emplacements are located in residential areas, we will have civilian casualties," James responded.

As soon as we boarded, James opened communication to the fleet, issuing the orders for the day. "Gentlemen, we are involved in a coordinated assault against a persistent enemy. Our objective here is to devastate their ability to wage war. There is to be no aggression against the citizens. They are not the objects of this exercise. I want the enemy's weapons off line, their military assets neutralized, and their Command and Control systems taken out before we arrive.

"Phase two of this exercise is a full assault on their military installations. If it even looks like it has a military use, destroy it. I want all roads leading to and from the installations removed. Warrior, Windsurfer, and Nighthawk, hold at 65,000, we'll join you in fifteen minutes. Donner, out."

"Will we be part of the assault wave?" asked Kyle.

"We will not. This ship serves as Command and Control for the exercise. Do you want me to tell the boys to save a couple of enemy fighters just for you to shoot down?" James smirked.

"You're a funny guy. The last time I looked, the Protectorate reported to the CRB. Is that true, Ryan?" Kyle asked sarcastically.

"Yes it is, Mister Chairman," I replied pointing at James.

When our Explorer arrived over Salmon, James gave the go-ahead order. I almost felt sorry for the innocents below. Wave after wave of Defenders soared in from all directions. The sky darkened until it seemed the sun had disappeared from the heavens. In minutes, the entire perimeter of the city was engulfed in flames.

People were dying below. I had this sickening feeling that mankind had stepped back five hundred years into the history texts. There was no longer any lighthearted banter in the viewing room. Each of us was fighting back our own emotional demons.

This was not a moment we would boast about to our children and grandchildren.

What was left of their air force was swept aside quickly. As James predicted, by the time we arrived, there was no defensive fire from the ground. Some of the bunkers had been in residential areas of the city, but the Disruptors were so precise they literally carved them out of their surroundings like a surgeon removing a cancer without harming the fragile skin around it.

"James, you seem almost resigned to destroying these people. I'm not sure I like this side of you. It's vengeful," I suggested.

"Killing their people to save our people was never going to be an easy decision. What I am resigned to is that this must end today. We can't spend our lives wondering when they'll attack again. I promise you guys we will only apply the force necessary to protect our citizens. That is our mandate. As soon as a white flag is waved, we'll not fire another volley," replied James.

"James, what happens now?" Marcus asked.

"That's up to them! I would expect their High Guard to be hailing us within minutes to request a cease fire. At that point, we'll insist they stand down and prepare to receive emissaries to discuss the terms of their surrender. I repeat—we are not here to murder people. We are here only to make sure they stop trying to murder us. At some point today, they will stand down because it's the only prudent course of action left to them," replied James.

A few minutes later, a voice came over the intercom indicating that the people below were hailing us across all bands. "Okay, this is what we've been waiting for. Kyle, we are not here to make friends or say we're sorry. We are here to negotiate terms of surrender," instructed James.

"I read you loud and clear," replied Kyle. "Commander, put the transmission through the video monitor in the viewing room."

A few seconds later, images appeared on the screen. It was the same five people we had spoken to less than two days ago while they were stalling us to set up another sneak attack. As passionate as Kyle was about preserving life and finding the good in all men, I knew this was not going to be a pleasant exchange.

"Mister Prime Minister, if this call is not to announce your wish to surrender, then prepare your people for a long and painful day," declared Kyle.

The people on the screen were clearly nervous, and when the Prime Minister spoke, his voice was unsteady and anxious. "Mr. Chandler, it would appear our options are limited, and you have the upper hand."

"So it would appear. We warned you once. Apparently not only are you liars, but you don't listen well either," Kyle answered.

"We wish to discuss terms of surrender and ask that you spare our people and our city. We are unable to defend ourselves any longer," pleaded the Prime Minister.

"We will stand down because too many innocents have already died because of your treachery. Please provide coordinates to our helmsman, and we will land to meet with you. Understand clearly, our resolve is unwavering. Should there be any attempt toward violent behavior, we will level your city and incinerate every person in it. Do you understand what I'm telling you?" demanded Kyle.

"We do, sir. No such action will be attempted," replied the Prime Minister.

"Prepare for our arrival in thirty minutes. Chandler, out!"

"Ryan, how does this surrender stuff usually get handled from your review of the ancient text?" Kyle asked.

"Typically, the victors—that would be us in this case—prepare a list of demands that form the terms of the surrender. This is followed by a period of discussion, not negotiation, between the sides, which is why it's important our demands be clearly defined," I counseled.

For the next twenty minutes, we huddled around the briefing table, making notes for Kyle. The coordinates took us to the city center. It was decided we would set our Explorer down in a park near the primary government buildings. From the park, we would be escorted across to their version of City Hall. James instructed three of the Defenders to follow us in and hover over the city as a visible reminder of what would happen if this did not go well.

As we began our vertical descent, we had our first close-up views of Salmon from an entirely different perspective. The images appearing on the monitor were of large structures in the city center. One thing was obvious; these people were decades ahead of us in their architecture and infrastructure. Where Bridgetown epitomized simplicity of design, Salmon was sophisticated to the point of being almost artistic. We could learn so much from each other; perhaps we might still.

I was happy we hadn't inflicted too much damage on the city core. We noticed there was a growing crowd of curious spectators surrounding the park to watch our arrival. This was a bit concerning since we had just destroyed a good portion of the cities perimeter and there might be emotions in play that could cause an unwanted incident.

James ordered a Defender to take a hovering position over the park just in case. Once we had landed, we could see on the monitor that a group of men dressed in military garb had formed a fifty-man escort a few yards from our ship. James wanted to make sure none of these soldiers were confused about the rules of the game, so he had the side Gatling guns activated, which made a very distinct noise and abrupt movement when initiated. The action startled everyone outside, and they looked genuinely frightened.

James wasn't taking any chances. Twenty Spider Drones were deployed around the Scorpion, purely for visual impact and to send a clear message to any would-be heroes that might want to take a shot at us as we exited. As we started down the corridor to the first air lock, there was no doubt James was concerned about the crowd reaction to our arrival.

Although it all seemed overly melodramatic, James knew his stuff and how to control a situation when the risks were unknown. As we emerged through the hatch, we could hear muffled rumblings from the crowd. At a rough guess, there must have been twenty thousand people watching and waiting. They seemed to be everywhere.

When we landed, the crowd was as close as a hundred feet from our ship. That lasted only until the Drones were deployed. Now the mass moved back toward the perimeter of the park a couple hundred yards away. This was a typical reaction whenever Spider Drones were introduced to a situation. James commented to Kyle that he was happy we had a few on every ship, and since they were built in Kyle's image, it was no surprise people were afraid of them.

The military escort seemed unsure of what to do when we finally made it to the bottom of the walkway. There we stood, there they stood, each side awkwardly waiting for the other to make the next move. At length, a middle-aged soldier stepped forward and spoke.

"We are your escort. If you will follow us, we will guide you to the Supreme Council Chambers."

James wasted little time setting the rules for this leisurely stroll. "Our escort team will follow and form on each side of our flank. Is there any problem with that?"

"No, sir. May we leave now?" the soldier responded, nervously glancing toward the Drones standing motionless near the ramp.

For effect, James looked back at the ship one last time, raised his hand, and the gangway began to retract back into the ship. Kyle, not to be outdone, removed his handheld keyboard and had the Spider Drones run forward thirty yards and form a line. That almost resulted in a stampede away from the park by the onlookers. The Salmon escort immediately dropped their side arms to the ground and raised their hands. James told them to pick up their weapons and get us where we needed to be.

"Kyle, just in case, have three of the Drones bring up our rear, but make sure you shut down their weapons systems. We don't want them picking off innocents," James instructed.

As we entered a rather tall, impressive building, the escort leader turned and advised us we would be taking turbo lifts to the Government Chambers. Marcus whispered to James that he was concerned we would be exposed once on the lift. James agreed and told the escort leader the arrangement was unacceptable. The soldier, already panic-stricken, fumbled to find the right response.

James wasn't waiting. "We will meet in the concourse over there. Tell your leaders these are the conditions we require. Tell them now!"

"Yes, sir! Yes, sir!" responded the soldier as he moved away to radio his superior.

Kyle went to James's side. "What's up?"

James explained the situation, and Kyle nodded his understanding.

"Our leaders will come here. Please be patient," said the soldier.

We waited for almost five minutes before any activity was detected. When it started, it was nonstop. A group of soldiers appeared from a room on the left, carrying a table so big we could have sat half the CRB at it and ten chairs somewhat out of portion to the table.

James chuckled at the chaos as the soldiers scuffled around trying to get it all set up. "Do you think if I asked we could get coffee and buns?"

I remember Kyle looking over at James with a fatherly expression on his face. "James, stop being a dick. We need to get on with this thing, but I could use a coffee."

About a minute later, we heard the distinct sound of an elevator door activating, and there they were. As the now familiar faces of the Council members approached, I could see on James's face that had we not been there, he would have drawn his sidearm and executed them one by one, beginning with the Prime Minister.

Dennison gestured for us to take our seats. Kyle wasted little time getting to the purpose of the meeting. "We can dispense with the ceremonial niceties and get directly to the matter at hand. We have prepared a document detailing the terms of your surrender. When you accept the terms—and you *will* accept them—we will mutually sign the document, and this meeting ends. If you refuse to sign, then we will deal with your refusal as a wish to continue the conflict."

Kyle continued, "Mr. Evans and Mr. Scott will pass the document around. I will read the terms and conditions, but before we begin, let me be perfectly clear. Should any attempt be made to harm us during this exercise, the five of you will be the first casualties, followed by the destruction of this city. Marcus, introduce the Council members to our insurance policy so they clearly understand the consequences of noncompliance."

Marcus stood up and walked toward the entrance, keying into the portable keyboard. I wondered what he was going to do. Suddenly the large set of entry doors were very literally blown away as one of the Spider Drones burst into the building and hopped forward until it stopped immediately in front of Marcus. The visual impact caused a chain reaction that even now so many years later still makes me giggle.

The Salmon escort once again dropped their weapons, but this time, they took to flight somewhere into the back area of the building. The five Council members jumped out of their chairs and dove under the meeting table. James's laughter was so robust I thought he might stroke out. Kyle tried to maintain his official posture, but it didn't last long before he too was doing the same. Marcus and I just looked at each other and smiled.

It took a few minutes for the situation to settle itself down. Kyle and James collected themselves, and things were ready to begin. Slowly, the Council members stood their chairs back up and sat down again, looking terrified. It was a cruel exhibition of power, but none of us felt any sympathy for the people across the table.

Kyle began, "The purpose of that exhibition was to make sure you understand; we don't, not even for a moment, think you people can be trusted. If something should happen to us, this robot will terminate each of you, and there is absolutely nothing you can do to stop it. We, unlike you, are not murderers of women and children, but that compassion does not extend to you. Do you clearly understand what you've seen and what I've said?"

"Yes, we do; there will be no such incidents," replied Dennison.

Kyle continued, "Good. Let's get on with this. Before we begin, could I suggest some coffee and buns be delivered?"

Again I looked over at James, and he had a grin from ear to ear. Dennison cocked his head to one side curiously and instructed a member of the escort team, now slowly regrouping from their hiding places, to get refreshments. The guard seemed frozen in time staring at the Drone. Kyle realized the guard would never even try passing by the Drone to retrieve the food. Rather than just continuing to terrorize the soldier, he asked Marcus to have the robot stand aside. As soon as the Drone moved, the room came alive again.

"Everyone can relax. We made our point," James announced.

Without further delay, Kyle began. "There are five fundamental articles to the surrender. I will read each one, and if you wish, you may ask for clarification. Your opportunity to ask for clarification will only be considered after I read each article. There will be no review permitted once the entire surrender has been read. Should we agree to amend an article, the document will be appropriately altered. There is no negotiation here. Is that understood?"

Dennison acknowledged his understanding and asked Kyle if he could remove the Spider Drone from the area altogether, because it was distracting.

Kyle refused to do so. "The Drone stays! Worry less about it and more about getting this surrender completed.

"Article one reads as follows: Salmon will no longer be permitted to maintain extensive military air assets. You will be permitted to retain sufficient assets to protect your city and supporting lands. This does not apply to unarmed air transportation assets, provided they are not used for military purposes."

Based on the Council's body language, this first requirement was something they weren't ready for, and that was confirmed by the first question. "We provide air protection for a number of villages to the south and east. What's to become of those people?" asked Dennison.

"Are they Salmon citizens?" James asked.

"They are not. They are part of the indigenous human population, not unlike the people of Draegon," he replied.

"What are you protecting them from? The only menaces I can think of are you. They didn't need your protection before you arrived on this planet. Why do they need it now?" James prodded.

"There is still a strong threat the winged predators will return. These simple farmers cannot repel the creatures," Dennison replied.

"How many villages are we talking about here, and what's the total human headcount?" asked Kyle.

The Prime Minister looked to his right to a middle-aged man dressed in military clothing and asked him to answer the question. "There are twenty-one villages and perhaps one hundred thousand people spread across an area of 250,000 miles. We are patrolling the area daily," he responded.

"Prime Minister, I find it difficult to come to grips with this contradiction. On one hand, you provide protection for innocent farmers and herdsmen, while on the other hand, you armed a tyrant who slaughtered thousands of innocent farmers and herdsmen. James, how do we deal with this? We cannot leave these people unprotected because of the actions of this government," Kyle said.

James's demeanor changed after he heard what was at stake. "I suggest we permit them to continue their patrols, but only below fifty thousand feet. We will use armed drones to patrol above that, since they have no need to patrol beyond the mountain range that separates us to the north. I think I'm okay with all this, but let's be clear, your air assets will be limited to only what is required to carry out the patrols," responded James.

"Ryan, please adjust the documents to reflect that understanding. Salmon will be permitted to continue the patrol of the air space over their city and the lands to the south and east below fifty thousand feet with limited assets, and we will patrol the skies above. We'll move on now," declared Kyle.

"Article Two: Salmon will be permitted to maintain ground forces and ground-based air-defense assets. You will not be permitted to maintain any weapons that could be deployed for long-range assaults against neighboring sites," Kyle read.

Just then, an aide appeared at a window, waving a piece of paper, trying to get someone's attention. There was no chance he was entering the building with the Drone standing watch. "Marcus, see what that soldier wants. He seems excited about something. I see our delivery boy too. Let him in with the food," James directed.

Marcus walked out through the hole in the wall where a large set of doors used to be. The soldier and he talked for a few seconds before Marcus took the note from him and walked back in with the guard and refreshments in tow. Without saying a word, he went directly to the woman at the end of the table, handed her the piece of paper, and then retook his seat. She, in turn, walked over to the Prime Minister's chair and whispered something into his ear. He nodded, and she returned to her seat.

"Colonel Donner, we understand your need to ensure your flank is protected, but the presence of the three war machines above our city has caused a mass exodus of the population to the forests because they fear imminent destruction."

Kyle looked directly at James and spoke, "James, it is not our intent to have people running for their lives because of us. They will be injured or worse, and that's unacceptable."

"I agree," responded James. With that, he touched his lapel communicator. "Commander Diamond, are you online? Please position Pegasus at twenty thousand feet over the city. Have all our other assets pull back to one hundred miles and maintain position. The Explorers are to return to their normal patrol grids, but stay on alert status," directed James.

"We are making this accommodation solely out of compassion for your citizens. Be advised the vessel I have directed into a fixed position over your city is a far worse nightmare than what you've seen so far. Do not put us into a situation where we have to provide an example of its destructive power," cautioned James.

"Mr. Chandler, we find it interesting that your airships and weapons are quite capable of mass destruction, and we wonder why you would believe there is a need to deploy such an arsenal just to protect your city," commented Dennison.

Before Kyle could answer, James was on another verbal offensive. "That *arsenal* is the only reason you murderers didn't kill all of our citizens when you decided that women and children were better targets of opportunity than military assets. That *arsenal* is the reason you didn't have better success the second time you tried to do it again, and that *arsenal* is what's going to put an end to you if this Council does not sign this document of surrender. Does that about sum it up for you, Mr. Prime Minister?"

There wasn't a sound in the room, and once again Kyle found himself having to move the focus away from James's eagerness to find an excuse, any excuse, to put these members down.

Kyle began again, "Okay, I'll assume Article Two is accepted as written, so we're moving on.

"Article Three obligates your government to provide engineering assets to assist in the reclamation of Bridgetown, which was badly damaged during your first attack. We can see that your architects possess all the skills to make this right. You will provide these resources because it represents the first honorable act we will have seen from you."

There were no comments from across the table. I think they were still trying to collect themselves after James's last salvo.

"Article Four speaks to the proliferation of advanced weaponry. This entire unfortunate series of events began because you provided lethal weapons to a society built on a culture of barbarism. We are not sure how many other farmers you've armed with similar equipment and manpower, but the practice ends today. You will make available a comprehensive list of all the settlements in possession of these weapons and an inventory of what they have. As far as Draegon is concerned, we will deal with them," stated Kyle.

"There are no inventories or lists to provide you, sir," replied the Prime Minister, cautious not to make eye contact with James. "Draegon was the exception, not the norm."

"Good. Let's move to Article Five," continued Kyle. "This article speaks to the establishment of a global governing body. Not to rule over the planet, but to discuss and pass resolutions to prevent the type of actions we're addressing today. Salmon will have a presence on this Council as voting members and status as one of the founding cities. For this organization to have teeth behind its resolutions, it must have the military might to enforce them, to your point about our weapons. We will provide that resource.

"Salmon and Bridgetown will provide members representing their cities and an oath to never again take provocative action that could upset the balance of the planet without clear resolution from the Council. These are the Articles of Surrender that must be signed. We will allow you five days to take this before your citizens. Should you refuse to sign, we will remove your government by force of arms. Until then, our fleet will remain in your air space to be sure you understand our resolve to get this done. I assume that's understood?" Kyle asked

"That is understood," replied Dennison.

"Marcus, withdraw the Drones back to the ship. Prime Minister, find our escort, please, and have them lead us back to our ship. Remember, five days," said Kyle.

As we lifted off, I noticed that James seemed withdrawn. Kyle finally took James aside to figure out what was bothering him. When they returned, Kyle gave Marcus and me a signal to keep the conversation low-key until we landed. As the Defender touched down at Bridgetown and we came down the ramp, James immediately left us without saying a word.

Kyle, Marcus, and I walked casually across the courtyard to where our scooters were parked. As we walked, Kyle shared with us that the admiral was in the hospital in dire condition and quite likely wouldn't survive the night. Apparently, James had received the news once we boarded our ship.

"I knew he was depressed and a bit weak, but not near death," I remarked.

"You're not alone! Apparently, ever since the attack on Bridgetown, the admiral's health has been worsening by the day. I think that partly explains why it seems James has absolutely no tolerance for these people. He holds them responsible for his father's health issues. The admiral has lost his will to live. At his age, that's a recipe for bad news," replied Kyle.

I suggested we attend the Medical Center to comfort James, but Kyle insisted that if the admiral did indeed succumb to his condition tonight, it would be better if only his loved ones were at his bedside. In the morning, we received the news by special messenger that the admiral had passed away quietly during the night, with his family at his side. As stubborn as he could be, he was one of us, and even Sabrina cried when the news was delivered.

We all decided to take the day off and be with our families. Cateria and I took the girls to the ranch to spend the day by the serenity of the river. Sabrina and Kyle were going to the Great Hall, where a shelter had been established for the homeless. Marcus suggested that he was just going to read and relax, but since the pretty nurse, Susan, told Sabrina she was doing the same, it was quite likely they would be doing it together. The drama was going to begin in earnest over the next few days, and this might be the last quiet time we'd have for a while.

The admiral had asked that his remains be placed in a capsule and propelled out toward the stars to be with Vanguard. An Explorer had been outfitted to accommodate friends and family for the trip and the celebration of the admiral's life. As much as it was a solemn time, it was a time to remember a man who truly epitomized the warrior mantra. He had spent his life in the service of the Children of Vanguard. It was time for these children to thank him for that service.

Twenty-One

The Vanguard Council

The following day, the CRB met in special session to discuss the best way to honor the admiral's memory. It was decided that a sculptured likeness would be commissioned and positioned as a cenotaph in the middle of a fountain of life. The site for this memorial would be outside the entrance to the Protectorate headquarters.

Kyle agreed to unveil the monument with a public ceremony to be broadcast throughout Bridgetown. With all this going on, it was very difficult to focus on our upcoming meeting to sign the Articles of Surrender, which we had postponed to get through the official mourning period. Time was catching up to us, and we weren't prepared for what had to be done.

After the statue discussion, we proceeded to update the members about our meetings in Salmon. Kyle also took the opportunity to introduce the CRB to the concept of the new Vanguard Council and his vision for its role in the global management of the planet. The CRB members were mildly interested; as long as it didn't affect them, they seemed indifferent. Kyle reminded them that the CRB would be working closely with this new entity on matters outside normal Bridgetown business. He suggested there would be an impact on the CRB and Bridgetown.

"Ryan and I will be resigning our seats on the CRB to become executive members of the new body. These resignations will be effective in one month. There will be other changes as well. The Protectorate will no longer act as a policing force solely for Bridgetown. Their responsibilities will now be on the global level, reporting to the new Council. In their place will be a new localized police force to be called the Bridgetown Police Command. The new force will serve the everyday needs of our citizens and will be made up of many of the same men and women currently serving with the Protectorate.

"Assets of the current Protectorate organization will be split out to ensure the new local police force has what they need to be effective. All air assets and your good friends, the Spider Drones, will remain the property of the Protectorate Air Command, headed by Colonel James Donner, who will resign his seat on the CRB. That will mean three vacant seats to fill. I recommend that the members use the voting system to fill two of them rather than appointees. James will identify the Protectorate replacement in the days to come. Once we have left our posts, your first order of business will be to vote in a new chairperson and secretary from within the membership. Are there any questions so far?" asked Kyle.

"Are we to assume the Protectorate and not the Bridgetown Police will be responsible for the city's security?" asked Senator Doctor Mary Jones, representing the Medical Community.

"You would assume correctly. The Spider Drones will continue to patrol the city, supported as always by the fly-over drone patrols. The only caveat to that is the Bridgetown Police will be required to man the Pulse Gatling gun emplacements should they be required," responded Kyle.

"Don't take this wrong, Kyle, because we owe you everything we have, but what authority allows you to decide where the Protectorate goes and who will replace them? For that matter, what the new landscape of Bridgetown will look like?" asked Senator Smith, one of the elected representatives.

"John, that's a legitimate question, and I'm not offended you've asked. My commitment to this Council and the citizens of Bridgetown has always been to act in their best interests, regardless of the political ramifications or my own well-being. Without the Vanguard Council, there is no global protection for Bridgetown, which we've all seen leaves us exposed and is not in the best interests of our people.

"If you would prefer, we can take this entire subject to referendum and let the people decide if I've overstepped my authority in this matter. That's the CRB's right, and I have always supported that right. Either way, Ryan, James, and I will resign our seats and join the Vanguard Council," declared Kyle.

"A vote by the people will not be necessary. I withdraw my question. You have always and continue to represent our best interests," responded Senator Smith.

I knew that once the Chambers closed business that day, Smith would suffer the indignation of the other Council members. Although it wasn't written anywhere, it was understood that challenging Kyle's right to do anything was just not done in public forum. For instance, once again he had volunteered James and me to be part of one of his audacious plans without asking us. Every time he did, it pissed us off, but we knew he needed us to help him, and we needed him to guide us.

Pissed or not, we would go where he went, plain and simple. Knowing that wasn't going to stop us from protesting his right to speak for us, but we knew he'd just say he was sorry, and we'd be sucked right in again. Shortly after this minor drama, the meeting was adjourned, and Kyle and I went to meet with James to go over strategies for the surrender signing. When we arrived at the briefing room, James was already there and almost his old self. He was friendly and loose, which seemed strange, but I guess he knew his duties had to be fulfilled whether his father was there or not. I was quick to tell him that Kyle had volunteered us yet again without asking. James just shook his head and shrugged.

"What difference does it make? We always do what he wants in the end anyway. At least when he volunteers us, we can use him as the excuse when things get all screwed up," responded James.

Most of the rest of the day was spent discussing how we saw all this working and how best to introduce the new Council to the citizens of both cities. It was well after dark by the time we decided to call it a day. When I arrived at my residence, Cateria and the girls were busily sewing a "quilt." I had never heard of a quilt and had no idea why anyone would want to work so hard making one when we had perfectly good blankets in the Supplies Center. Cateria schooled me that things of real quality came from the hands of real people and not a bunch of mechanical morons.

Although I had never heard the production robots referred to as "mechanical morons," she seemed intent on finishing this quilt thing. When I asked why we needed it in the middle of the summer, she glared at me, and just for a moment, I felt like one of those mechanical morons she was referring to.

"Ryan, this is our marriage quilt, which will be draped across our shoulders during the wedding ceremony," she snapped. There was no way I was going down that road.

I didn't sleep well that night. There was so much going on, and my brain was reeling from it all. Cateria was getting bigger and more emotional by the day. Put altogether, what you had was madness. I guess we were ready for her delivery as much as was possible, but when it came to this stuff, I was a babbling fool and would be even worse when the moment finally arrived. Cateria, on the other hand, was sleeping as soon as her head hit the pillow. She was taking the upcoming event in effortless stride. To her, it was what happened in life and something that was as normal as breathing in and out. I was doing a lot more breathing in lately than out, but God she was beautiful lying there beside me, softly snoring. How did I get this lucky anyway?

At 08:00 hours the next morning, James, Kyle, Marcus, and I were eating breakfast in the briefing room, going over the meeting plans one more time. Our objective was simple; we would have a signed surrender before noon, and we would be onto the next phase, which would be implementation of the agreement. Just over an hour later, an aide walked in and announced that the Defender with our guests was about to land. James instructed that as soon as it did, the passengers were to be brought directly to the briefing room by escort and without conversation of any kind.

When the Prime Minister and his entourage walked into the room, they weren't the same group that had seemed so confident when all this began. Their perceived supremacy over this virgin planet was surrendered as a consequence of bad judgment.

"I think we pretty well have agreement on all the articles of the surrender. Now we need to set our signatures to it, unless there are questions as yet unanswered," declared Kyle.

"Mr. Chandler, while we had this time apart, we took your document to the governing body of Salmon and our military establishment. We have a couple of points that require clarification before we affix our signatures," Dennison declared. "Is it your intent to occupy Salmon? Will you take reprisal actions against our government or military as a consequence of the events leading up to this surrender?"

Kyle answered immediately. "No, we have enough to fill our plates as it is without trying to manage someone else's affairs—and no, we have no intention of seeking a pound of flesh for crimes against us. What would be the point of punishing your people for actions they did not initiate?" responded Kyle. "Just as a sidebar, we thought *you guys* were the governing body. If you're not, why are you here?"

"We have confused you. We do speak for our people, but like your CRB, we must update the Salmon Council with our progress," he responded. "Our people in Draegon, what plans do you have for them when you displace Uthess?"

"That's entirely up to them. If they stand with him against us, they will suffer the same fate he does. If they stand down, they will be arrested and returned to you, where you will administer the appropriate justice for their actions against the innocents," replied James.

"Mr. Prime Minister, we can discuss the details of Draegon another time, and since it has nothing to do with this document, I must insist we get on with it. Will you sign?" Kyle said.

"We shall affix our signatures," Dennison replied.

"As shall we," Kyle declared. "James, call in our fleet over Salmon."

There it was. Signatures had been applied, hands were shaken, and a new order was created from the blood of others. There was a general sense of relief, closure, and anticipation.

Kyle continued, "Now I want to spend time speaking to this new Vanguard Council and its formation. The Council will be headquartered in Salmon."

James almost fell out of his chair, Marcus just stared blankly at Kyle, and I was too numb to speak. Kyle could see we were shocked by his announcement, and before he said another word about the Council, he knew we were owed an explanation for what amounted to a slap in the face. The other side of the table was grinning from ear to ear because their city would be the center of the most powerful group on the planet.

Kyle excused us, and we left the room. James had daggers in his eyes. I had never seen him so pissed. He acted like a man betrayed, and that isn't good for a warrior in control of the entire military might of the planet.

"Okay, guys, I can see you're really upset with me—and you should be. It was more than just a little presumptuous of me to make so important a decision without your counsel in advance. For that, I'm truly sorry, and it will never happen again," Kyle explained humbly.

James's face started to lose its bright red glow, and I was breathing a sigh of relief. Our initial shock was now being replaced with a "here we go again" acceptance of Kyle's antics.

"You're going to tell us this is just one of your practical jokes and you're not really considering this idea—right? People died for the right to have the new Council positioned in Bridgetown," James stated.

Kyle's expression went deadly serious, almost frightening. "James, that's bullshit, and you know it. People died because we were attacked, long before the idea of this Council was ever considered. Look around you, guys! Our city is in shambles. Our people are in shambles. This Council must have a forum that speaks to our authority and control. This little briefing room just doesn't cut it. Put aside your homophobic personalities for a moment, and let's look at the broader picture.

"The three of us and with Marcus's help will one day hold the fortunes of this planet in our hands, perhaps much of this end of the universe. Everyone else on this Council is merely a tool to that end, including their cities and their resources. A little geography is a small price to pay to get us there."

James said, "If you try to make us relocate our families there, we will assassinate you and steal your wife. No, wait a minute, not your wife. We'll steal your kid instead. By the way, we'd like to call your son by name, but apparently he doesn't have one. Is there something we should know? Are you the father?"

"His name is James Edward Chandler if you must know. The reason I never mentioned it is because I forgot. Simple as that, and by the way, I'm promoting you, so shut up. Now, are we a collective front going back into this meeting? Are we ready to take charge? If so, let's be done with this," ordered Kyle, smiling.

As soon as James heard that Kyle's son had his name, I could tell that Kyle had succeeded in stealing another piece of his soul. I have often wondered over the years if Kyle's son got his name in that split second so Kyle could win the day. I was going to ask Sabrina, but I was frankly not brave enough.

When we returned to the room, Kyle made no attempt to justify our absence. Without missing a beat, we were back at it. "The Protectorate, headed by Admiral James Donner, will be in the service of the Vanguard Council and will act on any and all resolutions involving the use of the military. Ryan and I have resigned our positions with the CRB to take seats on this newly formed body as voting members. Our respective cities will each seat seven members as the founding fathers of this institution. Your government can appoint three members, but the remaining four members from each city must be duly elected by the citizens. As we invite other members to join from the surrounding settlements, they will be given one seat each."

"Mr. Prime Minister, if you or any of the rest of your group wishes to be seated on the Council, you must resign from your government posts. We can have no conflicts of interest where the affairs of the planet are involved. Otherwise, please present your selections within sixty days. We must move with resolve to get this thing off the ground. Within the next 120 days, I want to call to order the first meeting of The Vanguard Council."

Things around Bridgetown were cautiously settled for the next few weeks, but not for our little group. Kyle had decided that any actions with respect to Draegon could wait and be dealt with as one of the first agenda items for the newly formed Council. He believed it would be a good test to see if emotions and personal agendas could be set aside to make rational decisions. James's position, on the other hand, was that we should take care of this and keep it out of the hands of the Council to avoid creating conflict in the voting so early in the game. One way or another, this was going to get done. I hoped it wouldn't result in the loss of any more lives.

So much was going on; it was hard to remain focused on any one thing. Kyle had already suggested that a high-speed rail system should be looked at to join Salmon and Bridgetown. Once again, he convinced the CRB and the citizens that this was the way of the future to promote interaction between the cities. Being Kyle, he formed a subcommittee to study the concept. This committee was made up of engineers and environmentalists from both cities. As much I think to piss off the engineering establishment as anything else, he asked Marcus to oversee their progress. Everything seemed to be unfolding as Kyle envisioned. James had agreed to establish a form of air transit service between the two cities. Both cities would become cojoined, and the citizenry on both sides would be given new freedom of movement and interaction.

True to his word, Kyle scheduled the first session of The Vanguard Council. As expected, he wasted little time seeking nominations and getting our voted representatives in place. Unexpectedly, the seven members from Salmon were all voted in by their citizens. For the most part, they were scholars, scientists, and physicians. Curious though was the absence of the five people who had signed the surrender.

Kyle's take on their absence was that it was a political and prudent strategy, given their involvement in the failed attacks. To present the members, we scheduled a formal dinner in Bridgetown on the eve of the first Vanguard Council meeting. This social interaction might offer a sense of how the different personalities might meld as we all took our seats in Chambers. So much had happened in what seemed so short a time, it made me dizzy, but Kyle never lost focus.

Time passed quickly and uneventfully. Before we had even taken a deep breath, the first meeting was only three days away. Prior to the event, we decided to collect the families, including Marcus and Susan, and spend a relaxing day at Joshal's ranch. Although it was not a working ranch, the house and barns were erected, and the scenery was so serene and beautiful near the river. It was a day of swimming in the river and drinking too much wine. Near dinner, neighboring settlers drifted in and brought a small hog to roast. As much as Sabrina liked to lecture us about the heart-killing effects of meat, she was covered in the same grease and fat as the rest of us.

Everyone but the settlers stayed the night because we were too drunk to do anything else. Once the neighbors drifted back to their farms, the girls went in to drink and giggle some more until they passed out. Us guys sat by the fading fire, lamenting all the events of the last twelve years. It was nice to joke and remember calmer times without making policy or posturing. We passed out just as the fire died. It was a good end to a good day.

Another interesting event occurred during our time off. By no one's insistence, Cateria's girls began to call me "Father." At first, I was a bit uncomfortable with it, but Cateria seemed supportive, as did our friends and the settlers. I had gone from a book nerd to a fully functioning father figure in what seemed a heartbeat.

The following day was much too short, and before we knew it, we were headed back to Bridgetown to prepare for the dinner. A Defender was tasked with retrieving our new members and their spouses from Salmon by seven in the evening, but before then, there was still much to do.

As the Defender touched down, James had a military color-guard escort the visitors to the dinner. Earlier in the evening, Sabrina had shamed Kyle into including some of the "common folk" on the invitee list. According to her, our heads were so swollen from all our newfound prestige that we were losing touch with the average citizen. She sure knew Kyle's trigger points. Although he pretended to be against it for a while, in the end, a few more bodies one way or another wasn't going to change anything. Cateria assured us that we needn't fret about the common folk being there because they would be kept in the background so as not to embarrass our menfolk.

Another sarcastic remark engineered no doubt by Sabrina. I think what peeved us off the most was the way the girls kept referring to themselves and everyone else as "common folk." Another ploy Sabrina surely engineered. I had come to believe that our women had signed some sort of secret witch's pact to keep us under control, and now they had sucked James's wife, Helen, and the pretty young nurse, Susan, into their conspiracies.

The dinner went surprising well, and it seemed like all the members of the new Council were genuinely committed to its success. Sabrina, of course, told Kyle that although all the members were brilliant scholars, she doubted that this group of eggheads could ever separate logic from compassion. Kyle assured her that beneath their outward demeanor, they were still men and women with the same compassions for their fellow man as us, or they would not have wanted to be on this Council. She wasn't convinced, but she trusted that he would be able to decide when to intervene.

Salmon architects were working feverishly to finish the official permanent home site for the Vanguard Council. To keep peace, Kyle declared that until completed, the initial meetings would take place in Bridgetown—to be precise, in the CRB chambers. It was a simple solution, and the room was already outfitted with the necessary furniture and electronic communication systems for such business. Salmon could have provided the same temporary meeting accommodations, but I think it was Kyle's way of trying to appease some strained egos.

Promptly at 09:00 hours the following morning, members of our newly formed body began filtering in. There was no particular seat assignment, but Kyle asked that, given our small size, we sit in the seats closest to floor level to keep the circle tight. The first item on the agenda was the consideration of the Council's charter, which Marcus and I had worked hard to put into a written document. We knew it would be edited, but it was at least something to bring forward for consideration. The only other item to be dealt with was the Draegon issue. We all agreed that for a first meeting, this was as complex as it should get. Just before hearing from James, an urgent message was delivered from the communications center in Salmon to their senior representative on the new Council. The message was handed to James, who read it aloud for the entire room to hear.

"Council members, thirty minutes ago, the emergency beacon was initiated from Draegon. There is no more detail because Draegon is not responding to Salmon's hails. The Protectorate will dispatch a recon team to the site to determine whether the emergency is real or just another Draegon lie," James declared.

Immediately after reading the message, James left to make the arrangements. Kyle continued to lead the meeting for another hour after James's departure and then advised that until the Draegon issue was resolved, we would adjourn. Arrangements were made to return the Salmon members to their city, and Kyle and I left to join up with James. When we arrived at the Control Center, James was there with Marcus, looking at some recon videos from Draegon.

"Moments ago, our recon video confirmed that a massive swarm of those mutated bats have laid siege to Draegon. As of yet, we have no clear estimates on the number of creatures involved, but it appears to be into the thousands," commented James.

Twenty-Two

We Were Responsible

"What actions are we considering, James?" asked Kyle.

"I have called in another ten Defenders to attend the site, and your timing is perfect because additional video is just streaming in," James responded.

We watched intently as the Defenders swooped in over the Draegon with their pulse weapons in full fire mode. As soon as the bats sensed they had become the hunted, their first instinct was to retreat toward the southern mountains. Our forces made no attempt to block their retreat. The mission at this initial stage was only to put an end to the loss of life on the ground. James tasked two surveillance drones to track the creatures' retreat from sixty thousand feet. With any luck, perhaps we would finally target where they were hiding.

Scattering the bats already on the ground proved to be a much tougher challenge. Terrified Draegon citizens were running everywhere, and structures made it virtually impossible to get weapon fixes on the predators in pursuit. We were left with little alternative but to wait until the creatures lifted off with their prey and took them out in flight. It was almost unbearable to watch the creatures through video zoom tearing living humans apart in front of us, defenseless to help. James instructed Defenders to get on the ground and deposit the five or six Spider Drones each carried as standard protocol. Kyle and Marcus went to sub-terminals and reprogrammed the Drones, using video images to attack the bats on sight. We all understood that the Drones would fire on the bats whether they had a victim or not. This would mean innocents would be caught in the crossfire. We had no alternative and no time.

The first Defender landed as close as it could to a large group of the bats feasting on their recent kills. As soon as the Spider Drones were deployed, the momentum began to change. Bats protected by the houses from the air were now cornered by the Spider Drones on the ground. In a few short minutes, the first five of Kyle's babies took down twenty-eight bats. The predators must have realized instinctively that a hunter even more dangerous than themselves was now in the game because they began to take to air.

Within an hour, fifty Drones were on the ground and had either killed or forced hundreds of bats back into the air. As the predators lifted off into the sky, Defenders and armed, airborne attack drones waited to finish the job. The citizens now safe from the bats were just as terrified by the Spider Drones and scurried into whatever shelters they could find. Although it was sad to watch them in this state, for the time being, it was for the best.

"We've got to put more resources on the ground—and quick! There are still hundreds of these fucking things down there. Every minute we waste is only adding to the body count," Kyle declared. "I think we had better increase the patrols around Bridgetown and Salmon, just in case we're next on the list."

James was sure that wouldn't happen but nonetheless decided it was easier to do it than to argue about the merits of doing it. Communications indicated that there were no responses to our hails from Draegon. We agreed that one of two conditions were in play here. Either Uthess was ignoring our hails because he didn't want our help, or the city infrastructure was in ruins and they couldn't answer. Soon after, low level recon videos were on our monitors. As the screens came to life again, the carnage was undeniable. Bodies and pieces of bodies were everywhere. It was almost impossible to determine if any were still alive, albeit, based on the rivers of blood flowing in the streets, the answer seemed obvious. Now was the time to get Sabrina involved to help organize medical and relief efforts.

"How soon can we get people down there to help?" I asked.

"If we focus on what must be done, we can be fully operational in Draegon by sunrise tomorrow. In the meantime, Kyle and Marcus can program a hundred more Spider Drones to help us. There are still bats on the ground scattered throughout the city. We need to battle one predator with another," responded James. "Let's reconvene in two hours with Sabrina present. Ryan, go to library, find everything you can about bats. We need to know their habits, weaknesses, nesting rituals, hunting tactics, and anything else that might help us destroy the bastards," James instructed.

By the time I finished at the library, I was already late for the meeting. When I entered the briefing room, all eyes turned in my direction, which left me a bit unnerved. I wasted little time finding a seat off to the side to avoid any direct eye contact with James and Kyle. Sabrina, as usual, came prepared for the meeting. With her was the Chief of Emergency Medicine, Doctor Elliot Mather, a hand-picked Triage Team made up of four general medicine doctors, four emergency trained nurses, and two technicians. The videos were replayed, and Sabrina and her team seemed stunned by the brutality of the event.

"This is monstrous!" Sabrina exclaimed. "We have to get our people on the ground and establish relief camps as quickly as possible. Elliot, how many people do you think we'll need? If we don't have enough, Kyle will get us help from Salmon."

"These people had no warning of this event. There must be five thousand people either dead or dying. I would suggest we put at least two hundred doctors and five hundred nurses in play, or we'll lose most of the wounded," responded Elliot.

"Kyle, can you help us out?" asked Sabrina.

"We'll find them! James, open up a communications link with Prime Minister Dennison right away, and I'll ask for his help," Kyle directed.

"Done!" responded James.

"James, how many Protectors can we send in to get and keep control of the survivors? Is there any risk of another attack while we're on the ground?" asked Sabrina.

"We have two thousand soldiers on their way. I'm leaving within the hour to coordinate the ground efforts. I've moved thirty Defenders around the perimeter of the city. Nothing gets through our net alive. Since we're getting no response from the ground, it suggests a total collapse of their infrastructure, which was already loosely managed before this.

"I have four field commanders assigned to quadrants of the city to bring order and management. Three Explorers are on the pad, ready to load all your personnel and equipment, Sabrina. I have scheduled your departure for thirty minutes from now. There is no time to waste. Marcus and Ryan, you will accompany Kyle and me," James summarized.

"We'll be ready," Sabrina assured us and then left.

"James, until we arrived, there didn't appear to be any resistance from the ground against these things. Where are the soldiers? Look at the videos; there isn't any evidence of a military presence anywhere. What do you make of that?" Marcus asked.

"I think we all know the answer to that. Uthess didn't send any, and we're going to find out why," James replied.

Kyle and James went to the communications room to speak with Salmon, while Marcus and I went over the data I had recorded at the library. Twenty minutes later, we were walking up the ramp of a Defender, officially initiating the relief effort. Thirty minutes later, we had joined the three Explorers hovering over Draegon with the Protectors aboard.

"How are we going to work this, James?" Kyle asked.

"This is the easy part! The Explorer Juggernaut is en-route and will land in the city center to disperse the Spider Drones.

The Drones' primary purpose will be to link up with those already there and sweep every inch of the city for any lingering bat presence. They will also patrol the streets and keep citizens safely locked in their homes until we can issue an 'all clear.' This action will be followed closely by the deployment of the Protectors and fire teams to assist in recovery of the wounded and the destruction of bat carcasses to avoid any disease risks. We should have the streets cleared within twelve hours and an established military government within twenty-four hours," said James.

Right on cue, the black mass of the Juggernaut hovered down to the surface. Once the ramps were extended, Spider Drones scurried down and immediately began darting up and down the streets in all directions. It left me remembering our first encounter with these metal menaces and our reaction to how they moved. I could only imagine the horror the citizens were feeling, trapped within their homes and fearing for their lives—first because of the bats, and now because of this new threat. If they only knew that Kyle's "babies" were there to protect them, perhaps it might be different.

Moments after the Drone deployment, the Windsurfer and Phoenix were hovering down to the east and west of the city center. Soon, streams of Protectors would be emerging and forming up into thirty-man platoons. Like the Drones, they would be dispersed, leaving a rear guard to secure the areas adjacent to their landing craft. I could tell by Kyle's expression that he was eager to get on the ground and be part of this mission.

As James was giving the order to land our ship, a message was received from one of the ground commanders indicating we might want to activate the video cams on Drones fifteen through twenty-one. The commander went on to say, "The Drones are sending back videos and are taking light defensive fire from the compound in the center of the city. We have dispatched two platoons to the area to take control of the situation."

"Make it quick! Once the Drones initiate their defensive programs, they'll terminate any aggressors and innocent citizens that might be in the area," Kyle warned.

James immediately activated the video monitors. It was a surreal sight! Draegon soldiers were positioned on the compound wall, firing down at the Drones. Not with sophisticated laser weapons, but with primitive crossbows and fire-tipped spears. If it wasn't so dangerous, it would have been comical to see ancient medieval weapons pitted against the power of modern technology. The Drone closest to the compound had activated its defensive programming and was already in full fire mode.

"Kyle, can you shut it down from here? The bloody thing is picking off humans for target practice. We don't need this; we're trying to help these people," pleaded James. Immediately, Kyle went to the Bridge to use their transmission equipment to shut the unit off.

"Helmsman, hover down into the compound. Kyle, as soon as we land, redirect the Drones away from the site before they destroy the place. We're going to have to get to whoever is left in charge and calm them down. Communications, get hold of the ground commander and have him surround the compound, but stand out of range of their weapons. I do not want another incident," ordered James.

Our ship veered sideways over to the compound and began a slow descent. As we were landing, the soldiers on the wall turned all their attention toward us in a futile attempt to chase us away. James went to the Bridge and began speaking over the loud speakers. "Soldiers of Draegon, we are here to help you. Stand down! We wish to speak to your king."

Nothing. They continued to rain arrows and spears down on us from the walls. It was a hopeless gesture, but they were clearly terrified. James had enough. "Weapons Officer, hit them with the Sonic Disrupter. Keep it within safe limits. I do not want any fatalities here. They're only trying to defend their king," ordered James.

Although we couldn't hear it inside the craft, we could see the effect over the monitors. The soldiers on the walls and in the courtyard began to drop to their knees, cradling their heads. This was over! James suggested we move now before they regained their equilibrium. With that, the ramp was extended, and we exited the craft with a small Protector escort and proceeded directly into the Great Hall.

The sonic weapon was remarkably effective. We met no resistance as we approached the throne room doors. As we burst through the doors, the shock of our unexpected arrival caused the guards within the room to draw their swords. All through this, Uthess sat calmly in his throne, surrounded by his advisors.

"King Uthess, have your personal guard stand down. We are here to help your people, nothing more. Do not create a situation that will only lead to unimaginable trouble for you and your men!" shouted Kyle.

The king, realizing no good could come from this, raised his hand, and the guards sheaved their swords.

"Uthess, we are pleased to find you safe. How many men have you lost defending the city?" asked Kyle.

"Lost? We have lost no men. We have beaten the beasts back into the sky and saved my throne. There is no loss here," replied Uthess.

"I meant the soldiers sent into the city to protect the citizens. Surely you must have hundreds of casualties?" Kyle asked again.

"I have sent no soldiers into the city. I have many subjects but few soldiers. I would not risk their lives to protect farmers. There are plenty of farmers, but they have but one king. It is only fitting they give their lives to preserve mine. I am divine, anointed by the gods. Even now they come to my aid. Have you not come at the command of The Vanguard?" Uthess asked in his most arrogant tone.

It happened so unexpectedly no one had a chance to react, and once done, we all just stood there paralyzed. No sooner had

Uthess uttered his arrogant words than James drew his sidearm and shot him through the center of his forehead. Just for a second, Uthess remained seated, staring blankly at James. Then, almost in slow motion, his lifeless body slid out of the throne and down the four steps, coming to rest virtually at our feet as a pool of blood formed around his body.

Once the king's security and advisors realized what had just happened, they reached for their weapons. Kyle moved as quickly as James to control the situation. "Rupert, tell your generals and guard to stand down or suffer the same fate as this lunatic at our feet!" commanded Kyle.

Slowly, the generals slid their weapons back into their hilts. "For this action, you will deal with The Vanguard, and I will be there when they crush your women and children under their feet!" spouted Prince Rupert.

"No you won't. Captain, shoot him directly through the heart," Kyle commanded.

I couldn't believe what was going on. Had we all gone mad? As soon as Kyle issued the order, the captain of our escort stepped forward and shot Rupert point blank through the chest.

"Stop it, Kyle! This is murder! This is not why we're here! We're not executioners!" I yelled.

Kyle lowered his head. "Captain, relieve the rest of them of their weapons and escort them to the ship. We're done here!"

While all of this was going on, James stood still, pointing his weapon in the direction of the lifeless body of the king. I reached out and gently pressed down on his arm, causing him to ever so slowly lower his sidearm. "Are you okay, James?" I asked.

"I'm okay," James responded meekly.

"Remind me never to piss you two off. You guys give a whole new meaning to the phrase 'take no prisoners,'" Marcus chirped.

Kyle immediately turned and faced us. "Gentlemen, this never happened, and anyone who says it did will deal with me. Have I made myself clear?" Everyone nodded. "Good. Let's get back to our ship and start doing what we came here to do before we were interrupted by this thing that never happened."

As we walked back toward our ship, James seemed to snap out of the moment. "I'm really sorry, guys! I can't believe I did that, but I just couldn't take another second of that asshole's crap, and I sure couldn't leave these poor people to suffer any more of his tyranny," James apologized.

"Admiral, you just make sure when we get to our ship you sit down and write fifty times, 'I will not kill tyrant kings.' Then you must give up sex for a week. No—make that a day! By the way, good shot! I think our big problem now is how we deal with the Draegon militia," replied Marcus.

"Why do I have to write lines and give up sex if Kyle doesn't?" James whined, now fully recovered and smiling.

"Because I'm the boss," Kyle piped in with a sly grin.

"You both should get your asses kicked. What was that anyway? Full-grown men having temper tantrums? You're not setting a very good example for the rest of us," I scolded. James and Kyle lowered their heads, pretending to be sorry. "Good—that's better," I closed.

As soon as we were safely back inside the Defender, James directed the loud speakers to be turned on so he could deliver a message to the soldiers just now recovering from the Sonic Disruptor effects.

"Soldiers of Draegon, your king is dead, as is his murderous consort, Price Rupert. This was the will of The Vanguard. Surrender your weapons and join us in saving your people, or die with them. You have one minute to decide."

Through the video monitors, we watched as one by one the soldiers dropped their weapons and made their way through the gates, where they were met by a platoon of Protectors. They were not greeted as prisoners but as comrades, and the groups moved away to continue saving the settlement.

With the aid of the Draegon militia, we were able to lock down the city in just over twelve hours. We also established four triage centers in preparation for Sabrina's arrival. Over eight hundred bat carcasses were torched where they lay. Sadly, over seven thousand human bodies were collected and moved to three large clearings outside of Draegon to await official declaration of death. Great care was taken to respect the corpses until loved ones could say their good-byes. No one would be there to grieve for Uthess and Rupert; their bodies were incinerated with the rest of the predators.

Slowly, the town's people that had been forced to stay in their homes for hours by the Spider Drones were allowed to start filtering into the streets. It was the most gut-wrenching sight we'd ever witnessed as the survivors searched through the collected remains for their loved ones, carrying them away to be mourned, each in their own way. James was concerned that if there was disease it would spread by allowing this. Kyle reminded him we had neither the right nor the heart to take away their need to honor their dead.

Sabrina's ship was the first of a steady stream of medical relief teams to arrive. As we watched Sabrina step onto the ramp with her team closely on her heels, I was almost knocked over with shock. There was Cateria. Why was she here? I wanted to run to her and plead she return to Bridgetown, but it wasn't the time, and as soon as Sabrina saw me staring in disbelief, she moved deliberately toward me.

"Ryan, she insisted on being a part of this humanitarian effort. Don't worry and don't be angry with her; she'll be fine. I'll make sure she doesn't leave my side. So, come on now. There's much to do if we are to save these people."

As she walked away to begin coordinating the effort, Kyle came up behind me and placed his hand on my shoulder. "My wife wouldn't bring her if she wasn't sure she could protect her. Not even ugly, man-eating, giant, fucking rodents will take on my Sabrina."

"I know that, but what help can Cateria be in the midst of all this death and suffering? Hasn't she already seen enough?" I moaned.

"This may be the best medicine for her. To be able to bring aid to others that have suffered the same loss as her will bring back meaning to her life. Ryan, I think this is a good thing," responded Kyle. We stood and watched for a couple more minutes before James yelled for us to get our asses moving and brought us back to the moment and the task at hand.

It would take over three months of around-the-clock efforts by all to bring a semblance of order back into the lives of the Draegon citizens. They had lost so much. These were long, grueling days, and we were all near exhaustion, but our resolve to save Draegon never waned. Beyond the seven thousand bodies that were found in the streets, another 2,600 would die on the operating tables. Twenty-three thousand were treated on site or sent to the medical centers in Bridgetown and Salmon. It was hard to believe all this happened in a six-hour span, and it brought into clear focus how deadly these creatures were. They had to be stopped!

I find it strange that even in the face of great tragedy, something good can emerge. We had been laboring for just over two months. Sometimes it seemed hopeless. Every chance I had, I spent at Cateria's side, but she kept scolding me for being overly protective. Even now, I remember with great clarity the moment Sabrina came into my tent and advised me that Cateria was having severe labor pains. I guess it was fortunate that James and Kyle were there to steady me because the shock of the announcement zapped whatever energy I had left, and I nearly fainted.

James made a Defender available. Cateria was carried onboard with a full medical team at her side, including Sabrina. Shortly after, Kyle, James, Marcus, and I paraded on board, and I went immediately to Cateria's side. Kyle then made the huge error of asking Sabrina how Cateria was doing. He should have known better.

"How do you think she's doing? She's in full labor five weeks early! If you want to be helpful, make sure James takes us directly to the Medical Center and lands this thing softly," she replied in an acidic tone.

The trip back to Bridgetown took only twenty minutes, which included a rather precise landing in the Medical Center garden. One thing was for sure—the garden wouldn't be a garden again for some time to come. I knew James would take heat for that once this was behind us because, of course, he was a man, and a man ruined the flowers in Sabrina's world. The efficiency of Sabrina and her team was a marvel of organization. From landing ramp to delivery room took less than five minutes. As soon as we entered the building, I was whisked away for a full body shower and clothing change while James and Kyle were dispatched on a top-secret mission for Sabrina. That left poor Marcus to sit with the love of his life, Susan, and drink coffee. He always seemed to get the tough jobs!

A few minutes later, I was stripped naked. Three nurses were washing me down head to toe and draping me in the traditional, ugly, pale blue gown. Just for a moment, I felt like the patient instead of the father-to-be. I was then escorted to the waiting room. Marcus was there waiting for me, minus Susan, who had been called to assist in the delivery preparation. I was so nervous!

Time was crawling by, and I probably checked the large clock on the wall fifty times in twenty minutes. I never realized just how long a minute could be when you're watching it go by. Where did James and Kyle go? Wherever it was, they left in a hurry, with Sabrina telling them there wasn't much time and she'd never forgive them if they were late. Another mystery!

Just when I thought this was never going to happen and I'd be doomed to waiting for the rest of my life with Marcus, who was never known for his light conversational skills, the main doors flung open. There were Kyle, James, Helen, and Cateria's girls, Dravon and Serri, almost running by me in the hall. In seconds, they disappeared around a corner. This was really nerve-racking, and I was about to walk down the hall and demand to know what was going on when two nurses walked into the room and instructed me to follow them.

I just about wet myself because the time had come. They requested Marcus come as well, which even in my state of mind I found strange. As we entered the delivery room, we were met by all our friends encircling Cateria's bed. A sense of doom was sucking my breath away. Something had gone wrong, and they were afraid to tell me.

"Ryan, come and sit beside Cateria on the bed. I made her a solemn promise that, come hell or high water, you two would be married before she gave birth—and you will. James, as chief authority of Bridgetown, will perform the service. Kyle, drape the quilt around their shoulders and hurry up. This baby is not going to wait much longer," ordered Sabrina.

At 10:34 on Friday, June 23, in the year 3617, Cateria and I were married, and at 10:41 the same night, my son, Joshal Kyle Evans, was born. Top that one, Kyle Chandler! While Cateria rested with the baby and girlfriends surrounding her bed, the menfolk, as Dravon described us, went out into the garden to get some cool evening air.

"Ryan, for a time there, we thought you were going to pass out again. That would have really have complicated this entire exercise. James and I were speaking a few minutes ago, and we noticed that your son is fairly well endowed. That kind of brought into question whether some tinkering was done with his DNA. Say it isn't so!" Kyle chuckled.

"Well, Mr. Chandler and Mr. Donner, you need not worry. The Evans clan is famous for the size of our genitals. I can't explain why, but the women seem to like it, assholes," I retorted.

Shortly after, my friends excused themselves and returned to Draegon. Sabrina sat with our son in the nursery for the rest of the night while Cateria fell into a deep sleep. I didn't fair too well in the sleep department. What relaxation I did get came from the realization that I had a son! Shit, I was so proud of

Cateria and myself for getting this done. All the other drama in our lives seemed to drift into the background . . . at least for the night.

In the morning, I had breakfast with Cateria and baby Joshal. It felt strange even saying it, but there we were. Just before we finished, four Protectors entered the room and advised me that I was required in the briefing room immediately. I hated when they used words like "immediately" or "urgently." I think it was their way of taking away any options you might have by making every event sound like life or death. I didn't want to leave my wife, but she insisted there was still much to do and I was important to getting it done.

When I arrived at the briefing room, the usual suspects were busy doing what had become the common exercise these days. Kyle, James, and Marcus were staring at another set of videos of yet another discovery that was sure to screw up my day.

"So, what's on the menu today?" I asked, trying to come across as someone who didn't have a care in the world.

"We found the colony of bats. The drones have sent us videos. You're not going to believe your eyes!" offered Marcus.

As I lowered myself into the only empty chair, right on cue, an aide walked through the door carrying another round of coffees and buns. If nothing else, James took care of even his reluctant guests. Finally I looked up at the screen and almost spit up my coffee. The videos showed a long, narrow gorge between two mountains. The gorge was perhaps twenty miles long and three miles wide. The most striking feature was that you couldn't see the mountain faces on either side because they were covered with hanging bats. Thousands of them! If that alone wasn't disgusting enough, some of the bats were small and obviously young. It was now apparent that the assumption about them being incapable of reproduction was wrong.

"Well, isn't this just bloody lovely!" I blurted out.

"Relax. This is perfect. We can wipe out the entire nest at one time and be done with them. I've already dispatched two

Defenders to the coordinates to end this bloody nightmare once and for all," responded James.

"You're assuming, of course, there aren't a hundred other nests just like this one," I replied.

"Maybe there are, and if so, we'll find them all, one at a time, until we're rid of this blight. For now, let's just be satisfied that this is, if nothing else, a damn good start," commented Kyle.

"I thought you guys were all in Draegon. Don't tell me you came back just to view these videos. You could have done that where you were," I commented.

"No, we weren't adding much value to what was going on there now that some semblance of order has been established," James replied.

James appointed Commander Diamond as Military Governor of the city, and it seemed we had left the beleaguered Draegon citizens in good hands. "Originally, we were coming back to bug your ass for the rest of the day, but then we received a message that these videos had been streamed to us. It's for the best anyway because I want to set up a video conference with members of the Vanguard Council to give them an update. I think now I'll wait until we watch our boys destroy the bat colony. Then I'll really have something to talk about," said Kyle.

"Where are the Defenders now?" I asked.

"Right in front of you on the screen. Don't worry; you're not going blind. They're cloaked! I didn't want to spook any of these things before we were ready to torch their asses," responded James.

The bats must have sensed our presence because they instinctively began to stir. Too late! In a heartbeat, ten Hades warheads streaked into the tight confines of the gorge, and a giant ball of flame erupted where once the bats had safe sanctuary. The valley was engulfed in a brilliant blue and red wall of superheated gases that rose over five thousand feet into the air.

As the smoke cleared, we could see thousands of blackened bat carcasses spread across the cavern floor like soot. James ordered the Defenders to lay down another barrage. He didn't want other animals feeding on the dead bat carcasses. As much as this action was necessary, it seemed cruel. These creatures were plucked from their home world by a devious enemy who used their instinctive survival traits as a weapon against a species on another world. I couldn't help but wonder what kind of a mind could conceive such a dark plan. How would we deal with them should these aliens once again come to claim the planet? We weren't unarmed farmers to be easily overcome. The price to take this planet from us would be high.

Kyle arranged the video address and advised the Council of the status of the Draegon emergency intervention and the bats. As soon as the update had finished, I was back at the hospital with Cateria. When I told her and Sabrina about our extermination of the bats, they were very pleased that Draegon was being revived and the flying predators would fly no more. Cateria was more upbeat than she had been in the morning, and Joshal was already kicking and screaming in her arms.

Sabrina's only comment about that was, like most men, Joshal was born complaining and feeling sorry for himself. In her opinion, that would never go away. I reminded her that I had heard female babies in the nursery putting up the same fuss. Her answer was typical feminism.

"Ryan, the reason you have trouble distinguishing the difference is because you're a man. Girl babies scream and carry on because boy babies piss them off with their silliness. That too is a condition that isn't likely to change as they get older," Sabrina retorted.

Twenty-Three

The Zorn Legacy

Now that another series of dramatic events had ended, Marcus and I were back to our examination of the Zorn discs. This time, we were jumping ahead to find out more about the workings of the Siltron extraction device and the particle accelerator. Although every disc had reference titles, they were not helpful. Jumping ahead was not anticipated by their creators. After two weeks of inserting each disc long enough to get a sense of subject matter, we got lucky. Finding one disc and checking references before and after got us a total of twenty-one discs relating to our requirements, but the last disc referenced "Siltron Cave Residents," and that tweaked our interest. We decided to make just a bit of a detour.

When we inserted the disc, the image of a man dressed in a white lab coat materialized. He began speaking immediately. "During our efforts to create the bore channel to the Siltron deposits, we broke through into a series of three large caves eight miles below the surface. The largest chamber of these caves was fifty-two miles wide, 112 miles long, and half a mile high. It was the last in a string of caves linked to the others by a subterranean waterway, which began in a mountain valley 200 miles south of our position. In the center of the primary chamber was a small lake fed by this river. Our discovery of the cave required our engineers to bore a new target entry hole into the lake bed, delaying Siltron extraction by eighty-one days.

"To establish the new bore hole, we transported heavy equipment from the southerly most entry, using large floating platforms fabricated on site. The platforms were then floated using the underground river leading to the main chamber lake. It was noted at that time there was an extensive indigenous bat population throughout all three caves, which complicated the entire engineering challenge.

"At first, the bat colony seemed almost indifferent to our presence in the caves, but as work began on the new bore hole, they began to become more excitable, almost to the point of being a nuisance. The engineers used flash guns to disperse them whenever we were working in the large cave, and it seemed to be working. Pictures of the cave structure and residents are contained on disc reference 'Cave Residents IA.'"

At that point, the disc ended and ejected. The search was on to find the referenced disc. About an hour later, Marcus raised his hand in victory and walked over, waving it above his head.

"Marcus, do you think there's any chance these bats are the same bats that have made our lives miserable over the last couple of years?" I asked.

"I'm not sure. The speaker didn't mention that the bats they found were anything other than common cave bats. You would think if they were huge, the guy would have pointed it out. Let's just look at the pictures on this disc, and we'll answer the question ourselves," replied Marcus.

When the next disc was loaded, it showed a video of the cave's interior. The site lighting was extremely powerful and lit up large portions of what had to be the primary chamber. The roof of the cave formed a natural dome, and it was clear where the tunneling device had broken through into the room. The lake was larger than we thought, given the description on the previous disc. The video gave us crystal clear images of the Zorn engineering group at work. As we suspected, they were humanoid, and apart from the fact we knew differently, they could have been us.

The video then focused more to the walls of the chamber, and we were amazed by what had to be the largest bat colony we had ever heard or read of in any book. There was no way of estimating the exact number, but it was certainly into the thousands. They didn't appear disturbed by the activities on the lake or the super-bright illumination, which was a bit astonishing. Much to our disappointment, they appeared to be regular cave bats. We watched the video to the end, at which point the same person as was on the previous disc reappeared and began to speak.

"The videos give us a fair indication of the size of the bat colony. As we began boring the new channel, the noise kept the bats in a constant state of distress. Their aggressiveness forced us to establish a sonic wall around our people. Contrary to Zorn protocols, interaction with this indigenous life form was unavoidable. On the eighty-second day, the channel reached the Siltron deposit, and extraction began. Please reference disc 'Cave Residents 1B.'"

Marcus wanted to go back to our original assignment and not waste any more time on what he described as, "the study of bats in their natural habitats." I, on the other hand, wasn't quite as eager to leave this before we had seen the entire series of discs on the subject.

"Marcus, there's a reason they have discs specifically referring to the subject of the bats. The Zorn wouldn't have wasted time and effort if that's all this was about. Let's watch at least one more before we pack it in," I pleaded.

"Ryan, because it means so much to you, and since the discs are only a few minutes long each, let's do it," he responded playfully.

Once again, the search was on, and we found the disc quite near where Marcus found the last one. The disc began much like its predecessors, with the engineer speaking, but this time, his manner was more strained, almost urgent.

"The Virtron radiation from our Siltron enrichment process is having an unexpected and unpleasant effect on the bat population in the caves. We have had to remove all personnel from the area for safety. The bats are growing larger each day and have become much more aggressive toward us. To date, we have lost six workers to their attacks. Our plan is to force the creatures into the adjacent caves and seal the entrance to the primary cave. The unfortunate consequence of our actions is many of the bats had to be exterminated to secure the chamber. We may have inadvertently created a new predatory hierarchy and introduced it into an existing ecosystem. The consequences could be dramatic unless we intervene, which would be another action contrary to Zorn off-world protocols.

"The creatures we have terminated and examined indicate the radiation has changed their physiological structure. They are mutating into something excessively large and out of scale for their environment. The examination has also brought to light another side effect. The radiation has destroyed the bats' reproductive abilities. Our scientists believe this may have a corrective impact over time. The Collective is debating whether we should eradicate all the creatures to prevent a potential global balancing problem or allow them to live out their life cycles, knowing they can't reproduce.

"Our tracking has determined that the bats' hunting grounds have expanded one hundred fold, and a large portion of the colony is no longer returning to the caves. Normally, bats of this order would feed on insect populations, but their prey may now be bigger to offset their mutation. To protect our settlers, we have relocated them to the far side of the planet beyond the range of the bats. This relocation will require us to increase the firing frequency of the accelerator to enable prevailing winds to spread the particles over a much wider area. Although the action is wasteful, we must preserve the colony until we relocate the complex. Please insert disc '1C.'"

There was a familiar hum, and the disc stopped and ejected. "Marcus, this is an enormous discovery. We thought these creatures were weapons from an alien invader! We were wrong! It took them this long to get this far from their original habitat, but they made it. They're likely following the food chain. I now know why there were no animal sounds or sightings at the Mountain site. There are no animals to make sounds. We've got to get this information to James and Kyle," I urged.

"You're right! Obviously, the Zorn Collective chose to let nature solve their problem, believing that without reproductive ability they would just die off. That's what we thought. It would appear that was wrong as well. Very likely, there are more of them between the original site and us. Without any other natural enemies to stop them, it's going to have to be us. Before we do that though, we should look at the next disc in the series," replied Marcus.

Disc "1C" was the last on the subject but informative. When the holographic image appeared, it was not the same man. Like all the speakers, this one was dressed in a long, white lab coat. He was considerably younger than his predecessor and came across as very calm and controlled. When he spoke, it was low-keyed but directly to the point.

"We are unable to relocate the Siltron extraction complex we moved our people to. We have been called back to Gaelon. We have calibrated the firing frequency to distribute at the minimum required density. It is hoped that those who find these discs will continue with the plan relocate. The bat population has evolved into a dangerous predatory species. We have attempted to use chemical sprays to control their numbers, but at this point, over 90 percent of the original colony have left the caves and not returned. Our scientists are confident that the bats will die off because the creature cannot reproduce. The settlers have been moved well beyond the range of the creatures' predatory hunting patterns. If these discs are being reviewed, then our actions to preserve our colony were successful."With that, the disc stopped and ejected.

I immediately dispatched a messenger to bring Kyle and James to the lab. When they arrived, both seemed in foul moods. I remember thinking to myself, *if you're pissed now, wait until you see and hear this shit.*

Kyle seemed impatient, even for him. Whatever was triggering this mood was obviously getting to James, or vice versa. "What's going on with you two?" I asked.

"It's not that important really. It's just a pain in the ass. The engineers asked James to have an Explorer tunnel a hole through a small mountain across the lake to speed up the equipment movement for our train project. We fly them there, and they point out the mountain. James makes the new tunnel, and then they decide it was the wrong mountain.

"I was there! I reminded the chief engineer that it was the mountain they identified. His response was, 'I guess they all look the same from up here.' Now we're going to have the do-gooders beating us up because we defaced the countryside for no good reason. We're considering boring a hole through the chief engineer. Anyway, what's got you guys so worked up?" Kyle asked.

"Well, rather than you two guys blaming us for this visit, we're just going to replay a couple of discs. We'll let you blame the hologram instead. Marcus, load up the first one, please," I said.

While the discs were playing, Kyle and James sat absolutely still and silent. There wasn't even any conversation as each disc was being changed for the next in the series. When the last disc ended, I looked at them, waiting for the questions to start. I had seen James quiet on numerous occasions, but I hadn't seen Kyle this withdrawn since the whole DNA issue years ago.

"Are you guys okay?" Marcus asked.

"I feel like taking out my sidearm and shooting each of you right through the head, then turning it on myself and doing the same thing. It's the only way I think we're ever going to get any peace in our lives. We've gone from some alien conspiracy, which I never believed in the first place, to mutated, flying, fucking rodents that eat men. I frankly don't know what to say. Kyle, if you're alive over there, say something," directed James.

"I don't know what to say either. I don't remember signing up for all this shit. My plan was simple! Find us a home, settle down, and rule the planet. Now it appears my plan has changed to running for my life and not attending any more of these sessions with you guys. There's never any good news. Marcus, you always see things differently. What does all this mean? And be gentle," Kyle requested.

"The way I see it, the Zorn accidently mutated a small animal and turned it into a giant, blood-thirsty predator. They then essentially said fuck it and flew away, leaving us to clean up their mess. And what a mess it is. We, being as naïve as we are, listened to some scientist, whose only claim to fame was to be part of a conspiracy against us for the last two hundred plus years. He convinced most of us, including yours truly, that these mutated creatures were transplanted here by some alien force bent on wiping out all humans before they arrived to assume ownership. We finally cornered a bunch of these giant flying rats and killed them. We patted ourselves on the back because we screwed the alien diabolical plan and saved mankind. Now we're just figuring out how ridiculously stupid we were. Does that about sum it up for you guys?" asked Marcus, smiling.

"Remind me never to ask this guy for an opinion again. That was brutal. Funny, but brutal, nonetheless! Assuming we're smarter now than we were three hours ago, what are we faced with here, Marcus?" Kyle asked.

"Joking aside, if we use what Joshal gave us indirectly as a timeline, the events on the disc occurred at least a thousand years ago. Under the assumption that's reasonably close and the creature has consumed all available food sources since it moved out from the caves, half this planet will have no large indigenous life left.

"I suspect that when they started, they did so in only one direction, moving as a colony. The good news is if that's true, we may have destroyed most of them. There will be stragglers that were hunting when we destroyed the nest. We're not completely free of these things. I think we're going to have to start preparing for that eventuality," suggested Marcus.

"I agree with Marcus; we must prepare. James, I will have the engineers begin enhancing our airborne drones. We have just under a thousand. We will need two thousand to cover the real estate we're talking here. The drones will take the fight to the bats, and any that get through will be dealt with by the Spider Drones. We'll do this through the authority of the Vanguard Council to make sure everyone is part of the solution."

"Another interesting, perhaps unrelated byline to all of this is Sabrina's comment about how much of the mineral being put into the atmosphere was going to waste," I commented.

"The original project was intended to seed the clouds directly near the accelerator because that's where the colony was to be. The bats changed the plan. We might very well be dangerously close to running the well dry. We're going to have to get back on what we can do to control the dispersion of the mineral. That might involve finding a source closer to us," Kyle said.

It was impressive how quickly Kyle was able to organize all the cities and settlements in this vital effort. Production plants were established in all three cities for the manufacture of both airborne and Spider Drones. This required extensive training of the citizens in each location. The cities would be producing the tools to protect themselves. It would take over a year to meet the inventory requirements of these robotic devices. An added benefit to all this was that as they worked together toward a common solution and against a common enemy, it brought the once distinctly different cultures closer together.

Twenty-Four

Shutting Down

While Kyle and James worked on beefing up our readiness, Marcus and I were back to the Zorn discs, attempting to learn more about how the Siltron powder was extracted and, more importantly, how to operate the futuristic equipment. Once we had found all the discs relating to the subject, we began the slow, arduous exercise of watching them and learning from the Zorn teachings.

One of our first lessons was that the accelerator tube did not go down to the extraction site. In fact, it began only a mile below the surface at a level described only as "Stage One." As we watched and learned, we discovered that the Siltron deposit was a raw, caked, organic powder and that the deposit was almost nine miles below the surface. The extractor was a sophisticated series of devices that began by piercing the vein and bombarding the deposit from within with a pulse ray described as a "Di-an Destabilization Field."

As near as we could gather from the schematics provided in the holographic library, this Di-an Field reduced the ore from a cake texture to coarse powder, which was then vacuumed up to the next stage in the process, identified as "Stage Two." At this stage, the powder was collected in two centrifuge devices, converting the powder to something that resembled slurry but was in fact made of particles so small it took on the appearance of liquid. It was here that the powder was enriched and activated with a radiation jumpstart.

The more we watched and listened, the more fascinating the process became. Marcus was almost spellbound by the pictures and tutorial that accompanied them. His genius was now working overtime, and his eyes were as big as saucers. The Siltron slurry was once again vacuumed upward another three miles to "Stage Three" of the processing cycle. The exaggerated trip allowed the now super-heated material to cool. At Stage Three, Siltron powder to be transported off the planet was pressured into large canisters and vacuum-sealed. These tanks were then moved by conveyance tubes to the surface for loading on starships for return to Gaelon. The Siltron to be used for seeding the atmosphere was moved by air pressure to the next stage, described as "Stage Four."

At this level, one mile below the surface, air was drawn by massive fans from the surface and pressurized to over five thousand pounds per square inch. This pressure served as the accelerator to shoot the material into the upper atmosphere.

The tutorial included detailed instructions of what was required to remove the entire processing plant and relocate it to a new site. It also described how to detect the existence of the powder when surveying new sites. So complex were the requirements for relocation, we agreed it would have to be the last resort, not the first option.

To Sabrina's point, the ideal method of introducing the refined powder to a human population was through city water systems in the form of showers or bathing. The mineral's value was greatly diminished if taken internally and could have a counter-effect if not regulated. There were even warnings concerning the effect on other living organisms should they be exposed to the powder. The examples provided suggested that cold-blooded animals did not react well to the mineral. It described the symptoms of exposure in these species as extensive skin cell destruction creating cancerous lesions, critical damage to internal organs, and blindness, followed by eventual death.

As soon as we heard that, we looked at each other as if the same light went off in our heads at exactly the same time. Joshal's story about the warrior invaders with the strange skin and how after time they were stricken by a plague affecting only them seemed to be too close to ignore. Could the invaders have been cold-blooded, and over time they developed the symptoms described because of the diluted powder raining down on them almost every day? I was so sad that Joshal was not with us. In this case, not only did the powder keep us healthy, but it would appear it saved the human race. The text went on to say that with concentrated distribution into city water purification systems, one canister could support a human population of one million for a period of one year. This could be our answer to conserving the resource. We couldn't wait to share this news with the group.

If we were to do any of this, we had to figure out how to reach these various levels in the site, but even that answer was right in front of us all the time. To get to the level where the cassettes were found, the keypad code was "Siltron." We assumed that's where the elevating device ended. The reality is if we had keyed in "Stage Two," it would have taken us to that level, and so on.

Immediately, I contacted our group and requested they meet us in the Science Center. Sabrina was so excited when I told her what we had found. This could be a way to shut down the accelerator and still have a predictable supply of the miracle powder. We were all joking around about Siltron cocktails and steaks over easy with a dash of Siltron sauce. It was silly of us to carry on like this, but the discovery was beyond anything we could have hoped for. Marcus had secured copies of the original, indigenous life samplings we had taken before landing to colonize the planet. I wasn't sure what he was getting at, but that was Marcus.

"I was anxious to investigate the Zorn statements concerning the effect of the powder on cold-blooded animals. What I discovered is of the thousands of indigenous life form samples collected and categorized, there were no land-based cold-blooded specimens on record. No snakes, lizards, frogs, and so on. The only anomaly appeared to be fish and some bird species. We had hundreds of specimens of fish. I thought about that for hours and came to the conclusion that because fish live under water, they were protected from the effects of the powder. I couldn't come to any conclusions about the birds. Was the Siltron the reason for the missing animal samples? We may never know, but it was interesting to speculate," explained Marcus.

"That's very interesting, Marcus, but I don't care. Those creatures on your missing list are all slimy anyway. None of us in this room, in Bridgetown, and for that matter, in Salmon have ever seen these creatures apart from books. The only important item on the table here is whether we can control the dispersion of the powder," Sabrina said.

Kyle couldn't hold back any longer. "What are we waiting for? Let's get our asses back there, fill up some canisters, and turn it off until we need more."

"I don't think it's quite that easy," Marcus corrected. "Apart from Salmon and Bridgetown, none of the other settlements have managed water systems, including Draegon. They're all using well and river water without managed purification systems. This is going to require an engineering study. If we only take care of ourselves, then what's the point? We should leave things the way they are until we have a solution that serves us all."

"How long will that take?" asked Sabrina.

"If Kyle can organize us, we can establish a team of engineers to study the best way to control and disperse the powder so it benefits everyone. I think if we get the right guys around the table, we can have a solution to present in a couple of months," responded Marcus.

"Couldn't we just move the entire mining operation closer to us and continue to seed the atmosphere and be done with it? The Zorn did indicate there were numerous deposits on the planet," Kyle suggested.

"We're not ready for that! The Zorn technology is way beyond where we are. If we start tinkering with something we don't completely understand, we may screw up what we have—and then what?" commented Marcus.

"We'll assemble a multicity team of engineers through the authority of the Council, led by Marcus. We'll set ourselves a target of three months for completion. The focus will be the dispersion of the powder without taking on the far riskier project of relocating the mining operation. Once we've solved the problem, we'll start examining and learning from the Zorn how to move the operation," directed Kyle.

Twenty-Five

The Siltron Solution

Kyle assembled a thirty-man engineering team made up of skillsets from a dozen different disciplines—from mining to irrigation to water treatment and hydraulics. These could be perhaps the thirty smartest men on the planet, but as we knew, the most brilliant of the lot was Marcus. Kyle was happy to set aside his authority to allow Marcus to lead the project. When I asked him how difficult it was to play a subordinate role, he answered as I knew he would.

"Marcus is the most brilliant engineer on the planet. Everyone knows it, and I would be foolish to think I could do a better job. We need to solve this problem, and I'd be willing to bet whatever solution is arrived at will be because Marcus figured it out with only minor contributions from the rest of us. All that said, Ryan, you will be part of the team too because we need to record how all this unfolds for future generations. For that type of stuff, you are the best secretary on the planet," stated Kyle.

I knew this was just another case of Kyle playing his influence card on me, but he was right. I was the best at what I did, but most times being the best nerd doesn't get you many compliments, outside family circles. Our first action was to revisit the site and study the various stages of the extraction process from raw cake to particle dispersion. Marcus suggested we establish a base camp on site because most of the study would require us to touch and feel every bit of the technology in play. When I told Cateria I would be away for a couple of months, she was less than enthusiastic, but she understood the importance of the project. I guess some of her initial reluctance was her sense of foreboding that we were violating the sanctuary of the gods.

Sabrina promised to watch over Cateria and the family while we did our work. A few days before leaving, I found my wife on her knees near Joshal's grave by the river, praying and softly weeping. When I asked her about it during a quiet moment, she was reluctant to answer, but with some prodding, she confessed to me, "Ryan, my love, I was praying for all of us and asking my father to plead with The Fathers not to be angry with us because we're trespassing in their most sacred places."

As much as I wanted to scold her for believing that the Zorn were gods and we needed their permission for all this, I thought better of it. Anyway, what could it hurt! We needed all the help we could get, and even a little divine intervention had to be a bonus.

With typical military efficiency, by the time we landed at the site, James's teams had already established a fully operational base camp just over three hundred yards from the Mountain of Light. Everything a group of engineering geniuses could ever want was there and set up. James had even considered our security needs with ten Spider Drones patrolling around the camp and airborne, armed drones patrolling the skies above the camp. Our military escort was one hundred of the most seasoned soldiers from the Protectorate ranks.

I asked James why such an elaborate security presence was necessary. His answer was plain and simple. "Ryan, I have the crappy task of protecting the thirty greatest engineering minds on this planet. Add to that the most influential human on the planet and his cranky wife watching my every move. What else would you have me do?" I reminded him that nowhere in his explanation was my presence a consideration. He just laughed.

Our first exercise was merely to tour each level of the Mountain of Light and try to understand exactly how each phase of the process worked. To assist, we had the Zorn discs brought from the Science Center as an immediate reference guide, should they be required. The stage was set for our first expedition into the bowels of the Mountain of Light. Everyone was excited about the adventure ahead. James stated that during these excursions he was going to lead the security escort, but for the nerdy crap later, he was going to return to Bridgetown so he wouldn't have to endure our ramblings. I wished I could adopt the same approach, but my role in this was seen by Kyle as essential. I told him anyone could take notes, and given the audience, I wasn't much more than another mouth to feed. His response was, "We have plenty of food."

There would be no walking to the elevator on this trip. James had made arrangements for three transport vehicles to move the team back and forth from the hatch. This was good news for me because, since my marriage to Cateria, she had made it her mission in life to fatten me up. I can safely say her plan was working. Sabrina kept crapping on me all the time to start eating healthier and exercising, but I wasn't buying into the lectures.

When we arrived at the hatch, Kyle pressed his palm to the scanner, but this time, as instructed by the Zorn discs, he selected the menu item identified as "Stage Two." When he was finished, he called Marcus and me over and asked us what the words on the small viewing screen meant. "Key in the number of units transporting." Marcus didn't even flinch! He turned and started counting the number of bodies in our group and then turned back to the keypad and entered "forty-one."

None of us was prepared for what happened next. Through the floor of the platform, forty-one half-dome modules emerged. As each module became fully raised, there was a very distinct *click* sound. We assumed that indicated the unit was locked in place. Each module had a small seat and an X harness meant to go over the shoulder, across the breast, and lock into the seat.

"Why didn't these come up the first time we used the elevating device?" I asked.

"I think it was because we were only going down five hundred feet. The device must move faster when the trip is farther down, and consequently, passengers need to be strapped in to avoid accidents. All that is just a guess of course," offered Kyle.

I didn't like his "guess" because I had this uncomfortable feeling this ride was going to be something I would rather avoid. Marcus, Kyle, and James, on the other hand, seemed exuberant about it. I'm not sure how the rest of our team felt, but based on facial expressions, it was a mixture of excitement and terror. I was on the terror side of the ledger. Marcus waited until we were all strapped in before taking his seat. He was going to be a wonderful leader as time went on. Once he strapped himself in, the platform slowly began to descend. As before, the cover moved with the platform until the entrance was sealed, and as before, the walls became fully illuminated. Almost immediately, puffs of cool, fresh air were injected into each module through a small vent in the dome portion. It should have been a warning, but I missed it.

From there on, it was to be the ride of our lives. Every second the platform descended, it doubled its speed. In less than a minute, we were moving so fast I had to close my eyes because the illuminated walls were becoming a blur and I could feel my stomach reminding me just how unnatural all this was. There was no physical sensation of how fast we were falling. We wouldn't have noticed at all if not for the illuminated walls.

A couple of minutes later, our descent began to slow. It wasn't a dramatic reduction in speed, but we were slowing, and my stomach was starting to recover. I could hear Marcus yelling over to Kyle that he'd love to know what propelled the elevating device. In just a little over three minutes, we came to an effortless stop. Three minutes to travel seven miles below the surface. Absolutely silliness!

Much like our first visit, the platform stopped adjacent to a long, illuminated corridor, and as before, it moved back toward the Mountain of Light. As each of us left our seats, the dome immediately withdrew back into the floor, becoming almost undetectable. With Marcus, Kyle, and James in the lead, we slowly made our way through the tunnel. At the end of the passageway was a scan pad imbedded into the wall. Kyle stepped forward and placed his palm on the screen, and immediately the wall vaporized in front of us. I hated when it did that.

The interior was considerably smaller than the top-level disc room we'd visited on our first trip to the Mountain, but it had more mechanical equipment. In one corner was a separate chamber surrounded by a transparent wall, which I thought might be glass or plastic. Marcus advised me it was the containment chamber for a small reactor that likely powered the installation, and the transparent material was probably a lead-embedded plastic with a transparent Teflon coating. I was sorry I asked.

In the center of the room were three oblong, cylinder shaped pieces of machinery in full operation. The numerous control panels showed all operations were in the green. We were making an assumption of course that "green" meant the same to the Zorn as it did to us. Marcus thought they were the centrifuges mentioned on the discs that converted the course sand into the slurry and then pumped it up to the Stage Three processing level.

Contained within this room, as well, were all the control panels to start, stop, and continuously monitor the extraction and the particle accelerator. This was the heart of the mining operation. A large wall-sized monitor was portraying a schematic style picture of the extraction progression in live time. Based on what we could make out, the deposit was over 60 percent depleted. Sabrina was right! For what could well be over a thousand years, the powder was being extracted and pumped into the upper atmosphere where most of it was wasted.

Kyle and Marcus decided we were going to have to start manning the station. Equipment left to operate on its own without technical support could be a problem, although it had been running problem-free for centuries. We could see from the control modules that it was possible to slow the extraction down without actually shutting it off, but for now, we were only observers. Marcus suggested we needed to understand more about the collecting of the powder for transport, which according to the Zorn discs was accomplished during Stage Three.

Kyle decided to leave half the team on this level for further study and to take notes on how all the control panels functioned. The rest of us were headed back down the tunnel to the waiting platform and the next adventure. Embedded in the wall directly beside the elevating device was another palm reader and viewing screen. Kyle quickly selected "Stage Three" from the menu, and again the screen prompted him to enter the number of units for transfer. He entered twenty-one, and immediately the platform floor came to life again.

Fifteen minutes later, we were entering another chamber. This room was much the same size as the lower level but with far fewer mechanicals. Three tubes, perhaps three feet in diameter, pierced through the floor from the lower chamber into what I can only describe as an enormous vat. The control panels gave the operator two choices; once the vat was filled, either divert the flow to a canister filling station, or bypass and continue the transfer of Siltron to Stage Four.

The canisters used to collect and transport the material were not as large as I expected they'd be, considering the contents of one canister circulated through the city water system could support a million people for one year. Marcus explained that the powder was packaged in concentrated form, and once mixed with water, it became diluted, and the water became the transport medium. To him and Kyle, it all made sense.

Each canister was about eight feet tall and perhaps three feet in diameter. They sat in a containment frame on a conveyor system. We assumed that when the system was operational, the conveyor moved each canister to the filling station where a shroud-like hood enclosed the top and transferred the powder and then resealed the unit under pressure. The filled canister then moved to where robotic arms lifted and placed it in a transport cradle. Once loaded, the cradle was tilted in line with a large channel that poked into the ceiling and launched the canister to the surface for loading.

I asked Marcus if he thought the powder had a useful life once pressured into the canister. His opinion was as long as it was kept under pressure, likely it would last forever. That made sense to me. The Zorn had been mining this material for centuries and transporting it from galaxy to galaxy. This was all speculation, of course, since we had no idea of how quickly their vessels moved through space. By the time we had returned to the base camp eleven hours later, the mood was upbeat, and we were ready to start trying to solve our dispersion problem. For now, it was a hot meal and hours of conversation about the sophistication of the Zorn technologies. Strangely, there seemed to be an unusual interest in the elevator device and how it operated. The engineers, including Marcus and Kyle, seemed stumped by what the propulsion drive mechanics were.

Feeling a bit brighter than normal, I suggested the descent was likely controlled gravity, and only the lifting required mechanical intervention. It was apparent I wasn't an engineer when they all looked at me as if I had lost my mind.

"Ryan, your opinion is imaginative but unfortunately flawed. Free fall using gravity and mass to promote speed would be too unpredictable. Our speed was controlled going down and much faster than mere gravity could have generated. There is a mechanical solution in play that pulls the platform down and pushes it up at defined speeds regardless of the payload. We do appreciate your input though," responded Marcus.

"Sure you do! I think I'm going to just shut up and scribe notes from now on," I replied.

The best theory bouncing around the table was some type of electromagnetic propulsion drive. The lift was being pulled by a system of electromagnets pulsating on and off, drawing the lift down or up. That partially explained how quiet the lift was and how effortlessly it stopped and started. Well, my idea was pretty good too!

After a big meal and some fireside chats, we were down for the night. It truly was a strange place. There were four short rainfalls as we slept. As I lay on my cot, the silence was almost unnatural. There were no animal sounds, not even the normal sounds common everywhere else on the planet. Surely the bats couldn't have killed every living creature, even bugs?

Over the next forty-five days, we made eighteen trips back to Stages Two and Three of the Mountain to confirm our findings. It was fascinating to watch these guys at work, drawing on their electronic tablets and flashing their brainstorming efforts up on the large monitors. Everyone seemed to talk at once, and I couldn't figure out how they ever decided or agreed on anything, but they did. After a few days, the fascination was gone for me, replaced by boredom and homesickness.

The engineers had examined and reexamined the data a thousand times until they had gone as far as they could. Now it was time to put it all in a form they could share with others. Marcus began the summary. "We all agree we do not have the wherewithal at this stage to move the mining operations closer to Bridgetown. Over time, we'll get there, but I think it's twenty years out." Everyone nodded agreement, and he continued.

"The only viable alternative is to do as the Zorn did, which is to fill canisters and bring them back for a more direct and controlled dispersion of the powder. Although it's a risk, we'll have to partially shut down the accelerator, which means partially shutting down the mining project. We cannot risk taking it completely offline because I don't think we fully understand the protocols for a cold restart. Do we agree?" Again, everyone nodded their agreement.

"The site cannot be left unmanned from here on. Admiral Donner has agreed to establish a Protectorate presence at this location. Kyle will advise the Vanguard Council that one of our recommendations is the establishment of a permanent mining colony. This will require a volunteer approach and extensive training. The primary issue still on the table is how we disperse the powder to our people in a controlled fashion to preserve the site for generations to come."

The original Zorn concept of seeding the atmosphere still made sense for the settlements without water management systems. How we accomplished this using aircrafts would need some additional thought, but it wasn't seen as an impasse. We would have to get the medical establishment involved to determine the appropriate concentration of powder to get the best results. Again, this was a simple series of tests and an ongoing management process. Kyle and Marcus had already committed to providing James with a mechanical powder delivery system for seeding the space over the settlements. We were still not convinced this form of seeding was the ideal solution, but until our technology caught up to our needs, it would have to do.

Ten of the engineers on the team agreed to stay behind to man the site on a rotating schedule. The ten Spider Drones would remain a security fixture for the new settlement, as would the airborne drones. Daily supply ships would visit the location to deliver critical equipment and other essential items. Kyle agreed to ask Sabrina to provide general medicine doctors on a rotating schedule to ensure we had an emergency medical solution at all times at the settlement. James committed to establishing a forward Protectorate outpost with one Explorer and ten Defenders with support staff and two hundred Protectors. This would be the first outpost we had ever attempted on the planet, and we wanted to do it right.

When we presented our plan to the Vanguard Council, there was a general sense of excitement and accomplishment. Sabrina arranged a medical study group to determine the most appropriate dispersion concentration of the Siltron. They spoke about the best time of day to disperse to gain maximum impact to health and even agreed when to increase the concentration during the working seasons for planting and harvesting to reduce the fatigue factors of the farmers.

As strange as it might seem, there was an endless line of volunteers to establish our new remote colony. There was even a name assigned to what someday might be a settlement of some significance. The final choice for a name brought Cateria to tears because of the connection to her father. The new settlement would hereafter be known as "New Beginnings."

Twenty-Six

They've Come Again

For months, the lives of the citizens of New Earth had been considered the best of times. With the development of the Siltron airborne dispersion system by Marcus and Kyle, all the known human settlements were prospering beyond even the most optimistic of expectations. The Vanguard Council served as the adhesive that held the cities and settlements together, and it was working. Our mandate that "no settlement would be without" had made us one culture with one goal—to prosper. We had become a true Collective.

Slowly, months turned into a year, and a year into two. Most of our drama seemed to evaporate into history, and there was seemingly nothing standing in our way. The predator bat dilemma had not completely ended because shortly after the establishment of New Beginnings, the settlers were attacked by the creatures. Thanks to the presence of the drones, these attacks did not result in a single human death. The drones killed over three hundred bats in the two recorded attacks. One of the patrolling airborne drones had tracked the creatures to a cave some two hundred miles south of the Mountain of Light, which turned out to be the same caves identified by the Zorn on the discs. James and Kyle vowed it would end there.

Three defenders fired thirty Hades rockets into the caves, creating a blast furnace effect. Nothing could have survived the super-heated air, but just in case, a hundred Spider Drones were programmed and sent into the caves to finish the job. Three weeks later, James led a team to examine the interior of the torched caves. As it turned out, the Zorn had sealed the main chamber just as was suggested on the disks, which made this entire cleansing much easier. After that day, there hadn't been any bat attacks against humans, but the search for other nests continued.

From time to time, small colonies of the beasts were found and dealt with quickly. The bats' new enemy became the airborne killer drones (ABKDs) as they were affectionately referred to by the citizens. The bats couldn't outrun the drones. They couldn't hide from them and were no match for the drones' arsenals of proximity missiles and pulse rays. Sabrina's people contributed to the bats' demise by developing an airborne virus that slowly interrupted the creatures' reproductive cycles, reducing the number of young born each year.

If we thought for a moment that dealing with the predators, solving the Siltron issue, and saving the planet meant the end of chaos for our little band of merry women and men, we were wrong. There was a period of calm reflection and predictability, but that was merely a precursor for what was still to come.

Commander Diamond, now Governor Diamond, had done a statesman-like job rebuilding Draegon and the surrounding settlements. The rail system between Salmon and Bridgetown was well on its way to realization, and there was already talk of expanding it to the west to incorporate Draegon. The introduction of an expanded rail system west would result in the joining of the three anchor cities of the Vanguard Council. These remarkable accomplishments all occurred within three years and were driven to completion by Kyle Chandler's unrelenting view of mankind's ability to adapt and prosper. I was proud to be a part of how far the planet had evolved. For a period, it seemed mankind could do no wrong and the future was ours to mold for our children.

New Beginnings had grown to a population of over thirty thousand, made up of a couple thousand technicians and engineers, a couple hundred soldiers, but mostly farmers looking to begin new lives in a virgin land. Sabrina had made arrangements with James to begin repopulating animals that the bats had pushed to the edge of extinction. Each daily shuttle contained not only supplies and equipment, but also a variety of small animals caught in live traps the day before. Although a slow process, when last I visited the site, there were birds in the skies near the settlement and forest hogs in the nearby woods. Oh, and yes, there were dogs everywhere.

Joshal, my son, was about to turn nine years old, and a celebration was being organized at the ranch. The Protectorate agreed to make vehicles available to deliver every child who wanted to attend. This domestication was not limited to just the citizens; even the once infamous Spider Drones were becoming a common fixture at all such events. The children were encouraged to create names for these metal monstrosities to help humanize them. Kyle, being who he was, would then take all the names and place each on a small plaque to affix to each machine. He even created a mechanical voice of sorts for each Drone, with a limited vocabulary of simple phrases to further try to get people past their ugliness. Phrases such as "Hello," "Boy, do you look good today," and "Always obey your parents" were commonly repeated by the Drones at special functions. It was amazing that adults were far more intimidated by them than the children were. Such is the luxury of innocence.

What wasn't being taken for granted were the air security patrols because we'd learned some hard lessons about letting down our guard over the years. The difference now was that they no longer were on missions to save the planet; they were just on watch. On the day of the celebration, there were over two hundred children and their parents at the ranch, and the festivities were proceeding as planned, of course, because Sabrina was spearheading the event. James, Kyle, and now newly married

Marcus, and I were drinking and recalling the days when all this would have seemed like a dream.

When we saw the military vehicle winding its way up the road from Bridgetown, no one paid much attention. It was likely some late arrivals. There were always late arrivals. We didn't even care when the two Protectors jumped out and started coming toward James, waving a piece of paper. That would be the last time anything would ever be taken for granted. James read the note almost without expression and told the soldiers he would be there shortly. Just after, the soldiers left as abruptly as they came. James made his apologies and indicated that something important had come up and he needed to tend to it. After a brief sidebar with Kyle, they gestured for Marcus and me to follow them to the transporter vehicle. I was starting to get that old doom and gloom feeling and had no idea why.

"James, what's so important that I had to leave my son's party to be with you clowns?" I asked.

"Just over an hour ago, one of our orbiting Explorers detected incoming crafts on a direct course to this planet. Four of these ships veered off and disappeared around the planet. An hour ago, our airborne drones detected these same four crafts crossing the desert equator on a direct path to Bridgetown. They landed just over one hundred miles west of our position. The orbiting Explorer has now reported that ten other unidentified ships have taken a fixed orbit in deep space. The only thing between these ships and our position is the Explorer Pegasus.

"The alien ships don't appear to be doing much of anything other than waiting. That's a problem because it rings of preparing for something. We need to challenge why they're here and figure out where we stand. I have instructed Command to scramble fifty Defenders and another four Explorers to join Pegasus."

"Do you think they're the same aliens Joshal referred to that tried to wipe out his people?" asked Marcus.

"Kid, I don't know. What I do know is if they're back for another shot, they're in for a big surprise," replied James.

Twenty-Seven

The Siege of Bridgetown

By the time we reached Command, the place was a beehive of activity. It wasn't frantic or disorganized. It was more like watching a well-practiced emergency response team going through their paces. As soon as James stepped into the room, one by one, officers stepped forward to give him the latest updates. Sometimes he asked questions, but mostly he just listened.

Drone videos were being streamed back from over the site of the alien landing. The scene clearly suggested they were preparing for a ground assault. The four ships were massive. Although difficult to accurately measure from fifty thousand feet, they were at least five to six times larger than an Explorer. These were not battle cruisers. They were armed but not mobile, and we surmised they were primarily used for the delivery of equipment and soldiers in a ground offensive. Based on the level of technology in the videos, the aliens must have been aware of our surveillance overhead, but they made no attempt to challenge our intrusion or mask what they were up to. This was a problem to James because he saw their lack of interest in what we were doing as evidence that they didn't think we could stop them. For two hours, the alien landing crafts deposited hundreds of transport vehicles and thousands of foot soldiers.

If we had thought the dense forest between us and them would hinder any meaningful advance on Bridgetown, we were wrong. The aliens had brought a number of vehicles that were designed to clear a path by removing trees and rendering them to dust. How this equipment worked couldn't be ascertained from the drones' altitude. What was evident was that these mechanical juggernauts were cutting a swath through the forest over a mile wide and two miles deep every hour.

James was of the opinion that the presence of our orbiting fleet was not the reason the alien ships were holding position. He was convinced the aliens were waiting for a defined set of events to be put into motion before they played their trump card. I didn't understand what he meant by that, but it sent shivers up my spine anyway.

"Guys, we're in a bit of trouble here. Unless I miss my guess, their battle cruisers are waiting for their ground forces to move closer to Bridgetown. Just before they arrive, I suspect their orbiting fleet will attempt to get by us and launch an air offensive to take out our ground defenses. That will be the signal for a ground assault to begin, but something is missing. The ships in orbit are too large and clearly not designed to attack from inside our atmosphere. They must have low-level attack fighters somewhere! Either they're staged inside the battle cruisers or they're in the background somewhere, awaiting instruction. If I'm right, we have to find and destroy them before this really turns to shit. Communications, contact our fleet in space. I want the fighters found.

"We can't allow their plan to unfold. I think we need to confront them now. If we force a fight early, maybe we catch them off guard. I'm less concerned about a space battle than I am about our ability to deal with their ground assault. At this stage, I think we just try to slow them down until we've dealt with their space armada. Besides sending in programmed ABKDs and nonstop Defender sorties, what else can we throw at them, guys?"

"Marcus and I can program all the Spider Drones we have in and around our city to converge on the alien position. Although they won't tip the scales, they will draw their attention and inflict enough damage to delay their advance. We follow them with the Defenders from high altitude and the ABKDs as a three-phase effort. I think our focus should be those machines carving through the forest. I have to think if we take them offline, this assault will come to a stop—at least until they figure out what to do next. This won't win the day, but it will buy us time until you take care of business up there," recommended Kyle.

"Based on their progress, it will take them over a day to get close enough for an artillery barrage. We might buy an extra twelve hours with this approach. James, we'll have to be back here to finish our work within thirty-six hours or they'll overrun the city. Is that even possible," asked Marcus?

"It's going to have to be," replied James.

"What if we're not the intended target?" I asked.

"The only settlement west of Bridgetown worthy of a force this size is Draegon, and they're on the wrong side of the mountains for that. It's us! Somehow they've figured out that taking Bridgetown will win the war. They're right! We need to start moving our citizens away from the city. Let's get as many soldiers in the streets as we can and begin relocating people to the farms and forests to the north. As soon as that's done, I want to put as many men on our western city perimeter as we can find," declared James.

"Communications Officer, send out a hail across all channels and demand to know their intentions or we'll open fire. Call in all available Defenders from patrol and every Explorer within an hour's flight time. I want them in orbit over our position between the aliens and us. I want all local Defender patrols in position over Bridgetown. When all that's been accomplished, find me," James directed.

The four of us proceeded to the briefing room to track the minute-by-minute activity of the aliens. A few minutes later, the communications officer came over James's communicator. "Sir, we are receiving a video response to our hails. They are demanding to speak to the leaders of our species."

"Put them through," James instructed. "Gentlemen, this is it. Over the next few hours, our time on this planet will be decided for better or worse. I have no intention of giving up what we fought so hard to create. The next few minutes begins our counter-offensive."

Almost as quickly as he said it, the large monitor came to life, and before us on the screen stood a single figure. Although the general torso was humanoid in appearance, the similarity ended there. The alien appeared to stand over eight feet tall, weighing in at perhaps three hundred pounds. It was covered in a kind of field armor complete with head protection and side arms unlike anything we'd seen before. The creature's hands were human-like but appeared to have only three digits on each hand. The skin was a strange brown color with what appeared to be a textured surface like a snake or lizard. The mouth was disproportionate to the size of the skull, with no evidence of lips or teeth. The eyes were a deep green, and the nose did not protrude like a human's, but was flat and barely discernable.

When the alien began to speak, the voice was broken, as if running out of breath. As it spoke, it was evident that the creature was using some sort of translation device. The words we were hearing were out of sequence with the gestures and facial movement.

James was not going to let this thing get the upper hand in the conversation. "You have violated our security perimeter and trespassed onto our planet. What is your intent?" challenged James.

"Silence! Do not dare to question our presence! You are trespassing on a world that is part of the Bergerac Empire. For your arrogance, you will be destroyed unless you leave this place before the next star cycle. You are a pestilence, as all your species before you were. Stand aside, and we will afford you safe passage out of this galaxy. Refuse, and we will exterminate you," the image replied.

"Give us time to consider your offer. We will respond shortly," replied James as the monitor went blank.

"That was a waste of time! They know we can't and won't leave the planet. They're here to wipe us out. Sorry, Kyle, there will be no diplomatic solution today. We're not waiting for any curfew or fighting this battle on their terms. Command, what are their ground forces doing?" asked James.

"Sir, they've advanced about six miles toward us. They have divided themselves into three fronts, and we have estimated their forces at forty thousand infantry, supported by three thousand pieces of mobile artillery and rocket launchers."

"What about our ships?" asked James.

"We're in position, sir. We have one hundred Defenders in close orbit and another fifty in the skies over Bridgetown. We'll do you proud, sir," responded the officer on watch in the Command Center.

"I know you will, son! Have a Defender ready for launch. I want to join our boys in orbit. Who has the lead for us up there?" asked James.

"Sir, the primary lead vessel is the Pegasus, commanded by Edwards."

"Good. Patch me through to him. Commander Edwards, this is Donner here. How does it look up there?"

"Well, sir, they're trying to look fearsome, but we're not intimidated. If they want our planet, they're going to have to be prepared to die to get it. James, sir, we will not surrender the line," responded Edwards.

"I never thought it would be any other way, Commander. A few of your friends and I are going to come up and share coffee and buns, but if you don't mind, I think we'll come through the back door as a kind of surprise. Would that be okay with you, Commander?" asked James.

"That, sir, would be just peachy. When might we expect you, so we can put on the kettle?" responded Edwards.

"Well, getting to the back door is going to delay our arrival for another hour, but watch as we set off the party favors. Then you're welcome to join in. Donner, out."

"The boys and I can hardly wait, sir! Edwards, out."

"Kyle, Ryan, I need you to stay here and coordinate activities in the city. If they get this far, I'll need clear minds to save as many of our people as possible. Marcus, I need you with me, just to keep me in line. Let's do this!" shouted James

"Before you go running off, Marcus and I will need an hour to program the drones," responded Kyle.

"An hour it is," replied James.

As a student of history, I always found it interesting that true warriors believe they'll win regardless of the odds. James epitomized that mantra to me. Our counter-offensive plan was to launch in two different directions with fifty Defenders and two Explorers in each formation. We would fly inside our atmosphere for ten thousand miles before entering space and then proceed to deep space, coming around at them from the rear.

Once within range, James would give the order to attack, and our efforts would continue in space and on the ground until either they destroyed us or we destroyed them. We hoped this would affectively fuck up their day. One thing was for sure; the aliens could not win this battle from the air because we had way too many assets to put in their way. James was still insistent that the aliens had other surprises in their back pockets, but for now, we could only deal with what was in front of us.

For the first time I could ever recall, Kyle seemed bewildered by it all. He had no tricks to save the day and no comforting words to share. James and Marcus were now airborne and on their way to meet their destiny and likely define ours.

"Ryan, I'm really uneasy about this. Not so much whether we win or lose, because I have to believe we will win. It's something else! I can't explain it, but you need to take a Defender and leave right now. Get back to the ranch and load our families and as many of the guests as you can. Have them transported to Salmon. Maybe you should leave with them," pleaded Kyle.

"I'll move our families, but there's no way I'm leaving you here to deal with this alone. We've always gone through this stuff together," I said.

"You might want to think about that. The city is going to get hit, and this installation is going to be high on their target list. I'm headed over to my office because I have an idea," replied Kyle.

"There's nothing to think about! I'll be back in a couple of hours. Don't do anything stupid while I'm gone," I scolded.

Just as I had thought, getting the families from the ranch was not as simple as explaining that it was Kyle's wish. Although it worked for Helen, Susan, and my family, Sabrina was another story.

"If Kyle is staying behind to help any way he can, then so am I. You can take our son, and Cateria can watch over him, but once this battle starts, there are going to be injured, and my place is here to help, not hiding out in some remote city thousands of miles from my husband. So get going; you're wasting time." That was the end of the conversation with Sabrina.

She was right about one thing. Arguing when she had her mind made up really was a waste of time. I decided I would let Kyle deal with his wife. My job was to get everyone as far away from Bridgetown as possible—as quickly as possible—and get back in time to help Kyle. The entire pick-up and delivery exercise took just over three hours. By the time I got back, Kyle was having a Defender loaded up with Siltron canisters. I didn't understand why he was doing this when we were on the verge of all-out war.

"It's simple, my friend. We know their Achilles' Heel. All we need to do is exploit it," he explained.

"I don't get it! What does any of this have to do with our current situation?" I asked, fearing my best friend had gone completely mad.

"You're not applying what we've learned. Joshal told us that the first alien attack on humans ended when the invaders came down with some kind of cancerous virus that was killing them off. Joshal guessed it was not the air, but something on the human skin. He was mostly right. What was killing them was on their skin and in the air—Siltron. We all guessed that but put it down as interesting, not necessarily relevant. Now it's relevant. When we were on the video call with the Bergerac, they appeared to have reptilian skin. Are you getting the connection now?" Kyle smirked.

"Well, now that you say it, I get it, but you're making some big assumptions here. Firstly, that the Bergerac are the same invaders Joshal alluded to, and secondly, they have lizard skin, not skin that just appears that way on a monitor. Even if they are one and the same, it took years for the Siltron to kill them off—if that indeed is what killed them. We don't have years. We may not even have many hours left," I replied.

"I think I've figured that out as well. I think Siltron is acid to them. It took years the first time because the powder was constantly being diluted by rain water. I believe a direct, pure concentration of Siltron is going to have an immediate effect. Here's the deal. We may or may not win the battle in space. If we don't and we survive their air assault, then we perish at the hands of these lizards on the ground—or, my idea, we fly over the area where their ground forces are, hit them with a blast of undiluted Siltron, and see if it does anything. What's the worst that can happen?

"It has no effect, and they march in and kill us all, in which case we won't need the Siltron anyway. Ryan, I know our air assault will slow down their advance, but I don't think it's enough. The Spider Drones will hold them up, but that's all they'll do in the face of what appears to be superior weaponry. It's worth a try," said Kyle.

He was right! At this point, what did we have to lose?

"How will you disperse the powder? The system you and Marcus developed was never meant to saturate an area," I said.

"Don't worry about it. I think I've got it figured out. It's an engineering thing," Kyle replied.

Just then, a Protector ran out onto the launch pad and requested we return to the Command Center because Admiral Donner was online and urgently wanted to speak to us. With that, we followed the soldier at a jog back into the Center. When we arrived, James was already on the monitor, issuing orders to a group of eight Defender captains. When the video cameras picked up on our arrival, he immediately turned his attention to Kyle and me.

"Boys, I was right! As we were approaching from deep space, we ran into their fighter formation hiding in a small asteroid belt behind one of our moons, about eight hundred thousand miles southwest of Bridgetown. I think their intent was to have the battle cruisers breach our space defenses and then fly the fighters to the planet through gaps in our lines. These are not star fighters; they're too small and too lightly armed. They're designed for low-level assaults inside an atmosphere, but not today. We're going to engage them in a few minutes, which will delay our arrival with the fleet above Bridgetown.

"I'm going to have to pull most of the Defenders up here with us. I want our offensive against their main fleet to occur coincidentally, with us taking out their rear guard. I want you guys to start our ground offensive on my command. You won't have as many Defenders as I'd hoped, but enough to send a message. We'll finish our work up here and rush our asses back to join in on your party," James told us.

Kyle quickly explained his Siltron idea to James, but James suggested we might consider it as a last resort. For now, he was not prepared to risk men and equipment on an untested theory.

He suggested that perhaps we could test it while he was kicking some ass in the stars. With that, the screen went dark.

Kyle and I went to the briefing room and had the feeds from the battle front piped directly through the intercom and on the monitor. On James's signal, the battle began. The element of surprise did buy us some quick kills against the alien primary fleet, but once they gathered themselves, we felt the full measure of their resolve. It took James six hours to dispose of the aliens' fighter fleet. Against the Defenders, these small fighters were out-gunned and out-classed, but destroying three hundred ships required more time than we could afford.

By the time James arrived to join the main fleet, the Bergerac had brought in another twelve battle cruisers. Their primary weapons were phaser beams and small, low-yield missiles. Although the technologies of their weapons were inferior, they had enough of them to be a problem. We were winning, but they were expensive victories.

Part of the challenge James faced in this battle was that, even with our superior weaponry, the shear mass of the alien cruisers made quick kills impossible. The battle seemed to be stalemated. After twenty hours, we had managed only twelve kills after thousands of direct hits. The Bergerac had other tricks up their sleeves that we hadn't considered. From the underside of their cruisers, they released unmanned sacrificial drones. Once launched, these star-shaped drones hurled themselves into our shields, causing momentary magnetic field interruptions and resulting in breaks to our shield integrity. Through these breaches, the alien mother ships launched missiles, crippling some of the Defenders. In defense, we were focusing all our weapons on taking these drones out of play.

For a while, each drone we destroyed was replaced by two more. The tide began to turn when Marcus noticed that in order to launch the drones, the Bergerac momentarily had to drop their own shields. As hard as it was to ignore the drones and the damage they caused, James instructed our fleet commanders to focus all our weapons on the ships launching them. The weakness in the alien process led to the destruction of seven of their cruisers within minutes. The five surviving battle cruisers began to pull back and finally retreated with Defenders hot on their heels. Although victory was sweet, the price was high in asset losses both in space and on the ground.

Our ground defensive tactics were not accomplishing what we had hoped. With most of the Defenders redirected into orbit, we were left with only a few fighters and the drones to slow the enemy advance. The Spider Drones fought valiantly, but their weapons were mostly ineffective against the aliens' armored vehicles. We had killed over ten thousand of their soldiers but had lost eight hundred Spider Drones. The airborne drones were modestly more effective against the alien equipment, but the sophistication of the alien tracking systems meant a short lifespan for our air assault.

Kyle was as white as a sheet. "Ryan, we can't hold them. Take two Protectors and get my wife—by force if necessary—along with as many other hospital personnel as you can. Squeeze them onto a Defender and get their asses out of here, now! We can't hold the line, and in a few minutes, their artillery barrage and missile attacks are going to lay waste to most of the city. I'll stay here and see if I can find enough soldiers to man our western perimeter. Hurry!"

I knew this wasn't a request or subject to discussion. I left immediately. Force was necessary to get Sabrina on the Defender. She was screaming for Kyle as inbound alien rockets started exploding around us. It took over thirty minutes to load the Defender and get it out of harm's way. When I radioed Command to ask Kyle to wait for me, I was told he had gone to the launch pad. Why in hell would he be at the launch pad? I didn't like it. Kyle was so convinced the Siltron was the answer, I just knew he was about to do something really stupid. I don't know why, but at that moment, I remembered something he said to me after Bridgetown was attacked by Salmon and he just had to stand there and watch.

"Ryan, the people depended on me, and I wasn't there for them. I was useless. That will never happen again, even if I die in the effort."

Now I was panicked! The sky was lit up with incoming missiles fired into the heart of Bridgetown. I remember thinking to myself, *not again, not again*—and then there was nothing.

Twenty-Eight

The Death of Innocence

As my eyes fluttered open, the first sensation that hit me was that I had a splitting headache and there was a nonstop ringing in my ears. I could feel the tube in my mouth but didn't pay much attention to it. I had a sense there were people around me, but they were like ghostly shadows speaking to me in a language I could barely hear and didn't understand. Then a black curtain rolled across my eyes, and I fell back into a realm of restless dreams.

When next I awoke, things were much clearer, and I wish now I had never regained consciousness. All I had known before would be replaced with the cruelties of reality. I recognized my surroundings as one of the critical care rooms at the Medical Center. Dippy or not, I knew this couldn't be good. The first person I recognized and understood as she spoke was Cateria. She looked drawn and defeated but summoned up everything she had to sound cheerful.

"Well, you're finally awake! I hope you don't feel like you look. I missed you! Welcome back!"

"I must look like shit, because that's how I feel. How long have I been here?" I asked.

"Three days, eleven hours, and wait for it, thirty-nine minutes of watching you catch your beauty sleep. How's that? We were really worried about you. The explosions threw you over two hundred feet into the side of the administration building. You don't have many bones left that aren't broken. Don't ever do that again!" she replied.

I tried to shift a bit to sit up, but there were so many traction lines and pulleys, it was a futile endeavor. "How many of the missiles hit?" I asked.

"Too many. Our civilian losses were over sixteen thousand that we know of, and the fires are just now being extinguished. We thought you were buried in the ruins somewhere, but they found you. Ryan, I have some bad news, and it's better you hear it from me," she said as the tears welled up in her eyes.

I knew in my heart what she was going to say, but I hoped beyond all hope I was wrong. "Is it about Kyle?" I asked.

"Yes. He saved us all, Ryan, but the Defender he was in exploded above the enemy forces. We haven't found him yet. We may never find him, Ryan. You have to prepare for the worst," she pleaded.

"Get James! I want James now!" I screamed as I collapsed back into my pillow. "Get him now!" And I was gone again.

The next time I opened my eyes, James and Marcus were standing on either side of the bed. Cateria was nowhere to be seen. My first words were to ask where she was. James told me that she was near exhaustion, having been by my bedside almost every minute of every day since the battle. Sabrina forced her into one of the empty rooms and gave her a sedative. She would be awake in a couple of hours. I was still a bit dopey, but not so out of it that I didn't remember about Kyle.

"Is there any news on finding Kyle? Whether he's alive or dead, we owe it to him to make sure we celebrate his life properly. We owe it to Sabrina to bring her husband back to her. What are we doing, James?" I demanded.

"We've found what's left of the Defender, but there's so much destruction in the area, it will be difficult. The dogs are sniffing twenty-four/seven. One way or another, we'll find him.

That, I promise you! Have you seen a doctor yet today?" asked James.

"I don't know! James, Marcus, I should have been there with him. He died alone. Our best friend died alone. Strange as it sounds, he said to me earlier that day he had a feeling something wasn't right. In fact, he made me move our families out of the city. How could he have known? What is the state of the battle? Is it over? How many men did we lose?" I was confused and babbling, asking questions I knew I didn't need to have answered right there and then.

"All your questions will be answered later. For now, you need to rest. If anything happens, we'll come to you," responded Marcus.

As he was saying the words, I was once again drifting back into the darkness. Every day after that, I grew stronger. Cateria thought bringing the children to see me might help my state of mind. She was right! For the first time in days, I felt like I had returned to the living. Cateria had done a good job shielding the children from the realities of what had happened. Oh, to be young again!

It was just over a week later on a dark rainy morning that James came to my room alone. I could tell immediately by the pale look on his face what we knew to be true was in fact true, and Kyle was dead.

"When did you find him, and what shape is his body in?" I asked before James could speak.

"The dogs sniffed out his body about an hour ago. He had written on both his palms. 'I was right again. Tell my family I love them. Good-bye, my friends!' When his ship exploded, he must have been thrown over a thousand feet into the forest. If not for the dogs, we might never have found his body. The only blessing is he got caught up in the branches, and apart from some deep lacerations, his body is in excellent shape.

"Ryan, he saved our city! I couldn't get the fleet back in time. It took us over forty hours to dispatch the Bergerac space armada. When Kyle realized we were out of time, he convinced Command to assign him two pilots to fly the Defender loaded with Siltron over the enemy position. We thought he would just disperse the powder and get out of there, but he told the pilots it wouldn't work. He insisted all the Siltron had to be released at once. Somewhere he got hold of a sidearm and forced the pilots to put the ship in auto pilot and eject. They tried desperately to convince him to stand down, but he wouldn't. The pilots ejected and made it back safely.

"You're not going to like this part, but we know what he was like and his love for all of us. Ryan, he was not shot down by the enemy. He engaged the self-destruct of the Defender. It appears he bailed out just before the explosion but hadn't cleared the blast zone. The concussion threw him over two thousand feet into the forest. We believe the fall through the tree limbs broke his neck. He must have died instantly, but he was right. The concentrated powder took less than an hour to invade the creatures' bodies. Most of their forces died where they stood. The rest tried to escape back to the landing vessels, but by then, we were back and destroyed those left before they got off the ground. He gave his life for us. It's what he always wanted," explained a now crying James.

"How is Sabrina coping with this?" I asked between my own sobs.

"Outwardly, in typical Sabrina style. Strong and bulletproof! Inside, it's ripping her apart. She won't let anyone touch his body, except her and Cateria. Right now, they're cleaning him up for his presentation to the world. I wouldn't want to be in the room for the next few hours because that's when all her armor is going to fall away. We owe her time with her husband," explained James as he again broke down crying.

"James, I have to see him! I can't get out of this bed, but if you make the arrangements, they can move my bed to where he is after Sabrina has had her time with him. Say you can make that happen, James. Say you can!" I pleaded with tears streaming down my face.

"I can, and I will," responded James.

Just over four hours later, James returned to my room with twelve of the biggest soldiers I had ever seen and a dozen nurses, including Cateria. With little fanfare, the soldiers surrounded the bed and lifted it off the floor while the nurses gathered the miles of tubes punched into my body from all directions. Not a word was said as they carried me out of the room and down the hall into a large, empty surgical theater. There in the center of the space lay Kyle's body, fully clothed and looking like he was fast asleep. They sat the bed down so my head and Kyle's were directly across from each other. Then everyone left the room.

For over an hour, I gave him shit, and then I began reminiscing about our long voyage together and the adventures along the way. Although I knew he was not with me in life, I had to believe he was still here in spirit. Later, Sabrina and all the families joined me, and we said our final good-byes to the greatest man we had ever known. I knew if he were watching, he would be laughing at us, but that was Kyle Chandler.

Kyle's body lay in state for three days in front of the Medical Center while millions of mourners from all over our known world flew in to show their respect and say their good-byes. The color guard for the ceremony was not soldiers in dress uniforms, but 10 Spider Drones. It was the perfect symbolic gesture, because these ugly pieces of hardware truly were Kyle's babies. James delivered a moving eulogy about all Kyle had done for the Children of Vanguard over the years and why we owed who we were today to his determination and never-say-die approach to getting it right.

Noticeably absent from these ceremonies were Sabrina and Cateria. Sabrina was absent because she preferred to grieve out of the public eye, and Cateria because she wouldn't leave Sabrina's side.

We buried Kyle by the river, under the ancient tree near his old friend Joshal, with this strange but simple engraving on his marker stone: "Kyle Chandler—Father, Husband, and Savior of the Human Race." Only our families attended. After the burial, we celebrated his life through the night and into the next day. That was ten years ago today.

Much has changed over the years since Kyle passed. Admiral Donner is now Chancellor Donner, and he and his family relocated to Salmon. When I asked James why he left, he simply replied, "The ghost of Kyle was haunting me everywhere I went in Bridgetown." James was not alone.

In memoriam to Kyle, a life-size statue of his sessions by the lake was sculpted. It portrayed Kyle standing under a tree with one foot resting on a rock and slightly hunched forward, speaking to a group of young men who were completely entranced by his every word. On the front of the display, etched in brass, is this inscription: "The People Have a Right to Know—Good or Bad—and We Have a Responsibility to Tell Them."

Bridgetown is no longer Bridgetown. By overwhelming support, the city's name was changed to Chandlerville. Sabrina lives a quiet life with their only son, James, who attends one of my classes at the university. He is an entirely different story. Cateria and Sabrina have remained inseparable friends, and we often gather at the farm for Sunday dinners.

Marcus is now chairman of the Vanguard Council. Although not the dynamic personality of Kyle, his demeanor is every bit that of his predecessor. He remains one of my very best friends. The Bergerac did not make another attempt to invade our planet, but James has been on high alert for ten years.

Cateria, with the help of Sabrina, fulfilled her dream of becoming a physician. She is now officially a Doctor of Pediatric Medicine at the Medical Center. She is no longer the innocent, brash country girl I fell head over heels in love with so many years ago, but that doesn't matter, because I'm no longer the naïve bookworm still learning the lessons of life.

As for me, well, I no longer involve myself in politics in any way other than to cast my vote when asked to do so. I teach Modern History classes at the university, and since a large portion of the material refers to Kyle's exploits, I am an expert on the subject. It is the best attended class on campus.

From time to time, I take my coffee and bun to Kyle's grave and update him with the current news. Then I lie down beside him, and together we watch as another day drifts into night.

Goodnight, Kyle Chandler. We'll speak again!

This isn't over yet!